# THE VALANCOURT BOOK OF
# VICTORIAN CHRISTMAS GHOST STORIES

# THE VALANCOURT BOOK OF

# VICTORIAN CHRISTMAS

# GHOST STORIES

*Edited with an introduction by*
TARA MOORE

VALANCOURT BOOKS
Richmond, Virginia
2016

# CONTENTS

# INTRODUCTION

## How to Read a Victorian Christmas Ghost Story

Imagine a midwinter night, an early sunset, a long, drafty evening spent by candlelight. The season of Christmas coincides with the shortest days of the year and, for middle-class Victorians, a chance for families to reconnect in story-telling circles. Urban dwellers, disconnected from village legends, simply picked up a magazine specially made to lace children's dreams with terror. The bleak, shadow-filled walk from the story circle to one's dark bedroom presented an uncomfortably eerie space to reflect on the mental images conveyed by those grisly tales.

To capture the Victorian ghost story experience is to whisper it by candlelight, to feel the tendrils of December's chill reaching from the darkness outside the hearth's glow. While our culture associates the summer campfire with this type of tale, the Victorians looked to Christmas fires instead. Walter Scott, at the opening of his ghostly tale "The Tapestried Chamber," bemoans how his written words will strip the story of its most satisfying chills. Read it aloud, he urges his readers. Read it at night.

## The History of Ghosts at Christmas

Ghosts had been a staple of both periodicals and Christmas for a century before the Victorian Christmas publishing boom, but the nineteenth century offered as a nexus for these two cultural icons. Eighteenth-century periodicals concerned with enlightenment had recognized that "ghosts were a problem to be solved" (Handley 113). While these periodical essays did confer a level of distinction on ghosts, they failed to fully harness the Christmas reading experience. When taxation on periodicals raised prices and circulations dropped, ghosts resorted to starring in oral accounts. The midwinter tradition of telling ghostly tales around the long evening fire satisfied both the poor and the rich. This tradition became entrenched in the printed accounts of Christmas. For example, when Washington Irving sought to capture the dignified glamour of the English country Christmas for his readers in 1820, he included the comfortable thrill of the ghost story circle as well as the boar's head and the wassail bowl.

The first literary genre to capitalize on this oral tradition, the Christmas literary annual, became especially popular in the 1820s and 1830s. Dozens of titles popped up to fill the desire of middle-class Victorians to present or display these lushly illustrated, gilded volumes. The gothic ghost story commonly featured in the table of contents of these decorative books. Literary annuals predated the mid-century Christmas book trend, but they further established the place of the ghost story in printed reading matter intended for Christmas use (Moore 81-82). By 1843, a young author would grasp at this genre when he needed some extra cash.

Charles Dickens did not invent the Victorian Christmas, but he did come to represent its commercial potential for publishing profit. Of his five small Christmas novellas, two contained outright ghosts, and another hinged on a supernatural scene. When Dickens found the work of publishing an annual Christmas book too exhausting (and not as profitable as he could have wished), he turned to preparing frame tales populated by the stories of some of the most popular writers of his day. These appeared as special Christmas numbers in the weekly magazines he edited: *Household Words* and, later, *All the Year Round*. Other magazines would follow suit, most of them soliciting authors to contribute ghost stories to add to the mix.

The real wellspring of Victorian Christmas spectres was the magazine. Periodicals began printing special Christmas numbers or simply tailoring their December and January numbers for Christmas reading, and that meant ghosts. Women contributed a large portion of these stories, and scholars have estimated that perhaps between fifty and seventy percent of all ghost fiction from the nineteenth century was written by women (Carpenter and Kolmar xvi). Readers wanted to read ghosts at Christmas, so that meant that authors dreamed up midwinter ghosts over the summer and into the early fall, preparing the way for those spooky holiday chills.

## Why Did the Victorians Love Ghost Stories?

Cultural elements contributed to the success of this transformed oral tradition. Authors who wrote about ghosts could have easily participated in the fad for séances that pervaded certain spheres of society. Nineteenth-century spiritualism shaped "a language of spectrality" which then influenced the production of ghosts in literature (Smith 97). Victorians, who enjoyed increasing levels of leisure and technology, devoted a portion of each to developing a robust culture of death and mourning, including photography of deceased children and picnicking in cemeteries (Carpenter and Kolmar xix). With their fascination with death and the afterlife, the Victorians appreciated when literature roamed into the realm of the uncanny. The following ghostly selections represent the style of ghost stories the Victorians could expect to find in the pages of their periodicals.

Most Victorian ghosts fail to provide the fright that modern audiences have come to expect. Horror fiction and films have no doubt desensitized us to the simple thrill of local ghost lore. The Victorians themselves were dealing with a debate over spiritualism and spirits which severely limited their ability to fully enjoy the ghostly horror story. Authors frequently wrote cautionary anti-ghost stories, the type that open with a sinister suggestion of a ghost, only to end with characters recognizing the foolishness of such a fear. For example, the bang in the night that caused the young bride to panic for five pages ends up being the fallen kitchen clock ("The Mystery"). Dickens used the pages of his periodicals to question the premise that ghosts had any basis in fact (Smajic 60). Disgusted with his culture's belief in ghosts, Dickens produced an entirely ghost-less Christmas number, *The Haunted House* (1859), in which a party of friends collect in a so-called haunted house to experience its thrill or demystify its reputation.

This volume gives preference to the eerier tales from the period, but several included here do hinge on an entirely rational explanation. It is as if authors knew that their readers demanded ghost stories, but the same authors simply could not bring themselves to further confirm the reality of ghosts. Looking back on the late-nineteenth-century ghost trend, one critic wrote, "story-writers found it as much as their place was worth to introduce any element of the apparently supernatural which was not capable of a severely practical explanation" (Berlyn). One story contained here, "How Peter Parley Laid a Ghost: A Story of Owl's Abbey," takes a highly didactic tone. Since *Peter Parley's Annual* was entrusted with teaching Victorian children the realities of their world, readers could be certain from the outset that the tease of a ghost would end with a very human lesson.

Several trends in Victorian ghost narratives rest on the premise that ghosts are real, at least in fiction. The emigrant's return is one such variety. In this brand of tale, the émigré's form appears to his lover or friend, typically at the moment of his death. These spectral visitants are nearly always male, and their appearance signifies their deep devotion to home and place of origin, no matter where in the Empire they have sought their fortune. In one tale, a press gang kidnaps a young man and drags him off to work on a navy vessel; his ghost appears to his fiancée three years later, conveying to her the instantaneous knowledge of his death (Sheehan). While this type of tale appeared throughout the year, the strong sentimentality regarding Christmas family unity made it especially fitting for holiday reading; at that time of the year, families of émigrés would have wanted to feel that they were still the focal point in the lives of their distant loved ones.

Another type of real ghost story involved "laying the ghost," a British phrase for releasing the ghost from whatever past crimes force it to roam the earth. Sometimes the ghost's crimes bind it to this plane, but, more often, the ghost wishes to help its relatives establish financial stability or peace. The ghost may continue to haunt until a particular wrong is righted, and then it is free to drift away. Several of the stories contained here deal with laying the ghost, either by solving a mystery or establishing financial security for the living.

While working-class ghosts rarely haunt anyone over a will, the spectres of the gentry carry the burden of seeing that their bequests are carried out. This otherworldly responsibility plays out in many country house hauntings, a subgenre well represented in this anthology. While working-class ghosts could be found in Victorian periodicals, their wealthier counterparts certainly received more attention. Indeed, readers seemed to idealize the country house Christmas, even though more and more readers celebrated the holiday in an urban setting, and few could boast of such a leisured lifestyle (Moore 89). Perhaps the idea of a haunted estate satisfied the voyeuristic middle class; after all, a haunting is certainly a disruption of a seemingly stable environment (Wolfreys 6). The ghost story offers readers a chance to fantasize about the destabilization of the powerful. Periodical readers could partake in this pastime by picking up their Christmas annual without ever having to leave town.

In his 1884 essay, "The Decay of the British Ghost," F. Anstey sardonically bemoans the loss of the real ghost: "There was something thoroughly Christmassy, for example, about the witchlike old lady, with a horrible dead rouged face, who looked out of a tarnished mirror and gibbered malevolently at somebody, for the excellent reason that he chanced to be her descendant" (252). Anstey's ironic assessment of the state of the ghost rings false in one way; ghosts certainly survived the mid-century boom and continued to feature during the last decades of the century and beyond. However, the ghost story did serve as a type of uncanny mirror, often showing subtle fissures in the society that produced it.

To revive the Victorian ghost, invite it in on its own terms. Wait for dark. Dim the lights. If you can arrange a draft to waft through the room, all the better. Meeting the ghosts of Christmas does not limit you to Dickens's edifying spirits; instead, prepare yourself for a sensual experience of midwinter leisure and Victorian story-telling tradition.

TARA MOORE
May 2016

TARA MOORE celebrates Christmas in central Pennsylvania where the whip-bearing, fur-clad Belsnickle still terrifies the children who know where to find him. Her publications include articles and books about Christmas, including *Victorian Christmas in Print* (2009) and *Christmas: The Sacred to Santa* (2014). She teaches writing and literature at Elizabethtown College.

## Works Cited

Anstey, F. "The Decay of the British Ghost," *Longman's Magazine* 3.145 (1 Jan. 1884): 251-259. *Periodicals Archive Online.* 9 April 2016. Web.

Berlyn, Alfred. "Ghosts Up-to-date," *The Academy* 2172 (20 Dec. 1913): 774-775.

Carpenter, Lynette and Wendy Kolmar. *Ghost Stories by British and American Women: A Selected, Annotated Bibliography.* New York: Garland, 1998.

Dickens, Charles, ed., *The Haunted House.* New York: Modern Library, 2004.

Handley, Sasha. *Visions of an Unseen World: Ghost Beliefs and Ghost Stories in Eighteenth-Century England.* London: Pickering & Chatto, 2007.

Irving, Washington. *The Sketch-book of Geoffrey Crayon, Gent.* [1820]. New York: Library of America, 1983.

Moore, Tara. *Victorian Christmas in Print.* New York: Palgrave Macmillan, 2009.

"The Mystery of the Old Grey House," *Tinsley's Magazine* 36 (Jan. 1885): 168-178.

Scott, Walter. "The Tapestried Chamber; or, The Lady in the Sacque," *The Keepsake for 1829.* London: Hurst, Chance & Co., 1828.

Smajic, Srdjan. *Ghost-Seers, Detectives and Spiritualists: Theories of Vision in Victorian Literature and Science.* New York: Cambridge University Press, 2010.

Sheehan, John. "A Ghostly Night at Ballyslaughter" *Temple Bar* 31 (January 1871): 227-236.

Smith, Andrew. *The Ghost Story, 1840-1920: A Cultural History.* New York: Manchester University Press, 2010.

Wolfreys, Julian. *Victorian Hauntings: Spectrality, Gothic, the Uncanny and Literature.* New York: Palgrave, 2002.

# Sir Walter Scott

## THE TAPESTRIED CHAMBER

*Testing out haunted houses featured frequently in ghost stories, but usually the brave soul made the decision willingly, either out of a desire to disprove spiritualism or to simply enjoy a thrill. With the creation of General Browne, an American War campaigner, WALTER SCOTT (1771-1832) describes a hearty, masculine character who also has access to an elegant country house. In this tale, General Browne returns from war only to face a trial for which his hardships in the Virginian wilds have not prepared him. This story first appeared in 1828 in* The Keepsake, *a literary annual that appeared at Christmas each year from 1828 to 1857.*

THE FOLLOWING NARRATIVE IS GIVEN FROM THE PEN, so far as memory permits, in the same character in which it was presented to the author's ear; nor has he claim to further praise, or to be more deeply censured, than in proportion to the good or bad judgment which he has employed in selecting his materials, as he has studiously avoided any attempt at ornament which might interfere with the simplicity of the tale.

At the same time it must be admitted, that the particular class of stories which turns on the marvellous, possesses a stronger influence when told, than when committed to print. The volume taken up at noonday, though rehearsing the same incidents, conveys a much more feeble impression, than is achieved by the voice of the speaker on a circle of fire-side auditors, who hang upon the narrative as the narrator details the minute incidents which serve to give it authenticity, and lowers his voice with an affectation of mystery while he approaches the fearful and wonderful part. It was with such advantages that the present writer heard the following events related, more than twenty years since, by the celebrated Miss Seward, of Lichfield, who, to her numerous accomplishments, added, in a remarkable degree, the power of narrative in private conversation. In its present form the tale must necessarily lose all the interest which was attached to it, by the flexible voice and intelligent features of the gifted narrator. Yet still, read aloud, to an undoubting audience by the doubtful light of the closing evening, or, in silence, by a decaying taper, and amidst the solitude of a half-lighted apartment, it may redeem its character as a good ghost-story. Miss Seward always affirmed that she had derived her information from an authentic source, although she suppressed the names of the two persons chiefly concerned. I will not avail myself of any particulars I may have since received concerning the localities of the detail, but suffer them to rest under the same general description in which they were first related to me; and, for the same reason, I will not add to, or diminish the narrative, by any circumstance, whether more or less material, but simply rehearse, as I heard it, a story of supernatural terror.

About the end of the American war, when the officers of Lord Cornwallis's army, which surrendered at Yorktown, and others, who had been made prisoners during the impolitic and ill-fated controversy, were returning to their own country, to relate their adventures, and repose themselves, after their fatigues; there was amongst them a general officer, to whom Miss S. gave the name of Browne, but merely, as I understood, to save the inconvenience of introducing a nameless agent in the narrative. He was an officer of merit, as well as a gentleman of high consideration for family and attainments.

Some business had carried General Browne upon a tour through the western counties, when, in the conclusion of a morning stage, he found himself in the vicinity of a small country town, which presented a scene of uncommon beauty, and of a character peculiarly English.

The little town, with its stately old church, whose tower bore testimony to the devotion of ages long past, lay amidst pastures and corn-fields of small extent, but bounded and divided with hedge-row timber of great age and size. There were few marks of modern improvement. The environs of the place intimated neither the solitude of decay, nor the bustle of novelty; the houses were old, but in good repair; and the beautiful little river murmured freely on its way to the left of the town, neither restrained by a dam, nor bordered by a towing-path.

Upon a gentle eminence, nearly a mile to the southward of the town, were seen, amongst many venerable oaks and tangled thickets, the turrets of a castle; as old as the wars of York and Lancaster, but which seemed to have received important alterations during the age of Elizabeth and her successor. It had not been a place of great size; but whatever accommodation it formerly afforded, was, it must be supposed, still to be obtained within its walls; at least, such was the inference which General Browne drew from observing the smoke arise merrily from several of the ancient wreathed and carved chimney-stalks. The wall of the park ran alongside of the highway for two or three hundred yards; and through the different points by which the eye found glimpses into the woodland scenery, it seemed to be well stocked. Other points of view opened in succession; now a full one, of the front of the old castle, and now a side glimpse at its particular towers; the former rich in all the bizarrerie of the Elizabethan school, while the simple and solid strength of other parts of the building seemed to show that they had been raised more for defence than ostentation.

Delighted with the partial glimpses which he obtained of the castle through the woods and glades by which this ancient feudal fortress was surrounded, our military traveller was determined to inquire whether it might not deserve a nearer view, and whether it contained family pictures or other objects of curiosity worthy of a stranger's visit; when, leaving the vicinity of the park, he rolled through a clean and well-paved street, and stopped at the door of a well-frequented inn.

Before ordering horses to proceed on his journey, General Browne made inquiries concerning the proprietor of the chateau which had so attracted his admiration; and was equally surprised and pleased at hearing in reply a nobleman named, whom we shall call Lord Woodville. How fortunate! Much of Browne's early recollections both at school, and at college, had been connected with young Woodville, whom, by a few questions, he now ascertained to be the same with the owner of this fair domain. He had been raised to the peerage by the decease of his father a few months before, and, as the general learned from the landlord, the term of mourning being ended, was now taking possession of his paternal estate, in the jovial season of merry autumn, accompanied by a select party of friends to enjoy the sports of a country famous for game.

This was delightful news to our traveller. Frank Woodville had been Richard Browne's fag at Eton, and his chosen intimate at Christ Church; their pleasures and their tasks had been the same; and the honest soldier's heart warmed to find his early friend in possession of so delightful a residence, and of an estate, as the landlord assured him with a nod and a wink, fully adequate to maintain and add to his dignity. Nothing was more natural than that the traveller should suspend a journey, which there was nothing to render hurried, to pay a visit to an old friend under such agreeable circumstances.

The fresh horses, therefore, had only the brief task of conveying the general's travelling carriage to Woodville Castle. A porter admitted them at a modern gothic lodge, built in that style to correspond with the castle itself, and at the same time rang a bell to give warning of the approach of visitors. Apparently the sound of the bell had suspended the separation of the company, bent on the various amusements of the morning; for, on entering the court of the chateau, several young men were lounging about in their sporting dresses, looking at, and criticising, the dogs which the keepers held in readiness to attend their pastime. As General Browne alighted, the young lord came to the gate of the hall, and for an instant gazed, as at a stranger, upon the countenance of his friend, on which, war, with its fatigues and its wounds, had made a great alteration. But the uncertainty lasted no longer than till the visitor had spoken, and the hearty greeting which followed was such as can only be exchanged betwixt those, who have passed together the merry days of careless boyhood or early youth.

"If I could have formed a wish, my dear Browne," said Lord Woodville, "it would have been to have you here, of all men, upon this occasion, which my friends are good enough to hold as a sort of holiday. Do not think you have been unwatched during the years you have been absent from us. I have traced you through your dangers, your triumphs, your misfortunes, and was delighted to see that, whether in victory or defeat, the name of my old friend was always distinguished with applause."

The general made a suitable reply, and congratulated his friend on his new dignities, and the possession of a place and domain so beautiful.

"Nay, you have seen nothing of it as yet," said Lord Woodville, "and I trust you do not mean to leave us till you are better acquainted with it. It is true, I confess, that my present party is pretty large, and the old house, like other places of the kind, does not possess so much accommodation as the extent of the outward walls appears to promise. But we can give you a comfortable old-fashioned room, and I venture to suppose that your campaigns have taught you to be glad of worse quarters."

The general shrugged his shoulders, and laughed. "I presume," he said, "the worst apartment in your chateau is considerably superior to the old tobacco-cask, in which I was fain to take up my night's lodging when I was in the Bush, as the Virginians call it, with the light corps. There I lay, like Diogenes himself, so delighted with my covering from the element, that I made a vain attempt to have it rolled on to my next quarters; but my commander for the time would give way to no such luxurious provision, and I took farewell of my beloved cask with tears in my eyes."

"Well, then, since you do not fear your quarters," said Lord Woodville, "you will stay with me a week at least. Of guns, dogs, fishing-rods, flies, and means of sport by sea and land, we have enough and to spare: you cannot pitch on an amusement but we will find the means of pursuing it. But if you prefer the gun and pointers, I will go with you myself, and see whether you have mended your shooting since you have been amongst the Indians of the back settlements."

The general gladly accepted his friendly host's proposal in all its points. After a morning of manly exercise, the company met at dinner, where it was the delight of Lord Woodville to conduce to the display of the high properties of his recovered friend, so as to recommend him to his guests, most of whom were persons of distinction. He led General Browne to speak of the scenes he had witnessed; and as every word marked alike the brave officer and the sensible man, who retained possession of his cool judgment under the most imminent dangers, the company looked upon the soldier with general respect, as on one who had proved himself possessed of an uncommon portion of personal courage; that attribute of all others, of which every body desires to be thought possessed.

The day at Woodville Castle ended as usual in such mansions. The hospitality stopped within the limits of good order: music, in which the young lord was a proficient, succeeded to the circulation of the bottle: cards and billiards, for those who preferred such amusements, were in readiness: but the exercise of the morning required early hours, and not long after eleven o'clock the guests began to retire to their several apartments.

The young lord himself conducted his friend, General Browne, to the chamber destined for him, which answered the description he had given of it, being comfortable, but old-fashioned. The bed was of the massive form used in the end of the seventeenth century, and the curtains of faded silk, heavily trimmed with tarnished gold. But then the sheets, pillows, and blankets looked delightful to the campaigner, when he thought of his "mansion, the cask." There was an air of gloom in the tapestry hangings, which, with their worn-out graces, curtained the walls of the little chamber, and gently undulated as the autumnal breeze found its way through the ancient lattice-window, which pattered and whistled as the air gained entrance. The toilette, too, with its mirror, turbaned, after the manner of the beginning of the century, with a coiffure of murrey-coloured silk, and its hundred strange-shaped boxes, providing for arrangements which had been obsolete for more than fifty years, had an antique, and in so far a melancholy, aspect. But nothing could blaze more brightly and cheerfully than the two large wax candles; or if aught could rival them, it was the flaming bickering faggots in the chimney, that sent at once their gleam and their warmth, through the snug apartment; which, notwithstanding the general antiquity of its appearance, was not wanting in the least convenience, that modern habits rendered either necessary or desirable.

"This is an old-fashioned sleeping apartment, general," said the young lord, "but I hope you find nothing that makes you envy your old tobacco-cask."

"I am not particular respecting my lodgings," replied the general; "yet were I to make any choice, I would prefer this chamber by many degrees, to the gayer and more modern rooms of your family mansion. Believe me, that when I unite its modern air of comfort with its venerable antiquity, and recollect that it is your lordship's property, I shall feel in better quarters here, than if I were in the best hotel London could afford."

"I trust—I have no doubt—that you will find yourself as comfortable as I wish you, my dear general," said the young nobleman; and once more bidding his guest good night, he shook him by the hand, and withdrew.

The general once more looked round him, and internally congratulating himself on his return to peaceful life, the comforts of which were endeared by the recollection of the hardships and dangers he had lately sustained, undressed himself, and prepared for a luxurious night's rest.

Here, contrary to the custom of this species of tale, we leave the general in possession of his apartment until the next morning.

The company assembled for breakfast at an early hour, but without the appearance of General Browne, who seemed the guest that Lord Woodville was desirous of honouring above all whom his hospitality had assembled around him. He more than once expressed surprise at the general's absence, and at length sent a servant to make inquiry after him. The man brought back information that General Browne had been walking abroad since an early hour of the morning, in defiance of the weather, which was misty and ungenial.

"The custom of a soldier,"—said the young nobleman to his friends; "many of them acquire habitual vigilance, and cannot sleep after the early hour at which their duty usually commands them to be alert."

Yet the explanation which Lord Woodville then offered to the company seemed hardly satisfactory to his own mind, and it was in a fit of silence and abstraction that he awaited the return of the general. It took place near an hour after the breakfast bell had rung. He looked fatigued and feverish. His hair, the powdering and arrangement of which was at this time one of the most important occupations of a man's whole day, and marked his fashion as much as, in the present time, the tying of a cravat, or the want of one, was dishevelled, uncurled, void of powder, and dank with dew. His clothes were huddled on with a careless negligence, remarkable in a military man, whose real or supposed duties are usually held to include some attention to the toilette; and his looks were haggard and ghastly in a peculiar degree.

"So you have stolen a march upon us this morning, my dear general," said Lord Woodville; "or you have not found your bed so much to your mind as I had hoped and you seemed to expect. How did you rest last night?"

"Oh, excellently well! remarkably well! never better in my life"—said General Browne rapidly, and yet with an air of embarrassment which was obvious to his friend. He then hastily swallowed a cup of tea, and, neglecting or refusing whatever else was offered, seemed to fall into a fit of abstraction.

"You will take the gun to-day, general?" said his friend and host, but had to repeat the question twice ere he received the abrupt answer, "No, my lord; I am sorry I cannot have the honour of spending another day with your lordship: my post horses are ordered, and will be here directly."

All who were present showed surprise, and Lord Woodville immediately replied, "Post horses, my good friend! what can you possibly want with them, when you promised to stay with me quietly for at least a week?"

"I believe," said the general, obviously much embarrassed, "that I might, in the pleasure of my first meeting with your lordship, have said something about stopping here a few days; but I have since found it altogether impossible."

"That is very extraordinary," answered the young nobleman. "You seemed quite disengaged yesterday, and you cannot have had a summons to-day; for our post has not come up from the town, and therefore you cannot have received any letters."

General Browne, without giving any further explanation, muttered something of indispensable business, and insisted on the absolute necessity of his departure in a manner which silenced all opposition on the part of his host, who saw that his resolution was taken, and forbore all further importunity.

"At least, however," he said, "permit me, my dear Browne, since go you will or must, to show you the view from the terrace, which the mist, that is now rising, will soon display."

He threw open a sash-window, and stepped down upon the terrace as he spoke. The general followed him mechanically, but seemed little to attend to what his host was saying, as, looking across an extended and rich prospect, he pointed out the different objects worthy of observation. Thus they moved on till Lord Woodville had attained his purpose of drawing his guest entirely apart from the rest of the company, when, turning round upon him with an air of great solemnity, he addressed him thus:

"Richard Browne, my old and very dear friend, we are now alone. Let me conjure you to answer me upon the word of a friend, and the honour of a soldier. How did you in reality rest during last night?"

"Most wretchedly indeed, my lord," answered the general, in the same tone of solemnity;—"so miserably, that I would not run the risk of such a second night, not only for all the lands belonging to this castle, but for all the country which I see from this elevated point of view."

"This is most extraordinary," said the young lord, as if speaking to himself; "then there must be something in the reports concerning that apartment." Again turning to the general, he said, "For God's sake, my dear friend, be candid with me, and let me know the disagreeable particulars which have befallen you under a roof where, with consent of the owner, you should have met nothing save comfort."

The general seemed distressed by this appeal, and paused a moment before he replied. "My dear lord," he at length said, "what happened to me last night is of a nature so peculiar and so unpleasant, that I could hardly bring myself to detail it even to your lordship, were it not that, independent of my wish to gratify any request of yours, I think that sincerity on my part may lead to some explanation about a circumstance equally painful and mysterious. To others, the communication I am about to make, might place me in the light of a weak-minded, superstitious fool, who suffered his own imagination to delude and bewilder him; but you have known me in childhood and youth, and will not suspect me of having adopted in manhood, the feelings and frailties from which my early years were free." Here he paused, and his friend replied:

"Do not doubt my perfect confidence in the truth of your communication, however strange it may be," replied Lord Woodville; "I know your firmness of disposition too well, to suspect you could be made the object of imposition, and am aware that your honour and your friendship will equally deter you from exaggerating whatever you may have witnessed."

"Well then," said the general, "I will proceed with my story as well as I can, relying upon your candour; and yet distinctly feeling that I would rather face a battery than recall to my mind the odious recollections of last night."

He paused a second time, and then perceiving that Lord Woodville remained silent and in an attitude of attention, he commenced, though not without obvious reluctance, the history of his night adventures in the Tapestried Chamber.

"I undressed and went to bed, so soon as your lordship left me yesterday evening; but the wood in the chimney, which nearly fronted my bed, blazed brightly and cheerfully, and, aided by a hundred exciting recollections of my childhood and youth, which had been recalled by the unexpected pleasure of meeting your lordship, prevented me from falling immediately asleep. I ought, however, to say, that these reflections were all of a pleasant and agreeable kind, grounded on a sense of having for a time exchanged the labour, fatigues, and dangers of my profession, for the enjoyments of a peaceful life, and the reunion of those friendly and affectionate ties, which I had torn asunder at the rude summons of war.

"While such pleasing reflections were stealing over my mind, and gradually lulling me to slumber, I was suddenly aroused by a sound like that of the rustling of a silken gown, and the tapping of a pair of high-heeled shoes, as if a woman were walking in the apartment. Ere I could draw the curtain to see what the matter was, the figure of a little woman passed between the bed and the fire. The back of this form was turned to me, and I could observe, from the shoulders and neck, it was that of an old woman, whose dress was an old-fashioned gown, which, I think, ladies call a sacque; that is, a sort of robe completely loose in the body, but gathered into broad plaits upon the neck and shoulders, which fall down to the ground, and terminate in a species of train.

"I thought the intrusion singular enough, but never harboured for a moment the idea that what I saw was any thing more than the mortal form of some old woman about the establishment, who had a fancy to dress like her grandmother, and who, having perhaps (as your lordship mentioned that you were rather strait-ened for room) been dislodged from her chamber for my accom-modation, had forgotten the circumstance, and returned by twelve, to her old haunt. Under this persuasion I moved myself in bed and coughed a little, to make the intruder sensible of my being in possession of the premises.—She turned slowly round, but, gracious heaven! my lord, what a countenance did she dis-play to me! There was no longer any question what she was, or any thought of her being a living being. Upon a face which wore the fixed features of a corpse were imprinted the traces of the vilest and most hideous passions which had animated her while she lived. The body of some atrocious criminal seemed to have been given up from the grave, and the soul restored from the penal fire, in order to form, for a space, an union with the ancient accomplice of its guilt. I started up in bed, and sat upright, sup-porting myself on my palms, as I gazed on this horrible spectre. The hag made, as it seemed, a single and swift stride to the bed where I lay, and squatted herself down upon it, in precisely the same attitude which I had assumed in the extremity of my horror, advancing her diabolical countenance within half a yard of mine, with a grin which seemed to intimate the malice and the derision of an incarnate fiend."

Here General Browne stopped, and wiped from his brow the cold perspiration with which the recollection of his horrible vision had covered it.

"My lord," he said, "I am no coward. I have been in all the mortal dangers incidental to my profession, and I may truly boast, that no man ever saw Richard Browne dishonour the sword he wears; but in these horrible circumstances, under the eyes, and, as it seemed, almost in the grasp of an incarnation of an evil spirit, all firmness forsook me, all manhood melted from me like wax in the furnace, and I felt my hair individually bristle. The current of my life-blood ceased to flow, and I sank back in a swoon, as very a victim to panic terror as ever was a village girl, or a child of ten years old. How long I lay in this condition I cannot pretend to guess.

"But I was roused by the castle clock striking one, so loud that it seemed as if it were in the very room. It was some time before I dared open my eyes, lest they should again encounter the horrible spectacle. When, however, I summoned courage to look up, she was no longer visible. My first idea was to pull my bell, wake the servants, and remove to a garret or a hay-loft, to be ensured against a second visitation. Nay, I will confess the truth, that my resolution was altered, not by the shame of exposing myself, but by the fear that, as the bell-cord hung by the chimney, I might, in making my way to it, be again crossed by the fiendish hag, who, I figured to myself, might be still lurking about some corner of the apartment.

"I will not pretend to describe what hot and cold fever-fits tormented me for the rest of the night, through broken sleep, weary vigils, and that dubious state which forms the neutral ground between them. An hundred terrible objects appeared to haunt me; but there was the great difference betwixt the vision which I have described, and those which followed, that I knew the last to be deceptions of my own fancy and over-excited nerves.

"Day at last appeared, and I rose from my bed ill in health, and humiliated in mind. I was ashamed of myself as a man and a soldier, and still more so, at feeling my own extreme desire to escape from the haunted apartment, which, however, conquered all other considerations; so that, huddling on my clothes with the most careless haste, I made my escape from your lordship's mansion, to seek in the open air some relief to my nervous system, shaken as it was by this horrible rencounter with a visitant, for such I must believe her, from the other world. Your lordship has now heard the cause of my discomposure, and of my sudden desire to leave your hospitable castle. In other places I trust we may often meet; but God protect me from ever spending a second night under that roof!"

Strange as the general's tale was, he spoke with such a deep air of conviction, that it cut short all the usual commentaries which are made on such stories. Lord Woodville never once asked him if he was sure he did not dream of the apparition, or suggested any of the possibilities by which it is fashionable to explain apparitions,—wild vagaries of the fancy, or deception of the optic nerves. On the contrary, he seemed deeply impressed with the truth and reality of what he had heard; and, after a considerable pause, regretted, with much appearance of sincerity, that his early friend should in his house have suffered so severely.

"I am the more sorry for your pain, my dear Browne," he continued, "that it is the unhappy, though most unexpected, result of an experiment of my own. You must know, that for my father and grandfather's time, at least, the apartment which was assigned to you last night, had been shut on account of reports that it was disturbed by supernatural sights and noises. When I came, a few weeks since, into possession of the estate, I thought the accommodation, which the castle afforded for my friends, was not extensive enough to permit the inhabitants of the invisible world to retain possession of a comfortable sleeping apartment. I therefore caused the Tapestried Chamber, as we call it, to be opened; and, without destroying its air of antiquity, I had such new articles of furniture placed in it as became the more modern times. Yet as the opinion that the room was haunted very strongly prevailed among the domestics, and was also known in the neighbourhood and to many of my friends, I feared some prejudice might be entertained by the first occupant of the Tapestried Chamber, which might tend to revive the evil report which it had laboured under, and so disappoint my purpose of rendering it an useful part of the house. I must confess, my dear Browne, that your arrival yesterday, agreeable to me for a thousand reasons besides, seemed the most favourable opportunity of removing the unpleasant rumours which attached to the room, since your courage was indubitable, and your mind free of any pre-occupation on the subject. I could not, therefore, have chosen a more fitting subject for my experiment."

"Upon my life," said General Browne, somewhat hastily, "I am infinitely obliged to your lordship—very particularly indebted indeed. I am likely to remember for some time the consequences of the experiment, as your lordship is pleased to call it."

"Nay, now you are unjust, my dear friend," said Lord Woodville. "You have only to reflect for a single moment, in order to be convinced that I could not augur the possibility of the pain to which you have been so unhappily exposed. I was yesterday morning a complete sceptic on the subject of supernatural appearances. Nay, I am sure that had I told you what was said about that room, those very reports would have induced you, by your own choice, to select it for your accommodation. It was my misfortune, perhaps my error, but really cannot be termed my fault, that you have been afflicted so strangely."

"Strangely indeed!" said the general, resuming his good temper; "and I acknowledge that I have no right to be offended with your lordship for treating me like what I used to think myself—a man of some firmness and courage.—But I see my post horses are arrived, and I must not detain your lordship from your amusement."

"Nay, my old friend," said Lord Woodville, "since you cannot stay with us another day, which, indeed, I can no longer urge, give me at least half an hour more. You used to love pictures, and I have a gallery of portraits, some of them by Vandyke, representing ancestry to whom this property and castle formerly belonged. I think that several of them will strike you as possessing merit."

General Browne accepted the invitation, though somewhat unwillingly. It was evident he was not to breathe freely or at ease, till he left Woodville Castle far behind him. He could not refuse his friend's invitation, however; and the less so, that he was a little ashamed of the peevishness which he had displayed towards his well-meaning entertainer.

The general, therefore, followed Lord Woodville through several rooms, into a long gallery hung with pictures, which the latter pointed out to his guest, telling the names, and giving some account of the personages whose portraits presented themselves in progression. General Browne was but little interested in the details which these accounts conveyed to him. They were, indeed, of the kind which are usually found in an old family gallery. Here, was a cavalier who had ruined the estate in the royal cause; there, a fine lady who had reinstated it by contracting a match with a wealthy round-head. There, hung a gallant who had been in danger for corresponding with the exiled court at Saint Germain's; here, one who had taken arms for William at the revolution; and there, a third that had thrown his weight alternately into the scale of whig and tory.

While Lord Woodville was cramming these words into his guest's ear, "against the stomach of his sense," they gained the middle of the gallery, when he beheld General Browne suddenly start, and assume an attitude of the utmost surprise, not unmixed with fear, as his eyes were caught and suddenly riveted by a portrait of an old lady in a sacque, the fashionable dress of the end of the seventeenth century.

"There she is!" he exclaimed, "there she is, in form and features, though inferior in demoniac expression to, the accursed hag who visited me last night."

"If that be the case," said the young nobleman, "there can remain no longer any doubt of the horrible reality of your apparition. That is the picture of a wretched ancestress of mine, of whose crimes a black and fearful catalogue is recorded in a family history in my charter-chest. The recital of them would be too horrible: it is enough to say, that in yon fatal apartment incest, and unnatural murder, were committed. I will restore it to the solitude to which the better judgment of those who preceded me had consigned it; and never shall any one, so long as I can prevent it, be exposed to a repetition of the supernatural horrors which could shake such courage as yours."

Thus the friends, who had met with such glee, parted in a very different mood; Lord Woodville to command the tapestried chamber to be unmantled, and the door built up; and General Browne to seek in some less beautiful country, and with some less dignified friend, forgetfulness of the painful night which he had passed in Woodville Castle.

# Elizabeth Gaskell

## THE OLD NURSE'S STORY

*Much attention has been given to this groundbreaking ghostly story, which appeared in 1852 in the very first special Christmas number of* Household Words, *Charles Dickens's periodical. By narrating a nurse's story,* ELIZABETH GASKELL (1810-1865) *places the ghost story within the sphere of women who might use such stories both to entertain their charges and caution them against dangerous behavior. Gaskell is well known for adept portrayal of women in novels such as* Cranford *and* North and South, *and her nonfiction work* The Life of Charlotte Brontë. *Though she won fame from her novels, her ghost stories offered her a space to treat themes of female sexuality with greater boldness.[1]*

YOU KNOW, MY DEARS, that your mother was an orphan, and an only child; and I dare say you have heard that your grandfather was a clergyman up in Westmoreland, where I come from. I was just a girl in the village school, when, one day, your grandmother came in to ask the mistress if there was any scholar there who would do for a nurse-maid; and mighty proud I was, I can tell ye, when the mistress called me up, and spoke to my being a good girl at my needle, and a steady honest girl, and one whose parents were very respectable, though they might be poor. I thought I should like nothing better than to serve the pretty young lady, who was blushing as deep as I was, as she spoke of the coming baby, and what I should have to do with it. However, I see you don't care so much for this part of my story, as for what you think is to come, so I'll tell you at once I was engaged, and settled at the parsonage before Miss Rosamond (that was the baby, who is now your mother) was born. To be sure, I had little enough to do with her when she came, for she was never out of her mother's

1 See Vanessa D. Dickerson, *Victorian Ghosts in the Noontide: Women Writers and the Supernatural*. Columbia: University of Missouri Press, 1996, 112, 115.

arms, and slept by her all night long; and proud enough was I sometimes when missis trusted her to me. There never was such a baby before or since, though you've all of you been fine enough in your turns; but for sweet winning ways, you've none of you come up to your mother. She took after her mother, who was a real lady born; a Miss Furnivall, a granddaughter of Lord Furnivall's in Northumberland. I believe she had neither brother nor sister, and had been brought up in my lord's family till she had married your grandfather, who was just a curate, son to a shopkeeper in Carlisle—but a clever fine gentleman as ever was—and one who was a right-down hard worker in his parish, which was very wide, and scattered all abroad over the Westmoreland Fells. When your mother, little Miss Rosamond, was about four or five years old, both her parents died in a fortnight—one after the other. Ah! that was a sad time! My pretty young mistress and me was looking for another baby, when my master came home from one of his long rides, wet and tired, and took the fever he died of; and then she never held up her head again, but just lived to see her dead baby, and have it laid on her breast before she sighed away her life. My mistress had asked me, on her death-bed, never to leave Miss Rosamond; but if she had never spoken a word, I would have gone with the little child to the end of the world.

The next thing, and before we had well stilled our sobs, the executors and guardians came to settle the affairs. They were my poor young mistress's own cousin, Lord Furnivall, and Mr. Esthwaite, my master's brother, a shopkeeper in Manchester; not so well to do then, as he was afterwards, and with a large family rising about him. Well! I don't know if it were their settling, or because of a letter my mistress wrote on her death-bed to her cousin, my lord; but somehow it was settled that Miss Rosamond and me were to go to Furnivall Manor House, in Northumberland, and my lord spoke as if it had been her mother's wish that she should live with his family, and as if he had no objections, for that one or two more or less could make no difference in so grand a household. So, though that was not the way in which I should have wished the coming of my bright and pretty pet to have been looked at—who was like a sunbeam in any family, be it never so grand—I was well pleased that all the folks in the Dale should stare and admire, when they heard I was going to be young lady's maid at my Lord Furnivall's at Furnivall Manor.

But I made a mistake in thinking we were to go and live where my lord did. It turned out that the family had left Furnivall Manor House fifty years or more. I could not hear that my poor young mistress had ever been there, though she had been brought up in the family; and I was sorry for that, for I should have liked Miss Rosamond's youth to have passed where her mother's had been.

My lord's gentleman, from whom I asked as many questions as I durst, said that the Manor House was at the foot of the Cumberland Fells, and a very grand place; that an old Miss Furnivall, a great-aunt of my lord's, lived there, with only a few servants; but that it was a very healthy place, and my lord had thought that it would suit Miss Rosamond very well for a few years, and that her being there might perhaps amuse his old aunt.

I was bidden by my lord to have Miss Rosamond's things ready by a certain day. He was a stern, proud man, as they say all the Lord Furnivalls were; and he never spoke a word more than was necessary. Folk did say he had loved my young mistress; but that, because she knew that his father would object, she would never listen to him, and married Mr. Esthwaite; but I don't know. He never married at any rate. But he never took much notice of Miss Rosamond; which I thought he might have done if he had cared for her dead mother. He sent his gentleman with us to the Manor House, telling him to join him at Newcastle that same evening; so there was no great length of time for him to make us known to all the strangers before he, too, shook us off; and we were led, two lonely young things (I was not eighteen), in the great old Manor House. It seems like yesterday that we drove there. We had left our own dear parsonage very early, and we had both cried as if our hearts would break, though we were travelling in my lord's carriage, which I had thought so much of once. And now it was long past noon on a September day, and we stopped to change horses for the last time at a little smoky town, all full of colliers and miners. Miss Rosamond had fallen asleep, but Mr. Henry told me to waken her, that she might see the park and the Manor House as we drove up. I thought it rather a pity; but I did what he bade me, for fear he should complain of me to my lord.

We had left all signs of a town or even a village, and were then inside the gates of a large wild park—not like the parks here in the south, but with rocks, and the noise of running water, and gnarled thorn-trees, and old oaks, all white and peeled with age.

The road went up about two miles, and then we saw a great and stately house, with many trees close around it, so close that in some places their branches dragged against the walls when the wind blew; and some hung broken down; for no one seemed to take much charge of the place;—to lop the wood, or to keep the moss-covered carriageway in order. Only in front of the house all was clear. The great oval drive was without a weed; and neither tree nor creeper was allowed to grow over the long, many-windowed front; at both sides of which a wing projected, which were each the ends of other side fronts; for the house, although it was so desolate, was even grander than I expected. Behind it rose the Fells, which seemed unenclosed and bare enough; and on the left hand of the house, as you stood facing it, was a little old-fashioned flower-garden, as I found out afterwards. A door opened out upon it from the west front; it had been scooped out of the thick dark wood for some old Lady Furnivall; but the branches of the great forest trees had grown and overshadowed it again, and there were very few flowers that would live there at that time.

When we drove up to the great front entrance, and went into the hall I thought we should be lost—it was so large, and vast, and grand. There was a chandelier all of bronze, hung down from the middle of the ceiling; and I had never seen one before, and looked at it all in amaze. Then, at one end of the hall, was a great fire-place, as large as the sides of the houses in my country, with many andirons and dogs to hold the wood; and by it were heavy old-fashioned sofas. At the opposite end of the hall, to the left as you went in—on the western side—was an organ built into the wall, and so large that it filled up the best part of that end. Beyond it, on the same side, was a door; and opposite, on each side of the fire-place, were also doors leading to the east front; but those I never went through as long as I stayed in the house, so I can't tell you what lay beyond.

The afternoon was closing in, and the hall, which had no fire lighted in it, looked dark and gloomy; but we did not stay there a moment. The old servant who had opened the door for us bowed to Mr. Henry, and took us in through the door at the further side of the great organ, and led us through several smaller halls and passages into the west drawing-room, where he said that Miss Furnivall was sitting. Poor little Miss Rosamond held very tight to me, as if she were scared and lost in that great place, and as for myself, I was not much better. The west drawing-room was very cheerful-looking, with a warm fire in it, and plenty of good, comfortable furniture about. Miss Furnivall was an old lady not far from eighty, I should think, but I do not know. She was thin and tall, and had a face as full of fine wrinkles as if they had been drawn all over it with a needle's point. Her eyes were very watchful, to make up, I suppose, for her being so deaf as to be obliged to use a trumpet. Sitting with her, working at the same great piece of tapestry, was Mrs. Stark, her maid and companion, and almost as old as she was. She had lived with Miss Furnivall ever since they both were young, and now she seemed more like a friend than a servant; she looked so cold, and grey, and stony, as if she had never loved or cared for any one; and I don't suppose she did care for any one, except her mistress; and, owing to the great deafness of the latter, Mrs. Stark treated her very much as if she were a child. Mr. Henry gave some message from my lord, and then he bowed good-bye to us all,—taking no notice of my sweet little Miss Rosamond's outstretched hand—and left us standing there, being looked at by the two old ladies through their spectacles.

I was right glad when they rung for the old footman who had shown us in at first, and told him to take us to our rooms. So we went out of that great drawing-room, and into another sitting-room, and out of that, and then up a great flight of stairs, and along a broad gallery—which was something like a library, having books all down one side, and windows and writing-tables all down the other—till we came to our rooms, which I was not sorry to hear were just over the kitchens; for I began to think I should be lost in that wilderness of a house. There was an old nursery, that had been used for all the little lords and ladies long ago, with a pleasant fire burning in the grate, and the kettle boiling on the bob, and tea things spread out on the table; and out of that room was the night-nursery, with a little crib for Miss Rosamond

close to my bed. And old James called up Dorothy, his wife, to bid
us welcome; and both he and she were so hospitable and kind,
that by and by Miss Rosamond and me felt quite at home; and
by the time tea was over, she was sitting on Dorothy's knee, and
chattering away as fast as her little tongue could go. I soon found
out that Dorothy was from Westmoreland, and that bound her
and me together, as it were; and I would never wish to meet with
kinder people than were old James and his wife. James had lived
pretty nearly all his life in my lord's family, and thought there was
no one so grand as they. He even looked down a little on his wife;
because, till he had married her, she had never lived in any but a
farmer's household. But he was very fond of her, as well he might
be. They had one servant under them, to do all the rough work.
Agnes they called her; and she and me, and James and Dorothy,
with Miss Furnivall and Mrs. Stark, made up the family; always
remembering my sweet little Miss Rosamond! I used to wonder
what they had done before she came, they thought so much of her
now. Kitchen and drawing-room, it was all the same. The hard,
sad Miss Furnivall, and the cold Mrs. Stark, looked pleased when
she came fluttering in like a bird, playing and pranking hither and
thither, with a continual murmur, and pretty prattle of gladness.
I am sure, they were sorry many a time when she flitted away into
the kitchen, though they were too proud to ask her to stay with
them, and were a little surprised at her taste; though to be sure, as
Mrs. Stark said, it was not to be wondered at, remembering what
stock her father had come of. The great, old rambling house was
a famous place for little Miss Rosamond. She made expeditions
all over it, with me at her heels; all, except the east wing, which
was never opened, and whither we never thought of going. But
in the western and northern part was many a pleasant room; full
of things that were curiosities to us, though they might not have
been to people who had seen more. The windows were darkened
by the sweeping boughs of the trees, and the ivy which had over-
grown them: but, in the green gloom, we could manage to see
old China jars and carved ivory boxes, and great, heavy books,
and, above all, the old pictures!

Once, I remember, my darling would have Dorothy go with
us to tell us who they all were; for they were all portraits of some

of my lord's family, though Dorothy could not tell us the names of every one. We had gone through most of the rooms, when we came to the old state drawing-room over the hall, and there was a picture of Miss Furnivall; or, as she was called in those days, Miss Grace, for she was the younger sister. Such a beauty she must have been! but with such a set, proud look, and such scorn looking out of her handsome eyes, with her eyebrows just a little raised, as if she wondered how any one could have the impertinence to look at her; and her lip curled at us, as we stood there gazing. She had a dress on, the like of which I had never seen before, but it was all the fashion when she was young: a hat of some soft, white stuff like beaver, pulled a little over her brows, and a beautiful plume of feathers sweeping round it on one side; and her gown of blue satin was open in front to a quilted, white stomacher.

"Well, to be sure!" said I, when I had gazed my fill. "Flesh is grass, they do say; but who would have thought that Miss Furnivall had been such an out-and-out beauty, to see her now?"

"Yes," said Dorothy. "Folks change sadly. But if what my master's father used to say was true, Miss Furnivall, the elder sister, was handsomer than Miss Grace. Her picture is here somewhere; but, if I show it you, you must never let on, even to James, that you have seen it. Can the little lady hold her tongue, think you?" asked she.

I was not so sure, for she was such a little, sweet, bold, open-spoken child, so I set her to hide herself; and then I helped Dorothy to turn a great picture, that leaned with its face towards the wall, and was not hung up as the others were. To be sure, it beat Miss Grace for beauty; and, I think, for scornful pride, too, though in that matter it might be hard to choose. I could have looked at it an hour, but Dorothy seemed half frightened at having shown it to me, and hurried it back again, and bade me run and find Miss Rosamond, for that there were some ugly places about the house, where she should like ill for the child to go. I was a brave, high-spirited girl, and thought little of what the old woman said, for I liked hide-and-seek as well as any child in the parish; so off I ran to find my little one.

As winter drew on, and the days grew shorter, I was some-times almost certain that I heard a noise as if some one was playing on the great organ in the hall. I did not hear it every evening; but, certainly, I did very often; usually when I was sitting with Miss Rosamond, after I had put her to bed, and keeping quite still and silent in the bed-room. Then I used to hear it booming and swelling away in the distance. The first night, when I went down to my supper, I asked Dorothy who had been playing music, and James said very shortly that I was a gowk to take the wind soughing among the trees for music: but I saw Dorothy look at him very fearfully, and Bessy, the kitchen-maid, said something beneath her breath, and went quite white. I saw they did not like my question, so I held my peace till I was with Dorothy alone, when I knew I could get a good deal out of her. So, the next day, I watched my time, and I coaxed and asked her who it was that played the organ; for I knew that it was the organ and not the wind well enough, for all I had kept silence before James. But Dorothy had had her lesson I'll warrant, and never a word could I get from her. So then I tried Bessy, though I had always held my head rather above her, as I was evened to James and Dorothy, and she was little better than their servant. So she said I must never, never tell; and if I ever told, I was never to say *she* had told me; but it was a very strange noise, and she had heard it many a time, but most of all on winter nights, and before storms; and folks did say, it was the old lord playing on the great organ in the hall, just as he used to do when he was alive; but who the old lord was, or why he played, and why he played on stormy winter evenings in particular, she either could not or would not tell me. Well! I told you I had a brave heart; and I thought it was rather pleasant to have that grand music rolling about the house, let who would be the player; for now it rose above the great gusts of wind, and wailed and triumphed just like a living creature, and then it fell to a softness most complete; only it was always music, and tunes, so it was nonsense to call it the wind. I thought, at first, that it might be Miss Furnivall who played, unknown to Bessy; but, one day when I was in the hall by myself, I opened the organ and peeped all about it, and around it, as I had done to the organ in Crosthwaite Church once before, and I saw it was all broken and destroyed inside, though it looked so brave and fine; and then, though it was noon-day, my flesh began to creep a little, and I shut it up, and run away pretty quickly to my own bright nursery; and I did not like hearing the music for some time after that, any more than James and Dorothy did. All this time Miss Rosamond was making herself more and more beloved. The old ladies liked her to dine with them at their early dinner; James stood behind Miss Furnivall's chair, and I behind Miss Rosamond's all in state; and, after dinner, she would play about in a corner of the great drawing-room, as still as any mouse, while Miss Furnivall slept, and I had my dinner in the kitchen. But she was glad enough to come to me in the nursery afterwards; for, as she said, Miss Furnivall was so sad, and Mrs. Stark so dull; but she and I were merry enough; and, by-and-by, I got not to care for that weird rolling music, which did one no harm, if we did not know where it came from.

That winter was very cold. In the middle of October the frosts began, and lasted many, many weeks. I remember, one day at dinner, Miss Furnivall lifted up her sad, heavy eyes, and said to Mrs. Stark, "I am afraid we shall have a terrible winter," in a strange kind of meaning way. But Mrs. Stark pretended not to hear, and talked very loud of something else. My little lady and I did not care for the frost; not we! As long as it was dry we climbed up the steep brows, behind the house, and went up on the Fells, which were bleak and bare enough, and there we ran races in the fresh, sharp air; and once we came down by a new path that took us past the two old, gnarled holly-trees, which grew about half-way down by the east side of the house. But the days grew shorter, and shorter; and the old lord, if it was he, played away more, and more stormily and sadly on the great organ. One Sunday afternoon,—it must have been towards the end of November—I asked Dorothy to take charge of little Missey when she came out of the drawing-room, after Miss Furnivall had had her nap; for it was too cold to take her with me to church, and yet I wanted to go. And Dorothy was glad enough to promise, and was so fond of the child that all seemed well; and Bessy and I set off very briskly, though the sky hung heavy and black over the white earth, as if the night had never fully gone away; and the air, though still, was very biting and keen.

"We shall have a fall of snow," said Bessy to me. And sure

enough, even while we were in church, it came down thick, in great, large flakes, so thick it almost darkened the windows. It had stopped snowing before we came out, but it lay soft, thick and deep beneath our feet, as we tramped home. Before we got to the hall the moon rose, and I think it was lighter then,—what with the moon, and what with the white dazzling snow—than it had been when we went to church, between two and three o'clock. I have not told you that Miss Furnivall and Mrs. Stark never went to church: they used to read the prayers together, in their quiet, gloomy way; they seemed to feel the Sunday very long without their tapestry-work to be busy at. So when I went to Dorothy in the kitchen, to fetch Miss Rosamond and take her up-stairs with me, I did not much wonder when the old woman told me that the ladies had kept the child with them, and that she had never come to the kitchen, as I had bidden her, when she was tired of behaving pretty in the drawing-room. So I took off my things and went to find her, and bring her to her supper in the nursery. But when I went into the best drawing-room, there sat the two old ladies, very still and quiet, dropping out a word now and then, but looking as if nothing so bright and merry as Miss Rosamond had ever been near them. Still I thought she might be hiding from me; it was one of her pretty ways; and that she had persuaded them to look as if they knew nothing about her; so I went softly peeping under this sofa, and behind that chair, making believe I was sadly frightened at not finding her.

"What's the matter, Hester?" said Mrs. Stark sharply. I don't know if Miss Furnivall had seen me, for, as I told you, she was very deaf, and she sat quite still, idly staring into the fire, with her hopeless face. "I'm only looking for my little Rosy-Posy," replied I, still thinking that the child was there, and near me, though I could not see her.

"Miss Rosamond is not here," said Mrs. Stark. "She went away more than an hour ago to find Dorothy." And she too turned and went on looking into the fire.

My heart sank at this, and I began to wish I had never left my darling. I went back to Dorothy and told her. James was gone out for the day, but she and me and Bessy took lights and went up into the nursery first, and then we roamed over the great large house, calling and entreating Miss Rosamond to come out of her hiding place, and not frighten us to death in that way. But there was no answer; no sound.

"Oh!" said I at last. "Can she have got into the east wing and hidden there?"

But Dorothy said it was not possible, for that she herself had never been in there; that the doors were always locked, and my lord's steward had the keys, she believed; at any rate, neither she nor James had ever seen them: so, I said I would go back, and see if, after all, she was not hidden in the drawing-room, unknown to the old ladies; and if I found her there, I said, I would whip her well for the fright she had given me; but I never meant to do it. Well, I went back to the west drawing-room, and I told Mrs. Stark we could not find her anywhere, and asked for leave to look all about the furniture there, for I thought now, that she might have fallen asleep in some warm, hidden corner; but no! we looked, Miss Furnivall got up and looked, trembling all over, and she was no where there; then we set off again, every one in the house, and looked in all the places we had searched before, but we could not find her. Miss Furnivall shivered and shook so much, that Mrs. Stark took her back into the warm drawing-room; but not before they had made me promise to bring her to them when she was found. Well-a-day! I began to think she never would be found, when I bethought me to look out into the great front court, all covered with snow. I was up-stairs when I looked out; but, it was such clear moonlight, I could see quite plain two little footprints, which might be traced from the hall door, and round the corner of the east wing. I don't know how I got down, but I tugged open the great, stiff hall door; and, throwing the skirt of my gown over head for a cloak, I ran out. I turned the east corner, and there a black shadow fell on the snow; but when I came again into the moonlight, there were the little footmarks going up—up to the Fells. It was bitter cold; so cold that the air almost took the skin off my face as I ran, but I ran on, crying to think how my poor little darling must be perished, and frightened. I was within sight of the holly-trees, when I saw a shepherd coming down the hill, bearing something in his arms wrapped in his maud. He shouted to me, and asked me if I had lost a bairn; and, when I could not speak

for crying, he bore towards me, and I saw my wee bairnie lying
still, and white, and stiff, in his arms, as if she had been dead. He
told me he had been up the Fells to gather in his sheep, before the
deep cold of night came on, and that under the holly-trees (black
marks on the hill-side, where no other bush was for miles around)
he had found my little lady—my lamb—my queen—my darling—stiff, and cold, in the terrible sleep which is frost-begotten.
Oh! the joy, and the tears, of having her in my arms once again!
for I would not let him carry her; but took her, maud and all, into
my own arms, and held her near my own warm neck, and heart,
and felt the life stealing slowly back again into her little, gentle
limbs. But she was still insensible when we reached the hall, and I
had no breath for speech. We went in by the kitchen door.

"Bring the warming-pan," said I; and I carried her up-stairs
and began undressing her by the nursery fire, which Bessy had
kept up. I called my little lammie all the sweet and playful names
I could think of,—even while my eyes were blinded by my tears;
and at last, oh! at length she opened her large, blue eyes. Then
I put her into her warm bed, and sent Dorothy down to tell
Miss Furnivall that all was well; and I made up my mind to sit
by my darling's bedside the live-long night. She fell away into
a soft sleep as soon as her pretty head had touched the pillow,
and I watched by her till morning light; when she wakened up
bright and clear—or so I thought at first—and, my dears, so I
think now.

She said, that she had fancied that she should like to go to
Dorothy, for that both the old ladies were asleep, and it was very
dull in the drawing-room; and that, as she was going through the
west lobby, she saw the snow through the high window falling—
falling—soft and steady; but she wanted to see it lying pretty and
white on the ground; so she made her way into the great hall;
and then, going to the window, she saw it bright and soft upon
the drive; but while she stood there, she saw a little girl, not as
old as she was, "but so pretty," said my darling, "and this little
girl beckoned to me to come out; and oh, she was so pretty and
so sweet, I could not choose but go." And then this other little
girl had taken her by the hand, and side by side the two had gone
round the east corner.

"Now, you are a naughty little girl, and telling stories," said I. "What would your good mamma, that is in heaven, and never told a story in her life, say to her little Rosamond, if she heard her—and I dare say she does—telling stories!"

"Indeed, Hester," sobbed out my child, "I'm telling you true. Indeed I am."

"Don't tell me!" said I, very stern. "I tracked you by your foot-marks through the snow; there were only yours to be seen: and if you had had a little girl to go hand-in-hand with you up the hill, don't you think the foot-prints would have gone along with yours?"

"I can't help it, dear, dear Hester," said she, crying, "if they did not; I never looked at her feet, but she held my hand fast and tight in her little one, and it was very, very cold. She took me up the Fell-path, up to the holly trees; and there I saw a lady weeping and crying; but when she saw me, she hushed her weeping, and smiled very proud and grand, and took me on her knee, and began to lull me to sleep; and that's all, Hester—but that is true; and my dear mamma knows it is," said she, crying. So I thought the child was in a fever, and pretended to believe her, as she went over her story—over and over again, and always the same. At last Dorothy knocked at the door with Miss Rosamond's breakfast; and she told me the old ladies were down in the eating parlour, and that they wanted to speak to me. They had both been into the night-nursery the evening before, but it was after Miss Rosamond was asleep; so they had only looked at her—not asked me any questions.

"I shall catch it," thought I to myself, as I went along the north gallery. "And yet," I thought, taking courage, "it was in their charge I left her; and it's they that's to blame for letting her steal away unknown and unwatched." So I went in boldly, and told my story. I told it all to Miss Furnivall, shouting it close to her ear; but when I came to the mention of the other little girl out in the snow, coaxing and tempting her out, and wiling her up to the grand and beautiful lady by the Holly-tree, she threw her arms up—her old and withered arms—and cried aloud, "Oh! Heaven, forgive! Have mercy!"

Mrs. Stark took hold of her; roughly enough, I thought; but

she was past Mrs. Stark's management, and spoke to me, in a kind of wild warning and authority.

"Hester! keep her from that child! It will lure her to her death! That evil child! Tell her it is a wicked, naughty child." Then, Mrs. Stark hurried me out of the room; where, indeed, I was glad enough to go; but Miss Furnivall kept shrieking out, "Oh! have mercy! Wilt Thou never forgive! It is many a long year ago——"

I was very uneasy in my mind after that. I durst never leave Miss Rosamond, night or day, for fear lest she might slip off again, after some fancy or other; and all the more, because I thought I could make out that Miss Furnivall was crazy, from their odd ways about her; and I was afraid lest something of the same kind (which might be in the family, you know) hung over my darling. And the great frost never ceased all this time; and, whenever it was a more stormy night than usual, between the gusts, and through the wind, we heard the old lord playing on the great organ. But, old lord, or not, wherever Miss Rosamond went, there I followed; for my love for her, pretty, helpless orphan, was stronger than my fear for the grand and terrible sound. Besides, it rested with me to keep her cheerful and merry, as beseemed her age. So we played together, and wandered together, here and there, and every-where; for I never dared to lose sight of her again in that large and rambling house. And so it happened, that one afternoon, not long before Christmas day, we were playing together on the billiard-table in the great hall (not that we knew the right way of playing, but she liked to roll the smooth ivory balls with her pretty hands, and I liked to do whatever she did); and, by-and-by, without our noticing it, it grew dusk indoors, though it was still light in the open air, and I was thinking of taking her back into the nursery, when, all of sudden, she cried out,

"Look, Hester! look! there is my poor little girl out in the snow!"

I turned towards the long, narrow windows, and there, sure enough, I saw a little girl, less than my Miss Rosamond—dressed all unfit to be out-of-doors such a bitter night—crying, and beating against the window-panes, as if she wanted to be let in. She seemed to sob and wail, till Miss Rosamond could bear it no longer, and was flying to the door to open it, when, all of a sudden, and close upon us, the great organ pealed out so loud and thundering, it fairly made me tremble; and all the more, when I remembered me that, even in the stillness of that dead-cold weather, I had heard no sound of little battering hands upon the window-glass, although the Phantom Child had seemed to put forth all its force; and, although I had seen it wail and cry, no faintest touch of sound had fallen upon my ears. Whether I remembered all this at the very moment, I do not know; the great organ sound had so stunned me into terror; but this I know, I caught up Miss Rosamond before she got the hall-door opened, and clutched her, and carried her away, kicking and screaming, into the large, bright kitchen, where Dorothy and Agnes were busy with their mince-pies.

"What is the matter with my sweet one?" cried Dorothy, as I bore in Miss Rosamond, who was sobbing as if her heart would break.

"She won't let me open the door for my little girl to come in; and she'll die if she is out on the Fells all night. Cruel, naughty Hester," she said, slapping me; but she might have struck harder, for I had seen a look of ghastly terror on Dorothy's face, which made my very blood run cold.

"Shut the back kitchen door fast, and bolt it well," said she to Agnes. She said no more; she gave me raisins and almonds to quiet Miss Rosamond: but she sobbed about the little girl in the snow, and would not touch any of the good things. I was thankful when she cried herself to sleep in bed. Then I stole down to the kitchen, and told Dorothy I had made up my mind. I would carry my darling back to my father's house in Applethwaite; where, if we lived humbly, we lived at peace. I said I had been frightened enough with the old lord's organ-playing; but now that I had seen for myself this little moaning child, all decked out as no child in the neighbourhood could be, beating and battering to get in, yet always without any sound or noise—with the dark wound on its right shoulder; and that Miss Rosamond had known it again for the phantom that had nearly lured her to her death (which Dorothy knew was true); I would stand it no longer.

I saw Dorothy change colour once or twice. When I had done, she told me she did not think I could take Miss Rosamond with me, for that she was my lord's ward, and I had no right over her; and she asked me, would I leave the child that I was so fond of, just for sounds and sights that could do me no harm; and that they had all had to get used to in their turns? I was all in a hot, trembling passion; and I said it was very well for her to talk, that knew what these sights and noises betokened, and that had, perhaps, had something to do with the Spectre-child while it was alive. And I taunted her so, that she told me all she knew, at last; and then I wished I had never been told, for it only made me more afraid than ever.

She said she had heard the tale from old neighbours, that were alive when she was first married; when folks used to come to the hall sometimes, before it had got such a bad name on the country side: it might not be true, or it might, what she had been told.

The old lord was Miss Furnivall's father—Miss Grace, as Dorothy called her, for Miss Maude was the elder, and Miss Furnivall by rights. The old lord was eaten up with pride. Such a proud man was never seen or heard of; and his daughters were like him. No one was good enough to wed them, although they had choice enough; for they were the great beauties of their day, as I had seen by their portraits, where they hung in the state drawing-room. But, as the old saying is, "Pride will have a fall;" and these two haughty beauties fell in love with the same man, and he no better than a foreign musician, whom their father had down from London to play music with him at the Manor House. For, above all things, next to his pride, the old lord loved music. He could play on nearly every instrument that ever was heard of: and it was a strange thing it did not soften him; but he was a fierce, dour, old man, and had broken his poor wife's heart with his cruelty, they said. He was mad after music, and would pay any money for it. So he got this foreigner to come; who made such beautiful music, that they said the very birds on the trees stopped their singing to listen. And, by degrees, this foreign gentleman got such a hold over the old lord, that nothing would serve him but that he must come every year; and it was he that had the great organ brought from Holland, and built up in the hall, where it stood now. He taught the old lord to play on it; but many and many a time, when Lord Furnivall was thinking of nothing but his fine organ, and his finer music, the dark foreigner was walking abroad in the woods with one of the young ladies; now Miss Maude, and then Miss Grace.

Miss Maude won the day and carried off the prize, such as it was; and he and she were married, all unknown to any one; and before he made his next yearly visit, she had been confined of a little girl at a farm-house on the Moors, while her father and Miss Grace thought she was away at Doncaster Races. But though she was a wife and a mother, she was not a bit softened, but as haughty and as passionate as ever; and perhaps more so, for she was jealous of Miss Grace, to whom her foreign husband paid a deal of court—by way of blinding her—as he told his wife. But Miss Grace triumphed over Miss Maude, and Miss Maude grew fiercer and fiercer, both with her husband and with her sister; and the former—who could easily shake off what was disagreeable, and hide himself in foreign countries—went away a month before his usual time that summer, and half-threatened that he would never come back again. Meanwhile, the little girl was left at the farm-house, and her mother used to have her horse saddled and gallop wildly over the hills to see her once every week, at the very least—for where she loved, she loved; and where she hated, she hated. And the old lord went on playing—playing on his organ; and the servants thought the sweet music he made had soothed down his awful temper, of which (Dorothy said) some terrible tales could be told. He grew infirm too, and had to walk with a crutch; and his son—that was the present Lord Furnivall's father—was with the army in America, and the other son at sea; so Miss Maude had it pretty much her own way, and she and Miss Grace grew colder and bitterer to each other every day; till at last they hardly ever spoke, except when the old lord was by. The foreign musician came again the next summer, but it was for the last time; for they led him such a life with their jealousy and their passions, that he grew weary, and went away, and never was heard of again. And Miss Maude, who had always meant to have her marriage acknowledged when her father should be dead, was left now a deserted wife—whom nobody knew to have been married—with a child that she dared not own, although she loved it to distraction; living with a father whom she feared, and a sister whom she hated. When the next summer passed over and the dark foreigner never came, both Miss Maude and Miss Grace grew gloomy and sad; they had a haggard look about them, though they looked handsome as ever. But by-and-by Miss Maude brightened; for her father grew more and more infirm, and more than ever carried away by his music; and she and Miss Grace lived almost entirely apart, having separate rooms, the one on the west side, Miss Maude on the east—those very rooms which were now shut up. So she thought she might have her little girl with her, and no one need ever know except those who dared not speak about it, and were bound to believe that it was, as she said, a cottager's child she had taken a fancy to. All this Dorothy said, was pretty well known; but what came afterwards no one knew, except Miss Grace, and Mrs. Stark, who was even then her maid, and much more of a friend to her than ever her sister had been. But the servants supposed, from words that were dropped, that Miss Maude had triumphed over Miss Grace, and told her that all the time the dark foreigner had been mocking her with pretended love—he was her own husband; the colour left Miss Grace's cheek and lips that very day for ever, and she was heard to say many a time that sooner or later she would have her revenge; and Mrs. Stark was for ever spying about the east rooms.

One fearful night, just after the New Year had come in, when the snow was lying thick and deep, and the flakes were still falling—fast enough to blind any one who might be out and abroad—there was a great and violent noise heard, and the old lord's voice above all, cursing and swearing awfully,—and the cries of a little child,—and the proud defiance of a fierce woman,—and the sound of a blow,—and a dead stillness,—and moans and wailings dying away on the hill-side! Then the old lord summoned all his servants, and told them, with terrible oaths, and words more terrible, that his daughter had disgraced herself, and that he had turned her out of doors,—her, and her child,—and that if ever they gave her help,—or food,—or shelter,—he prayed that they might never enter Heaven. And, all the while, Miss Grace stood by him, white and still as any stone; and when he had ended she heaved a great sigh, as much as to say her work was done, and her end was accomplished. But the old lord never touched his organ again, and died within the year; and no wonder! for, on the morrow of that wild and fearful night, the shepherds, coming down the Fell side, found Miss Maude sitting, all crazy and smiling, under the holly-trees, nursing a dead child,—with a terrible mark on its right shoulder. "But that was not what killed it," said Dorothy; "it was the frost and the cold;—every wild creature was in its hole, and every beast in its fold,—while the child and its mother were turned out to wander on the Fells! And now you know all! and I wonder if you are less frightened now?"

I was more frightened than ever; but I said I was not. I wished Miss Rosamond and myself well out of that dreadful house for ever; but I would not leave her, and I dared not take her away. But oh! how I watched her, and guarded her! We bolted the doors, and shut the window-shutters fast, an hour or more before dark, rather than leave them open five minutes too late. But my little lady still heard the weird child crying and mourning; and not all we could do or say, could keep her from wanting to go to her, and let her in from the cruel wind and the snow. All this time, I kept away from Miss Furnivall and Mrs. Stark, as much as ever I could; for I feared them—I knew no good could be about them, with their grey hard faces, and their dreamy eyes, looking back into the ghastly years that were gone. But, even in my fear, I had a kind of pity—for Miss Furnivall, at least. Those gone down to the pit can hardly have a more hopeless look than that which was ever on her face. At last I even got so sorry for her—who never said a word but what was quite forced from her—that I prayed for her; and I taught Miss Rosamond to pray for one who had done a deadly sin; but often when she came to those words, she would listen, and start up from her knees, and say, "I hear my little girl plaining and crying very sad—Oh! let her in, or she will die!"

One night—just after New Year's Day had come at last, and the long winter had taken a turn, as I hoped—I heard the west drawing-room bell ring three times, which was the signal for me. I would not leave Miss Rosamond alone, for all she was asleep— for the old lord had been playing wilder than ever—and I feared lest my darling should waken to hear the spectre child; see her I knew she could not, I had fastened the windows too well for that. So, I took her out of her bed and wrapped her up in such outer clothes as were most handy, and carried her down to the drawing-room, where the old ladies sat at their tapestry work as usual. They looked up when I came in, and Mrs. Stark asked, quite astounded, "Why did I bring Miss Rosamond there, out of her warm bed?" I had begun to whisper, "Because I was afraid of her being tempted out while I was away, by the wild child in the snow," when she stopped me short (with a glance at Miss Furnivall), and said Miss Furnivall wanted me to undo some work she had done wrong, and which neither of them could see to unpick. So, I laid my pretty dear on the sofa, and sat down on a stool by them, and hardened my heart against them as I heard the wind rising and howling.

Miss Rosamond slept on sound, for all the wind blew so; and Miss Furnivall said never a word, nor looked round when the gusts shook the windows. All at once she started up to her full height, and put up one hand, as if to bid us listen.

"I hear voices!" said she. "I hear terrible screams—I hear my father's voice!"

Just at that moment, my darling wakened with a sudden start: "My little girl is crying, oh, how she is crying!" and she tried to get up and go to her, but she got her feet entangled in the blanket, and I caught her up; for my flesh had begun to creep at these noises, which they heard while we could catch no sound. In a minute or two the noises came, and gathered fast, and filled our ears; we, too, heard voices and screams, and no longer heard the winter's wind that raged abroad. Mrs. Stark looked at me, and I at her, but we dared not speak. Suddenly Miss Furnivall went towards the door, out into the ante-room, through the west lobby, and opened the door into the great hall. Mrs. Stark followed, and I durst not be left, though my heart almost stopped beating for fear. I wrapped my darling tight in my arms, and went out with them. In the hall the screams were louder than ever; they sounded to come from the east wing—nearer and nearer—close on the other side of the locked-up doors—close behind them. Then I noticed that the great bronze chandelier seemed all alight, though the hall was dim, and that a fire was blazing in the vast hearth-place, though it gave no heat; and I shuddered up with terror, and folded my darling closer to me. But as I did so, the east door shook, and she, suddenly struggling to get free from me, cried, "Hester! I must go! My little girl is there; I hear her; she is coming! Hester, I must go!"

I held her tight with all my strength; with a set will, I held her. If I had died, my hands would have grasped her still, I was so resolved in my mind. Miss Furnivall stood listening, and paid no regard to my darling, who had got down to the ground, and whom I, upon my knees now, was holding with both my arms clasped round her neck; she still striving and crying to get free.

All at once, the east door gave way with a thundering crash, as if torn open in a violent passion, and there came into that broad and mysterious light, the figure of a tall old man, with grey hair and gleaming eyes. He drove before him, with many a relentless gesture of abhorrence, a stern and beautiful woman, with a little child clinging to her dress.

"Oh Hester! Hester!" cried Miss Rosamond. "It's the lady! the lady below the holly-trees; and my little girl is with her. Hester! Hester! let me go to her; they are drawing me to them. I feel them—I feel them. I must go!'

Again she was almost convulsed by her efforts to get away; but I held her tighter and tighter, till I feared I should do her a hurt; but rather that than let her go towards those terrible phantoms. They passed along towards the great hall-door, where the winds howled and ravened for their prey; but before they reached that, the lady turned; and I could see that she defied the old man with a fierce and proud defiance; but then she quailed—and then she threw her arms wildly and piteously to save her child—her little child—from a blow from his uplifted crutch.

And Miss Rosamond was torn as by a power stronger than mine, and writhed in my arms, and sobbed (for by this time the poor darling was growing faint).

"They want me to go with them on to the Fells—they are drawing me to them. Oh, my little girl! I would come, but cruel, wicked Hester holds me very tight." But when she saw the up-lifted crutch she swooned away, and I thanked God for it. Just at this moment—when the tall, old man, his hair streaming as in the blast of a furnace, was going to strike the little, shrinking child—Miss Furnivall, the old woman by my side, cried out, "Oh, father!

father! spare the little innocent child!" But just then I saw—we all saw—another phantom shape itself, and grow clear out of the blue and misty light that filled the hall; we had not seen her till now, for it was another lady who stood by the old man, with a look of relentless hate and triumphant scorn. That figure was very beautiful to look upon, with a soft, white hat drawn down over the proud brows, and a red and curling lip. It was dressed in an open robe of blue satin. I had seen that figure before. It was the likeness of Miss Furnivall in her youth; and the terrible phantoms moved on, regardless of old Miss Furnivall's wild entreaty, and the uplifted crutch fell on the right shoulder of the little child, and the younger sister looked on, stony and deadly serene. But at that moment, the dim lights, and the fire that gave no heat, went out of themselves, and Miss Furnivall lay at our feet stricken down by the palsy—death-stricken.

Yes! she was carried to her bed that night never to rise again. She lay with her face to the wall, muttering low, but muttering always: "Alas! alas! what is done in youth can never be undone in age! what is done in youth can never be undone in age!"

# John Berwick Harwood

## HORROR: A TRUE TALE

*Eighteenth-century novelists frequently presented their fiction as true accounts, or actual memoirs, in an attempt to raise the novel form from its then sordid status. Similarly, authors of nineteenth-century ghost tales sought to provide the authentic ghost story experience, even when the tale's credentials were dubious at best. In this case the story's subtitle, "A True Tale," offers readers a chance to enjoy someone else's uncanny experience, made all the more tantalizing by its promise of authenticity. While this eerie story was published anonymously, it has been attributed to* JOHN BERWICK HARWOOD *(1829-1899), who was certainly not an heiress of nineteen. He wrote other ghost stories, and he contributed "Picking up a Pocket Book," a rousing story of a bank clerk engaged in an American adventure, to the 1861 Christmas number for Dickens's* All the Year Round. *"Horror: A True Tale" first appeared in the January 1861 issue of* Blackwood's Magazine.

I WAS BUT NINETEEN YEARS OF AGE when the incident occurred which has thrown a shadow over my life; and, ah me! how many and many a weary year has dragged by since then! Young, happy, and beloved I was in those long-departed days. They said that I was beautiful. The mirror now reflects a haggard old woman, with ashen lips and face of deadly pallor. But do not fancy that you are listening to a mere puling lament. It is not the flight of years that has brought me to be this wreck of my former self: had it been so, I could have borne the loss cheerfully, patiently, as the common lot of all; but it was no natural progress of decay which has robbed me of bloom, of youth, of the hopes and joys that belong to youth, snapped the link that bound my heart to another's, and doomed me to a lone old age. I try to be patient, but my cross has been heavy, and my heart is empty and weary, and I long for the death that comes so slowly to those who pray to die.

I will try and relate, exactly as it happened, the event which blighted my life. Though it occurred many years ago, there is no fear that I should have forgotten any of the minutest circumstances: they were stamped on my brain too clearly and burningly, like the brand of a red-hot iron. I see them written in the wrinkles of my brow, in the dead whiteness of my hair, which was a glossy brown once, and has known no gradual change from dark to grey, from grey to white, as with those happy ones who were the companions of my girlhood, and whose honoured age is soothed by the love of children and grandchildren. But I must not envy them. I only meant to say that the difficulty of my task has no connection with want of memory—I remember but too well. But as I take the pen, my hand trembles, my head swims, the old rushing faintness and Horror comes over me again, and the well-remembered fear is upon me. Yet I will go on.

This, briefly, is my story: I was a great heiress, I believe, though I cared little for the fact, but so it was. My father had great possessions, and no son to inherit after him. His three daughters, of whom I was the youngest, were to share the broad acres among them. I have said, and truly, that I cared little for this circumstance; and, indeed, I was so rich then in health and youth and love, that I felt myself quite indifferent to all else. The possession of all the treasures of earth could never have made up for what I then had—and lost, as I am about to relate.

Of course, we girls knew that we were heiresses, but I do not think Lucy and Minnie were any the prouder or the happier on that account. I know I was not. Reginald did not court me for my money. Of *that* I felt assured. He proved it, Heaven be praised! when he shrank from my side after the change. Yes, in all my lonely age, I can still be thankful that he did not keep his word, as some would have done, did not clasp at the altar a hand he had learned to loathe and shudder at, because it was full of gold— much gold! At least, he spared me that. And I know that I was loved, and the knowledge has kept me from going mad through many a weary day and restless night, when my hot eyeballs had not a tear to shed, and even to weep was a luxury denied me.

Our house was an old Tudor mansion. My father was very particular in keeping the smallest peculiarities of his home unal-

Thus the many peaks and gables, the numerous turrets, ...the mullioned windows with their quaint lozenge panes set in lead, remained very nearly as they had been three centuries back. Over and above the quaint melancholy of our dwelling, with the deep woods of its park and the sullen waters of the mere, our neighbourhood was thinly peopled and primitive, and the people round us were ignorant, and tenacious of ancient ideas and traditions. Thus it was a superstitious atmosphere that we children were reared in, and we heard, from our infancy, countless tales of horror, some mere fables doubtless, others legends of dark deeds of the olden time, exaggerated by credulity and the love of the marvellous. Our mother had died when we were young, and our other parent being, though a kind father, much absorbed in affairs of various kinds, as an active magistrate and landlord, there was no one to check the unwholesome stream of tradition with which our plastic minds were inundated in the company of nurses and servants. As years went on, however, the old ghostly tales partially lost their effects, and our undisciplined minds were turned more towards balls, dress, and partners, and other matters airy and trivial, more welcome to our riper age.

It was at a county assembly that Reginald and I first met—met and loved. Yes, I am sure that he loved me with all his heart. It was not as deep a heart as some, I have thought in my grief and anger; but I never doubted its truth and honesty. Reginald's father and mine approved of our growing attachment; and as for myself, I know I was so happy then, that I look back upon those fleeting moments as on some delicious dream. I now come to the change. I have lingered on my childish reminiscences, my bright and happy youth, and now I must tell the rest—the blight and the sorrow.

It was Christmas, always a joyful and a hospitable time in the country, especially in such an old hall as our home, where quaint customs and frolics were much clung to, as part and parcel of the very dwelling itself. The hall was full of guests—so full, indeed, that there was great difficulty in providing sleeping accommodation for all. Several narrow and dark chambers in the turrets—mere pigeon-holes, as we irreverently called what had been thought good enough for the stately gentlemen of Elizabeth's reign—were now allotted to bachelor visitors, after having been empty for a century. All the spare rooms in the body and wings of the hall were occupied, of course; and the servants who had been brought down were lodged at the farm and at the keeper's, so great was the demand for space.

At last the unexpected arrival of an elderly relative, who had been asked months before, but scarcely expected, caused great commotion. My aunts went about wringing their hands distractedly. Lady Speldhurst was a personage of some consequence; she was a distant cousin, and had been for years on cool terms with us all, on account of some fancied affront or slight when she had paid her *last* visit, about the time of my christening. She was seventy years old; she was infirm, rich, and testy; moreover, she was my godmother, though I had forgotten the fact, but it seems that though I had formed no expectations of a legacy in my favour, my aunts had done so for me. Aunt Margaret was especially eloquent on the subject. "There isn't a room left," she said; "was ever anything so unfortunate! We cannot put Lady Speldhurst into the turrets, and yet where *is* she to sleep? And Rosa's godmother, too! poor dear child! how dreadful! After all these years of estrangement, and with a hundred thousand in the funds, and no comfortable warm room at her own unlimited disposal—and Christmas, of all times in the year!" What *was* to be done? My aunts could not resign their own chambers to Lady Speldhurst, because they had already given them up to some of the married guests. My father was the most hospitable of men, but he was rheumatic, gouty, and methodical. His sisters-in-law dared not propose to shift his quarters, and indeed he would have far sooner dined on prison fare than have been translated to a strange bed. The matter ended in my giving up my room. I had a strange reluctance to making the offer, which surprised myself. Was it a boding of evil to come? I cannot say. We are strangely and wonderfully made. It *may* have been. At any rate, I do not think it was any selfish unwillingness to make an old and infirm lady comfortable by a trifling sacrifice. I was perfectly healthy and strong. The weather was not cold for the time of year. It was a dark moist Yule—not a snowy one, though snow brooded overhead in the darkling clouds. I *did* make the offer, which became me, I said with a laugh, as the youngest. My sisters laughed too, and made a jest of my evident wish to propitiate my godmother.

"She is a fairy godmother, Rosa," said Minnie; "and you know she was affronted at your christening, and went away muttering vengeance. Here she is coming back to see you; I hope she brings golden gifts with her."

I thought little of Lady Speldhurst and her possible golden gifts. I cared nothing for the wonderful fortune in the funds that my aunts whispered and nodded about so mysteriously. But, since then, I have wondered whether, had I then shown myself peevish or obstinate, had I refused to give up my room for the expected kinswoman, it would not have altered the whole of my life? But then Lucy or Minnie would have offered in my stead, and been sacrificed—what do I say?—better that the blow should have fallen as it did, than on those dear ones.

The chamber to which I removed was a dim little triangular room in the western wing, and was only to be reached by traversing the picture-gallery, or by mounting a little flight of stone stairs which led directly upwards from the low-browed arch of a door that opened into the garden. There was one more room on the same landing-place, and this was a mere receptacle for broken furniture, shattered toys, and all the lumber that *will* accumulate in a country-house. The room I was to inhabit for a few nights was a tapestry-hung apartment, with faded green curtains of some costly stuff, contrasting oddly with a new carpet and the bright fresh hangings of the bed, which had been hurriedly erected. The furniture was half old, half new, and on the dressing-table stood a very quaint oval mirror, in a frame of black wood—unpolished ebony, I think. I can remember the very pattern of the carpet, the number of chairs, the situation of the bed, the figures on the tapestry. Nay, I can recollect not only the colour of the dress I wore on that fatal evening, but the arrangement of every scrap of lace and ribbon, of every flower, every jewel, with a memory but too perfect.

Scarcely had my maid finished spreading out my various articles of attire for the evening (when there was to be a great dinner-party), when the rumble of a carriage announced that Lady Speldhurst had arrived. The short winter's day drew to a

close, and a large number of guests were gathered together in
the ample drawing-room, around the blaze of the wood fire,
after dinner. My father, I recollect, was not with us at first. There
were some squires of the old hard-riding, hard-drinking stamp
still lingering over their port in the dining-room, and the host, of
course, could not leave them. But the ladies and all the younger
gentlemen—both those who slept under our roof, and those
who would have a dozen miles of fog and mire to encounter on
their road home—were all together. Need I say that Reginald was
there? He sat near me—my accepted lover, my plighted future
husband. We were to be married in the spring. My sisters were
not far off; they, too, had found eyes that sparkled and softened
in meeting theirs, had found hearts that beat responsive to their
own. And, in their cases, no rude frost nipped the blossom ere
it became the fruit; there was no canker in their flowerets of
young hope, no cloud in their sky. Innocent and loving, they were
beloved by men worthy their esteem.

The room, a large and lofty one, with an arched roof, had
somewhat of a sombre character from being wainscoted and
ceiled with polished black oak of a great age. There were mirrors,
and there were pictures on the walls, and handsome furniture,
and marble chimney-pieces, and a gay Toumay carpet; but these
merely appeared as bright spots on the dark background of the
Elizabethan woodwork. Many lights were burning, but the blackness of the walls and roof seemed absolutely to swallow up their
rays, like the mouth of a cavern. A hundred candles could not
have given that apartment the cheerful lightness of a modern
drawing-room. But the gloomy richness of the panels matched
well with the ruddy gleam from the enormous wood fire, in
which, crackling and glowing, now lay the mighty Yule log. Quite
a blood-red lustre poured forth from the fire, and quivered on the
walls and the groined roof.

We had gathered round the vast antique hearth in a wide
circle. The quivering light of the fire and candles fell upon us all,
but not equally, for some were in shadow. I remember still how
tall and manly and handsome Reginald looked that night, taller
by the head than any there, and full of high spirits and gaiety. I,
too, was in the highest spirits; never had my bosom felt lighter,

and I believe it was my mirth which gradually gained the rest, for I recollect what a blithe, joyous company we seemed. All save one. Lady Speldhurst, dressed in grey silk and wearing a quaint head-dress, sat in her armchair, facing the fire, very silent, with her hands and her sharp chin propped on a sort of ivory-handled crutch that she walked with (for she was lame), peering at me with half-shut eyes. She was a little spare old woman, with very keen delicate features of the French type. Her grey silk dress, her spotless lace, old-fashioned jewels, and prim neatness of array, were well suited to the intelligence of her face, with its thin lips, and eyes of a piercing black, undimmed by age. Those eyes made me uncomfortable, in spite of my gaiety, as they followed my every movement with curious scrutiny. Still I was very merry and gay; my sisters even wondered at my ever-ready mirth, which was almost wild in its excess. I have heard since then of the Scottish belief that those doomed to some great calamity become *fey*, and are never so disposed for merriment and laughter as just before the blow falls. If ever mortal was *fey*, then, I was so on that evening. Still, though I strove to shake it off, the pertinacious observation of old Lady Speldhurst's eyes *did* make an impression on me of a vaguely disagreeable nature. Others, too, noticed her scrutiny of me, but set it down as a mere eccentricity of a person always reputed whimsical, to say the least of it.

However, this disagreeable sensation lasted but a few moments. After a short pause my aunt took her part in the conversation, and we found ourselves listening to a weird legend which the old lady told exceedingly well. One tale led to another. Every one was called on in turn to contribute to the public entertainment, and story after story, always relating to demonology and witchcraft, succeeded. It was Christmas, the season for such tales; and the old room, with its dusky walls and pictures, and vaulted roof, drinking up the light so greedily, seemed just fitted to give effect to such legendary lore. The huge logs crackled and burnt with glowing warmth; the blood-red glare of the Yule log flashed on the faces of the listeners and narrator, on the portraits, and the holly wreathed about their frames, and the upright old dame in her antiquated dress and trinkets, like one of the originals of the pictures stepped from the canvas to join our circle. It threw a shimmering lustre of an ominously ruddy hue upon the oaken panels. No wonder that the ghost and goblin stories had a new zest. No wonder that the blood of the more timid grew chill and curdled, that their flesh crept, and their hearts beat irregularly, and the girls peeped fearfully over their shoulders, and huddled close together like frightened sheep, and half-fancied they beheld some impish and malignant face gibbering at them from the darkling corners of the old room. By degrees my high spirits died out, and I felt the childish tremors, long latent, long forgotten, coming over me. I followed each story with painful interest; I did not ask myself if I believed the dismal tales. I listened, and fear grew upon me—the blind, irrational fear of our nursery days. I am sure most of the other ladies present, young or middle-aged, were affected by the circumstances under which these traditions were heard, no less than by the wild and fantastic character of them. But with them the impression would die out next morning, when the bright sun should shine on the frosted boughs, and the rime on the grass, and the scarlet berries and green spikelets of the holly; and with me—but, ah! what was to happen ere another day dawn? Before we had made an end of this talk, my father and the other squires came in, and we ceased our ghost stories, ashamed to speak of such matters before these new-comers—hard-headed, unimaginative men, who had no sympathy with idle legends. There was now a stir and bustle.

Servants were handing round tea and coffee, and other refreshments. Then there was a little music and singing. I sang a duet with Reginald, who had a fine voice and good musical skill. I remember that my singing was much praised, and indeed I was surprised at the power and pathos of my own voice, doubtless due to my excited nerves and mind. Then I heard some one say to another that I was by far the cleverest of the Squire's daughters, as well as the prettiest. It did not make me vain. I had no rivalry with Lucy and Minnie. But Reginald whispered some soft fond words in my ear, a little before he mounted his horse to set off homewards, which *did* make me happy and proud. And to think that the next time we met—but I forgave him long ago. Poor Reginald! And now shawls and cloaks were in request, and carriages rolled up to the porch, and the guests gradually departed.

At last no one was left but those visitors staying in the house. Then my father, who had been called out to speak with the bailiff of the estate, came back with a look of annoyance on his face.

"A strange story I have just been told," said he; "here has been my bailiff to inform me of the loss of four of the choicest ewes out of that little flock of Southdowns I set such store by, and which arrived in the north but two months since. And the poor creatures have been destroyed in so strange a manner, for their carcasses are horribly mangled."

Most of us uttered some expression of pity or surprise, and some suggested that a vicious dog was probably the culprit.

"It would seem so," said my father; "it certainly seems the work of a dog; and yet all the men agree that no dog of such habits exists near us, where, indeed, dogs are scarce, excepting the shepherds' collies and the sporting dogs secured in yards. Yet the sheep are gnawed and bitten, for they show the marks of teeth. Something has done this, and has torn their bodies wolf-ishly; but apparently it has been only to suck the blood, for little or no flesh is gone."

"How strange!" cried several voices. Then some of the gentle-men remembered to have heard of cases when dogs addicted to sheep-killing had destroyed whole flocks, as if in sheer wanton-ness, scarcely deigning to taste a morsel of each slain wether.

My father shook his head. "I have heard of such cases, too," he said; "but in this instance I am tempted to think the malice of some unknown enemy has been at work. The teeth of a dog have been busy no doubt, but the poor sheep have been mutilated in a fantastic manner, as strange as horrible; their hearts, in especial, have been torn out, and left at some paces off, half-gnawed. Also, the men persist that they found the print of a naked human foot in the soft mud of the ditch, and near it—this." And he held up what seemed a broken link of a rusted iron chain. Many were the ejaculations of wonder and alarm, and many and shrewd the conjectures, but none seemed exactly to suit the bearings of the case. And when my father went on to say that two lambs of the same valuable breed had perished in the same singular manner three days previously, and that they also were found mangled and gore-stained, the amazement reached a higher pitch.

Old Lady Speldhurst listened with calm intelligent attention, but joined in none of our exclamations. At length she said to my father, "Try and recollect—have you no enemy among your neighbours?"

My father started, and knit his brows. "Not one that I know of," he replied; and indeed he was a popular man and a kind landlord.

"The more lucky you," said the old dame, with one of her grim smiles.

It was now late, and we retired to rest before long. One by one the guests dropped off. I was the member of the family selected to escort old Lady Speldhurst to her room—the room I had vacated in her favour. I did not much like the office. I felt a remarkable repugnance to my godmother, but my worthy aunts insisted so much that I should ingratiate myself with one who had so much to leave, that I could not but comply. The visitor hobbled up the broad oaken stairs actively enough, propped on my arm and her ivory crutch. The room never had looked more genial and pretty, with its brisk fire, modern furniture, and the gay French paper on the walls.

"A nice room, my dear, and I ought to be much obliged to you for it, since my maid tells me it is yours," said her ladyship; "but I am pretty sure you repent your generosity to me, after all those ghost stories, and tremble to think of a strange bed and chamber, eh?" I made some commonplace reply. The old lady arched her eyebrows. "Where have they put you, child?" she asked; "in some cockloft of the turrets, eh? or in a lumber-room—a regular ghost-trap? I can hear your heart beating with fear this moment. You are not fit to be alone."

I tried to call up my pride, and laugh off the accusation against my courage, all the more, perhaps, because I felt its truth. "Do you want anything more that I can get you, Lady Speldhurst?" I asked, trying to feign a yawn of sleepiness.

The old dame's keen eyes were upon me. "I rather like you, my dear," she said, "and I liked your mamma well enough before she treated me so shamefully about the christening dinner. Now, I know you are frightened and fearful, and if an owl should but flap your window to-night, it might drive you into fits. There is a nice little sofa-bed in this dressing-closet—call your maid to arrange it for you, and you can sleep there snugly, under the old witch's protection, and then no goblin dare harm you, and nobody will be a bit the wiser, or quiz you for being afraid."

How little I knew what hung in the balance of my refusal or acceptance of that trivial proffer! Had the veil of the future been lifted for one instant! but that veil is impenetrable to our gaze. Yet, perhaps, *she* had a glimpse of the dim vista beyond, *she* who made the offer; for when I declined, with an affected laugh, she said, in a thoughtful, half abstracted manner, "Well, well! we must all take our own way through life. Good-night, child—pleasant dreams!" And I softly closed the door. As I did so, she looked round at me rapidly, with a glance I have never forgotten, half malicious, half sad, as if she had divined the yawning gulf that was to devour my young hopes. It may have been mere eccentricity, the odd phantasy of a crooked mind, the whimsical conduct of a cynical person, triumphant in the power of affrighting youth and beauty. Or, I have since thought, it *may* have been that this singular guest possessed some such gift as the Highland "second-sight," a gift vague, sad, and useless to the possessor, but still sufficient to convey a dim sense of coming evil and boding doom. And yet, had she really known *what* was in store for me, *what* lurked behind the veil of the future, not even that arid heart could have remained impassive to the cry of humanity. She would, she *must* have snatched me back, even from the edge of the black pit of misery. But, doubtless, she had not the power. Doubtless she had but a shadowy presentiment, at any rate, of some harm to happen, and could not see, save darkly, into the viewless void where the wisest stumble.

I left her door. As I crossed the landing a bright gleam came from another room, whose door was left ajar; it (the light) fell like a bar of golden sheen across my path. As I approached, the door opened, and my sister Lucy, who had been watching for me, came out. She was already in a white cashmere wrapper, over which her loosened hair hung darkly and heavily, like tangles of silk.

"Rosa, love," she whispered, "Minnie and I can't bear the idea of your sleeping out there, all alone, in that solitary room—the very room, too, nurse Sherrard used to talk about! So, as you know Minnie has given up her room, and come to sleep in mine, still we should so wish you to stop with us to-night at any rate, and I could make up a bed on the sofa for myself, or you—and——"

I stopped Lucy's mouth with a kiss. I declined her offer. I would not listen to it. In fact, my pride was up in arms, and I felt I would rather pass the night in the churchyard itself than accept a proposal dictated, I felt sure, by the notion that my nerves were shaken by the ghostly lore we had been raking up, that I was a weak, superstitious creature, unable to pass a night in a strange chamber. So I would not listen to Lucy, but kissed her, bade her good-night, and went on my way laughing, to show my light heart. Yet, as I looked back in the dark corridor, and saw the friendly door still ajar, the yellow bar of light still crossing from wall to wall, the sweet kind face still peering after me from amid its clustering curls, I felt a thrill of sympathy, a wish to return, a yearning after human love and companionship. False shame was strongest, and conquered. I waved a gay adieu. I turned the corner, and, peeping over my shoulder, I saw the door close; the bar of yellow light was there no longer in the darkness of the passage.

I thought, at that instant, that I heard a heavy sigh. I looked sharply round. No one was there. No door was open, yet I fancied, and fancied with a wonderful vividness, that I did hear an actual sigh breathed not far off, and plainly distinguishable from the groan of the sycamore branches, as the wind tossed them to and fro in the outer blackness. If ever a mortal's good angel had cause to sigh for sorrow, not sin, mine had cause to mourn that night. But imagination plays us strange tricks, and my nervous system was not over-composed, or very fitted for judicial analysis. I had to go through the picture-gallery. I had never entered this apartment by candle-light before, and I was struck by the gloomy array of the tall portraits, gazing moodily from the canvas on the lozenge-paned or painted windows, which rattled to the blast as it swept howling by. Many of the faces looked stern, and very different from their daylight expression. In others, a furtive flickering smile seemed to mock me, as my candle illumined them; and in all, the eyes, as usual with artistic portraits, seemed to follow my motions with a scrutiny and an interest the more marked for the apathetic immovability of the other features. I felt ill at ease under this stony gaze, though conscious how absurd were my apprehensions; and I called up a smile and an air of mirth, more as if acting a part under the eyes of human beings, than of their mere shadows on the wall. I even laughed as I confronted them. No echo had my short-lived laughter but from the hollow armour and arching roof, and I continued on my way in silence. I have spoken of the armour. Indeed, there was a fine collection of plate and mail, for my father was an enthusiastic antiquary. In especial there were two suits of black armour, erect, and surmounted by helmets with closed visors, which stood as if two mailed champions were guarding the gallery and its treasures. I had often seen these, of course, but never by night, and never when my whole organisation was so overwrought and tremulous as it then was. As I approached the Black Knights, as we had dubbed them, a wild notion seized on me that the figures moved, that men were concealed in the hollow shells which had once been borne in battle and tourney. I knew the idea was childish, yet I approached in irrational alarm, and fancied I absolutely beheld eyes glaring on me from the eyelet-holes in the visors. I passed them by, and then my excited fancy told me that the figures were following me with stealthy strides. I heard a clatter of steel, caused, I am sure, by some more violent gust of wind sweeping the gallery through the crevices of the old windows, and with a smothered shriek I rushed to the door, opened it, darted out, and clapped it to with a bang that reechoed through the whole wing of the house. Then by a sudden and not uncommon revulsion of feeling, I shook off my aimless terrors, blushed at my weakness, and sought my chamber only too glad that I had been the only witness of my late tremors.

As I entered my chamber, I thought I heard something stir in the neglected lumber-room, which was the only neighbouring apartment. But I was determined to have no more panics, and resolutely shut my ears to this slight and transient noise, which had nothing unnatural in it; for surely, between rats and wind, an old manor-house on a stormy night needs no sprites to disturb it. So I entered my room, and rang for my maid. As I did so, I looked

around me, and a most unaccountable repugnance to my temporary abode came over me, in spite of my efforts. It was no more
to be shaken off than a chill is to be shaken off when we enter
some damp cave. And, rely upon it, the feeling of dislike and
apprehension with which we regard, at first sight, certain places
and people, was not implanted in us without some wholesome
purpose. I grant it is irrational—mere animal instinct—but is not
instinct God's gift, and is it for us to despise it? It is by instinct that
children know their friends from their enemies—that they distinguish with such unerring accuracy between those who like them
and those who only flatter and hate them. Dogs do the same; they
will fawn on one person, they slink snarling from another. Show
me a man whom children and dogs shrink from, and I will show
you a false, bad man—lies on his lips, and murder at his heart. No;
let none despise the heaven-sent gift of innate antipathy, which
makes the horse quail when the lion crouches in the thicket—
which makes the cattle scent the shambles from afar, and low in
terror and disgust as their nostrils snuff the blood-polluted air.
I felt this antipathy strongly as I looked around me in my new
sleeping-room, and yet I could find no reasonable pretext for my
dislike. A very good room it was, after all, now that the green
damask curtains were drawn, the fire burning bright and clear,
candles burning on the mantelpiece, and the various familiar articles of toilet arranged as usual. The bed, too, looked peaceful and
inviting—a pretty little white bed, not at all the gaunt funereal
sort of couch which haunted apartments generally contain.

My maid entered, and assisted me to lay aside the dress and
ornaments I had worn, and arranged my hair, as usual, prattling
the while, in Abigail fashion. I seldom cared to converse with
servants; but on that night a sort of dread of being left alone—a
longing to keep some human being near me—possessed me, and
I encouraged the girl to gossip, so that her duties took her half an
hour longer to get through than usual. At last, however, she had
done all that could be done, and all my questions were answered,
and my orders for the morrow reiterated and vowed obedience
to, and the clock on the turret struck one. Then Mary, yawning
a little, asked if I wanted anything more, and I was obliged to
answer No, for very shame's sake; and she went. The shutting of

the door, gently as it was closed, affected me unpleasantly. I took a dislike to the curtains, the tapestry, the dingy pictures—everything. I hated the room. I felt a temptation to put on a cloak, run, half-dressed, to my sisters' chamber, and say I had changed my mind, and come for shelter. But they must be asleep, I thought, and I could not be so unkind as to wake them. I said my prayers with unusual earnestness and a heavy heart. I extinguished the candles, and was just about to lay my head on my pillow, when the idea seized me that I would fasten the door. The candles were extinguished, but the fire-light was amply sufficient to guide me.

I gained the door. There was a lock, but it was rusty or hampered; my utmost strength could not turn the key. The bolt was broken and worthless. Baulked of my intention, I consoled myself by remembering that I had never had need of fastenings yet, and returned to my bed. I lay awake for a good while, watching the red glow of the burning coals in the grate. I was quiet now, and more composed. Even the light gossip of the maid, full of petty human cares and joys, had done me good—diverted my thoughts from brooding. I was on the point of dropping asleep, when I was twice disturbed. Once, by an owl, hooting in the ivy outside—no unaccustomed sound, but harsh and melancholy; once, by a long and mournful howling set up by the mastiff, chained in the yard beyond the wing I occupied. A long-drawn, lugubrious howling, was this latter; and much such a note as the vulgar declare to herald a death in the family. This was a fancy I had never shared; but yet I could not help feeling that the dog's mournful moans were sad, and expressive of terror, not at all like his fierce, honest bark of anger, but rather as if something evil and unwonted were abroad. But soon I fell asleep.

How long I slept, I never knew. I awoke at once, with that abrupt start which we all know well, and which carries us in a second from utter unconsciousness to the full use of our faculties. The fire was still burning, but was very low, and half the room or more was in deep shadow. I knew, I felt, that some person or thing was in the room, although nothing unusual was to be seen by the feeble light. Yet it was a sense of danger that had aroused me from slumber. I experienced, while yet asleep, the chill and shock of sudden alarm, and I knew, even in the act of throwing off sleep like a mantle, *why* I awoke, and that some intruder was present. Yet, though I listened intently, no sound was audible, except the faint murmur of the fire,—the dropping of a cinder from the bars—the loud irregular beatings of my own heart.

Notwithstanding this silence, by some intuition I knew that I had not been deceived by a dream, and felt certain that I was not alone. I waited. My heart beat on; quicker, more sudden grew its pulsations, as a bird in a cage might flutter in presence of the hawk. And then I heard a sound, faint, but quite distinct, the clank of iron, the rattling of a chain! I ventured to lift my head from the pillow. Dim and uncertain as the light was, I saw the curtains of my bed shake, and caught a glimpse of something beyond, a darker spot in the darkness. This confirmation of my fears did not surprise me so much as it shocked me. I strove to cry aloud, but could not utter a word. The chain rattled again, and this time the noise was louder and clearer. But though I strained my eyes, they could not penetrate the obscurity that shrouded the other end of the chamber, whence came the sullen clanking. In a moment several distinct trains of thought, like many-coloured strands of thread twining into one, became palpable to my mental vision. Was it a robber? could it be a supernatural visitant? or was I the victim of a cruel trick, such as I had heard of, and which some thoughtless persons love to practise on the timid, reckless of its dangerous results? And then a new idea, with some ray of comfort in it, suggested itself. There was a fine young dog of the Newfoundland breed, a favourite of my father's, which was usually chained by night in an outhouse. Neptune might have broken loose, found his way to my room, and, finding the door imperfectly closed, have pushed it open and entered. I breathed more freely as this harmless interpretation of the noise forced itself upon me. It was—it must be—the dog, and I was distressing myself uselessly. I resolved to call to him; I strove to utter his name—"Neptune, Neptune!" but a secret apprehension restrained me, and I was mute. Then the chain clanked nearer and nearer to the bed, and presently I saw a dusky shapeless mass appear between the curtains on the opposite side to where I was lying. How I longed to hear the whine of the poor animal that I hoped might be the cause of my alarm. But no; I heard no sound save the rustle of the curtains and the clash of the iron chain. Just then the dying flame of the fire leaped up, and with one sweeping hurried glance I saw that the door was shut, and, horror! it is not the dog! it is the semblance of a human form that now throws itself heavily on the bed, outside the clothes, and lies there, huge and swart, in the red gleam that treacherously dies away after showing so much to affright, and sinks into dull darkness.

There was now no light left, though the red cinders yet glowed with a ruddy gleam, like the eyes of wild beasts. The chain rattled no more. I tried to speak, to scream wildly for help; my mouth was parched, my tongue refused to obey. I could not utter a cry, and, indeed, who could have heard me, alone as I was in that solitary chamber, with no living neighbour, and the picture-gallery between me and any aid that even the loudest, most piercing shriek could summon. And the storm that howled without would have drowned my voice, even if help had been at hand. To call aloud—to demand who was there—alas! how useless, how perilous! If the intruder were a robber, my outcries would but goad him to fury; but what robber would act thus? As for a trick, that seemed impossible. And yet, *what* lay by my side, now wholly unseen? I strove to pray aloud, as there rushed on my memory a flood of weird legends—the dreaded yet fascinating lore of my childhood. I had heard and read of the spirits of wicked men forced to revisit the scenes of their earthly crimes—of demons that lurked in certain accursed spots—of the ghoul and vampire of the East, stealing amid the graves they rifled for their ghostly banquets; and I shuddered as I gazed on the blank darkness where I knew it lay. It stirred—it moaned hoarsely; and again I heard the chain clank close beside me—so close that it must almost have touched me. I drew myself from it, shrinking away in loathing and terror of the evil thing—what, I knew not, but felt that something malignant was near. And yet, in the extremity of my fear, I dared not speak; I was strangely cautious to be silent, even in moving farther off; for I had a wild hope that it—the phantom, the creature, whichever it was—had not discovered my presence in the room. And then I remembered all the events of the night— Lady Speldhurst's ill-omened vaticinations, her half-warnings, her singular look as we parted, my sister's persuasions, my terror in the gallery, the remark that "this was the room nurse Sherrard used to talk of." And then memory, stimulated by fear, recalled the long forgotten past, the ill-repute of this disused chamber, the sins it had witnessed, the blood spilled, the poison administered by unnatural hate within its walls, and the tradition which called it haunted. The green room—I remembered now how fearfully the servants avoided it—how it was mentioned rarely, and in whispers, when we were children, and how we had regarded it as a mysterious region, unfit for mortal habitation. Was It—the dark form with the chain—a creature of this world, or a spectre? And again—more dreadful still—could it be that the corpses of wicked men were forced to rise, and haunt in the body the places where they had wrought their evil deeds? And was such as these my grisly neighbour?

The chain faintly rattled. My hair bristled; my eyeballs seemed starting from their sockets; the damps of a great anguish were on my brow. My heart laboured as if I were crushed beneath some vast weight. Sometimes it appeared to stop its frenzied beatings, sometimes its pulsations were fierce and hurried; my breath came short and with extreme difficulty, and I shivered as if with cold; yet I feared to stir. *It* moved, it moaned, its fetters clanked dismally, the couch creaked and shook. This was no phantom, then—no air-drawn spectre. But its very solidity, its palpable presence, were a thousand times more terrible. I felt that I was in the very grasp of what could not only affright, but harm; of something whose contact sickened the soul with deathly fear. I made a desperate resolve: I glided from the bed, I seized a warm wrapper, threw it around me, and tried to grope, with extended hands, my way to the door. My heart beat high at the hope of escape.

But I had scarcely taken one step, before the moaning was renewed, it changed into a threatening growl that would have suited a wolf's throat, and a hand clutched at my sleeve. I stood motionless. The muttering growl sank to a moan again, the chain sounded no more, but still the hand held its gripe of my garment, and I feared to move. It knew of my presence, then. My brain reeled, the blood boiled in my ears, and my knees lost all strength, while my heart panted like that of a deer in the wolf's jaws. I sank back, and the benumbing influence of excessive terror reduced me to a state of stupor.

When my full consciousness returned, I was sitting on the edge of the bed, shivering with cold, and barefooted. All was silent, but I felt that my sleeve was still clutched by my unearthly visitant. The silence lasted a long time. Then followed a chuckling laugh, that froze my very marrow, and the gnashing of teeth as in demoniac frenzy; and then a wailing moan, and this was succeeded by silence. Hours may have passed—nay, though the tumult of my own heart prevented my hearing the clock strike, must have passed—but they seemed ages to me. And how were they spent? Hideous visions passed before the aching eyes that I dared not close, but which gazed ever into the dumb darkness where It lay—my dread companion through the watches of the night. I pictured It in every abhorrent form which an excited fancy could summon up: now as a skeleton, with hollow eyeholes and grinning fleshless jaws; now as a vampire, with livid face and bloated form, and dripping mouth wet with blood. Would it never be light! And yet, when day should dawn, I should be forced to see It face to face. I had heard that spectre and fiend were compelled to fade as morning brightened, but this creature was too real, too foul a thing of earth, to vanish at cockcrow. No! I should see it—the horror—face to face! And then the cold prevailed, and my teeth chattered, and shiverings ran through me, and yet there was the damp of agony on my bursting brow. Some instinct made me snatch at a shawl or cloak that lay on a chair within reach, and wrap it round me. The moan was renewed, and the chain just stirred. Then I sank into apathy, like an Indian at the stake, in the intervals of torture.

Hours fled by, and I remained like a statue of ice, rigid and mute. I even slept, for I remember that I started to find the cold grey light of an early winter's day was on my face, and stealing around the room from between the heavy curtains of the window. Shuddering, but urged by the impulse that rivets the gaze of the bird upon the snake, I turned to see the Horror of the night. Yes, it was no fevered dream, no hallucination of sickness, no airy phantom unable to face the dawn. In the sickly light I saw it lying on the bed, with its grim head on the pillow. A man? Or a corpse arisen from its unhallowed grave, and awaiting the demon that animated it? There it lay—a gaunt gigantic form, wasted to a skeleton, half clad, foul with dust and clotted gore, its huge limbs flung upon the couch as if at random, its shaggy hair streaming over the pillows like a lion's mane. Its face was towards me. Oh, the wild hideousness of that face, even in sleep! In features it was human, even through its horrid mask of mud and half-dried bloody gouts, but the expression was brutish and savagely fierce; the white teeth were visible between the parted lips, in a malignant grin; the tangled hair and beard were mixed in leonine confusion, and there were scars disfiguring the brow. Round the creature's waist was a ring of iron, to which was attached a heavy but broken chain—the chain I had heard clanking. With a second glance I noted that part of the chain was wrapped in straw, to prevent its galling the wearer. The creature—I cannot call it a man—had the marks of fetters on its wrists, the bony arm that protruded through one tattered sleeve was scarred and bruised; the feet were bare, and lacerated by pebbles and briers, and one of them was wounded, and wrapped in a morsel of rag. And the lean hands, one of which held my sleeve, were armed with talons like an eagle's. In an instant the horrid truth flashed upon me—I was in the grasp of a madman. Better the phantom that scares the sight than the wild beast that rends and tears the quivering flesh—the pitiless human brute that has no heart to be softened, no reason at whose bar to plead, no compassion, nought of man save the form and the cunning. I gasped in terror. Ah! the mystery of those ensanguined fingers, those gory wolfish jaws! that face, all besmeared with blackening blood, is revealed!

The slain sheep, so mangled and rent—the fantastic butchery—the print of the naked foot—all, all were explained; and the chain, the broken link of which was found near the slaughtered animals—it came from *his* broken chain—the chain he had snapped, doubtless, in his escape from the asylum where his raging frenzy had been fettered and bound. In vain! in vain! Ah, me! how had this grisly Samson broken manacles and prison bars—how had he eluded guardian and keeper and a hostile world, and come hither on his wild way, hunted like a beast of prey, and snatching his hideous banquet like a beast of prey, too?

Yes, through the tatters of his mean and ragged garb I could see the marks of the severities, cruel and foolish, with which men in that time tried to tame the might of madness. The scourge—its marks were there; and the scars of the hard iron fetters, and many a cicatrice and welt, that told a dismal tale of harsh usage.

But now he was loose, free to play the brute—the baited, tortured brute that they had made him—now without the cage, and ready to gloat over the victims his strength should overpower. Horror! horror! I was the prey—the victim—already in the tiger's clutch; and a deadly sickness came over me, and the iron entered into my soul, and I longed to scream, and was dumb! I died a thousand deaths as that awful morning wore on. I *dared not* faint. But words cannot paint what I suffered as I waited—waited till the moment when he should open his eyes and be aware of my presence; for I was assured he knew it not. He had entered the chamber as a lair, when weary and gorged with his horrid orgie; and he had flung himself down to sleep without a suspicion that he was not alone. Even his grasping my sleeve was doubtless an act done betwixt sleeping and waking, like his unconscious moans and laughter, in some frightful dream.

Hours went on; then I trembled as I thought that soon the house would be astir, that my maid would come to call me as usual, and awake that ghastly sleeper. And might he not have time to tear me, as he tore the sheep, before any aid could arrive? At last what I dreaded came to pass—a light footstep on the landing—there is a tap at the door. A pause succeeds, and then the tapping is renewed, and this time more loudly. Then the madman stretched his limbs and uttered his moaning cry, and his eyes slowly opened—very slowly opened, and met mine. The girl waited awhile ere she knocked for the third time. I trembled lest she should open the door unbidden—see that grim thing, and by her idle screams and terror bring about the worst. Long before strong men could arrive I knew that I should be dead—and what a death!

The maid waited, no doubt surprised at my unusually sound slumbers, for I was in general a light sleeper and an early riser, but reluctant to deviate from habit by entering without permission. I was still alone with the thing in man's shape, but he was awake now. I saw the wondering surprise in his haggard bloodshot eyes; I saw him stare at me half vacantly, then with a crafty yet wondering look; and then I saw the devil of murder begin to peep forth from those hideous eyes, and the lips to part as in a sneer, and the wolfish teeth to bare themselves. But I was not what I had been. Fear gave me a new and a desperate composure—a courage foreign to my nature. I had heard of the best method of managing the insane; I could but try; I *did* try. Calmly, wondering at my own feigned calm, I fronted the glare of those terrible eyes. Steady and undaunted was my gaze—motionless my attitude. I marvelled at myself, but in that agony of sickening terror I was *outwardly* firm. They sink, they quail abashed, those dreadful eyes, before the gaze of a helpless girl; and the shame that is never absent from insanity bears down the pride of strength, the bloody cravings of the wild beast. The lunatic moaned and drooped his shaggy head between his gaunt squalid hands. I lost not an instant. I rose, and with one spring reached the door, tore it open, and, with a shriek, rushed through, caught the wondering girl by the arm, and, crying to her to run for her life, rushed like the wind along the gallery, down the corridor, down the stairs. Mary's screams filled the house as she fled beside me. I heard a long-drawn, raging cry, the roar of a wild animal mocked of its prey, and I knew what was behind me. I never turned my head—I flew rather than ran. I was in the hall already; there was a rush of many feet, an outcry of many voices, a sound of scuffling feet, and brutal yells, and oaths, and heavy blows, and I fell to the ground, crying, "Save me!" and lay in a swoon.

I awoke from a delirious trance. Kind faces were around my bed, loving looks were bent on me by all, by my dear father and dear sisters, but I scarcely saw them before I swooned again. . . .

When I recovered from that long illness, through which I had been nursed so tenderly, the pitying looks I met made me tremble. I asked for a looking-glass. It was long denied me, but my importunity prevailed at last—a mirror was brought. My youth was gone at one fell swoop. The glass showed me a livid and haggard face, blanched and bloodless as of one who sees a spectre; and in the ashen lips, and wrinkled brow, and dim eyes, I could trace nothing of my old self. The hair, too, jetty and rich before, was now as white as snow, and in one night the ravages of half a century had passed over my face. Nor have my nerves ever recovered their tone after that dire shock. Can you wonder that my life was blighted, that my lover shrank from me, so sad a wreck was I?

I am old now—old and alone. My sisters would have had me to live with them, but I chose not to sadden their genial homes with my phantom face and dead eyes. Reginald married another. He has been dead many years. I never ceased to pray for him, though he left me when I was bereft of all. The sad weird is nearly over now. I am old, and near the end, and wishful for it. I have not been bitter or hard, but I cannot bear to see many people, and am best alone. I try to do what good I can with the worthless wealth Lady Speldhurst left me, for at my wish my portion was shared between my sisters. What need had I of inheritances?—I, the shattered wreck made by that one night of horror!

# "BRING ME A LIGHT!"

## A GHOST STORY

*Once a* Week *(1859-1880), the periodical in which this story first appeared in January 1861, originated from a dispute over celebrity publicity. Publishers Bradbury and Evans refused to print Charles Dickens's defense of his marital separation, and their successful joint endeavor* Household Words *was the casualty. Bradbury and Evans found a new editor and started* Once a Week, *which became an outlet for* Punch *writers and illustrators.[1] This story appeared during the magazine's most successful period.*

*This story plays on the realistic nineteenth-century fear of death by fire. Between 1848 and 1861, nearly 40,000 people in England were burned alive or scalded to death; after the breeching age of five, girls were 60% more susceptible to this end than boys due to their flammable clothing; the danger was also higher for older women.[2] Authorities recommended that Victorians starch cotton, linen, and muslin dresses with fire-resistant chemicals to avoid this danger.*

MY NAME IS THOMAS WHINMORE, and when I was a young man I went to spend a college vacation with a gentleman in Westmoreland. He had known my father's family, and had been appointed the trustee of a small estate left me by my great aunt, Lady Jane Whinmore. At the time I speak of I was one-and-twenty, and he was anxious to give up the property into my hands. I accepted his invitation to "come down to the old place and look about me." When I arrived at the nearest point to the said "old place," to which the Carlisle coach would carry me, I and my portmanteau were put into a little cart, which was the

1 John Sutherland, "Once a Week" in *The Stanford Companion to Victorian Fiction.* Stanford: Stanford University Press, 1989. 479-480.
2 "Death by Fire—In the 14 Years 1848-61." *The Times* (London) 24537 (20 April 1863): 5.

only wheeled thing I could get at the little way-side inn.

"How far is it to Whinmore?" I asked of a tall grave-looking lad, who had already informed me I could have "t'horse and cairt" for a shilling a mile.

"Twal mile to t'ould Hall gaet—a mile ayont that to Squire Erle's farm."

As I looked at the shaggy wild horse, just caught from the moor for the purpose of drawing "t'cairt," I felt doubtful as to which of us would be the master on the road. I had ascertained that the said road lay over moor and mountain—just the sort of ground on which such a steed would gambol away at his own sweet will. I had no desire to be run away with.

"Is there any one here who can drive me to Mr. Erle's?" I asked of the tall grave lad.

"Nobbut fayther."

I was puzzled; and was about to ask for an explanation, when a tall, strong old man, as like the young one as might be, came out from the door of the house with his hat on, and a whip in his hand. He got up into the cart, and looking at me, said,

"Ye munna stan here, sir. We shan't pass Whinmore Hall afore t'deevil brings a light."

"But I want something to eat before we start," I remonstrated. "I've had no dinner."

"Then ye maun keep your appetite till supper time," replied the old man. "I canna gae past Whinmore lights for na man—nor t'horse neither. Get up wi' ye! Joe, lend t'gentleman a hand."

Joe did as he was desired, and then said—

"Will ye be home the night, fayther?"

"May be yees, may be na, lad; take care of t'place."

In a moment the horse started, and we were rattling over the moor at the rate of eight miles an hour. Surprise, indignation, and hunger possessed me. Was it possible I had been whirled off dinnerless into this wilderness against my own desire?

"I say, my good man," I began.

"My name is Ralph Thirlston."

"Well! Mr. Thirlston, I want something to eat. Is there any inn between this desert and Mr. Erle's house!"

"Nobbut Whinmore Hall," said the old man, with a grin.

"I suppose I can get something to eat there, without being obliged to anybody. It is my own property."

Mr. Thirlston glanced at me sharply.

"Be ye t'maister, lad?"

"I am, Mr. Thirlston," said I. "My name is Whinmore."

"Maister Tom!"

"The same. Do you know anything about me and my old house?"

" 'Deed do I. You're the heir of t'ould leddy. Mr. Erle is your guardian, and farms your lands."

"I know so much, myself," I replied. "I want you to tell me who lives in Whinmore Hall now, and whether I can get a dinner there, for I'm *clem*, as you say here."

"Weel, weel. It is a sore trial to a young stomach! You must e'en bear it till we get to Mr. Erle's."

"But surely there is somebody, some old woman or other, who lives in the old house and airs the rooms!"

" 'Deed is there. But it's nobbut ghosts and deevil's spawn of that sort."

"I am surprised, Mr. Thirlston, to hear a man like you talk such nonsense."

"What like man do ye happen know that I am, Maister Whinmore? Tho' if I talk nonsense (and I'm no gainsaying what a learned colleger like you can tell about nonsense), yet it's just the things I have heard and seen mysell I am speaking of."

"What have you heard and seen at Whinmore Hall?"

"What a' body hears and sees to Whinmore, 'twixt sunset and moonlight;—and what I used to see times and oft, when I lived there farming-man to t'ould Leddy Jane,—what I'm not curious to see again, now. So get on, Timothy," he added to the horse, "or we may chance to come in for a fright."

I did not trouble myself about the delay, as he did, but watched him.

This man is no fool, I thought. I wonder what strange delusion has got possession of the people about this old house of mine. I remembered that Mr. Erle had told me in one of the very few letters I ever received from him, that it was difficult to find a tenant for Whinmore Hall. Curiosity took precedence of hunger, and I began to think how I could best soothe my irritated companion, and get him to tell me what he believed.

We were back on the road again, and going across the shoulder of a great fell;—the sun had just disappeared behind a distant range of similar fells; it left no rosy clouds, no orange streaks in the sky—black rain-clouds spread all over the great concave, and in a very few minutes they burst upon us. There was a cold, piercing wind in our teeth. I felt my spirits rise. The vast monotonous moor, the threatening sky, and the fierce rushing blast had something for me sublime and invigorating. I looked round at the new range of moorland which we were gradually commanding, as we rounded the hill.

"I like this wild place, Mr. Thirlston," I said.

"Wild enough!" he grumbled in reply. " 'Tis college learning is a deal better than such house and land. Beggars won't live in th' house, and th' land is the poorest in all England."

"Is that the house, yonder, on the right?"

"There's na ither house, good or bad, to be seen from this," he replied: but I observed that he did not turn his head in the direction I had indicated. He kept a look-out straight between the horse's ears; I, on the contrary, never took my eyes off the grey building which we were approaching. Nearer and nearer we came, and I saw that there was a sort of large garden or pleasure-ground enclosed round the house, and that the road ran past a part of this enclosure, and also past a large open-worked iron gate, which was the chief entrance. Very desolate, cold, and inhospitable looked this old house of mine; wild and tangled looked the garden. The tall, smokeless chimneys were numerous, and stood up white against the blackness of the sky; the windows, more numerous still, looked black, in contrast with the whitish-grey stone of the walls. Just as we entered the shadow cast by the trees of the shrubbery, our horse snorted, and sprang several yards from the enclosure.

"Now for it! It is your own fault for running away, and bringing us late," muttered Ralph Thirlston, grasping the reins and standing up to get a better hold of the horse. Timothy now stood still; and to my surprise he was trembling in every limb, and shaking with terror.

"Something has frightened the beast," said I. "I shall just go and see what it was," and was about to jump down, when I felt Ralph Thirlston's great hand on my arm: it was a powerful grip.

"For the love of God, lad, stay where ye are!" he said, in a frightened whisper. "It's just here that my brother met his death, for doing what you want to do now."

"What! For walking up to that fence and seeing what trifle frightened a skittish horse?" And I looked at the fence intently. There was nothing to be seen but a straggling bough of an elder bush which had forced its way through a chink in the rotten wood and was waving in the wind.

Finding that the man was really frightened as well as the horse, I humoured him. He still held my arm.

"There is no need for any one to go closer to see the cause of poor Timothy's fear," I said, laughing. "If you will look, Mr. Thirlston, you will see what it was."

"Na! lad, na! I'm not going to turn my face towards the deevil and his works. 'Lord have mercy upon us! Christ have mercy upon us! Our Father which art in heaven—'" and he repeated the whole prayer with emphasis, slowness, and with his eyes closed. I sat still, an amazed witness of his state of mind. When he had said "Amen," he opened his eyes, and looking down at the horse, who seemed to have recovered, as I judged by his putting his head down to graze, he gave a low whistle, and tightening the reins once more, Timothy allowed himself to be driven forward. Thirlston kept his face away from the enclosure on his right hand, and looked steadily at Timothy. I gave another glance towards the innocent elder bough,—but what was my astonishment to see where it had been, or seemed to be, the figure of a man with a drawn sword in his hand.

"Stop, Thirlston! stop!" I cried. "There is somebody there. I see a man with a sword. Look! Turn back, and I'll soon see what he is doing there."

"Na! na! Never turn back to meet the deevil, when ye have once got past him!" And Thirlston drove on rapidly.

"But he may overtake you," I cried, laughing. But as I looked back I saw that a pursuit was not intended, for the figure I had seen was gone. "I'll pay a visit to that devil to-morrow," I added. "I shall not harbour such game in my preserves."

"Lord's sake, don't talk like that, Maister Whinmore!" whispered Thirlston. "We're just coming to the gaet! May be they may strike Timothy dead!"

"They?—who? Not the ghosts, surely?" I looked through the great gate as we passed, and saw the whole front of the house. "Why, Mr. Thirlston, you said no one lived in the old Hall! Look! There are lights in the windows."

"Ay! ay! I thought you would see them," he said, in a terrified whisper, without turning his head.

"Why, look at them yourself," cried I, pointing to the house.

"God forbid!" he exclaimed; and he gave Timothy a stroke with the whip, that sent him flying past the rest of the garden of the Hall. Our ground rose again, and in a few minutes a good view of the place was obtained. I looked back at it with vivid interest. No lights were to be seen now; no moving thing; the black windows contrasted with the grey walls, and the grey chimneys with the black clouds, as when the place first appeared to me. The moon now rose above a dark hill on our left. Thirlston allowed Timothy to slacken his speed, and, turning round his head, he also looked back at Whinmore Hall.

"We are safe enough now," he said. "The only dangerous time is betwixt sunset and moonrise, when people are passing close to the accursed ould place."

About a mile further, the barking of a housedog indicated that we were approaching Mr. Erle's. The driver stopped at a small wicket-gate leading into a shrubbery, got down, and invited me to do the same. He then fastened Timothy to the gatepost. The garden and the house have nothing to do with my present tale, and are far too dear to me to be flung in as an episodical adornment. They form the scenery of the romantic part of my own life; for Miss Erle became my wife a few years after this first visit to Whinmore. I saw her that evening, and forgot Ralph Thirlston, the old Hall, its ghosts and mysterious lights. However, the next morning I was forced back to this work-a-day world in her father's study. There I heard Mr. Erle's account of my property. All the land was farmed by himself, except the few acres round the Hall, which no one would take because it was not worth tillage, and because of the evil name of the house itself.

"I suppose you know why no tenant can be found for the Hall, since Ralph Thirlston drove you over?"

"Yes," I said, smiling. "But I could get no rational account from him. What is this nonsense about ghosts and lights? Who lives in the Hall?"

"No one, my good fellow. Why, you would not get the stoutest man in the parish, and that's Thirlston, to go into the house after sunset, much less live in it."

"But I have seen lights in some of the windows myself."

"So have I," he replied.

"Do you mean to say that no human beings make use of the house, in virtue of the superstition about it? Tricks of this kind are not uncommon."

"At the risk of seeming foolish in your eyes, I must reply, that I believe no human beings now living have any hand in the operations which go on in Whinmore Hall." Mr. Erle looked perfectly grave as he said this.

"I saw a man with a sword in his hand start from a part of the fence. I think he frightened our horse."

"I, too, have seen the figure you speak of. But I do not think it is a living man."

"What do you suppose it to be?" I asked, in amazement; for Mr. Erle was no ignorant or weak-minded person. He had already impressed me with real respect for his character and intellect.

He smiled at my impetuous tone.

"I live apart from what is called the world," said he. "Grace and I are not polite enough to think everything which we cannot account for either impossible or ridiculous. Ten years ago, I myself was a new resident in this county, and wishing to improve your property, I determined to occupy the old Hall myself. I had it prepared for my family. No mechanic would work about the place after sunset. However, I brought all my servants from a distance; and took care that they should have no intercourse with any neighbour for the first three days. On the third evening they all came to me and said that they must leave the next morning— all but Grace's nurse, who had been her mother's attendant, and was attached to the family. She told me that she did not think it safe for the child to remain another night, and that I must give her permission to take her away."

"What did you do?" said I.

"I asked for some account of the things that had frightened them. Of course, I heard some wild and exaggerated tales; but the main phenomena related were what I myself had seen and heard, and which I was as fully determined as they were not to see and hear again, or to let my child have a chance of encountering. I told them so, candidly; and at the same time declared that it was my belief God's Providence or punishment was at work in that old house, as everywhere else in creation, and not the devil's mischievous hand. Once more I made a rigorous search for secret devices and means for producing the sights and sounds which so many had heard and seen; but without any discovery: and before sunset that afternoon the Hall was cleared of all human occupants. And so it has remained until this day."

"Will you tell me the things you saw and heard?"

"Nay, you had better see and hear them for yourself. We have plenty of time before sunset. I can show you over the whole house, and if your courage holds good, I will leave you there to pass an hour or so between sunset and moonrise. You can come back here when you like; and if you are in a condition to hear, and care to hear, the story which peoples your old Hall with horrors, I will tell it you."

"Thank you," said I. "Will you lend me a gun and pistols to assist me in my investigations?"

"Surely." And taking down the weapons I had pointed out, he began to examine them.

"You want them loaded?"

"Certainly, and with bullets. I am not going to play."

Mr. Erle loaded both gun and pistols. I put the latter into my pocket, and we left the room by the window. Grace Erle met us on the moor, riding a shaggy pony.

"Where are you going, so near dinner time?" she asked.

"Mr. Whinmore is going to look at the old Hall."

"And his gun?" she asked, smiling.

"I want to shoot vermin there."

She looked as if she were about to say something eagerly, but checked herself, and rode slowly away. I looked after her, and wondered what she was going to say. Perhaps she wished to prevent me from going.

Presently we stood before the great iron gate of Whinmore. Mr. Erle took two keys from his pocket. With one he unlocked the gate, with the other the chief door. There were no other fastenings. These were very rusty, and were moved with difficulty.

"People don't get in this way," said I. "That is clear."

The garden was a sad wilderness, and grass grew on the broad steps which led up to the door.

As soon as we had crossed the threshold, I felt the influence of that desolate dwelling creep over my spirits. There was a cold stagnation in the air—a deathly stillness—a murky light in the old rooms that was indescribably depressing. All the lower windows had their pierced shutters fastened, and cobwebs and dust adorned them plentifully.

Yet I could have sworn I saw lights in two, at least, of these lower windows. I said so to my companion. He replied—

"Yes. It was in this very room you saw a light, I dare say. This is one in which I have seen lights myself. But I do not wish to spoil my dinner by seeing anything supernatural now. We will leave it, and I will hasten to the lady's bed-chamber and dressing-room, where the apparitions and noises are most numerous."

I followed him, but cast a glance round the room before I shut the door carefully. It was partly furnished like a library, but on one side was a bed, and beside it an easy-chair. "What name is given to this room? It looks ominous of some evil deed," I said.

"It is called 't'ould Squire's Murder Room,' by the people who know the story connected with it."

"Ah!" I said; "then I may look for a ghost there?"

"You will perhaps see one, or more, if you stay long enough," said Mr. Erle, with the utmost composure. "This way."

I followed him along a gallery on the first floor to the door of a room. He opened it, and we entered what had been apparently one of the principal bedrooms. It was a regular lady's chamber, of the seventeenth century, with dark plumes waving on the top of the bed-pillars of black oak. The massy toilette, with its oval looking-glass, set in silver and shrouded in old lace—the carved chairs and lofty mantelpiece—gave an air of quaint elegance to the dignity of the apartment. I had but little time to examine the objects here, for Mr. Erle had passed on to an inner room, which was reached by ascending a short flight of steps.

"Come up here," cried a voice which did not sound like Mr. Erle's. I ran up the stairs and I found him alone in a small room which contained little else than an escritoire, a cabinet, and two great chairs. On one side, a large Parisian looking-glass, *à la Régence*, was fixed on the wall. The branches for lights still held some yellow bits of wax-candle covered with dust. I joined Mr. Erle, who was looking through the window over a vast expanse of mountainous moorland. "What a grand prospect!" I exclaimed. "I like these two rooms very much. I shall certainly come and live here."

"You shall tell me your opinion about that to-morrow," said Mr. Erle. "I must go now."

Concealing as much as possible the contempt I felt for his absurd superstition, I accompanied him down-stairs again. "Are these the only rooms worth looking at?" I asked.

"No; most of the rooms are good enough for a gentleman's household. The rooms I have shown you, and the passages and staircase which lead from one to the other, are the only portions of the house in which you are subjected to annoyance. I have slept in both the rooms, and advise no one else to do so."

"You had bad dreams?" I asked, with an involuntary smile, as I took my gun from the hall-table, where I had left it.

"As you please," said Mr. Erle, smiling also.

I stretched out my hand to him when we stood at the gate together.

"Good night!" said I. "I think I shall sleep in one of those rooms, and return to you in the morning."

Mr. Erle shook his head. "You will be back at my house within three hours, Tom Whinmore; so, *au revoir!*"

He strode away over the moor. His fine figure appeared almost gigantic as it moved between me and the setting sun.

"That does not look like a man who should be a prey to weak superstition, any more than good Ralph Thirlston, who drove home alone willingly enough past this same gate and fence at nine o'clock last night! The witching hour, it seems, is just after sunset. Well, it wants a quarter of an hour of that now," I continued, thinking silently. "There will be time enough for me to explore the garden a little, before I return to the house and wait for my evening's entertainment."

As I walked through the shrubbery, I recollected the figure I had seen outside the fence on the previous evening. I must find out how *that* trick is managed, thought I, and if I get a chance I will certainly wing that ghost, *pour encourager les autres*.

Ascertaining, as well as I was able, the part of the shrubbery near which I saw the man, I began to search for footsteps or marks of human ingenuity. I soon discovered the elder bush that had sent some of its branches through a hole in the fence. I crept round it, and examined the fence. No plank was loose, though some boughs had grown through the hole. I could see no footstep except my own on the moist, dank leafy mould. I got over the fence and saw no marks outside. Baffled, and yet suspicious, I went back and continued my walk, in the course of which I came upon sundry broken and decayed summer-houses and seats. In the tangled flower-garden, on the south-west side, were a few rich blossoms, growing amicably with the vilest weeds. I tore up a great root of hemlock to get at a branch of Provence rose, and then seeing that the sun had disappeared below the opposite fell, I pursued my course and arrived again at the broad gravel path leading from the gate to the hall-door.

Both stood open, as I had left them. I lingered on the grass-grown steps to look at the last rays of the sun, reddening the heather on the distant fell. As I leaned on my gun enjoying the profound stillness of this place, far from all sounds of village, or wood, or sea—a stillness that seemed to deepen and deepen into unearthly intensity—the charm was broken by a human voice speaking near me—the tone was hollow and full of agony— *"Bring me a light! Bring me a light!"* it cried. It was like a sick or dying man. The voice came, I thought, from the room next to me on the right hand of the Hall. I rushed into the house and to the door of that room; it was the first which Mr. Erle had shown me. I remembered shutting the door—it now stood wide open; and there was a sound of hurrying footsteps within.

"Who is there?" I shouted. No answer came. But there passed by me, as it were, in the very doorway, the figure of a young and, as I could see at a glance, very beautiful woman.

When she moved onwards I could not choose but follow, trembling with an indefinable fear, yet borne on by a mystic attraction. At the foot of the stairs she turned on me again, and smiled, and beckoned me with an upraised arm, whereon great jewels flashed in the gloom. I followed her quickly, but could not overtake her. My limbs—I am not ashamed to say it—shook with strange fear; yet I could not turn back from following that fair form. Onward she led me—up the stairs and through the gallery to the door of the lady's chamber. There she paused a moment, and again turned her bewitching face, radiant with smiles, upon me before she disappeared within the dark doorway. I followed into the room, and saw her stand before the antique toilette and arrange in her bosom a spray of roses—the very spray that I had so lately pulled in the garden, it seemed—then she kissed her hand to me and glided to the narrow stairs that led to the little room above. Then came a loud haughty voice—the voice of a woman accustomed to command. It sounded from the little room above, and it could not be the voice of that fair girl, I felt sure. It said:

"*Bring me a light! Bring me a light!*"

I shuddered at the sound; I knew not why, but I stood there still. I then saw the figure of an old female servant, rise from a chair by one of the windows. She approached the toilette, and there I saw her light two tapers, with her breath, it seemed.

"*Bring me a light!*" was repeated in an angry tone from the upper room.

The old woman passed rapidly to the stairs. Thither I followed in obedience to a sign from her; and, mounting to the top, saw into the room.

That beautiful girl stood in the centre, with her costly lace gown sweeping the floor, and her bright curls drooping to the waist. Her back was towards me, but I could see her innocent, sweet face in the great glass. What a lovely, happy face it was!

Behind her stood another lady, taller, and more majestic. She pretended to caress her, but her proud eyes, unseen by the young lady, brightened with triumphant malice. They danced gladly in the light of the taper which she took from the maid. "God of heaven! can a woman look so wicked?" I thought.

"*Watch her!*" whispered a voice in my ear—a voice that stirred my hair.

I did watch her. Would to God I could forget that vision! She— the woman, the fiend—bent carefully to the floor, as though to set right something amiss in the border of the fair bride's robe. I saw her lower the flame of the candle, and set fire to the dress of the smiling, trusting girl. Ere I could move she was enveloped in flames, and I heard her wild shrieks mingling with the low demo- niac laughter of her murderess.

I remember suddenly raising the gun in my hand and firing at the horrid apparition. But still she laughed and pointed with mocking gestures to the flames and the writhing figure they enveloped. I ran forward to extinguish them;—my arms struck against the wall, and I fell down insensible.

When I recovered my senses I found myself lying on the floor of that little room, with the bright cold moon looking in on me. I waited without moving, listening for some more of those demon sounds. All was still. I rose—went to the window—the moon was high in heaven, and all the great moor seemed light as day. The air of that room was stifling. I turned and fled. Hastily I ran down those few steps—quicker yet through the great chamber and out into the gallery. As I began to go down the stairs, I saw a figure coming up.

I was now a very coward. Grasping the banister with one hand, and feeling for the unused pistol with the other, I called out—

"Who are you?" and with stupid terror I fired at the thing, without pausing.

There was a slight cry; a very human one. Then a little laugh.

"Don't fire any more pistols at me, Mr. Whinmore. I'm not a ghost."

Something in the voice sent the blood once more coursing through my veins.

"Is it ——?" I could not utter another word.

"It is I, Grace Erle."

"What brought you here?" I said, at length, after I had descended the stairs, and had seized her hand that I might feel sure it was of flesh and blood.

"My pony. We began to get uneasy about you. It is nearly midnight. So papa and I set off to see what you were doing."

"What the devil are you firing at, Whinmore?" asked Mr. Erle, coming hurriedly from a search in the lower rooms.

"Only at *me*, papa!" answered his daughter, archly, glancing up at my face. "But he is a bad shot, for he didn't hit me."

"Thank God!" I ejaculated—"Miss Erle, I was mad."

"No, only very frightened. Look at him, papa!"

Mr. Erle looked at me. He took my arm.

"Why! Whinmore, you don't look the better for seeing the spirits of your ancestors. However, I see it is no longer a joking matter with you. You do not wish to take up your abode here immediately."

I rallied under their kindly *badinage*.

"Let me get out of this horrible place," said I.

Mr. Erle led me beyond the gate. I leaned against it, in a state of exhaustion.

"Here. Try your hand at my other pocket-pistol!" said Mr. Erle, as he put a precious flask of that kind to my lips. After a second application of the remedy I was decidedly better.

Miss Erle mounted her pony, and we set off across the moor. I was very silent, and my companions talked a little with each other. My mind was too confused to recollect just then all that I had experienced during my stay in the house, and I wished to arrange my thoughts and compose my nerves before I conversed with Mr. Erle on the strange visions of that night.

I excused myself to my host and his daughter, in the best way I could, and after taking a slice of bread and a glass of water, I went to bed.

The next day I rose late; but in my right mind. I was much shocked to think of the cowardly fear which had led me to fire a pistol at Miss Erle. I began my interview with my host, by uttering some expressions of this feeling. But it was an awkward thing to declare myself a fool and a coward.

"The less we say about that the better," said her father, gravely. "Fear is the strongest human passion, my boy; and will lead us to commit the vilest acts, if we let it get the mastery."

"I acknowledge that I was beside myself with terror at the sights and sounds of that accursed house. I was not sane, at the moment I saw your daughter! I shall never—"

"Whinmore, she hopes you will never mention it again! *We* certainly shall not. Now, if you are disposed to hear the story of your ancestor's evil deeds, I am ready to fulfil the promise I made you last night. I see you know too much, now, to think me a fool for believing my own senses, and keeping clear of disagreeable creatures that will not trouble themselves about me. I don't raise the question of *what* they are, or *how* they exist—nor even whether they exist at all. It is sufficient that they appear; and that by their appearance they put a stop to normal human life. You may be a philosopher; and may find some means of banishing these supernatural horrors. I shall like you none the less, if you can do what I cannot."

"I will try. Will you tell the story?"

"Yes, if you will take a cigar with me first."

After we had composed ourselves comfortably before the fire in his study, Mr. Erle began.

"How long ago, I can't exactly find out, but some time between the Reformation and the Great Rebellion, the Whinmores settled in this part of the county, and owned a large tract of land. They were of gentle blood, and most ungentle manners; for they quarrelled with every one, and carried themselves in an insolent fashion, to the simple below them, and to the noble above. The Whinmores were iron-handed and iron-hearted, staunch Catholics and staunch Jacobites, during the religious and political dissensions of the end of the seventeenth and beginning of the eighteenth centuries. After the establishment of Protestantism in the reigns of William III. and Anne, the position of the proud house of Whinmore was materially altered. The cadets went early into foreign service as soldiers and priests, and the first born remained at home to keep up a blighted dignity. After the establishment of the Hanoverian dynasty, the Whinmores of

Whinmore ceased to take any part in public affairs. They were too proud to farm their own land; and putting trust in a nefarious steward, the Whinmore who reigned at the Hall when King George the Second reigned over England was compelled to keep up appearances by selling half the family estate.

"The Whinmore in question, 't'ould squire,' as the people call him, was a melancholy man, not much blest in the matrimonial lottery. His wife, Lady Henrietta Whinmore, was the daughter of a poor Catholic Earl. Tradition says she was equally beautiful and proud; and I believe it.

"To return. This couple had only one child, a son. When Lady Henrietta found that her husband was a gentleman of a moping and unenterprising turn of mind, that she could not persuade him to compromise his principles, and so find favour with the new government, she devoted herself to the education of her son, Graham. As he was a clever boy, with strong health and good looks, she determined that he should retrieve the fortunes of the family. She kept him under her own superintendence till he was ten years of age. She then sent him to Eton, with his cousin the little Earl of ——. He was brought up a Protestant, and thus the civil disabilities of the family would be removed. He was early accustomed to the society of all ranks, to be found in a first-class English public school; and his personal gifts as well as his mental excellence helped to win him the good opinion of others. Graham came home from Oxford in his twenty-third year, a first-class man."

"Indeed!" I exclaimed. "I hope I am descended from him, and that his good luck will be a part of my inheritance. Is there any portrait of this fine young English gentleman of the olden time?"

"A very good one. It is in my daughter's sitting-room. We are both struck by your likeness to your grandfather, Graham Whinmore."

"I shall never take a first-class," I sighed; "but go on."

"When Graham returned home after his success at college, he found his father a hopeless valetudinarian, who had had his bed brought down to his library, because he thought himself too feeble to go up and down stairs. He showed little emotion at sight of his son, and seemed to be fast sinking to idiotcy. His mother, on the contrary, was radiant with joy; and had made the old ruined house look its best to welcome the heir. For, at that time, the place was much dilapidated, and only a small portion was habitable, that is the part you saw yesterday, the south front.

"And Graham stayed at home for a month or two in repose, after the fatigues of study. One afternoon as he rode home from a distant town, he paused on the top of Whinmore Hill, which commands a good view of the Hall. The simple bareness of the great hills around, the antique beauty and retirement of the Hall—above all, the sweet impressive stillness of the place, had often charmed Graham, as a boy. Now he gazed with far stronger feeling at it all.

"'It shall *not* be lost to me and my children,' he vowed, inwardly. 'I will redeem the mortgage on the house, I will win back every acre of the old Whinmore land. Yes, I will work for wealth; but I must lose no time, or my opportunity will be gone.'

"He looked at the ruined part of the house, and began to calculate the cost of rebuilding as he hastened forward. As soon as he entered the house he went to see his father, whom he had not seen that day. He found him in his bed, with the nurse asleep in the easy chair beside it. His father did not recognise him, and to Graham's mind, looked very much changed since the previous day. He left the room in search of his mother; thinking, in spite of his love for her, that she neglected her duty as a wife. 'She should be beside him now,' he thought. Still, he framed the best excuse he could for her then, for he loved and reverenced her. She was so strong-minded, so beautiful. Above all, she loved him with such passionate devotion. He dreaded to tell her the resolution he had formed. She was an aristocrat and a woman. She did not understand the mutation of things in that day; she would not believe that the best way to wealth and power was not through the Court influence, but by commercial enterprise. He went to her bedroom, the Lady's Chamber, in which you were last night. She was not there, and he was about to retreat, when he heard her voice in anger speaking to some one, in the dressing-room or oratory above. Graham went towards the stairs, and was met by an old female servant who was in his mother's confidence, and acted as her maid and head-nurse to his father. She came down in tears, murmuring, 'I cannot bear it. It was you gave me the draught for him. I will send for a doctor.'

" 'A doctor, indeed! He wants no doctor,' cried the angry mistress. 'And don't talk any more nonsense, my good woman, if you value your place.'

"In her agitation the woman did not see her young master, and hastily left the room.

"Astonished at the woman's words, he slowly ascended the steps to the dressing-room. He found his mother standing before the long looking-glass arrayed in a rich dress of old point lace, over a brocaded petticoat, with necklace, bracelets, and tiara of diamonds. She looked very handsome as her great eyes still flashed and her cheek was yet crimson with anger. She turned hastily as her son's foot was heard on the topmost stair. When she saw who it was her face softened with a smile.

" 'You here, Graham! I have been wanting you. Read that.'

"He could scarcely take his admiring eyes from the brilliant figure before him as he received the letter.

"It was addressed to his mother, and came from his cousin, the Earl, informing her that he had obtained a certain post under government for Graham.

"She kissed him as he sat down after reading the letter.

" 'There is your first step on fortune's ladder, my son. You are sure to rise.'

" 'I hope so, mother. But where are you going decked out in the family diamonds and lace?'

" 'Have you forgotten?—To the ball at the Lord-Lieutenant's. You must dress quickly, or we shall be late. Your cousin will be there, and we must thank him for that letter.'

" 'Yes, mother,' he replied, 'but we must refuse the place—I have other views.'

"Lady Henrietta's brow darkened.

" 'Mother! I have vowed to recover the estate of my ancestors. It will require a large fortune to do this. I cannot get a large fortune by dangling about the Court—I am going to turn merchant.'

"Lady Henrietta stared at him in amazement.

" 'You?—My son become a merchant?'

" 'Why not, mother? Sons of nobler houses have done so; and

I have advantages that few have ever had. Listen, dear mother. I saved the life of a college friend, who was drowning. His father is one of the wealthiest merchants in London—in all England. He wrote to tell me that if it suited my views and those of my family, he was ready to receive me, at once, as a junior partner in his firm. He had learned from his son that I wished to become rich that I might buy back my ancestral estate. His offer puts it in my power to become rich in a comparatively short space of time.—I intend to accept his munificent offer.'

"Lady Henrietta's proud bosom swelled; but there was something in her son's tone which made her feel that anger and persuasion were alike vain. After some minutes' silence, she said bitterly:

"'The world is changed indeed, Graham, if men of gentle blood can become traders and not lose their gentility.'

"'They can, mother. And I do not think the world can be much changed in that particular. A man of gentle blood, who is, in very truth, a gentleman, cannot lose that distinction in any occupation. Come, good mother, give me a smile! I am about to go forth to win an inheritance. I shall fight with modern weapons—the pen and the ledger—instead of sword and shield.'

"At that moment hasty steps were heard in the chamber below, and a voice called:

"'My lady! my lady! come quick! The Squire is dying!'

"Mother and son went fast to Mr. Whinmore's room. They arrived in time to see the old man die. He pointed to her, and cried with his last breath,

"'*She did it! She did it!*'

"Lady Henrietta sat beside his bed and listened to these incoherent words without any outward emotion. She watched the breath leave the body, and then closed the eyes herself. But though she kept up so bravely then, she was dangerously ill for several months after her husband's death, and was lovingly tended by her son and the old servant.

\*　　\*　　\*　　\*

"I must now pass over ten years. Before the end of that time

Graham Whinmore had become rich enough to buy back every acre of the land and to build a brand new house, twenty times finer than the old one, if he were so minded. But he was by no means so minded. He restored the old house—made it what it now is. He would not have accepted Chatsworth or Stowe in exchange.

"The Lady Henrietta lived there still; and superintended all the improvements. She had become reconciled to her son's occupation for the sake of the result in wealth. She entered eagerly into all his plans for the improvement of his property, and she had some of her own to propose.

"It was the autumn of the tenth year since her husband's death, and she was expecting Graham shortly for his yearly visit to the Hall. She sat looking over papers of importance in her dressing-room; the old servant (who seems to have grown no older) sat sewing in the bedroom below, when a housemaid brought in a letter which the old servant took immediately to her mistress.

"Lady Henrietta opened the letter quickly, for she saw that the handwriting was her son's. 'Perhaps he is coming this week,' she thought with a thrill of delight. 'Yes, he will come to take me to the Lord-Lieutenant's ball. He is proud of his mother yet, and I must look my best.' But she had not read a dozen words before the expression of her face changed. Surprise darkened into contempt and anger—anger deepened into rage and hatred. She uttered a sharp cry of pain. The old servant ran to her in alarm; but her mistress had composed herself, though her cheek was livid.

" 'Did your ladyship call me?'

" 'Yes. Bring me a light!'

"In this letter Graham announced his return home the following week—with a wife;—a beautiful girl—penniless and without connections of gentility. No words can describe the bitter rage and disappointment of this proud woman. He had a second time thwarted her plans for his welfare, and each time he had outraged her strongest feelings. He had turned merchant, and by his plebeian peddling had bought the land which his ancestors had won at the point of the sword. She had borne that, and had submitted to help him in his schemes. But receive a beggarly, low-born

wench for her daughter-in-law?—No! She would never do that.
She paced the room with soft, firm steps, like a panther. After a
time thought became clearer, and she saw that there was no question of her willingness to receive her daughter-in-law, but of that
daughter-in-law's willingness to allow her to remain in the house.
Ah! but it was an awful thing to see the proud woman when she
looked that fact fully in the face. She hated her unseen daughter
with a keen cold hate—a remorseless hate born of that terrible
sin, Pride. But she was not a woman to hate passively. She paced
to and fro, turning and returning with savage, stealthy quickness.
The day waned, and night began. Her servant came to see if she
were wanted, and was sent away with a haughty negative. 'She
is busy with some wicked thought,' murmured the old woman.

★ ★ ★ ★

"Graham Whinmore's bride was, as he had said, 'so good and
so lovely,' that no one ever thought of asking who were her parents. She was also accomplished and elegant in manner. She was
in all respects but birth superior to the Duke's daughter whom
Lady Henrietta had selected for her son's wife. The beautiful
Lilian's father was a music master, and she had given lessons in
singing herself. Lady Henrietta learned this and everything else
concerning her young daughter-in-law that could be considered
disgraceful in her present station. But she put restraint on her
contempt, and received her with an outward show of courtesy
and stately kindness. Graham believed that for his sake his
mother was determined to forget his wife's low origin, and he
became easy about the result of their connection after he had
seen his mother caress his wife once or twice. He felt sure that no
one could know Lilian and not love her. He was proud and happy
to think that two such beautiful women belonged to him.

"The Lord-Lieutenant's ball was expected to be unusually brilliant that year, and Graham was anxious that his wife should be
the queen of the assembly.

" 'I should like her to wear the old lace and the jewels, mother,'
said Graham.

"The Lady Henrietta's eyebrows were contracted for a moment, and she shot forth a furtive glance at Lilian, who sat near, playing with a greyhound.

"If Graham had seen that glance! But her words he believed.

" 'Certainly, my son. It is quite proper that your wife should wear such magnificent heirlooms. There is no woman of quality in this county that can match them. I am proud to abdicate my right in her favour.'

" 'There, Lilian! Do you hear, you are to eclipse the Duchess herself!'

"I will do so, if you wish it,' said Lilian. 'But I do not think that will amuse me so much as dancing.'

\* \* \* \*

"Balls, in those times, began at a reasonable hour. Ladies who went to a ball early in November, began to dress by daylight.

"Lilian had been dressed by her maid. Owing to a certain sentimental secret between her and her husband, she wore her wedding-dress of white Indian muslin, instead of a rich brocaded silk petticoat, underneath the grand lace robe. The diamonds glittered gaily round her head and her softly-rounded throat and arms. She went to the old library, where Graham sat awaiting the ladies. She wanted his opinion concerning her appearance. The legend does not tell how he behaved on this occasion, but leaves it to young husbands to imagine.

" 'You must go to my mother, and let her see how lovely you look. Walk first, that I may see how you look behind.' So she took from his hand a spray of roses he had gathered, and preceded him from the room, and up the staircase to his mother's chamber. She was in the dressing-room above.

" 'Go up by yourself,' said Graham; 'I will remain on the stairs, and watch you both. I should like to hear what she says, when she does not think I hear; for she never praises you much to me, for fear of increasing my blind adoration, I suppose.'

"Lilian smiled at him, and disappeared up the stairs. It was now becoming dark, and as he approached the stairs, a few minutes afterwards, to hear what was said, his mother's voice, in a strange, eager tone, called from above,

"*'Bring me a light! Bring me a light!'*

"Then Graham saw his mother's old servant run quickly from her seat by the window, and light a tall taper on the toilette. She carried this up to her mistress, and found Graham on the stair on her return. She grasped his arm, and whispered fearfully,

"'Watch her! Watch her!'

"He did watch, and saw—"

"For God's sake, Mr. Erle," I interrupted, "don't tell me what he saw—for I saw the same dreadful sight!"

"I have no doubt you did, since you say so; and because I have seen it myself."

We were silent for some moments, and then I asked if he knew anything more of these people.

"Yes—the rest is well known to every one who lives within twenty miles. Graham Whinmore vowed not to remain under the same roof with his mother, after he had seen his wife's blackened corpse. His grief and resentment were quiet and enduring. He would not leave the corpse in the house; but before midnight had it carried to a summer-house in the shrubbery, where he watched beside it, and allowed no one to approach, except the old servant who figures in this story. She brought him food, and carried his commands to the household. From the day of Lilian's death till the day of her burial in the family vault at Whinmore Church, Graham guarded the summer-house where his wife lay, with his drawn sword as he walked by night round about. It was known that he would not allow the family jewels to be taken from the body, and that they were to be buried with it. Some say that he finally took them from the body himself, and buried them in the shrubbery, lest the undertakers, tempted by the sight of the jewels on the corpse, might desecrate her tomb afterwards for the sake of stealing them. This opinion is supported by the fact that a portion of the shrubbery is haunted by the apparition of Graham Whinmore, in mourning garments, and with a drawn sword in his hand.

"Would you advise me to institute a search for those old jewels?" I asked smiling.

"I would," said he. "But take no one into your confidence,

Tom Whinmore. You may raise a laugh against you, if you are unsuccessful. And if you find them, and take them away—"

"Which I certainly should do," I interrupted.

"You will raise a popular outcry against you. The superstitious people will believe that you have outraged the ghost of your great-grandfather, who will become mischievous, in consequence."

I saw the prudence of this remark; and it was agreed between us, that we should do all the digging ourselves, unknown to any one. I then asked how it was that I was descended from this unfortunate gentleman.

Mr. Erle's story continued thus:—

"After his wife's funeral, Graham Whinmore did not return to the Hall, but went away to the south, and never came here again, not even to visit his mother on her death-bed, a year after. In a few years he married again, and had sons and daughters. To an unmarried daughter, Jane Whinmore,—always called 'Leddy Jane' by our neighbours,—he left the house and lands. He did not care to keep it in the family, and she might leave it to a stranger, or sell it, if she pleased. It was but a small portion of Graham Whinmore's property, as you must know. She, however—this 'Leddy Jane'—took a great fancy to the old place. She is said to have lived on terms of familiarity with the ghost of her grandmother, and still more affectionately with her father's first wife. She heard nothing of the buried jewels, and saw nothing of her own father's ghost during his lifetime. That part of the story did not come to light until after the death of Graham Whinmore; when the 'Leddy Jane' herself was startled one evening in the shrubbery, by meeting the apparition of her father. It is said that she left her property to her youngest nephew's youngest son, in obedience to his injunctions during that interview."

"So that though unborn at the time, I may consider myself lord of Whinmore Hall, by the will of my great-grandfather!" I said.

"Precisely so. I think it an indication that the ghostly power is to die out in your time. The last year of the wicked Lady Henrietta's life was very wretched, as you may suppose. Her besetting and cherished sins brought their own reward—and her crowning crime was avenged without the terror of the law. For it is said that every evening at sunset the apparition of her murdered daughter-in-law came before her, wearing the rich dress which was so dear to the proud woman; and that she was compelled to repeat the cruel act, and to hear her screams and the farewell curses of her adored son. The servants all left the Hall in affright; and no one lived with the wicked Lady except the faithful old servant, Margaret Thirlston, who stayed with her to the last, followed her to the grave, and died soon after.

"Her son and his wife were sought for by Jane Whinmore on her arrival here. She gave them a home and everything they wanted as house-keeper and farm-manager at the Hall. And at the death of Giles Thirlston, his son Ralph became farm-manager in his place. He continued there till 't' Leddy's' death, when he settled at the little wayside inn which you have seen, and which he calls 'Leddy Jane's Gift.' "

\*   \*   \*   \*

I have but little more to say. Mr. Erle and I sought long for the hidden treasure. We found it, after reading a letter secreted in the escritoire, addressed to 'My youngest nephew's youngest son.' In that letter directions were given for recovering the hidden jewels of the family. They were buried outside the garden fence, on the open moor, on the very spot where I can swear I saw the figure of a man with a sword—my great-grandfather, Graham Whinmore.

After I married, we came to live in the south; and I took every means to let my little estate of Whinmore. To my regret the Hall has never found a tenant, and it is still without a tenant after these twenty-five years.

Will any reader of ONCE A WEEK make me an offer? They shall have it cheap.

J. M. H.

# OLD HOOKER'S GHOST

## or, CHRISTMAS GAMBOLS AT HUNTINGFIELD HALL

Bentley's Miscellany, *a monthly magazine, became known for serializing long, illustrated novels. By the 1840s its following had dropped off, but it continued to entertain middle-class readers until the title ceased in 1868.*[1] *The following story, originally published in 1865, contains all of the ingredients of a decorous country-house Christmas: church-going, alms-bearing, mumming, as well as a Christmas dinner, a ghost-story circle, and a masquerade. The perfect Christmas setting serves as a frame tale for a tragic story and a family supposedly haunted by an avenging spirit. When the ghost narrative begins to invade the frame tale, the memories of past indiscretions disturb the jollity of the holiday proceedings.*

## CHAPTER I

### AN INTRODUCTION TO HUNTINGFIELD HALL AND ITS INHABITANTS

A T THAT PERIOD OF THE YEAR when rain, wind, and frost have, by their combined powers, stripped the trees of their foliage and plucked even the last rose of autumn from its stem, a large merry party of all ages were collected under the hospitable roof of the warm-hearted, generous Sir Gilbert Ilderton, of Huntingfield Hall, prepared for a Christmas campaign of fun and jollity. Sir Gilbert should be described before his mansion. He stood six feet two in his stockings; his figure was broad, stout, and well built; his countenance oblong, with blue eyes, large and expressive, a longish well-formed nose, and a mouth from which a benignant smile was seldom absent. He might be taken as the beau ideal of an English country gentleman.

---

1 John Sutherland, "Bentley's Miscellany" in *The Stanford Companion to Victorian Fiction*. Stanford: Stanford University Press, 1989. 58-59.

His eldest son, Gilbert, a fine handsome young fellow, very like him in appearance and manners, was at college, and soon about to come of age; his next was in the army; and the third, Charley—the delight of his mother, the favourite of the household, and of the whole neighbourhood—was serving his country at sea in the exalted position of a midshipman; but never mind, he intended some day to be an admiral, and to thrash the French or any other enemies of Old England with right good will. There were several other younger boys, and three daughters, known to the country round as the Three Graces, lovely young creatures, fair and gentle, with refined, elegant figures. It would have been difficult to find a more beautiful girl than Mary Ilderton, the eldest—she was a year older than Gilbert—and the others promised to equal her. Then there was Lady Ilderton—a true English matron, kind, and gentle, and thoughtful, dignified and courteous, utterly above the littlenesses of common minds—she was the very antipodes of vulgarity, yet she was full of animation and humour also, and could keep everybody alive and make them happy—at least, it was their own fault if they were not so.

The Hall at Christmas was always full of guests, for Sir Gilbert delighted in seeing happy joyous faces around him, and relations and friends, old and young, of high and of humble degree, as far as purses were concerned, were assembled. The life and spirit of the house was a certain Mr. Giles Markland. Everybody called him Cousin Giles. All the young people, not learned in genealogies, thought that he was their cousin, though they did not know how. He was, however, really a cousin of Sir Gilbert's, who valued him more for the qualities of honesty, simplicity, and kindness of heart which he possessed, than on account of his relationship. The Miss Ildertons were not looked upon as clever, though there could be no doubt that they were well brought up, and possessed the usual accomplishments of young ladies of the nineteenth century, but among the guests was a niece of Lady Ilderton's, Miss Jane Otterburn, who was considered a genius, for she wrote poetry, had a vast amount of imagination, acted well, got up charades, invented games and amusements of all sorts, and indeed, in the house, ably seconded Cousin Giles, who was himself the prime mover of all out-of-door sports. She was a small, dark, quick, active, bright-eyed girl, or rather young woman, for she was well out of her teens, and acknowledged by all to be very pretty—indeed, in that respect she might have vied with the Miss Ildertons, and as a partner was a greater favourite than they were. She was an orphan, and had a good fortune, which made her doubly interesting. In the art of weaving an extemporary tale of fact or fiction, Jane Otterburn's fertile imagination burst forth with a brilliancy which few could equal.

The most complete contrast to her in the house was also a distant cousin of Sir Gilbert's, Susan Langdon. She was good natured, and fair, and fat, and deliciously dull, as Cousin Giles used to say. She was a general and well-satisfied butt, for she was, he added, too obtuse to observe the shafts aimed at her, or too good natured to mind them when they struck her harder than usual. She had a mother very like her, and a brother Simon possessed of the same characteristics, who always chuckled and rubbed his hands when he discovered any tricks played on Susan, not perceiving that similar ones were practised on himself. However, the individual members of the party must be made to appear as they are required.

Christmas-day arrived. Everybody went to church over the hard crisp ground, and the sacred edifice was decked with holly and bright red berries, and there were appropriate inscriptions under the organ gallery, and the subject of the sermon inculcated on the congregation was peace and good will towards their fellow-men, and no one would doubt what Sir Gilbert practised as they saw the smiling, pleased countenances of the villagers as he passed among them. Then there was a luncheon and a brisk walk taken by the younger people, Cousin Giles leading, among hedges no longer green and woods denuded of leaves, and by ponds, to judge how soon the ice would bear, and a dozen or more cottages visited, and gifts bestowed on old people unable to move out, he singing joyous carols, and Jane Otterburn discoursing learnedly on the nature of frost and snow, and hibernating animals, and on other topics suggested by the season, and Susan Langdon, laughing she knew not why, except that she felt happy, and Simon trying to play her a trick, but not having the wit to invent one. The Miss Ildertons talked pleasantly, listening to their brother Gilbert's remarks, or conversed with young Lord Harston and Captain Fotheringsail of the navy, dividing their attentions with praiseworthy impartiality. Then came the dinner—old English fare, but better cooked than formerly—roast beef and turkey, and plum-puddings and mince-pies, all decked with holly, and lighted brandy to warm the pies and puddings, and no lack of generous wine of the best, and a real grace said by the minister, present with his family, and a blessing asked. Little attendance was demanded from the servants when the cloth was removed, for they, too, were enjoying Heaven's bounteous gifts, bestowed through their kind master's hand, in their hall below, decked with holly, one end, with the aid of screens and boughs, forming a tasteful stage.

Their repast over, voices outside announced the arrival of the carol-singers, and they being speedily admitted, and, after partaking of refreshment, arranged on the stage, the whole family from the drawing-room assembled in the hall to hear them, Sir Gilbert sitting in front, with purse in hand, giving many an encouraging and approving smile. They gave place to mummers, to the great satisfaction of the younger part of the audience. There was Father Christmas and his attendant sprites, Hail, Frost, and Snow, and heroes innumerable, dressed in paper hats, helmets, and armour decked with spangles and ribbons, and swords of wood, and long spears, altogether a motley group; the Duke of Wellington and Napoleon Bonaparte; Nelson, Soult, and Blucher; the Black Prince and Julius Caesar; the Duke of Marlborough and Richard of the Lion Heart; and numerous other men of renown of all ages, brought together with delightful disregard to historical correctness. They fought one with the other, and fell mortally wounded, the Great Duke of modern days alone surviving, when a new character rushed in—a doctor with a nostrum to cure all complaints—and, applying it to their noses, with some words of a cabalistic character, which sounded like "Take some of this riff-raff up thy sniff-snaff," he set each dead hero on his feet ready to fight another day.

"That gentleman would have wonderful practice if he could be as successful among the public as he has been to-night," observed

Cousin Giles, while Sir Gilbert was bestowing his largesse on the performers. "Let's have it all over again!"

"Ancore!—ancore!" was shouted by the younger members of the audience; and not unwillingly the actors, with the utmost gravity, went through their parts without the slightest variation of word or gesture.

Tea over, the juveniles were invited into the dining-room, where at the farther end of the table a hideous witch was seen presiding over a huge bowl, from which suddenly, as the lights were withdrawn, blue flames burst forth, and the witch, her long brown arms extending over the bowl, grew more hideous still, and a voice was heard inviting them all to partake of the contents—"Hot raisins—sweet raisins—nice burning raisins"— and but few hung back, for the voice was not unfriendly, and was easily recognised as that of Cousin Giles; and when they had seen their own faces turn blue and yellow and green, and the raisins were all gone, the witch sunk down under the table and Cousin Giles popped up, and the witch was gone. Then came games of all sorts, old and young joining with equal zest, led by Cousin Giles and Jane Otterburn. Now all were silent to listen to, and many to join in, a Christmas carol sweetly sung, and family prayers were held and the Scriptures read, and Christmas-day was over, and all retired, with grateful hearts and kindly thoughts of one another, to rest.

# CHAPTER II

### A TALE OF A GHOST

There is said to be a skeleton in some out-of-the-way cupboard of every house. There was one in Huntingfield Hall. No one liked to speak of it, though. Even the jovial Sir Gilbert shunned the subject. The morning had been spent on the ice—several of the ladies had put on skates for the first time, and the gentlemen had exerted themselves till all were tolerably tired. Still games of all sorts had gone on as usual for the sake of the younger members of the party, blindman's-buff and hide-and-seek suiting best the taste of most of them, no one thinking of the tale of the Old Oak Chest, or dreading a fate similar to that of the heroine. At length even the most active had had enough of movement, and a general cry was raised for a story from Jane Otterburn. Cousin Giles pressed the point, and Jane was led within a large semicircle formed round the fire, Sir Gilbert taking his usual seat on one side, and Lady Ilderton on the other. She took a low seat, with one arm resting on Miss Ilderton's chair, her dark locks falling over the light-blue dress of her fair cousin, while her other hand held a feather-screen to guard her eyes from the fire.

"Now, Jane—now Miss Otterburn, your story—your story!" cried several voices, old and young.

Jane waited a moment in silence, gazing at the fire, and began:

There was an old, old family, whose ancestors were among the Norman conquerors of Britain, and who had ever since owned the same estate in the centre of England. The ladies were fair and virtuous, the men brave and upright, but proud of their birth, and somewhat haughty withal. They had fought for King Charles, and sided with James to the last, though they became loyal subjects of William of Orange, and, whatever their sympathies, having sworn to acknowledge him, they took no part with the supporters of the Pretender.

At length, a certain Sir Hugh Oswald became the head of the house. He had a son and daughter, of whose good looks, manners, and general bearing, he was justly proud. He was proud, indeed, of all things belonging to himself, and it would have been difficult to persuade him that they were otherwise than perfection.

It was on a dark night in November, the wind was howling and whistling through the trees, and the sleet and rain came pelting down with a fury which drove even the most hardy under shelter, that young Hugh Oswald left the Hall by a side-door, and took his way across the park towards a keeper's cottage. At his tap the door opened, and a young girl, fair and beautiful as a Houri, who had been sitting reading by a lamp, stood ready to receive him.

"Dearest Hugh, you know I love to see you, but what a night

for you to come out, and leave the gay party assembled at the Hall."

"The very reason that I came, as no one will suspect, even if I am missed, that I have left the Hall, my own sweet May," answered Hugh, folding her in his arms.

What more was said I need not describe. This was only one of many stolen visits to the keeper's lodge, strange as it may seem, known of and suspected by no one at the Hall. At length Hugh obtained leave from his father to travel. He had seen little of England, nothing of the Continent. He was absent for some time, and then he wrote to say that he had taken a step he hoped his father would forgive, though he had acted without first seeking his sanction. He had married a girl, young, lovely, and amiable. It was only necessary to see her to love her. He entreated forgiveness, and hoped that his father would receive her as his bride.

The answer Sir Hugh sent was more favourable than might have been expected, still he remarked that his forgiveness must of necessity depend on circumstances. Hugh, on one pretence or another, delayed returning home, not trusting, apparently, to the circumstances on which his forgiveness depended. At last, Sir Hugh, losing patience, or suspecting that all was not right, peremptorily ordered his son to return. The young couple came. Hugh had not overpraised his wife's beauty. Sir Hugh gazed at her earnestly without speaking, then took his son aside.

"Hugh," he said, "you do not know whom you have married, but I do. There is no happiness for you on this side the grave."

Not another word would he say, notwithstanding all his son's solicitations for an explanation. Little did he know what at that very moment was taking place.

It was summer. In a distant part of the shrubbery, in a bower covered with roses, jasmine, and other creeping plants, stood Emily Oswald, waiting with anxious gaze and beating heart the coming of one who had declared himself her lover. He came; his dress was rustic, but his figure was refined, his countenance eminently handsome, and his bearing manly. He showed no timidity as he approached the young lady, for he was evidently confident of her love. He urged her to fly with him. He pleaded his devoted love and affection. He told her that he knew her father would never consent to their union, and that it would be better to marry without his sanction than after he had refused it. She listened credulously and too readily. She fled with him; her subsequent history I will not detail. She had believed that the peasant youth, the keeper's pretended son, was a noble in disguise.

She was not missed till late at night, and when sought for throughout the house and grounds no trace of her could be found. Not till two days afterwards did Sir Hugh discover that his only daughter, the beautiful child of whom he was so proud, had fled with the keeper's son, the brother of the girl his own boy Hugh had married, and thereby entailed, as he conceived, eternal disgrace on his family; yet, as if that were not enough, Emily, his trusted child, must commit an act to increase the stigma tenfold. He suspected, too, that the wound to his feelings had been premeditated, and he knew, too, the foe by whose machinations it had been accomplished. The baronet took his gun and wandered forth into the grounds. Such was his constant custom. He seldom went out without his weapon.

It was said that he met the keeper, a man who had strangely come to the place and sought for employment in that situation, that Sir Hugh had charged the keeper with acts of villany and treachery, that the other had insultingly retorted, that a fierce struggle had ensued. Two days afterwards the body of the keeper had been found, shot through the breast, in a remote part of the grounds. Rumour pointed to Sir Hugh as the murderer, but he was never accused openly. It was further asserted that the dying man had foretold that his spirit would haunt the Hall for ten generations, and that during that time the eldest son should never succeed to his inheritance. Sir Hugh appears to have been severely punished, at all events.

The fate of his beautiful and beloved daughter was a sad one. The keeper's son, though talented, was utterly unprincipled, and she died young, from a broken heart. His sister, too, did not turn out as well as her young husband had anticipated. As she grew older, and more was expected of her, tastes and manners became apparent which had been overlooked in a young and pretty girl. Hugh died before his father, and Sir Hugh lived long, a sad and childless old man, and his estate descended to a brother's son.

"Where did you get that story, Jane?" asked the baronet, in a tone of annoyance, very unlike that in which he usually spoke.

"My dear Jane, where could you possibly have heard that tale?" exclaimed her aunt.

"That is more than I can tell you," answered Miss Otterburn. "I thought that I had invented it, and I certainly drew on my imagination for the names, but I confess that it is possible I may have heard it somewhere. I often, when I fancy that I am inventing, find that I have heard the outline of the tale before."

Neither Sir Gilbert nor Lady Ilderton said anything more on the subject, though both were unusually grave. Other tales were told, in many of which ghosts and goblins played a prominent part. During the course of the evening, Cousin Giles took an opportunity of drawing Miss Otterburn aside.

"What in the name of wonder, my dear Jane, induced you to tell that story?" he exclaimed. "Don't you know that it is connected with this house and Sir Gilbert's ancestors? You gave even the right Christian names of father and son. There can be no doubt that Sir Hugh really did shoot the keeper, old Hooker, as he was called, and it is asserted and believed that his ghost haunts, as he threatened, the mansion of his murderer."

"What! this very house!" exclaimed Jane, with a look of astonishment, and it might have been terror, or some other uncomfortable feeling, in her countenance.

"Yes, if old women, housekeepers, and superannuated butlers can be believed, old Hooker's ghost has appeared more than once or twice stalking through the Hall at midnight, no one daring to speak to it or attempt to stop it. You must understand that the family give a different version of the story. They say that old Hooker committed suicide, in consequence of his daughter running off with young Hugh, who, they state, did not marry her, and of his son, of whom he was very proud, being transported for the abduction of Miss Ilderton. With regard to the son, it is difficult to say who was most to blame. The young man had, I believe, raised himself by his extraordinary talents far above his former position, and he might have supposed that a marriage with her would have advanced his ambitious projects; or he might have run off with her and treated her as he ultimately did in retaliation for the way his sister had been treated by young Hugh. Still I suspect that, at the best, he was an unprincipled fellow, and that not much can be said in favour of any of the parties concerned. However, they are all long ago dead and buried, and waiting to be tried by a tribunal which will measure out even justice to all men; so do not let us condemn them undefended."

## CHAPTER III

### PREPARATIONS FOR TWELFTH-NIGHT

The story of old Hooker's Ghost was not again alluded to in the presence of any of the Ilderton family, as the subject was evidently distasteful to them; but it formed the subject of conversation among the guests when only two or three were together, and at length, through one or two of the ladies'-maids, the story reached the servants'-hall, where, of course, it was eagerly received. Lampet, the butler, however, shook his head when he heard it, and advised that it should not be talked about.

"It may be true, or it may not be true, but there'll be no harm come of letting it alone," he observed.

Notwithstanding the wisdom of this remark, neither in the servants'-hall nor above-stairs would people let it alone, till at length many began to feel uncomfortable as night drew on, and preferred having a companion when they had to traverse the long passages and corridors which led from wing to wing of the mansion. Jane Otterburn found that she had indeed raised a ghost of a character she had little anticipated. All this time none of the family knew what was going on, as, after it had been understood that Sir Gilbert and Lady Ilderton disliked the subject, when any of them approached it was instantly dropped. In time even the costume old Hooker had worn was minutely described: a hunting-frock of Lincoln green, with leathern belt; a cap with iron bands, shaped somewhat like a Mambrino's helmet, or the hat of a policeman of modern days; a powder-horn at his back, high leathern boots, and a huge spear, which it must have required two hands to wield. This showed that he was a head keeper—a person of no little consequence, and one who must have proved a formidable opponent to deerstalkers and poachers of all descriptions. That he was above the ordinary keepers, accounted for the superior education he had managed to give his son.

Jane had talked so much and thought so much about the story, that she was not quite comfortable herself, and more than once, when going somewhat late to bed, her door having suddenly burst open as she went to shut it, she thought she saw— the moonlight streaming through a window—a strange figure moving along the passage in the distance. She was a courageous girl, though imaginative in the extreme, so she watched the figure, wondering if it would turn, but it vanished apparently through the window at the farther end of the passage. She told no one what she had seen, believing that her senses had deceived her; but three nights afterwards, when, under precisely the same circumstances, the figure again appeared and disappeared, she was, to say the least of it, extremely puzzled and secretly agitated, though she still determined not to mention the occurrence. By the morning she had recovered her equanimity, and was as lively and agreeable as usual. The gentlemen thought her especially so, and the light-hearted merry Captain Fotheringsail, whose breast when in uniform was covered with orders, seemed to have ears and thoughts for no one else. Jane liked him, but had a fancy that he had come to the Hall as a suitor for the hand of one of her cousins. She was one of those happy beings who think so little of self that she always fancied that, if attentions were paid, they must be intended for some other person present. It might have been very stupid in the captain not to make his intentions more clear, but so it was, and Jane thought herself heart free.

It should have been mentioned that, on Christmas-day, Sir Gilbert and Lady Ilderton had had their hearts made glad by the announcement that their sailor son, Charley, was on his way to England, and, as he would soon get leave, might be expected shortly at the Hall.

Several of the proposed amusements were put off till his arrival; among them was a fancy ball, or masquerade rather, which it was settled should take place on Twelfth Night, should he write word that he could come in time.

"Hurra! Charley is coming!" cried Gilbert, on opening a letter at the breakfast-table—that delightful period of the day in a well-ordered English household, when, rising refreshed by sleep, all the members meet round the snow-white board, laden with sweet-smelling bread and rolls of all shapes, and toast and butter in fanciful pats swimming in crystal bowls of pure water, and preserves in cut glasses, and, maybe, some delicate sausages or cutlets kept hot under covers, and fragrant tea and coffee, and china of elegant pattern, all so cool, and fresh, and bright, and then the sideboard groaning with substantial viands. "Yes, he'll be here by the fifth at latest, and, depend on it, if any one is inclined to be slow, he'll stir them up."

Charley was a general favourite, though it must be acknowledged, when he went to sea, he was a somewhat harum-scarum fellow.

Now great preparations were making for the ball, and the costumes which were to be worn at it. There were to be knights in armour, and a Robin Hood and Maid Marian, and Turks, and Greeks, and Albanians, and Circassians, and Hamlets, and an Othello, a Rolla, and a Young Norval, and a Virgin of the Sun, and Night and Morning, and the Four Seasons, and a Harlequin, and a Clown, and Columbine—indeed, it was difficult to say what characters were not to appear; but the best of it was, that no one knew who was to be who, except, perhaps, Cousin Giles, and Jane Otterburn, and Gilbert, who were among the initiated. The ball-room was a magnificent hall—the pride of the county—and that was to be decked with evergreens, with lamps placed amidst them, and bowers of flowers which the hothouses alone could provide at that season of the year.

"It would be great fun," said Cousin Giles to Jane, as they were busy over some of their plans. "I don't think, really, that Sir Gilbert would be annoyed. What vexes him is to have the matter taken in earnest. I rather fancy that he doesn't believe the story himself. The dress is that of a society of Foresters in this party of the country, and I can easily procure it."

Jane looked thoughtful. Could it have been any one masquerading at night whom she had seen in the passage? Had she seen it but one night that might have been the solution of the mystery.

She did not like to mention the subject, even to Cousin Giles, for she had an idea that he would laugh at her, so she said nothing, and kept wondering on.

The fifth of January came, and the preparations were in a forward state, but Charley had not arrived, though Gilbert did not seem much concerned, and said that he was sure that he would make his appearance, at all events, in time for the ball.

## CHAPTER IV

### A MASQUERADE, AND AN ACCOUNT OF THE PART THE GHOST PLAYED AT IT

It was Twelfth-night, and people from all the country round were assembling at Huntingfield Hall—some few in a sober, modern costume, but the greater number in all varieties of fantastic dresses. A Lady Abbess came chaperoning a Columbine, an Italian Flower-girl, and a fair Circassian; and a magnificently-robed Pasha supported on one arm a demure Quakeress, and on the other a sombre-clad Nun; but some glittering trimming, which could be seen under her cloak, showed that she was not likely to remain long in that costume. A Virgin of the Sun entered arm in arm with Don Juan, and a Greek Pirate with the Maid of Orleans; a Circassian chief and a Russian noble were hand and glove, and a bog-trotting Irishman, with a doodeen in his mouth and a shillelagh in his fist, supported the arm of a somewhat stout Queen Elizabeth. Sir Gilbert and Lady Ilderton appeared as a gentleman and lady of the time of Henry the Eighth, and their daughters, with another young lady, as the Four Seasons, without masks.

The fun began, and every effort was made to discover who was who, but so well disguised were many of the guests that this was often no easy task. Not only animals, but even senseless objects were represented; and among other things, a huge cask glided into the room. Remarks not over-complimentary to the talent of the occupant were made as it circled its way on, as if moved by human hands outside, in the usual fashion of making a cask progress, when a voice invariably replied, "I may be stupid, for I am a butt for the wit of others." After turning round and round through the room for some time, resting occasionally near some couple engaged in interesting conversation, a voice from within seldom failing to make some appropriate comment, it stopped near one of the evergreen bowers, exhibiting a smiling ruddy countenance, with a huge mouth, to the company, from which a loud peal of laughter burst forth. From that moment it remained stationary, and when soon afterwards a Clown, who had been inquisitively prying into every corner, began to knock at it, and at length attempted to get in, it was found to be empty. He on this set to work to trundle it away, and as if fatigued, stopped again near the wall to be out of the way; a Columbine passing engaged his attention, when, to his apparent dismay and the astonishment of the guests, the tub began to move on of itself, he following, and pretending to be unable to overtake it, while he shouted "Hillo, you mesmerised butt, you—stop—stop! Hillo, you spirit of a tun, a pipe, a cask, or whatever you are, or call yourself—stop, I say—stop!" But the butt would not stop till it reached a deep recess, when he overtook it, and, pulling away at it, upset it, when, as before, it was seen to be empty.

Meantime, an admirably-dressed hunchback Gipsy had been going about telling fortunes. Although she had no mask, so well was her face disguised that no one seemed to know who she was—whether old, or young, or tall, or short. She had not to seek people out, but one after the other they came up to her, and with wonderful accuracy she told them who they were, and mostly what were their aims and wishes, what they had done, and what they proposed doing. Among others, a jovial sailor rolled up, pipe in mouth, and asked to what part of the world he should next be sent, how long he should remain, and when he came back whether he should find his black-eyed Susan faithful and true? To the answer he got to the first question he paid little attention. Instead of replying to the second, she desired him to describe his black-eyed Susan, to say how long he had been attached, and whether she returned his affection. His description answered exactly to that of Jane Otterburn. Three weeks only had passed since he had seen her for the first time; but sailors can seldom enjoy more than a brief time of courtship, and have to sing "Happy's the wooing that's not long a doing." The point, in truth, about which he was most anxious, was the return he might expect to his affection. The Gipsy hesitated a little, and her voice was scarcely as clear and high as it had previously been, as she replied:

"True honest love, when it meets with a free heart and disengaged hand, seldom fails to obtain a return, and the honest love of a brave man, when no return can be given, changes to friendship, and he seeks wisely and soon some other object on whom to bestow his affections."

"But Mistress Gipsy," persisted Jack, "suppose I cares for Sue, and I does care for her, and for the very ground she treads on, does Sue care for me? That's the gist of the matter, and what I wants to know."

"Ask her yourself. If she is what you describe, she'll give you a sincere answer," answered the Gipsy, and her voice was still lower than before; "but not this evening—not this evening. You have nothing to dread, I suspect," she added.

The sailor gave a sudden start, and seemed very unwilling to quit the side of the Gipsy, who, after this little occurrence, greatly lost her loquacity and power of repartee, and she was voted by those who had not before spoken to her to be a very dull and uninteresting Gipsy. Her conversation with the sailor was interrupted by a cry from several of the guests, and from one end of the room there stalked forth a figure in a suit of Lincoln green, with hunting-cap on head and spear in hand. The face of the figure was properly whitened, but there was a jauntiness in the walk and a twinkle in the eyes, as the ghost moved among the crowd, which soon betrayed the true character of the supposed visitant from the grave. He had not, however, reached one end of the hall before the eyes of the guests were turned towards the other end, where there appeared a figure in a similar costume, but more worn and stained, with what was evidently a winding-sheet trailing behind; the countenance was deadly pale, and there was an unnatural glare in the eyes which it was painful to look at, while the features were rigid and fixed in an extraordinary manner. A curious halo, or mist it seemed, surrounded the figure as it stalked along, turning neither to the right hand nor to the left, nor appearing to notice any one in the room. No one ventured to speak to it and ask it whence it came, but two or three gentlemen, who had come in characters of a doubtful nature, crept hurriedly out of its way. One was in black, with a pair of small chamois horns on his head, hoofs on his feet, and a long tail, which he carried gracefully coiled round his arm; another was a wood-demon, a green monster with wings, and claws, and horns, he was accompanied by a troop of imps, all of different colours, though bearing many of his characteristics; while a third represented a leaden blue-coloured demon, produced in the unwholesome imaginations of German poets. Everything about him was blue—watch, snuff-box, and toothpick-case. He got out of the way with even more haste than the rest, to the great amusement of the little imps, who did not appear to have the same dread of the awful-looking being as the rest.

On it came, slowly and silently, people making a broad way for it, and some even hurrying out of the room with looks indicative of terror; the bright lights grew dim as it passed, so many afterwards declared. The Gipsy, when she saw it, started, and, after scrutinising it for a moment, became so agitated that, had it not been for her companion, who was evidently a fellow not to be daunted by even his Satanic Majesty himself, she would have fallen. The sailor, on seeing this, looked very much inclined to rush forward and bring the ghost, if such it were, to action, but the Gipsy, grasping his arm, held him back.

"No, no. Do not interfere with it," she exclaimed. "There may be more of reality in it than you suppose."

The sailor, on hearing this, burst into a hearty merry laugh, which seemed to have some influence on the ghost, for it slowly turned its fearful eyes towards him, then turned back its head, and stalked or rather glided on.

"Never fear, my fine fellow, but I'll find you out, and prove that a ghost can squeak if he can't speak," cried the sailor, still undaunted. "Avast there! Heave-to, I say! I want to light my pipe, and your goggles will just suit my purpose."

To this address the ghost paid no attention, and the sailor seemed very much inclined to give chase, when, as it had got about three-quarters of the way down the room, Sir Gilbert, who had left it for a short time, re-entered.

"What gramarye[1] is this?" he exclaimed, with a look of astonishment and annoyance. "I did not suppose that any visitor to this house would have taken so unwarrantable a liberty. Whoever you are, I must beg that you will instantly retire, and only appear again in your proper costume. We have all assembled to enjoy ourselves in an evening of harmless amusement, and I cannot allow the opportunity to be taken to try the nerves of ladies and children; for I hope all the men present will perceive that it is only a remarkably well got-up piece of mummery."

The figure stopped for an instant listening to this address, and then turned round so withering a glance that even the baronet was put out of countenance. He soon recovered himself, however, exclaiming:

"Nonsense! Such things cannot be!" But the unusual expression of doubt and vexation which his countenance wore showed too plainly what were his real feelings. To have a ghost walk into his room without his will, or to receive a visit from any unwelcome visitor, is enough to annoy any man, and this post-sepulchral visit of old Hooker, if such it was, certainly was anything but pleasant. But, besides this, Sir Gilbert had been vexed at the non-arrival of his son Charley, whom, in spite of his wildness, he dearly loved. He could not help fearing that he might have got into some scrape at Portsmouth, or have been detained elsewhere by some escapade or other. Probably, had Lady Ilderton seen the ghost and been alarmed at it, he would have been still more angry than he was—that is to say, as far as his kind, genial nature would allow him to be angry.

There was a dead silence after Sir Gilbert had spoken, but no one stepped forward to confront or stop the ghost, probably from the impression that such things cannot be stopped, or that unpleasant consequences would ensue if the attempt were to be made. At all events, the appearance of old Hooker passed on unimpeded, until it reached one of the bowers at the end of the room where no seats had been placed. When it got there, suddenly a blue flame burst forth, surrounded by which it vanished.

"The mummery has been admirably got up, I must confess,"

1 Occult learning; magic.

observed Sir Gilbert. "Some of my household have, of course, been in the secret, though I wish that I had first been consulted. And now, my friends, let the dancing commence, as I must before long request you all to unmask."

Some little time, however, elapsed before the equanimity of many of the guests was restored. At length the gay strains of the dance music, and the exertions of Cousin Peter, who had re-appeared as Robin Hood, and others, put them into their former good spirits, and they began to talk, and laugh, and joke as if no such unpleasant visitor as the long-buried old Hooker had appeared. When Cousin Giles was asked what he thought of the matter, he shook his head, and declared that he was in a very great hurry to get out of the room and out of the clothes when the real thing so unexpectedly appeared. Sir Gilbert, as soon as he had seen his guests once more amusing themselves as if nothing had happened, sent his steward and two or three other trusty people to endeavour to discover what had become of the person, if person it was, who had represented old Hooker's ghost. They returned after searching in every possible place, declaring that they could find no one hid away, nor had they seen any one pass in any similar costume except Mr. Peter, who had taken no pains to conceal himself.

"Very strange—very strange indeed!" muttered Sir Gilbert. "Did you examine the attics, Masham?" he asked his steward. "There are several old chests in the north lumber-attic. Several of them contain dresses, and if they have been disturbed, it may give us a clue to the culprit, for a culprit I consider whoever played the trick, admirably as I must own it was done."

"As to that, Sir Gilbert, with due respect to your opinion, I don't exactly like to be certain," answered Masham, with a bow. "I *have* heard of a gentleman who came down to these parts with a Scotch name, I think, who could make tables turn, and articles of furniture and musical instruments fly about the room, and spirits of persons a long time dead, some of them in foreign parts, come and talk and say all sorts of things to people who like to ask them questions. Now, if this is true—and it is extraordinary how many gentlefolks believe in it—I do not see why the ghost of old Hooker shouldn't walk about the house, or even through the ball-room, especially when he knew that somebody had been dressing up like himself, which of course wouldn't be pleasant to him; and besides, Sir Gilbert—I didn't like to say it before—this is the very day, so it is reported, that he came to his end, and that's another reason why he wouldn't like people to be dancing and jigging away like mummers over his grave, so to speak."

Masham was a dissenter of the puritan school—an honest, upright man, always accustomed to speak his mind to his employer, by whom he was highly esteemed. In this instance, however, he went a little too far, and he acknowledged afterwards that he had never before seen his master in such a taking.

"Nonsense, man—nonsense!" exclaimed Sir Gilbert. "The fellow you speak of is an impostor, an arrant humbug, and the people are geese who believe in him, whatever their station in life—more shame to them if they are well educated. That is a poor reason for believing that old Hooker's ghost should haunt the Hall. Go and search again. I am resolved to have the trick discovered before the guests leave the house. They shall not go away, and spread all over the country the story of its being haunted. Look first into the north attic. Take care, Masham, that none of the servants set the place on fire by letting a candle fall in their fright, should a cat jump up or a rat move. I conclude that you know the chests I mean?"

"Oh yes, Sir Gilbert; I helped Master Charles to overhaul one of them three years ago, when he wanted to collect some dresses for a play, and I went up with the housekeeper, and we put them all safe back again the day after," answered the steward, hurrying off.

Sir Gilbert was joined soon afterwards by Lady Ilderton, who came to ask him the particulars of the strange story of which she had heard rumours, but which no one had ventured directly to tell her.

"Merely, my dear lady, that some one has walked through the ball-room in a hunting costume to represent the old keeper Hooker, and because no one spoke to him, or tried to stop him, they have taken it into their heads that what they saw was no living being, but a ghost or spirit."

"How very extraordinary—and that it should have taken place

during the few minutes we were both together out of the room," observed Lady Ilderton, in a low voice. "I am disinclined to believe in such things, and yet this is more than I can well account for."

"Oh, nonsense—nonsense, Lady Ilderton!" exclaimed Sir Gilbert; and yet his tone was not quite so firm as usual. "Depend on it, Masham will find it all out before long, and, if he does not, Cousin Giles will tomorrow, though of course I would rather the trick had not been played. And now let us go back into the drawing-room."

Not long after this, two most riotous sailors rushed into the room, insisting on playing leap-frog, tumbling over each other, and committing a variety of eccentricities unheard of in a ball-room. At last one of them rushed up to Lady Ilderton, and, throwing his arms round her neck, gave her a hearty kiss, when his mask falling off, displayed the well-bronzed, merry countenance of her son Charley. He introduced his companion as a brother-officer, whom he had invited to spend a few days at the Hall.

He was heartily welcomed by his father, who loved him in spite of his occasional wild proceedings, and of course his mother and sisters doted on him, and fully believed that he would turn out a second Nelson if he had the opportunity.

The ball went off with the greatest possible spirit, and without any other contretemps, could the incident which has been described, be considered one. Masham came back, and reported that the old chests had undoubtedly been opened and the contents tumbled out, as there were marks where the dust had been disturbed, but that he had discovered no trace of the person who had represented old Hooker's ghost.

## CHAPTER V

MORE OF THE GHOST'S PRANKS, AND HOW HE WAS FINALLY LAID

Sir Gilbert had allowed the adornments of the ball-room to remain undisturbed, that his tenants and others might see them—a favour which was sure to be highly prized.

The following evening a large party were assembled in the ball-room, for the young people had declared that they should be far too tired to do anything but dance, and musicians were, therefore, retained, and all the people in the immediate neighbourhood invited to come back. Lord Harston was glad of it, because he had made up his mind to propose to Miss Ilderton, and, as other young men have done, fancied that a ball-room was a very good place for the purpose. Captain Fotheringsail might possibly have had some similar ideas on the same subject with regard to Jane Otterburn. Charley and his brother-midshipman declared that they were ready for a dance every night of their lives. Jane had gone to her room after dinner, which was in a wing of the house away from the ball-room, and at this time as silent as at midnight; the evening guests had not yet arrived. A cheerful fire was burning, the flames from which sent at times a flickering and uncertain light through the room, but were generally bright enough to enable her to dispense with the light of her candles, as she sat down in an arm-chair to meditate pleasantly, as young ladies who have made a satisfactory conquest are apt to do. Though reveries of that description are pleasant, realities are pleasanter, and so she was about to get up to go down into the ball-room, when a feeling that she was not alone made her turn her head, and there, standing at the open door, was the figure of old Hooker the keeper, exactly as it had appeared on the previous evening.

She was a courageous girl, but her heart beat quick, and she felt that she would very much rather it had not been there. She rose from her seat, determined to confront it, when, with a sound which might be described as a plaintive cry, it glided from the door. She bravely hurried after it, exclaiming, "Stop! stop! I must insist on knowing who you are." But the passage was in total darkness, and the figure had disappeared. She had heard of the phantoms of the imagination to which some few people are subject when out of health, but she felt perfectly well, and had never had any visitation of the sort, and so, discarding all idea of a supernatural appearance, she felt convinced that somebody who had played off the trick on the previous evening had again dressed up to carry it on further. Still, therefore, undaunted by what might have frightened some ladies into hysterics, she lighted her candle, and drawing a large shawl over her shoulders, for the passages were cold, she prepared to descend to the ball-room.

It would be too much to say that she had no uncomfortable sensation, or that she did not peer into the darkness ahead, and occasionally take an anxious glance over her shoulder, or that she altogether felt sure that she should not see old Hooker gliding before her, or noiselessly coming up behind her. She could not help allowing all the ghost stories she had ever heard to pass in ghastly review through her mind. Still she tried not to walk faster than she should otherwise have done; indeed, she foresaw that if she attempted to run, the wax taper she held would most probably be blown out. This, strong-minded as she was, she would very much rather should not happen. The keen wind of Christmas was blowing outside, and blasts here and there found their way along the passages, in consequence of one or two doors which ought to have been shut having been left open.

Huntingfield Hall was an old edifice, and the same attention to warming the passages and shutting out the wind had not been paid when it was constructed as is the case in more modern buildings. The young lady saw before her a door partly open, but which seemed at that moment about to close with a slam. To prevent this, forgetting her former caution, she darted forward, when the same blast which, as she supposed, was moving the door, blew out her candle. She knew her way, and remembered that a few paces farther on there were two steps, down which she might fall if not careful. A creeping feeling of horror, however, stole over her when, as she attempted to advance, she felt herself held back. It must be fancy. She made another effort, and again was unable to move forward. Her heart did, indeed, now beat quickly. She would have screamed for help, but she was not given to screaming, and her voice failed her. Once more she tried to run on, but she felt herself in the grasp of some supernatural power, as a person feels in a dream when unable to proceed. Her courage at length gave way, every moment she expected to hear a peal of mocking laughter from the fiend who held her, for her imagination was now worked up to a pitch which would have made anything, however dreadful, appear possible. At length, by an effort, she cried out:

"Help me! help! Pray come here!"

The words had scarcely left her lips when a door in the passage opened, and she saw a person hurrying with a light towards her.

"Thanks, thanks, Henry!" she exclaimed, giving way to an hysterical laugh, as she sank into the arms of Captain Fothering-sail, feeling now perfectly secure against all enemies, either of a supernatural or natural character.

"What is the matter, dearest?" he asked, in a voice of alarm.

"Oh, nothing, nothing. My candle went out, and I felt myself unable to move on," she answered.

"I see you could not, for the skirt of your dress and your shawl have both caught in the door," he exclaimed, with a merry laugh, which did more than a dose of sal volatile or camphor would have done to dispel her fears, and, taking his arm, she accompanied him to the ball-room.

Should she tell him of the reappearance of old Hooker, or some living representative? Why not? She hoped always to have the privilege of enjoying his perfect confidence, and giving hers in return, so she told him what she had seen, or fancied that she had seen, assuring him at the same time that she did not believe her visitor had intended to come to her room. Again he gave way to a peal of merry laughter, and exclaimed:

"I am delighted to hear it, for now he will be caught to a cer-tainty. I have not the slightest doubt that he intends again to visit either the ball-room or the servants'-hall, but whenever he comes we will be ready for him. I have an idea that your wild young cousin and his friend have no little to do with the trick, for I have ascertained that they arrived at the Hall some hours before they made their appearance in the ball-room in the character of sail-ors. When I saw their proceedings I rather regretted the character I had assumed, lest I should have been taken for one of the party."

The guests were assembling in the ball-room as the captain and Jane reached it. People looked at them and smiled significantly, and some of them said, "I thought it would be so." One or two remarked, "Well, it is curious how the dark girls cut out the fair ones. Who would have thought that that little Miss Otterburn would have been preferred to her cousins the Ildertons? Lady Ilderton won't thank her, I think." However, Lady Ilderton was as much pleased when she heard that Captain Fotheringsail, whom she liked very much, had proposed to her niece, as if he had made an offer to one of her daughters; and so people, for once in a way, were wrong.

Captain Fotheringsail and Jane at once separated from each other, and went round to each of the guests separately, whispering in their ears. They instantly formed themselves into a quadrille, and the musicians struck up. On this the captain slipped from the side of his partner, and adroitly ran a dark thin line across the room, almost the height of a man's knee from the floor.

The quadrille was concluded and nothing happened. A valse was gone through, and then another quadrille was played. It seemed, however, that if the captain had hopes of catching the ghost, the ghost was not to be caught. He begged Cousin Giles to ascertain whether old Hooker had appeared in the servants'-hall, or anywhere about the house. Cousin Giles had assured him that he knew nothing at all about the matter, and was on the point of going to perform his commission, when, from the exact spot where the ghost had appeared on the previous day, forth he stalked, looking quite as dreadful as before. The guests ran from side to side to let him pass, when just as he reached the middle of the room he stumbled, made an attempt to jump, and then down he came full length on the floor. Off came a head and a pair of shoulders, and then was seen the astonished and somewhat frightened countenance of the simple Simon Langdon, who exclaimed, "Oh, Charley, Charley, I didn't think you were going to play me that trick." Finding that the trick was discovered, Charley dashed out from behind a screen with a tin tube and lamp in his hand, and blew a superb blue flame over Simon, who was quickly divested of his hunting-dress amid the laughter of the guests. Charley and his friend confessed that they had induced Simon to act the ghost that evening, though who had played it the previous one they did not say.

"Well, young gentlemen, you have had your fun, and no harm has been done, though the consequences might have been more serious than you anticipated," said Sir Gilbert. "It requires no large amount of wit to impose on the credulous, as the spirit-rappers and mediums have shown us, and as we may learn by the exhibition of my young friend here and his coadjutors." And the baronet looked very hard at Simon and Charley. He then added, in his usual good-natured tone, "However, as I said, no mischief has been done, though I must have it clearly understood that I cannot again allow old Hooker's ghost to make his appearance at Huntingfield Hall."

*Note*.—The author has to state, that there is more truth in this story than may generally be supposed. A ghost, or spirit of some sort, was believed by a whole neighbourhood to have paid occasional visits to members of his own family, and it was not till after the lapse of many years that one of them by chance heard of the story, which had not even the shadow of a foundation.

# Ada Buisson

## THE GHOST'S SUMMONS

*It was common for the ghostly tales in periodicals to be narrated by domestic servants. In Gaskell's "The Old Nurse's Story," for example, the nurse has intimate access to the family but remains outside of their confidence. In this dramatic tale, a rich man employs a doctor to serve in a similar role; the doctor witnesses a confusing, uncanny scene, but he remains ignorant of the full story. The scant details of the scene merely suggest the story behind an unusual deathbed, one that seems to have been brought about by an act both premeditated and unavenged. This story originally appeared in* Belgravia *in January 1868.*

"WANTED, SIR—A PATIENT."

It was in the early days of my professional career, when patients were scarce and fees scarcer; and though I was in the act of sitting down to my chop, and had promised myself a glass of steaming punch afterwards, in honour of the Christmas season, I hurried instantly into my surgery.

I entered briskly; but no sooner did I catch sight of the figure standing leaning against the counter than I started back with a strange feeling of horror which for the life of me I could not comprehend.

Never shall I forget the ghastliness of that face—the white horror stamped upon every feature—the agony which seemed to sink the very eyes beneath the contracted brows; it was awful to me to behold, accustomed as I was to scenes of terror.

"You seek advice," I began, with some hesitation.

"No; I am not ill."

"You require then—"

"Hush!" he interrupted, approaching more nearly, and dropping his already low murmur to a mere whisper. "I believe you are not rich. Would you be willing to earn a thousand pounds?"

A thousand pounds! His words seemed to burn my very ears.

"I should be thankful, if I could do so honestly," I replied with dignity. "What is the service required of me?"

A peculiar look of intense horror passed over the white face before me; but the blue-black lips answered firmly, "To attend a death-bed."

"A thousand pounds to attend a death-bed! Where am I to go, then?—whose is it?"

"*Mine.*"

The voice in which this was said sounded so hollow and distant, that involuntarily I shrank back. "Yours! What nonsense! You are not a dying man. You are pale, but you appear perfectly healthy. You—"

"Hush!" he interrupted; "I know all this. You cannot be more convinced of my physical health than I am myself; yet I know that before the clock tolls the first hour after midnight I shall be a dead man."

"But—"

He shuddered slightly; but stretching out his hand commandingly, motioned me to be silent. "I am but too well informed of what I affirm," he said quietly; "I have received a mysterious summons from the dead. No mortal aid can avail me. I am as doomed as the wretch on whom the judge has passed sentence. I do not come either to seek your advice or to argue the matter with you, but simply to buy your services. I offer you a thousand pounds to pass the night in my chamber, and witness the scene which takes place. The sum may appear to you extravagant. But I have no further need to count the cost of any gratification; and the spectacle you will have to witness is no common sight of horror."

The words, strange as they were, were spoken calmly enough; but as the last sentence dropped slowly from the livid lips, an expression of such wild horror again passed over the stranger's face, that, in spite of the immense fee, I hesitated to answer.

"You fear to trust to the promise of a dead man! See here, and be convinced," he exclaimed eagerly; and the next instant, on the counter between us lay a parchment document; and following the indication of that white muscular hand, I read the words, "And to Mr. Frederick Read, of 14 High-street, Alton, I bequeath the sum of one thousand pounds for certain service rendered to me."

"I have had that will drawn up within the last twenty-four hours, and I signed it an hour ago, in the presence of competent witnesses. I am prepared, you see. Now, do you accept my offer, or not?"

My answer was to walk across the room and take down my hat, and then lock the door of the surgery communicating with the house.

It was a dark, icy-cold night, and somehow the courage and determination which the sight of my own name in connection with a thousand pounds had given me, flagged considerably as I found myself hurried along through the silent darkness by a man whose death-bed I was about to attend.

He was grimly silent; but as his hand touched mine, in spite of the frost, it felt like a burning coal.

On we went—tramp, tramp, through the snow—on, on, till even I grew weary, and at length on my appalled ear struck the chimes of a church-clock; whilst close at hand I distinguished the snowy hillocks of a churchyard.

Heavens! was this awful scene of which I was to be the witness to take place veritably amongst the dead?

"Eleven," groaned the doomed man. "Gracious God! but two hours more, and that ghostly messenger will bring the summons. Come, come; for mercy's sake, let us hasten."

There was but a short road separating us now from a wall which surrounded a large mansion, and along this we hastened until we reached a small door.

Passing through this, in a few minutes we were stealthily ascending the private staircase to a splendidly-furnished apartment, which left no doubt of the wealth of its owner.

All was intensely silent, however, through the house; and about this room in particular there was a stillness that, as I gazed around, struck me as almost ghastly.

My companion glanced at the clock on the mantelshelf, and sank into a large chair by the side of the fire with a shudder. "Only an hour and a half longer," he muttered. "Great heaven! I thought

I had more fortitude. This horror unmans me." Then, in a fiercer tone, and clutching my arm, he added, "Ha! you mock me, you think me mad; but wait till you see—wait till you see!"

I put my hand on his wrist; for there was now a fever in his sunken eyes which checked the superstitious chill which had been gathering over me, and made me hope that, after all, my first suspicion was correct, and that my patient was but the victim of some fearful hallucination.

"Mock you!" I answered soothingly. "Far from it; I sympathise intensely with you, and would do much to aid you. You require sleep. Lie down, and leave me to watch."

He groaned, but rose, and began throwing off his clothes; and watching my opportunity, I slipped a sleeping-powder, which I had managed to put in my pocket before leaving the surgery, into the tumbler of claret that stood beside him.

The more I saw, the more I felt convinced that it was the nervous system of my patient which required my attention; and it was with sincere satisfaction I saw him drink the wine, and then stretch himself on the luxurious bed.

"Ha," thought I, as the clock struck twelve, and instead of a groan, the deep breathing of the sleeper sounded through the room; "you won't receive any summons to-night, and I may make myself comfortable."

Noiselessly, therefore, I replenished the fire, poured myself out a large glass of wine, and drawing the curtain so that the fire-light should not disturb the sleeper, I put myself in a position to follow his example.

How long I slept I know not, but suddenly I aroused with a start and as ghostly a thrill of horror as ever I remember to have felt in my life.

*Something*—what, I knew not—seemed near, something nameless, but unutterably awful.

I gazed round.

The fire emitted a faint blue glow, just sufficient to enable me to see that the room was exactly the same as when I fell asleep, but that the long hand of the clock wanted but five minutes of the mysterious hour which was to be the death-moment of the "summoned" man!

Was there anything in it, then?—any truth in the strange story he had told?

The silence was intense.

I could not even hear a breath from the bed; and I was about to rise and approach, when again that awful horror seized me, and at the same moment my eye fell upon the mirror opposite the door, and I saw—

Great heaven! that awful Shape—that ghastly mockery of what had been humanity—was it really a messenger from the buried, quiet dead?

It stood there in visible death-clothes; but the awful face was ghastly with corruption, and the sunken eyes gleamed forth a green glassy glare which seemed a veritable blast from the infernal fires below.

To move or utter a sound in that hideous presence was impossible; and like a statue I sat and saw that horrid Shape move slowly towards the bed.

What was the awful scene enacted there, I know not. I heard nothing, except a low stifled agonised groan; and I saw the shadow of that ghastly messenger bending over the bed.

Whether it was some dreadful but wordless sentence its breathless lips conveyed as it stood there, I know not; but for an instant the shadow of a claw-like hand, from which the third finger was missing, appeared extended over the doomed man's head; and then, as the clock struck one clear silvery stroke, it fell, and a wild shriek rang through the room—a death-shriek.

I am not given to fainting, but I certainly confess that the next ten minutes of my existence was a cold blank; and even when I did manage to stagger to my feet, I gazed round, vainly endeavouring to understand the chilly horror which still possessed me.

Thank God! the room was rid of that awful presence—I saw that; so, gulping down some wine, I lighted a wax-taper and staggered towards the bed. Ah, how I prayed that, after all, I might have been dreaming, and that my own excited imagination had but conjured up some hideous memory of the dissecting-room!

But one glance was sufficient to answer that.

No! The summons had indeed been given and answered.

I flashed the light over the dead face, swollen, convulsed still with the death-agony; but suddenly I shrank back.

Even as I gazed, the expression of the face seemed to change: the blackness faded into a deathly whiteness; the convulsed features relaxed, and, even as if the victim of that dread apparition still lived, a sad solemn smile stole over the pale lips.

I was intensely horrified, but still I retained sufficient self-consciousness to be struck professionally by such a phenomenon.

Surely there was something more than supernatural agency in all this?

Again I scrutinised the dead face, and even the throat and chest; but, with the exception of a tiny pimple on one temple beneath a cluster of hair, not a mark appeared. To look at the corpse, one would have believed that this man had indeed died by the visitation of God, peacefully, whilst sleeping.

How long I stood there I know not, but time enough to gather my scattered senses and to reflect that, all things considered, my own position would be very unpleasant if I was found thus unexpectedly in the room of the mysteriously dead man.

So, as noiselessly as I could, I made my way out of the house. No one met me on the private staircase; the little door opening into the road was easily unfastened; and thankful indeed was I to feel again the fresh wintry air as I hurried along that road by the churchyard.

There was a magnificent funeral soon in that church; and it was said that the young widow of the buried man was inconsolable; and then rumours got abroad of a horrible apparition which had been seen on the night of the death; and it was whispered the young widow was terrified, and insisted upon leaving her splendid mansion.

I was too mystified with the whole affair to risk my reputation by saying what I knew, and I should have allowed my share in it to remain for ever buried in oblivion, had I not suddenly heard that the widow, objecting to many of the legacies in the last will of her husband, intended to dispute it on the score of insanity, and then there gradually arose the rumour of his belief in having received a mysterious summons.

On this I went to the lawyer, and sent a message to the lady, that, as the *last person* who had attended her husband, I undertook to prove his sanity; and I besought her to grant me an interview, in which I would relate as strange and horrible a story as ear had ever heard.

The same evening I received an invitation to go to the mansion.

I was ushered immediately into a splendid room, and there, standing before the fire, was the most dazzlingly beautiful young creature I had ever seen.

She was very small, but exquisitely made; had it not been for the dignity of her carriage, I should have believed her a mere child.

With a stately bow she advanced, but did not speak.

"I come on a strange and painful errand," I began, and then I started, for I happened to glance full into her eyes, and from them down to the small right hand grasping the chair. The *wedding-ring* was on that hand!

"I conclude you are the Mr. Read who requested permission to tell me some absurd ghost-story, and whom my late husband mentions here." And as she spoke she stretched out her left hand towards something—but what I knew not, for my eyes were fixed on that hand.

Horror! White and delicate it might be, but it was shaped like a claw, and the third finger was missing!

One sentence was enough after that. "Madam, all I can tell you is, that the ghost who summoned your husband was marked by a singular deformity. The third finger of the left hand was missing," I said sternly; and the next instant I had left that beautiful sinful presence.

That will was never disputed. The next morning, too, I received a check for a thousand pounds; and the next news I heard of the widow was, that she had herself seen that awful apparition, and had left the mansion immediately.

# JACK LAYFORD'S FRIEND

WITH AN ACCOUNT OF HOW HE LAID THE GHOST

A Christmas Story

*When Mary Elizabeth Braddon named her monthly magazine Bel-*
*gravia, she had every intention of harnessing the elegance associated*
*with that London neighborhood. This story by an anonymous author*
*certainly emphasizes class boundaries as it demonizes the governess*
*in a number of ways. The description of her appearance includes a*
*racial slur; the offensive term appears four times in that 1869 volume*
*of* Belgravia, *attesting to its perceived acceptance among middle-*
*class Victorian readers.*

## CHAPTER I

"I'M AFRAID YOU'LL HAVE BUT A DULL TIME OF IT, old fellow; it isn't too late to write, and say we find we can't manage it, even now; not but that the poor old guv would be awfully cut up, and the girls too, for that matter."

"I wouldn't disappoint them for the world," broke in the individual addressed; "so that's settled. As for being slow, or anything of that sort, it's never slow with plenty of girls in the house."

"O, there's plenty of 'em, if that's all," rejoined the first speaker; and his tone, to one who did not know him as his friend did, might perhaps have sounded just a trifle unappreciative of the blessing; "but when it's a fellow's sisters, you know—"

"Yes, but then you see, my dear Jack, in my case it's another fellow's sisters. So, come, pack up your traps; and then hurrah for the governor and the girls!"

Jack, thus adjured, said no more. The hint that even now, at the eleventh hour, there was yet time to reconsider their plans, had been thrown out, truth to tell, and his friend knew, in no anxiety of Jack's for himself. Indeed it is to be more than doubted if the disappointment of either the "governor" or the girls would have greatly exceeded Jack's own, had his suggestion of giving up the projected home-visit been differently received. So that was settled. An hour or so later, and the December fog was stealing down on the dingy London streets and over its murky river; but Jack Layford and his friend were leaving it all—river, streets, and fog—fast behind them, as, tearing, puffing, snorting, they sped on their iron road eastward.

"Only a couple of years," Jack is saying from his snug corner of the first-class G. E. railway carriage that they have contrived to secure all to themselves,—"only a couple of years! I can scarcely believe it; and to think that we might never have known each other at all, Phil, if it hadn't been for that jolly old umbrella of mine!"

And Jack spoke truth; but for the said umbrella the two friends might never have been even acquaintances. East and west, just so far apart, had their courses lain. East, Jack Layford; west, Philip Carlyon. So far west indeed the latter, that he could not well have made it farther; unless, that is, he had quitted *terra firma* altogether and taken to the sea. East and west through school-days and college-days. Then had come the world (which was London) and Jack Layford's umbrella (on Phil Carlyon's toes); and east and west had met at last, to be east and west no longer.

Jack loved to go over the story of that first meeting; how, seated side by side in the pit of the Haymarket one raw November evening, strangers both in the great city, they had stolen shy glances at one another, it might be, but nothing more; until the row at the end, "when I brought that umbrella of mine down on your 'patents,' Phil, and you swore; and then there was supper together at Evans's; and that's how it all came about, eh, old fellow?"

But, as Jack says, two years ago all this. Friends now; Damon and Pythias, with various other small and harmless jokes at the two's expense; but Damon and Pythias knowing very little of one another's personal history and belongings, as is not unfrequently the case when the surnames of those gentlemen happen to be *Bull*. Layford, for instance, knew in a kind of general way that his friend Carlyon was an only child, with an adoring mother down at some outlandish-sounding place in Cornwall, to which he vanished now and then for a week or so, as the fit took him; knew also that he had an income of some sort, and concluded it to be a good one; rides in the Row, balls, fêtes, &c. in the season, with the moors or Norway for the vacation months, being a state of things scarcely attainable by the present means of so many dinners a week during term-time, with a remote contingency of *briefs* in the future. Again, with Carlyon, he, for his part, had a kind of vague knowledge of his friend Jack being one of a large family, the rest of which were girls; knew, furthermore, that there was no mother, and that "the guv," as Jack was irreverently given to term him, was the best of old fellows, and farmed some hundreds of acres down in Suffolk, as other Layfords had done before him time out of mind; and lastly, though not least, that he made the said Jack a very fair allowance, though he had been ever so little disappointed when that young gentleman had suddenly announced his intention of renouncing the church for something more substantial in the shape of common law.

"Here we are, old fellow, home at last!"

And how home-like the old house gleamed through the winter's night! a little foggy, even down here. Home-like even to Philip Carlyon's eyes, to whom it brought no memories, no associations; home-like indeed to honest Jack's, to whom it brought both things.

Jack scarcely waited for the dog-cart to stop; down went the reins, and Philip saw his big friend standing in a flood of light, the centre of a grand complication of female arms and heads, in the old-fashioned hall, before he himself had time to make his more leisurely descent. The young Cornishman stood for a moment irresolute, and with a feeling of something very like shyness, in the open doorway. But it was only for a moment. The old Squire had spied him out.

"Come in, sir; come in!" cried Jack's governor, dragging his visitor by the hand, and shaking it warmly at the same time. "Why, Jack, sir, what are you thinking about, eh?"

"I can't help it, sir," cried poor Jack deprecatingly, and making an effort at freedom; "it's the girls."

But the girls had caught sight of the stranger by this time, and falling back, a laughing, blushing group, gave Jack his liberty.

"I see I needn't introduce you to the governor, Carlyon," said Jack with a nod, as he endeavoured to restore to something like order his ruffled plumes; "and these are the girls." Having said which, Jack appeared to consider that he had fulfilled the whole duty of man under the circumstances, and proceeded forthwith to suggest hot water in the bedrooms, and something to eat in the dining-room as soon as practicable.

If Philip Carlyon had found the old house home-like in that view of it from the outside, he found the great dining-room with its panelled walls, blazing fire, and soft lamp-light, with tea awaiting them, more home-like still. Perhaps it was not just these things alone that served to give the home-like look. There was a something there that Philip Carlyon's home, happy as it might have been, had never known. There was the old Squire, firm and stalwart still, with his cheery voice and bright keen eyes, and hair too that was crisp as ever, if the dark brown was here and there streaked with gray. And there were the girls. Philip began counting them to himself, and wondering which was which, for Jack had in a measure accustomed him to their names. There was one Phil knew must be Miss Layford. She it was who made the tea, attended to the Squire, and was moreover evidently an authority with the rest. Jack sat next her; and Phil thought that if the choice had been given him, he might perhaps have chosen that seat too. She was not much like Jack, this eldest sister, excepting that she was rather tall, taller by some inches than any of the other girls— though more than half of them, it is true, had not yet done growing, even among the bigger ones. Then if she was not exactly what could be called dark—nothing like so dark as Philip himself, for instance—she had certainly nothing of Jack's fairness.

Philip came to the decision, by the time that tea was over, that Miss Layford's hair must be chestnut, and her eyes—well, chestnut too. Great soft brown eyes, with a dash of red gold in them—he had a favourite dog at home with just such eyes. But Miss Layford's guest—desirable in his eyes as that occupation might have seemed—could not sit staring at her all tea-time.

There was a lady seated opposite him, at whom—had his

taste in the matter been consulted—Philip Carlyon would perhaps rather not have looked at all; and yet he did look more than
once, and was savage with himself in consequence. Not one of
the family, as he easily discovered, for she was addressed as Miss
Dormer. She appeared to have the charge of the half-dozen or
so of girls seated near; among them two little ones, twins evidently—with round curly heads, fair, like Jack's, and very round
eyes, blue, also like Jack's—who stared shyly at the strange guest,
reminding him forcibly of two little robins on the look-out for
crumbs. "She's the governess," said Phil to himself; "but then
why is she here in the holidays?"

After a time he found himself asking why she was there at all,
and finally came to the decision that he would not sit opposite her
again if he could help it. Her eyes offended him. "Confound her,
why can't she keep 'em to herself!" he growled; "they're like gim-
lets, by Jove!" Even the unfortunate young woman's hair must
needs irritate him; and yet it was such hair as all the "Macassar"
of Rowland[1] and his tribe could scarcely have induced on half-
a-dozen heads in the United Kingdom,—luxuriant, black—raven
black. "She's a nigger, I believe," was Phil's final conclusion; "only
she's managed to get some of the dye out of her hands and face."
But the round of observation was not yet complete—"the girls"
were by no means exhausted. There was one, for instance, seated
next Philip, Flop by name—self-achieved, as he shortly discovered—with whom—after she had all but deposited a cup of tea
in his lap, and had dropped her spoon, knife, and various other
trifles below the table, which he had been under the necessity of
diving for and recovering—he found himself on terms of almost
brotherly intimacy. Then there was Emmy, and Lotty, and Bessie;
though which was which, together with a few other little details
connected with them, was a subject upon which our friend
Philip's ideas were at present a trifle misty.

In the drawing-room, after tea, Phil found these little matters
gradually resolving themselves, as was natural. And now, if Jack
Layford's friend had been disposed to envy him his position at the
tea-table, how much more so when, Miss Layford having seated

1  A hair oil much advertised in the Victorian period.

herself at the piano, that lucky young giant was at her side once more, turning over the leaves and calling her Margaret, while she, smiling and obedient, gave him song after song as it was called for! And all this while Phil was being literally held by the button by the somewhat prosy old Squire. After a time Miss Dormer went to the piano, but Jack did not turn over the leaves for her; and Philip, free by this time—feeling horribly rude all the while—would not make the offer; so it fell to the lot of the good-natured Flop—after, it is to be premised, she had by way of inauguration brought down the walnut-wood "what-not" and its load with a horrible crash to the ground. Nor had Philip Miss Layford even for an excuse, she having been called from the room just at the moment at which she rose from the piano; and although Phil kept a sharp look-out on the door, she did not return until the innocent Squire had once more captured his unwary guest. On the whole, perhaps the evening might, so far as our friend was concerned, have been more successful; but Phil consoled himself with the determination before he went to sleep that night to manage affairs better in future.

In accordance with which resolution, when Jack Layford descended to the breakfast-table the next morning, resplendent in pink and cords, he found another figure—not quite such a massive or brilliant one it may be, but quite as faultlessly turned out—in the field before him. There, seated at Margaret's side, assisting her with the coffee-pot, buttering her toast, laughing, talking the while, doing everything in short just as if he had been the veritable Jack himself, sat Mr. Philip Carlyon. Was it Philip's fancy, or did Jack's bright face really cloud over at the sight? But for the utter absurdity of the thing, Philip could almost have said that it was so. Jack was certainly restless that morning. He wandered from the table to the sideboard, fluttered from cold meat to hot, and ended by eating neither. His principal occupation seemed to be watching the two at the head of the table; while Miss Dormer's attention appeared to be divided among the three.

"Come, Carlyon," cried Jack at last, "I think before the day is over you will wish you had eaten your breakfast instead of talking."

But Carlyon only laughed.

"Mr. Carlyon does not agree with you." The voice was Miss Dormer's.

Mr. Carlyon was looking red now, Jack black, and Miss Layford—well, rather red also. At this moment the Squire came innocently to the general rescue.

"Well, if you won't really take any more, Mr. Carlyon, I think we may as well be getting off."

"I am ready, sir," said Phil, rising.

Jack had already disappeared; and in a few minutes the girls had the old house to themselves.

There was a late dinner that day; and the evening was passed much the same as the previous one had been, with this exception, that Philip, strong in his resolution of the past night, did somehow contrive to manage affairs more to his own satisfaction. In the first place, he secured the much-desired post at Miss Layford's piano, turned over the leaves and chose the songs, just as that lucky Jack had done the night before. He even condescended so far as to smile on his pet aversion, the governess, when her turn came; and, sitting by Margaret's side in some far-off corner, made no sign of impatience throughout the entire performance. And Jack? From the chess-table, over which he sat with the "guv," he cast so many restless glances at the far-off corner, made so many extraordinary moves, and was finally so evidently lost as to his own position in the game, or his adversary's either, that the Squire at last good-naturedly sent him off to join his friend. But of this permission Jack did not avail himself. He made his way to the piano instead, dethroned Flop, again on duty, not in the gentlest manner, and was Miss Dormer's humble slave for the rest of the evening.

The little black-eyed governess flushed a little as Jack came up.

"You find it dull," she said softly; "and you want poor little nobody to take pity on you; so even I am of use sometimes, Mr. Layford?"

She was not looking at him; the dark eyes, with a strange light in them, were on the stray couple, whispering and smiling together in the distant corner. Jack's eyes followed hers, as it was just possible she had intended they should do. It was only for a moment; then he turned them once more on her, and Miss

Dormer knew that there was an angry flash in them, but not for her.

"Pray don't talk like that, Miss Dormer," stammered poor foolish Jack, "about being nobody, and—and that sort of thing. I'm sure you're as good a friend as a fellow ever had; and while a fellow has a friend like you, by Jove!" cried Jack, almost aloud in his defiance, "I don't see what he need care for any other."

"O hush, pray hush!" cried Miss Dormer softly, with a little sigh. But Jack would not hush.

What more he said need not be set down here; poor foolish fly, he knew the web was there, and the spider too, for that matter. He had known it before to-night; and yet he had only to be asked in a few soft words—combined with certain influences from without, of which Madame Spider knew the full worth—and he was ready to walk in. Poor foolish fly indeed! Mr. Jack Layford, then, having made about as great a fool of himself as a young man could well be expected to do in the time, Miss Dormer wisely determined to let well alone; but if she did not vouchsafe her cavalier any amount of conversation, she took care to keep him by her side. As for her silence, perhaps Miss Dormer was of opinion that the little tableau afforded by the handsome couple in the far-off corner was calculated to assist her plans, whatever they might be, more than any mere words of hers could do. And perhaps Miss Dormer was right.

"The glass is falling," said the old Squire, as he bade his guest good-night. "We shall have snow before morning."

Mr. Carlyon gave a little shiver.

"Does the idea of being snowed-up in a dull country-house quite give you the horrors, Mr. Carlyon?" asked Miss Layford laughingly, as she gave him her hand.

Philip laughed too.

"On the contrary, Miss Layford, I should only be too happy could it snow for ever."

The Squire had moved off, but Jack stood near.

"Come and have a pipe, Carlyon. You would stand paying compliments until to-morrow morning."

"Well, you needn't stay to hear them, my dear fellow.—Now, need he, Miss Layford?"

"O, come along!" growled Jack.

"What a bear you are, Jack!—Now, isn't he, Miss Layford?"

"O, dreadful!" and Miss Layford gave the "bear" her hand; but Jack would scarcely take the little hand that lay in his.

"Good-night," he said; and then he marched out of the room. Philip followed him. In the hall, Jack turned:

"I don't think I shall smoke to-night; you know the way if you care to; there's tobacco and things about."

"No, thank you," said Carlyon; "if you're not that way inclined, I'm off to bed; though I don't see why you need have been in such a deuce of a hurry, if you didn't mean to smoke after all."

"O, there's such lots to do to-morrow; the place to get done —holly, and all that sort of thing; then there's people coming in the evening; Christmas-eve, you know; and the girls are best in bed."

"I'm sure I didn't want to keep the girls up," said Philip, with a little twinkle in his dark eyes.

Jack gave a grunt; and Phil, unable to contain himself any longer, burst out laughing. Jack joined in.

"I'm in a beast of a temper, I know," said poor Jack; "but I can't help it."

"Well, I won't contradict you," replied his friend; "and, as I fancy, the best place for you will be bed—like the girls, you know. Good-night."

Jack was soon beyond the reach of his troubles; but his friend Carlyon did not find sleep come so easily. Jack puzzled him; many things puzzled him; but, there, it was no use bothering himself, he was no nearer any solution of the mystery. Phil decided that the only thing left for him to do was to look to time and chance—or even, should such a course seem advisable, to Jack himself—for an explanation.

The morning brought a fulfilment of the Squire's prophecy. Philip Carlyon looked from his bedroom window on to a world of white—such a world as the young Cornishman had not often seen. "What," Phil asked himself, as he went through the rather difficult operation of shaving, "what if they really were to be snowed-up? And what was the longest possible time such a state of things could be expected to last—a week, for instance—a month?" Then Phil laughed at his own folly. "Never mind; I must make the best of what time I have," said he. And in a few minutes he was making the best of it accordingly, over the dining-room fire, with Miss Layford and a small detachment of the girls, cold, but merry as usual. In a minute or two Miss Dormer and her charges came in, after her the Squire; and then they sat down to breakfast. "Jack was always late," Miss Layford said; and so was Flop. Not that Flop loved her bed particularly, but she always contrived to meet with so many checks and misfortunes in the course of her toilette, that it was like struggling against fate to get through it at all. Jack appeared in tolerably good time, for him, looking, as Phil was glad to think, decidedly improved in temper by the night's rest. There was to be no getting out of the house that day for any one—at least, no one seemed disposed to try it. But there was plenty to be done in it, as Jack had said. There was work for all, even for the two round-headed, round-eyed little girls, who looked, Phil thought, more like two little robins than ever, as they went hopping about here and there, laden with bits of shining evergreen, as if bent on that fabled errand of mercy so dear to nursery days.

So the snow lay white and untrodden outside the old country-house, and within there was laughter and life and bustle. The little black-eyed governess was as busy as any one. Those sharp orbs of hers seemed never at fault; and did the general committee of management find themselves at a stand-still, as was sometimes the case, there was always Miss Dormer to the rescue. But Philip Carlyon's experiences of Miss Dormer's skill and usefulness were of a far more personal kind. More than once in the little occurrences of the day he recognised the little governess's hand. Did Miss Layford, for instance, engaged upon the decoration of the large oil-paintings in the dining-room, require an extra nail, there was Miss Dormer at Philip's elbow, with a whole boxful to be sent to her assistance. Was there a decoration requiring the skill or power of more than one pair of hands, Mr. Carlyon and Miss Layford were decided by Miss Dormer to be the very couple to execute it the most successfully. And these were but solitary instances in the day's work. When Philip came to look back upon it, it seemed to be made up of such. And what was the mean-

ing of it all? "Not any disinterested affection for me," said Philip;
"nor for Miss Layford either, for I believe she hates both of us.
Is it Jack? and does her ladyship find us rather in the way?" Here
Phil paused, for it struck him just at this point that he might have
made a good many shots and not come nearer the mark. "Have I
hit it?" quoth Jack's friend. "Well, keep your eye on him, madame;
but I shall keep an eye on him too." It was quite dark before all
was done; but the *débris* of leaves and berries was swept away at
last. The younger girls and Miss Dormer had gone to their tea
in the schoolroom; Miss Layford drew one of the comfortable
old-fashioned chairs to the hall-fire, and seated herself with the
grateful air of one whose task is done.

"You are tired," said Philip, coming to her side.

"Well, yes, just a wee bit; aren't you?"

"I! not a bit. I am only sorry it's over."

"You had better go over and help them at the church; I'll
engage to say they won't have done there for the next two hours;"
and Jack smiled grimly at his own pleasantry.

"Thank you, my dear Jack; but I think, unless Miss Layford
particularly wishes to get rid of me, I'll stay where I am."

"I can tell you what Miss Layford does particularly wish,"
interposed Margaret, "and that is for some tea. If you will ring
that bell at your elbow, Mr. Carlyon, we'll have it here. There will
be plenty of time to dress afterwards; the people won't be here
before seven. Early hours, you think, Mr. Carlyon; but we keep
old Christmas in an old-fashioned way."

"I am delighted to hear it," Mr. Carlyon answered. Perhaps he
was bethinking himself of a certain green-leaved, glistening, ber-
ried bough he himself had hung not so very far from where Miss
Layford was sitting now. Who knows?

At this moment a little figure appeared in the circle. It was the
most round-headed and round-eyed of the little robins. "I want
Margaret, please," lisped the little bird shyly from Mr. Carlyon's
arms, for he had caught her up.

"You can't have Margaret," said Tiny's captor, blushing in the
dark at his own temerity. Perhaps some one else blushed too; but,
as I have said, it was in the dark, so who can tell? But Miss Tiny
evidently did not intend to allow the remark to pass.

"She isn't *your* Margaret!" she said, fired with a sudden boldness; "put me down!" And then Miss Tiny actually kicked.

"*Encore*, Tiny!" cried Jack. But Tiny was released.

"That was naughty!" said Margaret, trying to look solemn.

Tiny put up a pitiable lip that threatened tears, seeing which, cruel Margaret took her in her lap and kissed her.

"I don't like him!" Tiny confided, in perfectly distinct tones.

"Hush!" whispered Margaret.

But Tiny was not to be so easily extinguished. "Why, do you?" And Tiny started bolt upright, her tears and troubles alike forgotten before this new, and evidently objectionable, phase of the affair. Flop came to the rescue; and very much after the Flop fashion it proved.

"Tiny dear," said she, "you must not talk like that; ladies never like gentlemen, unless," added the oracle, as a brilliant afterthought, "unless they ask them to—you know."

After which words of wisdom, Flop smilingly proceeded to hand round the tea, which had just arrived, calmly wondering to herself the while what it was that seemed to be amusing every one so much.

But satisfactory as Flop's argument might be to herself, to Tiny's comprehension it by no means mended matters; and for poor Margaret, she was not safe out of the little affair yet.

Tiny's voice was again uplifted; it was very plaintive this time.

"You won't like him, not even if he does ask you, will you, Margey? Margey!" It was no use saying, Hush!

Tiny was not looking at all like a shy little robin now, much more indeed like an inquisitive pert little sparrow. But happily at this juncture Miss Dormer's voice was heard inquiring for her stray pupil.

"Tea is quite over in the schoolroom," said the governess, making her way into the circle.

"And we have not even heard to what we are indebted for the honour of Miss Tiny's visit," said Mr. Carlyon.

"I think Tiny must stop and have tea here, if you please, Miss Dormer," said Margaret; "then she can tell us what she wants."

So it was settled, and the invitation being extended to Miss Dormer, she remained also; and then, between delicious morsels of thin bread-and-butter from Margaret's own plate, Tiny proffered her request: "Please, Margaret, may we sit up to supper?"

Margaret looked grave and shook her head.

"I am afraid not, Tiny."

"Just this once;" it was Mr. Carlyon.

"Well, just this once then," Margaret yielded; "to oblige Mr. Carlyon, you know, Tiny."

Tiny rounded her great blue eyes as if she did not know anything of the kind, and then she actually condescended so far as to smile on her former enemy.

"I wish I had such a good sister," said Mr. Carlyon.

"She's as good as a sister," said Tiny, laying her soft cheek caressingly to Margaret's face.

"Is she?" Mr. Carlyon answered, with a little flush and laugh, though no one else appeared to see anything that was noticeable in the little girl's simple speech.

"You have no sister, Mr. Carlyon?" asked Margaret's soft voice a moment or two later.

"I had one; but she is dead."

"I—I am very sorry; I beg your pardon," stammered Margaret, red and troubled.

"Pray don't, Miss Layford," Philip interposed. "My poor sister has been dead many years now. I often speak of her," he went on, anxious, as Margaret felt, to reassure her. "Her life was not of the happiest; she married against my father's wishes a cousin of ours, and was never forgiven, poor soul, until too late."

Philip Carlyon ended with a little sigh, and for a moment no one seemed inclined to speak.

"And you, Mr. Carlyon," a voice asked presently, "do you too object—to this marrying of cousins, I mean?"

Perhaps Miss Dormer, for she it was, took Mr. Carlyon a little by surprise; at any rate he paused a moment or two before replying.

"I object to it, Miss Dormer, so far that I would never encourage it."

"You would interfere even to prevent it?"

"That would depend entirely upon my right to do so or not."

"But you think it wrong?" persisted the wiry voice.

"I have said that I object," answered Mr. Carlyon sharply, with a wild inclination upon him to say something more, and what he would have called 'shut the woman up.'

What, on earth, did she mean by pestering him for his opinions like that! But 'the woman' was not to be shut up.

"Ah, yes, you object," she echoed softly, happily ignorant of the precise nature of Mr. Carlyon's ruminations; "many people do, you know—most people."

"I don't think you know anything about it, Miss Dormer," broke in Jack bluntly; "it's a thing that's done every day; and I don't see what you, nor Carlyon either, for that matter, have got to do with it, that you should go prejudicing people's minds."

"I, my good fellow!" cried Phil, in a positive whirl of amazement. But Miss Dormer said nothing.

Margaret Layford rose: "I think it is time to dress," she said quietly, and broke up the circle.


## CHAPTER II

The Layfords' guests that Christmas-eve consisted merely of some half-dozen or so of near neighbours with their families, and, it may be, here and there a chance nephew, niece, or visitor. It was an annual affair, this Layford gathering, and was just what all such gatherings should be, if they are not; and Jack Layford's friend was not the man to feel, or to let others feel him, a stranger in such scenes. He was one of themselves from the very first, ready for anything and everything; the only wonder appeared to be, how they had ever done without him. The charades, for instance, had never been so successful. The way in which Mr. Carlyon made love to Margaret Layford! "O, really, you know," as one fat old lady observed, "one felt almost as if they hadn't any business to be looking!" And then there was Jack. The way in which Jack glared as the crest-fallen rival in the last scene—the word was "checkmate"—no one had ever seen him act anything like it before. After the charades, there was a game in which two of the company left the room, whilst the others fixed upon some proverb to be afterwards discovered by the banished ones. Mr.

Carlyon, when his turn came, found himself with Miss Layford for companion; and with the consciousness, moreover, that it was somehow or other Miss Dormer's handiwork again. But he was not going to trouble himself as to the how or even the wherefore of his bit of good fortune; his only anxiety just now was to make the best use of it.

Do you want to know how our friend set to work? Would you like very much to hear what took place under the holly and mistletoe in the old hall, where these two young people found themselves alone? I think I know some one who would have given his ears to know. But if the dear old holly, or mistletoe either, only whispered one-half of what goes on under their green boughs, who would have faith in them any longer? Should we not rather come to hate the sight of them for their treachery? I shall only tell you that there was a mistletoe-bough—but that you already know—and that it was very near, very near indeed, that Jack found the two standing, when he suddenly opened the drawing-room door, and in rather a surly voice bade them come in. Perhaps the culprits themselves looked a little bit conscious; but what was it to Jack if they did? What was it to any one, if you come to that! You may shake your head and look pious, Miss Propriety; but what was mistletoe made for, do you suppose? and above all, what was it hung under the lamp in the old hall for, that Christmas-eve—can you tell me that?

Love—and whatever the answer to the above questions may be, from mistletoe to love is not such a very great stretch, even for the imagination—love, I was about to observe, is apt to make us all somewhat selfish, even the best of us; and so occupied was Philip Carlyon with his own affairs this same snowy Christmas-eve, that he had little or no eyes for those of his friend. Had it not been so, he must have seen that this same friend of his was being thrown in the little black-eyed governess's way a great deal more than was at all desirable. The great burly fly was setting his feet farther and farther in the cunningly-spread web, with the little spider smiling to herself at the other end, to see what a great stupid fly it was; and there was no one to the rescue.

To Phil Carlyon this night there was a glamour over every-thing. The people—kindly commonplace people enough probably—were the nicest people he had ever met. The old ones, the best, the most genial of old souls; the girls, the nicest and prettiest of young ones; even Miss Dormer, viewed in the universal rose-tint, was almost tolerable. But somehow it never got beyond the *almost* with her. It seemed to Phil, as he went over it all that night, or rather morning, by his own fire, like a page out of a fairy-tale or a scene out of a pantomime; for, you see, he knew what had taken place under the mistletoe in the great hall, if we do not. The prince and princess had met at last, and now there was nothing to do but to live happily ever after. Bed seemed a grand mistake to Philip that night. "To sleep; perchance to dream!" Why, what dreams, the wildest, the most blissful, could come up to this grand reality of his? But he turned in at last, nevertheless, and went to sleep; and dreamt too, for that matter. He had been asleep, and dreaming, perhaps an hour, when the door of his room was suddenly opened, and Phil—who was at this moment being united to Miss Dormer, gracefully attired in the dining-room curtains, with the lamp and its bunch of mistletoe by way of head-dress—awoke with a start to see his friend Jack standing, candle in hand, by his bed-side.

Bewildered by the sudden apparition, and but half awake, Phil sat up, blinking owl-like and silent at Jack and his candle.

"By Jove!" he cried at length, "then *that* was the hall-lamp!" And then Phil, moved thereto by the recollection of his dream, fell back upon his pillow and fairly roared.

It was Jack's turn to stare now; and there is no saying how long Phil's fit might have continued, had not his eyes suddenly fallen on the white face still by his bed-side.

"What is it, Jack?" he cried, starting up, sobered and wide awake.

Jack went over to the mantelshelf and put down his candle, then he came back to the bed.

"Phil," he said, "do you believe in ghosts?"

If Jack had not been so evidently in earnest, it is more than probable that his friend would have had another relapse. As it was, he only answered, "I never have done;" as if, with Jack's face before him, he would not take upon himself to say what he might not do before the interview was over.

"Phil," said white-faced Jack, "if there are such things, I have seen one to-night."

"Bad dreams," suggested Phil, thinking of his own, perhaps.

But Jack shook his head. "I was as wide awake as you are."

Carlyon lay looking at him for a moment or two silently. "Wait a bit," said he at last; "I see there's a little fire still; poke it up, Jack, and I'll get into my dressing-gown. Give me my slippers, there's a good fellow; and now let's talk it over comfortably."

Jack had got up a tolerably cheerful fire, and the two drew their chairs before it.

"Now then, Jack, for the ghost."

"Don't laugh, old fellow. I give you my word I wouldn't go through it again for a fortune—ghost or no ghost."

"I'm not going to laugh, Jack, I promise you; so there now, fire away!"

"Well then, to begin at the beginning, I was not long getting into bed; and I should say that my getting to bed and to sleep were about one and the same thing. I must have been asleep some time, for at first I thought it was morning, and that it was Blake outside with the shaving-water."

"Thought what was?"

"Why, the ghost, or whatever it was. I woke up in a sudden kind of way—all in a moment, you know—and there it stood, just at the foot of the bed, so that the light from the window close by fell right on it, and I could see that it, whatever it was, was all white, and staring, and wrapped up in what looked like grave-clothes; that is, the head was all wrapped up. I haven't got over it yet." Jack shivered in a kind of apology.

"Never mind, old man; I daresay it was deuced unpleasant." And Phil gave a sturdy poke at the logs before them, as if even he would not be quite beyond the influences of a cheering blaze.

"At first," Jack went on, "I thought if it would only speak, it would be better than the horrible silence; but when it did speak, it was more horrible still. I may as well make a clean breast of it, and tell you that I fairly bolted under the bedclothes. When I could positively bear it no longer, I screwed up my courage and came to the surface once more; but the thing was gone."

"But not before you had heard what it had got to say?"

Jack stammered and flushed in an unaccountable manner.

"Phil," he said earnestly, laying his hand on his friend's knee, "there's not another man in this world I would have told all this to."

"I can believe it, Jack, and I shouldn't have liked it a bit more than you did; so tell me all about it, old boy, what it said, and everything."

"That's the queerest part of it," Jack began, anything but white-faced now. "You remember what you were telling us in the hall,—about your sister and your cousin, you know?"

Phil nodded, a trifle wonderingly.

"Well, that's what it was."

Phil could only stare at Jack blankly.

"You take me?" the latter asked.

"Can't say I do—unless," Phil added, "you mean me to understand that a visitant from the other world comes to talk to you about my relations, which, to say the least of it, sounds rather unlikely."

"I didn't mean that—at least, not exactly; it was a kind of—in short, a warning—there!"

"Concerning marriage and cousinship?"

Jack nodded.

Phil came bolt upright in his chair. "Supper," he said shortly.

Jack made a movement of impatience.

"My dear Jack, there's no other way out of it—there really isn't. Now, just ask yourself, for one moment, who should come, on the strength of my poor sister's story, from the other world, to trouble you with the desirability or undesirability of a match between you and any cousin in Christendom?"

"My mother." Jack's voice was very low, and Jack's face, that had been very red, was white again. His companion gave a long low whistle. "I daresay you think me mad or an idiot, Phil; but I have seen it, and that makes all the difference."

"And I'll see it too, Jack; somebody's been playing you a trick, depend upon it. They may try it again probably; and then we'll be even with 'em, or at least we'll try."

"But I sleep with my door locked."

"Humph! where did you find your key—just now, I mean?"

"Why, that was rather funny, now you mention it—on the floor."

"And the door was still locked?"

"Yes, it was locked all right. But why do you ask? Have you got some wonderful idea in that long head of yours?"

"Never you mind my head; we aren't going to talk any more about this affair to-night; and as I don't suppose you care exactly to go back to your own room, do you take my bed; I shall do very well on this chair."

But Jack would not hear of this arrangement; so Philip himself went back to his bed and his dreams, while Jack sat on by the dying fire, sleep coming once more, even to him, at last.

Before the two descended to breakfast the next morning, it was agreed between them that nothing more should be said concerning the mystery of the night. Whatever poor Jack may have done, his friend did not let the night's events or their solution interfere in any way with his appetite for breakfast, or with his enjoyment of the walk after it to the church by the side of his newly-discovered princess. For him the fairy tale was going on still, and Jack and his troubles had, for the time, no place in it.

It was not the pleasantest of wintry days. The sky promised more snow, and a cutting north wind drove the stray flakes that were already falling into the faces of the Manor party like bits of veritable ice, till poor Flop's nose threatened to leave her face altogether. But to Philip Carlyon the day was perfect, and the blasts of north wind might have been zephyrs from Paradise itself. Miss Layford, too, looked warm and smiling, but that might have been only the reflection of her companion's face—at times, it must be confessed, rather near to hers. There was the Squire, beaming and cheery, surrounded by his laughing, chatting ones. Miss Dormer, too, was bright and cheerful; so, perhaps, it was only poor Jack who really felt what an unpleasant day it was. "The sort of weather one would like to kick, by Jove!" growled Jack. But even Jack thawed into a happier frame of mind under Miss Dormer's care. Besides, returning, the wind was no longer in their faces, and it was decidedly pleasanter.

Philip Carlyon and Margaret, dropping behind, soon lost sight of the rest of the party; and when next a turn of the road brought them again to view, they saw that Jack and Miss Dormer had detached themselves from the rest, and were walking briskly on ahead. At the sight all Philip's misgivings touching the little governess and his friend came back to him. In his own happiness poor foolish Jack's had been well-nigh overlooked altogether. Philip stole an inquiring glance at the face by his side; he saw quite enough to know that he need not be afraid to speak.

"How long has this been going on?"

Margaret knew what *this* meant, and answered at once.

"I can't say—not exactly, that is—but it has never been as bad as this before. O Phil, can't you save him?" and Margaret's soft brown eyes, with the bright tear-drops in them, were lifted beseechingly to her companion's face.

What man, so adjured, would not have pledged himself to an even less-hopeful task? Of course Phil promised.

"You remember our charade last night? It shall be 'checkmate' with my lady yet; never fear."

"Poor dear Jack, only fancy his marrying that dreadful woman!"

"She must go," said Phil; "that's settled. By the way, that reminds me to ask why she is not away for her holidays, like other people?"

"She always says she has nowhere to go."

"Humph! I'm afraid we must trouble her to find somewhere."

They were in sight of the house now, and Philip Carlyon stopped.

"Wait a moment, Margaret," he said; "you know who I am going to see this morning, and what I am going to say; you don't repent?"

"Repent! O Phil!"

She said nothing more; but Mr. Philip Carlyon appeared to be more than satisfied.

## CHAPTER III

Coming out from the library some half-hour later, Philip Carlyon stumbled on, or rather was stumbled upon by, the inevitable Flop, and a shower of miscellaneous articles—books, a drawing-board, paint-pencils, and so forth—were incontinently delivered at his feet.

"Dear me!" bleated poor Flop, when the din had a little subsided, "how the things in this house *do* tumble about! And perhaps you've got corns, and that drawing-board is dreadfully sharp and heavy too; it nearly cut poor little Tiny's head open the other day; she'd got right under it when I let it fall, you know—poor silly little dear!"

"Nearly as silly as I was," said Philip, laughing. "I believe the confounded thing has all but taken my foot off."

"Has it really, though? O dear, dear, I'm so sorry! And the paint-box—it's one of those tin things—moist colours, you know—has cut my finger, I think, see!" and Flop thrust forth a bleeding digit to within an inch of Phil's nose; for poor Flop, short of sight herself, laboured under the delusion that all her fellow-mortals were similarly afflicted.

"So it is!" cried Phil. "Here, let me wrap it up, poor thing!"

They were standing in one of the hall-windows, and Philip—poor Flop's wounded hand in his—was making some laughing comment, when a shadow from outside fell upon them, and, looking up, there was Jack's fair face, with the honest blue eyes opened to their utmost, staring at them in a kind of blank amaze.

"Come in!" cried Philip. "I want to speak to you."

Jack, thus called upon, marched round to the great door, kicking off the snow from his boots as he went. Flop was gone, and Philip was standing by the hall-fire making a little pretence of warming himself as Jack entered.

"Well?" inquired Jack, the surprised stare not quite gone out of his blue eyes yet.

"The fact is, Jack, I've got something to say to you—something to tell you. Can't you guess within a little what it's about, old fellow?"

But Jack only stared still more, and shook his head.

"I think you could guess if you liked, Jack; but if you won't, why I suppose I must tell you. I have asked your sister, and—she is going to take me for better for worse—there!"

The stare of amazement on Jack's face had been as noth-

ing compared to that which it now wore. For the best part of a
minute Jack seemed, in his astonishment, utterly speechless. At
the end of that time he had managed to recover himself sufficiently to utter the one word, "Flop!" It was really not so very
surprising when you consider the little picture Jack had looked
upon a moment since from the great hall-window; and yet Phil
found something so irresistibly comic in the idea, that he burst
into one of his roars, to poor Jack's still greater mystification.

"Flop's one of the best souls going," said Phil, when he had
sufficiently recovered himself to attempt an explanation; "but it
isn't Flop; and not being Flop, my dear Jack, and Tiny not looking
upon me in quite the favourable light that I could wish—why, it's
Margaret!"

The old uneasiness, all that has so puzzled him in his friend
Jack—but laid aside in these later hours—flashed back upon
Philip Carlyon the moment Margaret's name had left his lips. A
white face fronted him, but it was only for a moment; the next it
was buried in Jack's sturdy arms upon the old carved mantleshelf
before him.

"Jack, Jack, what is it? For heaven's sake, speak, man!"

But Jack neither spoke nor moved.

"There's a mystery somewhere," cried Philip desperately;
"I've felt it all along; I saw it the first day I came; what is it, old
man? Jack, dear old Jack, what is it?"

At the touch of Phil's hand, at the sound of his troubled voice,
poor Jack lifted his face. With a great effort he looked straight at
Philip, and put out one hand towards him.

"Phil," he said, with a little attempt at a smile, "never mind me.
I shall be all right in a minute or two. I see it all now. I thought you
were trying to cut me out, old fellow, and got savage. I thought
you knew—everybody does; I daresay I never told you; I took it
for granted you knew—Margaret is my cousin. She has always
lived here, one of us, and I have been fool enough to fancy she
always might; that is all, that is the grand mystery, Phil. I have
been a fool!" and poor Jack tried a laugh that was more dreary
even than the smile had been.

"If I had only known," Philip began.

"It wouldn't have made any difference. I see it now; she could never have cared for me, Phil; don't say any more about it. I must get over it as best I can."

"Come for a walk," said Philip; "there's nothing like a good stretch; try it, old fellow!"

"Not with you, Phil; let me go by myself. I shall turn up again at dinner; and," these were Jack's parting words at the open door, "whatever you do, don't trouble yourself about—about *this*, you know, Phil; I shall be all right."

Philip Carlyon stood watching poor Jack's big figure striding over the snow; he stood looking out over the white stretch of lawn and meadow long after the lonely figure had vanished from the scene. He was going over in his own mind the events of these past few days. The grand tangle of it all—poor Jack's irritation, little Tiny's simple speech, even the ghost mystery itself,—all lay unravelled at Philip Carlyon's finger-ends. Margaret Layford not Jack's *sister*, but his *cousin;* what was there that the simple fact did not explain? There was one thing now quite clear to Philip's mind: if that small Macchiavelli, Miss Dormer, got hold of poor miserable Jack in his present frame of mind, the checkmate Phil had so glibly promised himself and Margaret would not be so easy of accomplishment. One result of his cogitations was, that Philip decided to take Miss Layford into his confidence with regard to the little affair of the previous night. A walk after luncheon was easily arranged, and then Margaret learned the whole story.

"Jack was his poor mother's favourite," she said. "Miss Dormer, I suppose, has managed to learn so much; our conversation of last evening must have suggested to her scheming little brain the idea of making the use of the knowledge she has done."

"And will do again, depend upon it," rejoined Philip. "Meanwhile not a word of our engagement, nor of our suspicions of herself; of the latter not a hint even to Jack. I shall change rooms with him to-night; and I think I may venture to say that, for the future, we shall find our friend the ghost tolerably well laid."

So it was arranged. Jack appeared at the dinner-table in decidedly higher spirits than was customary even with him. As for the little governess, it was just as Philip had predicted. The great stupid fly was hers past all doubt; and as the evening wore on, there was a flash of triumph in the dark eyes that their owner was scarcely at pains to conceal.

"Patience!" whispered Philip, as he pressed Margaret's hand at parting, and saw the anxious glances she was casting towards her cousin and Miss Dormer, who were also saying good-night at the farther end of the great drawing-room—"patience; it will be our turn soon!"

"But if she should—O Phil!"

"But she sha'n't; she shall marry me first—there!"

Whereupon Margaret laughed, and going her way, with Miss Dormer following her, left the coast clear to the two young men. Jack came up to the fireplace, where his friend Philip stood, looking rather foolish—feeling even more foolish than he looked, if the truth were told. Philip made way for him, but said nothing.

"Can you do nothing but stare at a fellow?" growled Jack at length; "if you must stare at somebody, there's the glass!"

"Thank you, my dear Jack," returned Philip blandly; "I don't doubt the sight would be charming; but just at this present moment I am wanting to look at the biggest, blindest"—and here Phil was speaking in the biggest capitals—"dearest, blundering young fool the World ever turned out; and she has done pretty well in that way."

Jack was for a moment inclined to be very wrathful, but the glamour of the day was falling from him—as also of the champagne at dinner—and he was by this time almost, if not quite, like the possessed of old, "in his right mind," which for the last few hours or so he most certainly had not been.

"Phil," he said sadly, "I know you would help me if you could, and so would Margaret; but it's too late."

"Don't tell me it's gone so far as that," cried Phil savagely.

Jack's face grew very red.

"It's gone so far, that, in honour—"

"Honour—bah!" echoed his companion contemptuously. "But there, go to bed, go to bed, and pray Heaven to help the greatest fool ever made;" which was a mistake of Phil's; for Heaven had had nothing to do with it, as he ought to have known.

"You're going to my room, you know!" he called out, as Jack moved off.

"I know!" Jack made answer dismally.

All the ghosts in the universe would have been welcome to him beside this new horror he had been at such pains to raise.

When, some quarter of an hour after, Philip Carlyon followed his friend to the room he had made over to him for the night, he found Jack still dressed, seated upon the bed-side, one of the dreariest objects he had ever had the misfortune to gaze upon.

"Come, Jack," cried he cheerily, "aren't you going to bed to-night?"

But Jack was not to be cheered.

"Bed!" groaned the wretched young fellow; "what's the good of bed, or anything else? I wish I was dead and buried."

"I daresay you'll be accommodated some day; so don't let that distress you, unless you are in a very particular hurry and can't afford to wait."

"O Phil, old man, don't chaff a fellow! I verily believe I'm the most miserable dog alive."

"It's well Miss Dormer does not hear you!" laughed the unsympathising Phil.

"Don't mention her!" cried Jack, with a genuine shiver.

"I'll tell you what it is, Jack," said Philip, seating himself by his friend's side; "if you'll go to bed like a Christian, instead of sitting groaning there like an old woman at a prayer-meeting, I'll do what I can to get you out of this hobble; and I think I see a way. But if you don't—by Jove!" cried Philip threateningly, "the little governess shall marry you to-morrow if she likes. So now, good-night."

Jack, another man in these last few seconds, started up.

"Do you really mean it, though? I'll bless you for ever and a day!"

"You turn-in, then," said Phil.

"All right!" said Jack; and Philip actually heard him whistling as he went his way to Jack's late bedroom.

Here it appeared that our friend had taken care to provide himself with the various trifling necessaries for a comfortable night—for it was not his intention either to go to bed or to sleep, as you may suppose. His first move was to lock the door; having done which, he discovered with a smile that the key was brought into such a position that another applied from without would send it out softly upon the mat beneath. So far so good. Philip then doctored the fire, exchanged his coat for the more luxuriant folds of the most inviting of dressing-gowns, and lastly, after mixing himself a glass of something steaming and fragrant enough to have tempted even a ghost itself to become for the time mortal, sat himself down in his easy-chair, and with slippered feet upon the fender, set himself to read. Twelve, one, two, from the clock on the landing outside, and still Mr. Carlyon read on. Three. Mr. Carlyon closed his book, and seemed to listen. There was some little life in the fire still, and this he left burning. The candles he carefully extinguished; and then stretched himself upon the bed. It was not too soon; there was the the soft opening of a distant door, a scarcely audible footstep creeping cautiously towards his own, a halt on the mat outside, a moment's breathing space. Then the key that was within the room fell, not noisily, but dulled by the soft carpeting, the lock was turned, the door crept slowly open, and then—enter ghost! Philip, waiting expectant as he was, felt himself giving an involuntary shiver. Prepared even to get some enjoyment out of the affair, Phil felt that he could for the moment realise just a something of what poor Jack's feelings had been. But it must be allowed that this was only for a moment. With a smile that surely meant mischief, could the poor ghost but have seen it, Philip followed with his half-closed eyes the white-draperied one's progress until the position between the window and the bed was gained. Yes, there it stood, just as Jack had described it; not tall certainly, but ghostly enough for twenty ghosts.

"Now for act the second," said Phil to himself.

Act the second commenced by the utterance of Jack Layford's name twice, thrice it may be, in the most sepulchral tones of which a rather soprano voice is capable. At the third call, the occupant of the bed showed signs of consciousness, as it was evidently necessary he should do if the play was to be properly carried out.

As Philip had calculated, the cue was taken. It was probably much the same oration as that to which the room's owner of the previous night had been treated, and Philip Carlyon heard it politely to the end.

Suddenly through the room there rang a stifled cry, almost shriek, but it certainly did not proceed from Mr. Carlyon. That gentleman—polite, smiling—stood, one hand upon the fast-closed door, the other waving a courteous adieu to poor Jack's terror, now white, appealing, frantic, all but at his feet. Her retreat thus cut off, Miss Dormer—for of course it was she—as the only thing left her to do, was down on her knees, imploring piteously for mercy at her captor's hands. Alas, poor ghost! There was not much pretence of disguise or concealment now; the time for that was past.

"I will promise anything," groaned the wretched little woman, "only let me go, dear Mr. Carlyon! I will leave the house to-morrow—to-night! I will never see John Layford again! Only let me go!"

Mr. Carlyon was not so terrible as he looked—and the firelight showed him awfully dark and stern to the miserable woman at his feet. "Get up, Miss Dormer!" he said authoritatively. "Don't kneel there! You shall go, on your own terms—that is, you leave this place at once, and never see my friend Jack again. The Squire must of course know all; but it shall go no further. And now go."

So, defeated, humbled, almost pitiable in her humiliation, the poor plotter slunk out.

"Check, I think," said Phil, with a grim smile, as he once more closed the door, not taking the trouble this time to lock it.

And now what more is there to tell? At the breakfast-table that morning there was no Miss Dormer, but there was a clamour and babel of voices quite beyond all the endeavours of Flop to still; and when the two little robins came to be informed, in answer to their wondering inquiries, that Miss Dormer would be no more seen by them on that, or indeed any other, morning, however future, the tumult was redoubled. Little Tiny, for her part, at once arriving at the melancholy conclusion of Miss Dormer's having unexpectedly deceased during the night—after the manner of a favourite canary about a month since—commenced a tributary howl to the memory of the departed, but suddenly stopped short—moved, possibly, by some flash of consolation concerning lessons that would *not* have to be said; and, changing her small mind altogether upon the subject, laughed instead, greatly to the comfort of all parties.

"That's right," cried Flop approvingly. "Of course we are all very sorry; but we aren't going to cry, are we, Jack?"

Jack, very red, mumbled something about "girls" and "nonsense;" and Philip and Margaret were fain to hide their heads behind the great silver tea-urn.

After breakfast, and when the two were standing alone by the dining-room fire, talking together in the low-voiced happy way peculiar to young people in their situation, Jack came in equipped for a journey. There was a certain sad look in the young fellow's eyes as they fell upon the two, but he went bravely up to where they stood and put out his hand. "Good-bye, Margey," he said; "and good-bye to you, too, old fellow. I'm going back to town; but you needn't follow yet. I shall be down at Easter, Meg; and I suppose," said Jack, with a little smile, and laying a kindly hand on Phil Carlyon's shoulder, "that I may bring with me the best friend I ever had."

L. N.

# HOW PETER PARLEY LAID A GHOST

## A STORY OF OWLS' ABBEY

*Peter Parley was a transatlantic, unprotected brand. The original idea for nourishing writing for children came from an American, Samuel Goodrich. His brand of common-sense, educational fare became so popular that imitators adopted his style, and his pseudonym. William Martin, a British editor, published* Peter Parley's Magazine *from 1839 to 1863. While it was in operation, the magazine put out a Christmas annual, and this tradition continued even after the magazine itself had been discontinued. This annual endeavor appeared each Christmas season from 1840 to 1892, and, with colored plates after 1845, it sold very well as a Christmas and New Year's gift.[1] The story here (first published in 1875) represents a wealth of similar ghost stories intended for Christmas reading in that it seeks to build tension while teaching a lesson about the reality of ghosts.*

I KNOW IT HAS BEEN THE HABIT of young people to speak of me and think of me as having been always an old man. Certainly, since I began to talk to my young friends, I have got considerably older than I was when I first introduced myself to them. But I have been a boy like themselves for all that, and I still appreciate and sympathise with all the delights and sorrows of boyhood and girlhood; with an exception, however; I do *not* appreciate and sympathise with delights or sorrows which have cruelty, falsehood, or indeed any vice as their cause or consequence. Some follies, also, I am fain to overlook; but folly which endangers life, or places people in peril which would not otherwise approach them, or folly which believes not in the sufferings of others I am very severe upon. Practical joking, a very common and often a very fatal folly, is my special abhorrence. As a boy, I was not cleverer nor more book-learned, nor more perfect than my contem-

1 Carol A. Bock, *"Peter Parley's Magazine"* in *The Oxford Encyclopedia of Children's Literature.* Edited by Jack Zipes. Oxford: Oxford University Press, 2006.

poraries, nor than my present reader perhaps; but I kept myself clear, either by inclination or by force of advice, from certain follies which I now undertake to reprehend. I hope I have been just, during these many years; for I have never rebuked boys for faults which I was partial to in *my* early youth.

All this is vastly dry, you'll say; and more like Peter Prosy than Peter Parley; but I never begin a story wherein I have been myself concerned without telling my young friends that I don't profess to have been the perfection of boyhood, but that I vividly remember my youth, and am, as far as kindliness to youth is concerned, and thorough sympathy with its pleasures and pains, a boy in heart still. Now, having said my prefatory say, I will go on to relate a little adventure which befell me some—well, never mind *how* many—years ago.

Near the village where I was born there used to stand the remains of an old Gothic abbey, formerly dedicated, I believe, to some saint, by name Olaus. In mediæval times this name was all very well, but as centuries crept on, so fell away the appellation, as the stones of the abbey themselves; and St. Olaus' Abbey was speedily corrupted into St. Owls', and, finally, into Owls' Abbey. Perhaps the advanced state of decay in which this old ruin was in my day had helped to favour this title, for Owls' Abbey deserved its name on account of the thousands of night-birds which infested and built in it. At the time of which I write some respectable vestiges still remained of the old pile; a broken arch, a crumbling window, and so on. And I will take this opportunity of instructing my young friends in some of the points whereby they will in future be able to distinguish Gothic from Norman ruins.

I often hear youths, otherwise well-informed, commit sad blunders in their wild guesses at the different styles of architecture, so I will briefly tell them how to avoid such exposures of ignorance for the rest of their lives. Gothic architecture is often called—and very properly—"POINTED architecture;" this one name will help as a guide; for by the term "Gothic" we understand that style wherein the *pointed arch* as applied to various purposes of construction becomes a leading characteristic of the edifice. This sort of pointed architecture dates from the rise of

Christianity itself, and was probably devised in opposition to the
Pagan form of building. Some say that an avenue of overbranch-
ing trees was the object which suggested the Gothic arch; but
though authorities are not agreed upon its origin, it is sufficient
to remember that Gothic architecture is *pointed;* while Norman
architecture has round arches.

The splendid aisles of Westminster Abbey are almost un-
equalled as specimens of pointed arches; and you will know now
that they are Gothic. Specimens of Norman arches you will find
in Waltham Abbey, and, nearer home, at at Saint Bartholomew's
Church, West Smithfield; and these are in contradistinction
*round.* There are many sub-divisions of both Gothic and Norman,
of course, but I have merely laid down the broad lines by which
you will be able to decide on the architecture of this sort of ruin
whenever you meet with it, in your rambles or at pic-nics.

Owls' Abbey, then, was an old Gothic ruin; standing at the foot
of a pleasant green hill, and embosomed in fine trees, it was a
picturesque spot, and used to attract many visitors, pedestrian
tourists, and even our own village folk; who would frequently
take an al-fresco dinner within the old grey walls, while summer
time and *daylight* lasted. While there was bright sun to light up
the dark ivy and keep the bats and owls in their hiding places,
such pic-nics were not rare. Nutting parties would often wander
amidst the ruins, and adventurous seekers of nests, and trappers
of rats and rabbits, penetrated the dim recesses of Owls' Abbey
at just periods of the year. But when winter stripped the fading
trees, and beneath the cold winter's moon the ruins looked
ghastly white, and skeleton-like in their leaflessness, there was no
villager hardy enough to venture even at sunset into the dismal
abbey; and as to passing through it by night, though the "short
cut" to many places lay thereby, that was out of the question. And
why, do you suppose? Because the simple villagers would have it
that the abbey was HAUNTED.

Superstition is almost invariably the result of the want of
education; or, in plain English, the ignorant are almost always
credulous. You will readily understand this by referring to many
wonderful appliances of this day; such as gas, steam, electricity as
applied to telegraphs, and so on; the which, if discovered only a

hundred years ago would certainly have brought their inventors to the stake as sorcerers. Yet the world, better informed in these times, regards such men as benefactors to their country and to the world.

The old belief in ghosts, goblins, sprites, and elves has helped to produce some very pretty poetry, but beyond this I cannot possibly see what gain there could be out of such folly. In these days, when science shows us *what* ghosts and apparitions really are; namely, creations of a disordered body, or disordered mind, we seldom come across a haunted house in cities. In villages, however, where education grows but slowly, you will generally find some spot supposed to be frequented by spirits, and discover amongst the less-informed folk a tendency to accept any foolish tale of hobgoblins as serious truth. I don't believe that any of my readers are so silly as to feel alarm at passing through dim and silent places by night; they have advantages now which make my belief in their good sense quite secure.

The foolish people of the village round and about Owls' Abbey were firmly persuaded that the old ruin was haunted, by not only the traditional old abbot—who had been barbarously slain at the sacking of the abbey by Oliver Cromwell—but by a more modern apparition, reported to be the wraith of an unfortunate Irish pedler, who had been waylaid, robbed, and beaten to death by some desperadoes, for the sake of his few brooches, etc. This renowned spectre was called "Barney's Ghost," and there were not a few who could declare they had seen this ghost apparently hunting amongst the underwood of the abbey for the contents of his pack. Wonders did not cease here, for even the little white stone bridge which spanned the village stream hard by the valley wherein the abbey stood, had its mysterious visitor, in the impalpable person of a White Lady, who sat on the keystone of the arch, engaged in the doleful but tidy duty of combing her long golden hair, for the better accomplishment of which occupation the lady carried her head in her lap. Altogether, Owls' Abbey and its precincts supplied ample material for making the foolish villagers afraid of their own shadows. I was about fifteen when the events which I shall now relate took place.

One fine evening in summer-time, as I was returning from a

day's fishing in the mill-stream, about a mile from the village, I
saw a lot of men talking earnestly to old Lapp, the cobbler, who
was seated outside his little cottage, working in the cool of the
day. I knew most of the men by sight, for the village was not a
very extensive place. There were Joe Barratt, the blacksmith—
his forge-fire was out for that evening; old Abel Tandy, who was
supposed to be the oldest inhabitant, and lived very well on the
strength of being too decrepit to work; Dick Millet, assistant at
the flour factory; Jim Lantern, the town-crier, and others; but
amongst them was a man whom I had never seen before, and
who was evidently a traveller only passing through the village.
He had, it seems, from the conversation which I overheard, been
enquiring into the village news and the village "lions;" amongst
which, you may be sure, Barney's ghost, and the White Lady had
been trotted out with great effect. The stranger had a smile on his
face while old Lapp was holding forth.

"Never you mind, mister! I *see* it: that's enough!"

"Ah!" said the new comer, "what was it that you say you
saw?"

"Say I saw?" retorted old Lapp. "I *did* see it. There was Barney's
ghost a-hunting about in the ferns for the lockets and chains as
was dropped thereabouts; a white misty sort of figure; not of this
world, I know, and I knew it at once for Barney's spirit!"

"Ah!" chorussed the bystanders. "You're right, old Lapp!"

"When was the said Barney murdered then?" enquired the
stranger.

"Ask Abel Tandy," said Barratt, in a solemn voice.

All eyes turned to the aged man, who, with considerable pride
at such a recollection, replied, shrilly—"Eighty year ago, come
Michaelmas!—eight-y year ago! I were a boy then, and had seen
Barney ever so many times! Ay, ay! it's all that time! Eight-y year!"

"Why, then," said the traveller, turning to old Lapp, "you can't
be more than fifty-eight or so, and couldn't have seen Barney
alive. How did you manage to recognise him?"

"Hadn't I been told that his spirit haunted the abbey, and was
to be seen groping about for his jewellery? and when I see the
figure a-doing so, wasn't I right in supposing it were Barney's
ghost?"

"Ah! sure!" repeated the chorus, delighted to see the champion of the ghost in the ascendant.

"And you mean to tell me that this abbey is haunted?"

"Surely!" shouted the chorus, in perfect time.

"And you firmly believe it?"

"Ah! sure-ly! Why not? We've all seen it!"

"And you wouldn't pass through the ruins by night?"

"Not for all the wureld!" was the unanimous shout.

"Ah! well!" sneered the stranger. "I'm sorry for you! It's my nearest cut, I'm told, and through the abbey I go, Barney and the White Lady notwithstanding! Good bye, and more sense to you!"

So saying, the traveller shouldered his way out of the gaping bystanders, and briefly asking if he was right in his direction, passed on whistling. Abel and old Lapp were speechless at their own particular ghost being so pooh-poohed by a stranger; and all the gossips shook their foolish heads, and hoped that nothing more would come of it. I went home much amused, but still thinking of the stranger's face, which seemed to haunt me. It was not a good face; but sly, cunning, and I thought cruel. When I rose next morning, I found on passing the village on my way to the little settlement which lay on the other side of Owls' Abbey, another gathering of the worthies of the night before, their faces graver than ever. They had a strange story to tell to everyone who would listen to them. The bank had been robbed! and, more than that, several of the villagers' houses, including the sagacious old Lapp's, had been entered, and whatever was of the least value stolen. There was enough here, you will say, to satisfy the most gossiping of our village; but superior to this excitement was the feeling of triumph at the signal defeat of the traveller of the night before, who it appears had returned to the village, about two hours after he left the discussion I have recorded, trembling with fear, white as a sheet, and with teeth chattering. Twaddleton (our village) was avenged; its legends had been verified, and the fool-hardy stranger had been rewarded for his sneers by being frightened almost out of his wits at the sight of the White Lady and Barney's ghost. This victory almost eclipsed the excitement of the robberies, but soon the reality of their losses wakened the silly gossips to a due sense of precaution. The stranger left the village by daylight, and no more was heard of him. Next night Dick Millet's grey mare disappeared from her paddock. Soon after, Joe Barratt's tools were missing from the forge, and positively Jim Lantern's brass bell was carried off. Twaddleton was aghast; watch was set, but, in unguarded places the thief, or thieves, showed that they laughed Twaddleton to scorn, and every night some new robbery was to be bewailed. Things had gone on thus for a week, when the magistrate determined to send for a Bow-street runner—a "detective" we should call him now—from London. On the day that the man was sent for, my father permitted me to spend an evening with an uncle of mine, who lived at the neighbouring hamlet beyond Owls' Abbey. I was delighted at the holiday, and when I prepared to return I found that evening had overtaken me, and as I promised to be at home by a certain hour, there was nothing for it but to borrow a lantern from my uncle and take the short cut through the wood, and—worse still—through Owls' Abbey. On being laughingly asked "if I were afraid?" of course I was bound to say "not a bit!" and with many "good nights," and a bulls-eye lantern, I set off for Twaddleton. I was not superstitious, and I didn't for an instant believe in the apparitions of Barney or the White Lady, but I am willing to confess to my feeling a sense of loneliness and helplessness, when I found myself in the dark wood, with nothing to show the pathway but the little tunnel of light thrown by my lantern; which, naturally, made surrounding objects blacker still. Sometimes a hare would dart across the narrow footway, and sometimes an owl would flit before my face like a cloud of feathers, and startle me as I ran. But now I approached Owls' Abbey, and my journey became interesting.

As I got inside the territory of the ruins I stumbled over a broken stone and my light was extinguished. Fortunately the wood was past, and there was quite enough light left for me to pick my way in safety homewards. On I went, stepping from stone to stone, and listening to the hooting of owls. Suddenly I heard a laugh!—distinctly a laugh; and close by me. I own that I was greatly startled, but I stood still, and listened again. The laugh was repeated, but this time I heard voices, apparently under ground. I was not a little dismayed now, and all the village stories rushed across my brain, and I thought of Barney and the old abbot. Fear was, I confess it, getting the better of me, when I heard the neigh of a horse! somehow this touch of mortality—for I had never heard of the ghost of a horse in the abbey—re-assured me, and I listened with greater intentness. The sound of hoofs trampling, and some loud voices in correction now followed, and guided by them, I found that they proceeded from the old cellars in the "refectory" of the abbey. Kneeling down cautiously, I peeped through two worn-out pillars and saw—what? The stranger-traveller, another man whom I had never before seen, and Millet's grey mare. There sat the men squabbling over certain property, pilfered, no doubt, from our villagers, and there, tethered up to a stone, was the unhappy old nag, who missed her warm quarters and regular feeds greatly.

In a moment I was decided. Stepping cautiously away I posted out of Owls' Abbey, perfectly free from alarm now, full of joy at having found out the robbers, and determined to lose no time in setting justice on their track. On I ran, and on reaching the White Lady's Bridge, there, sure enough, was a white figure sitting on the key-stone of the arch! Mindful of my late experience, I went unflinchingly on. A cheery voice bade me "good night!" It was a countryman in a smock-frock, resting on the bridge; evidently a stranger, or he would have respected the local tradition more. I told him what I had seen, and he kindly returned with me. On reaching Twaddleton I told my story, and to my delight a quiet man who had listened carefully to my narrative, turned out to be the Bow-street runner. A cavalcade now formed; Barratt, and Millett, and Jim Lantern and many more, shamed out of their compunctions by my experience, joined the troop, and without losing time we returned to Owls' Abbey. Here, cautiously dividing our forces, the detective made me lead the way to the spot where I had heard the voices. As we approached a neigh was heard.

"My old mare, for ninepence!" roared Millett in extacy.

In a moment there was a rush—a struggle—and the two rogues, regular London thieves, were collared and handcuffed. Having paved the way to plunder by trading on the foolish superstitions of the villagers, the principal robber had feigned alarm

to disarm suspicion, and used to return nightly to thieve, knowing that while he and his accomplice and his plunder lay in Owls'
Abbey they were safe enough.

The villains were punished in due course, and Twaddleton,
having seen for itself that the reputed ghosts were all a myth,
returned to its senses, and used the short-cut ever afterwards.

And this is how the Twaddleton ghost was laid.

# Ellen Wood

## A MYSTERIOUS VISITOR

*Beginning in May 1857, the Indian Mutiny was an uprising of Indian regiments who began to expel or put to death European residents. The uprising effectively ended the East India Company's dominance in India. It took two months for the news of this upheaval to reach the United Kingdom, but, once it did, it became a focal point for periodicals, entirely dominating foreign affairs articles for the rest of the year. Known for her sensation novels, including* East Lynne, ELLEN WOOD *(1814-1887) developed a knack for wringing the greatest amount of pathos and tragedy out of the page: "Her books are pure soap operas".[1] This short story appeared first in* Bentley's Miscellany *in 1857 and later, in a bowdlerized version, in* Argosy, *the magazine she bought and edited. It certainly emphasizes the British perspective of the Indian Mutiny's tragic violence for readers far removed from the danger. The soldier-husband involves his wife in the mutiny by visiting her on the night of its occurrence. While this seems like gritty Christmas reading, the highly emotional quality of the story would have been fitting for the midwinter reading circle during the charged period of Christmas 1857.*

O N MONDAY MORNING, THE 11TH OF MAY LAST, there sat in one of the quiet rooms of Enton parsonage a young and pretty woman, playing with her baby. It was Mrs. Ordie. The incumbent of Enton was Dr. Ling, an honorary canon of the county cathedral, and rather given, of late years, to certain church innovations. He called himself a high churchman, his friends a Tractarian, and his enemies a Puseyite. However, Puseyite or not, he was the spiritual director of Enton, which brought him in a good round income, every farthing of which he lived up to, some people said to more. Mrs. Ling was from India; her

---

1 Winifred Hughes. *The Maniac in the Cellar: Sensation Novels of the 1860s.* Princeton: Princeton University Press, 1980.

family connexions lived there; father, uncles, brothers, and cousins, had been, or were, in the civil or military service of Bengal. Consequently, as the daughters of Dr. Ling had grown towards womanhood, they were severally shipped off, with high matrimonial views, according to a fashion that extensively prevails among certain of our British families.

Miss Ling, Louisa, had gone out first, and had secured Captain Ordie. Constance had gone out next, and espoused Lieutenant Main, to the indignation of all her relatives, both at home and out, for she was a handsome girl, and had been set down for nothing less than a major. Lieutenant Main, who was attached to Captain Ordie's regiment, had been home on sick leave, and was unfortunately returning in the very ship that took Constance. Before they had come to the end of their voyage, they had agreed that Main was a prettier name for the young lady than Ling, and although everybody assured her that he had no interest and would never get promoted, she married him. The third daughter, Sarah Ann, very young and pretty she was, went out the following year, with a stern injunction not to do as Constance had done. Sarah Ann, probably, would not have gone so soon, but that Mrs. Ordie had urged it. Her own health was not good; she was returning to Europe; let Sarah Ann come and be introduced under *her* auspices, before she left, otherwise she would be consigned to the charge and bad example of Mrs. Main. And Sarah Ann was despatched at the age of fifteen: Dr. and Mrs. Ling had three other daughters yet.

It happened, however, before Sarah Ann could get there, that Mrs. Ordie's health grew worse, and she was ordered immediately to her native climate, so, after all, Sarah Ann had to be received by Mrs. Main. Mrs. Ordie, upon landing in England, proceeded to Enton. The voyage had been of much service to her, and her health was improved. And there we see her sitting, on the morning of the 11th of last May, nearly twelve months after her arrival, playing with her infant, who was nine months old. She was well now, and in August she and the child were going back to India.

Mrs. Ordie was much attached to this child, very anxious and fidgety over it; her first child had died in India, so perhaps that was the reason. She fancied, this morning, that it was not well, and had been sending in haste for Mrs. Beecher, who lived close by. The honorary canon, Mrs. Ling, and two of the remaining daughters, had gone, the previous Saturday, to spend a week in the county town, where he had some "honorary" duty to perform in the cathedral.

Mrs. Beecher came running in without her bonnet. She had been governess to Louisa and Constance when they were young, had married the curate, and remained the deeply-attached friend and adviser of the Ling family. In any emergency Mrs. Beecher was appealed to, and she proved herself equal to all.

"I am sure baby's ill," was Mrs. Ordie's salutation. "I have been playing with her, and doing all I can to excite her notice, but she will keep her head down. See how hot her cheeks are."

"I think she is sleepy," said Mrs. Beecher. "And perhaps a very little feverish."

"*Do* you think her feverish? Whatever shall I do? Good mercy, if she should die as the other did!"

"Louisa," remonstrated Mrs. Beecher, "do not excite yourself causelessly. I thought you had left that off before you went out: you promised me you had."

"Oh, but you don't know what it is to lose a child, you never had one," returned Mrs. Ordie, giving way to her excitement. "If she dies, I can tell you I shall die with her."

"Hush," interrupted Mrs. Beecher. "In the first place, I believe there is little, if anything, the matter with the child, except cutting her teeth, which renders all children somewhat feverish. In the second, if she were dangerously ill, you have no right to say what you have just said."

"Oh yes, I have a right, for it is truth. I would rather lose everything I possess in the world, than my baby."

"Not everything, I hope, Louisa," quietly remarked Mrs. Beecher.

"Yes, everything. I would. I like nothing half so well. What a while Mr. Percival is!" she added, walking to the window and looking out.

"You surely have not sent for Mr. Percival?"

"I surely have. And if he does not soon make his appearance, I shall send again."

Mrs. Beecher sighed. "I am sorry to see this, Louisa. You will get into your old nervous state again."

Mrs. Ordie would not hear reason. She had taken up the idea that the child *was* ill, and at length told Mrs. Beecher that as she had never had any children herself, she could not feel for her. She had always been of most excitable temperament. As a girl, her imagination was so vivid, so prone to the marvellous, that story books and fairy tales were obliged to be kept from her. She would seek to get them unknown to her parents, and, when successful, would wake up in the night, shrieking with terror at what she had read. Hers was indeed a peculiarly active brain. It is necessary to mention this, as it may account, in some degree, for what follows.

There was really nothing the matter with the child, but Mrs. Ordie insisted that there was, and made herself miserable all the day. The surgeon, Mr. Percival, came; he saw little the matter with it, either, but he ordered it a warm bath, and sent in some medicine—probably distilled water and sugar: mothers and nurses must be humored.

Mrs. Beecher called in, in the evening. Mrs. Ordie hinted that she might as well remain for the night, to be on the spot should baby be taken worse.

Mrs. Beecher laughed. "I think I can promise you that there will be no danger, Louisa. You may cease to torment yourself; if she was not quite well this morning, I can see that she is perfectly so to-night. You may go to sleep in peace."

"You might as well stay. However, if any thing does happen, I shall send to your house, and call you up."

The Lings kept four servants. Of these, two, a man and maid, were with their master and mistress, the other two were at home. And there was the child's nurse. After Mrs. Beecher left, Mrs. Ordie crept along the corridor to the nurse's room, where the baby slept, and found the nurse undressing herself.

"What are you doing that for?" she indignantly exclaimed. "Of course you will sit up to-night, and watch by baby."

"Sit up for what, ma'am?" returned the nurse.

"I would not leave the child unwatched to-night for any thing. My other baby died of convulsions, and the same thing may attack this. They come on in a moment. I have ordered Martha to sit up in the kitchen and keep hot water in readiness."

"Why, ma'am, there's no cause in the world for it. The baby is as well as you or I, and has never woke up since I laid her down at eight o'clock."

"She shall be watched this night," persisted Mrs. Ordie. "So dress yourself again."

"I must say it's a shame," grumbled the nurse, who had grown tired of her mistress's capricious ways, and had privately told the other servants that she did not care how soon she left the situation. "I'd sit up for a week, if there was a call for it, but to be deprived of one's natural rest, for nothing, is too bad. I'll sit myself in the old rocking-chair, if I must sit up," added the servant, half to herself, half to her mistress, "and get asleep that way."

Mrs. Ordie's eyes flashed anger. The fact was, the slavery of Eastern servants had a little spoiled her for the independence of European ones. She accused the girl of every crime that was unfeeling, short of child-murder, and concluded by having the infant's crib carried down to her own room. She would sit up herself and watch it.

The child still slept calmly and quietly, and Mrs. Ordie sat quietly by it. But she began to find it rather dull, and she went to the book-shelves and got a book. It was then striking eleven. Setting the lamp on a small table at her elbow, she began to read.

She had pitched upon the "Vicar of Wakefield." She had not opened the book for years, and she read on with interest, all her old pleasure in the tale revived. Suddenly she heard footsteps on the gravel path outside, advancing down it, and she looked off and listened. The first thought that struck her was, that one of the servants had been out without permission, and was coming in at that late hour, which, as her hanging watch, opposite, told her, was twenty-five minutes past eleven. It must be explained that Enton parsonage stood a little back from the high road, and was surrounded by trees. Two iron gates gave ingress from the road, by a broad, half-circular carriage path, which swept round close by the house, between it and the thick trees. A lawn and garden were at the back of the house, but there was no ingress there, or to any part of the premises, save through the iron gates. A narrow gravel path, branching off from the portico, led to the small house of the curate, not a hundred yards off, and *that* house was connected with the high road by one iron gate, and a straight walk. Broad enough for carriages also, but none ever went down it, for they could not turn. These iron gates—the rector's two and the curate's one—were invariably locked at sunset, all the year round: did any visitors approach either house, after that, they had to ring for admittance.

Mrs. Ordie heard footsteps in the stillness of the night, and her eyes glanced to her watch. Twenty-five minutes after eleven. But immediately an expression of astonishment rose to her face, and her eyes dilated and her lips opened, and her ears were strained to the sound. If ever she heard the footsteps of her husband, she was sure she heard them then.

She drew in her breath and listened still. They were coming nearer, close upon the house, his own sharp, quick, firm step, which she had never heard since she left him in Calcutta: they were right underneath her window now, on their way to the door. With a cry of joy she rose, and softly opened the window.

"George! dear George! I knew your step. Whatever brings you home?"

There was no answer, except the sound of the footsteps, but she leaned out, and by the rays, cast outside from the kitchen window, which was well lighted within, and stood far back, at right angles with the house door, she saw the form of the visitor. Rather dimly to be sure, but there was no mistaking it for any other than Captain Ordie, and he wore his regimentals. She watched him leave the broad path, and halt at the entrance to the portico, which was situated on the side of the house. She spoke again:

"George, you did not hear me. Don't knock—baby's ill. Wait a moment, and I will let you in."

She sprang to the door. Her lamp was not one suitable for carrying, and she would not stay to light a taper: she knew every stair well, and sped down them. But she was awkward at the fastenings of the front door, and could not undo them in the dark. She ran into the kitchen for a light. The servant, sitting up in obedience to her orders, was lying back in a chair, her feet stretched out upon another. She was fast asleep and snoring. A large fire burnt in the grate, and two candles were alight on the ironing-board underneath the window, one of them guttering down. Servants will be wasteful.

"Martha! Martha!" she exclaimed, "rouse up. My husband's come."

"What!" cried the woman, starting up in affright, and evidently forgetting where she was, "who's come?"

"Come and open the hall-door. Captain Ordie is there."

She snatched one of the candles from the table, and bore to the door again. The servant followed, rubbing her eyes.

The door was unlocked and thrown open, and Mrs. Ordie drew a little back to give space for him to enter. No one came in. Mrs. Ordie looked out then, holding the candle above her head. She could not see him anywhere.

"Take the light," she said to the maid, and she stepped outside beyond the portico, and looked about. "George!" she called out, "where are you? The door is open." But Captain Ordie neither appeared nor answered.

"Well, I never knew such an extraordinary thing!" exclaimed Mrs. Ordie. "Where can he have gone?"

"Ma'am," said the servant, who began now to be pretty well awake, "I don't understand. Did you say any body was come?"

"My husband is come. Captain Ordie."

"From Mrs. Beecher's?" asked the woman.

"Mrs. Beecher's, no! What should bring him at Mrs. Beecher's? He must have come direct from Portsmouth."

"But he must have come to the door here from the Beechers'," continued the servant. "He couldn't have come any other how. The gates are locked."

In her wonder at his appearance, this fact had not struck Mrs. Ordie. "One of them must have been left unfastened," she said, after thinking. "That was very careless, Martha. It is your place to see to it when Richard's out. Papa once turned a servant away for leaving the gates open at night."

"I locked both the gates at sundown," was the woman's reply. "And the key's hanging up in its place in the kitchen."

"Impossible," repeated Mrs. Ordie. "The Captain came in by the upper one, the furthest from here. I heard him the minute he put his foot on the gravel, and knew his step. You must have thought you locked it. George!" added Mrs. Ordie, in a louder tone. "George!"

There was no answer. No sound whatever broke the stillness of the night.

"Captain Ordie!" she repeated, "Captain Ordie!"

The servant was laughing to herself, taking care that her young mistress did not see her. She believed that Mrs. Ordie had been doing what she did—dropping asleep; and had *dreamt* she heard somebody on the gravel.

"I know what it is," cried Mrs. Ordie, briskly. "He has never been here before, and finding the door was not immediately opened to him, has gone on to the Beechers, thinking this the wrong house."

She ran down the narrow path as she spoke, which branched off from the portico, round by the kitchen window; and the maid followed her, first stopping to put the candle inside the hall. It was light, now they were out.

But nothing was to be seen of George Ordie. The curate's house, a small one, was closed, and presented the appearance of a dwelling whose inmates were at rest; the blinds were drawn before the windows, and all was still. Mrs. Ordie ran over probabilities in her mind, and came to the conclusion that he could not have gone there. The Beechers were early people, and had no doubt been in bed an hour ago; and had her husband knocked there, he would be waiting at the door still, for they had not had time to come down and let him in.

"It could only have been fancy, ma'am," cried Martha.

"Silence," said Mrs. Ordie; "how can it have been fancy? I heard my husband, and saw him."

"Well, ma'am, I argue so from the gates being fast. He couldn't have got over 'em because of the spikes."

"The gates can not be fast," returned Mrs. Ordie, "and it is foolish in you to persist in the falsehood—only to screen your own carelessness."

"I wish you'd just please to come and look at the gates," retorted Martha.

"I will," said Mrs. Ordie, starting off with alacrity, anxious to convict Martha to her face. "It is an utter impossibility that Captain Ordie could have come in at a high, locked gate, with spikes on the top; he would not attempt to do so."

"That's just what I say," answered Martha. "I dreamt t'other night," she muttered to herself, as she followed her mistress, "that a man came down that there path with lovely gownd pieces to sell: I might just as well have riz up the house, and had *him* routed for."

They gained the broad walk, and proceeded round towards the gate. Mrs. Ordie put out her hand and tried it. It was locked. Martha sniffed.

"Why, it is like magic!" uttered Mrs. Ordie.

"I was positive and certain about its being locked, ma'am. And that's why I said it must be fancy. I think it couldn't have been nothing else."

Mrs. Ordie was indignant. "Is this gate fancy?" she said, shaking it, in her anger.

"No, that's a real gate."

"Then don't tell me again that my husband is fancy. How could I have seen and heard him if he were not come? Captain Ordie!" she called out, once more. "George! where can you have gone to?"

"If he is on the premises, he must *be* on 'em," logically argued the servant. "Because there's no outlet out of 'em, but by these gates."

"Come to the other gate," said Mrs. Ordie.

They retraced their steps round the circular path, Mrs. Ordie looking in all directions for a gleam of scarlet, and reached the other gate. It was also locked. Then she went and tried Mr. Beecher's gate; it was likewise fast; and then she went to their own garden, at the back of the house, and looked and called. She even went into the summer-house, but there was no trace of Captain Ordie. The servant walked with her, half-amused, half-provoked.

"Can he have slipped in-doors," murmured Mrs. Ordie, "that first time when we had gone down to the Beechers?" And she went in, looked in the sitting-rooms, ascended the stairs to her own room, where the light was, taking the opportunity to glance at her child, and then looked in the kitchen. But Captain Ordie was nowhere to be seen, and she had never been so much perplexed and puzzled in all her life.

"Then he must have gone on, as I thought, to Mr. Beecher's," was her last solution of the enigma. "They were possibly up, and let him in directly. And they are keeping him there till morning, that he may not disturb us, knowing that baby is ill."

"But about the gate," interrupted the servant, returning to her stumbling-block, "how could he have got through it?"

"I know he did get through it, and that's enough," responded Mrs. Ordie. "He may have managed to climb over it, not finding the bell. Soldiers have venturesome spirits. I will go and fetch him. You stop here, Martha, and listen to baby."

Once more Mrs. Ordie sped to the curate's. She knocked at the door, and stood back to look up at the house. "They have put him into their spare bed," she soliloquized; "Mrs. Beecher has kept it made up this fortnight past, expecting their invalid from India. My goodness! I never thought of it! they have no doubt come together, in the same ship. George may have gone up to Calcutta, and finding James Beecher was coming, have got leave, all in a hurry, and accompanied him."

But there was still no sign of light or life in the house, and Mrs. Ordie picked up some bits of gravel, and threw them at Mrs. Beecher's bed-room window. This brought forth the curate, in his nightcap, peeping through the curtains.

"It is I, Mr. Beecher," she called out. "Have you got Captain Ordie here?"

"Make haste, Anne," cried the curate, turning his head round to speak to his wife. "It's Mrs. Ordie. Perhaps the child is in a fit."

"My husband is come," repeated Mrs. Ordie. "He is here, is he not?"

"Yes, directly," answered the curate, imperfectly understanding, but opening the casement about an inch, to speak.

"Is she really worse, Louisa?" exclaimed Mrs. Beecher, who now appeared at the window. "I will just throw on a few things, and be with you."

The curate, believing the matter to be settled, drew in his

nightcap, and closed the casement. But Mrs. Ordie's voice was again heard. "Mr. Beecher! Mr. Beecher! I want you."

"Dress yourself, my dear," cried Mrs. Beecher to him, in a flurry. "I dare say they want you to go for Mr. Percival. If the baby is really worse, and it is not Louisa's fancy, I shall never boast of knowing children again. It looked as cool and well in the evening as it need look. She is calling again."

Mr. Beecher reopened the casement. "I am putting on my clothes, Mrs. Ordie. I am coming."

"But you need not do that. Has your brother come?"

"Who?"

"Your brother: James Beecher."

"No. Not yet."

"There's a ship in, as my husband has arrived. Tell him I am here."

"We'll be down in a minute," called out Mr. Beecher, retiring from the window, and making desperate haste. "Anne, Captain Ordie's come."

"Captain Ordie!" exclaimed Mrs. Beecher.

"Mrs. Ordie says so."

"Then we shall have James here to-morrow. How very unexpected Captain Ordie's arrival must have been to his wife! And to find his child ill!"

Mrs. Ordie waited. Mrs. Beecher came down first, in a large shawl, and her bonnet tied over her nightcap. They began to speak at cross purposes.

"Is he coming? Have you told him?" impatiently asked Mrs. Ordie.

"My dear, yes. But he had gone upstairs in slippers, and his shoes were in the back kitchen. Louisa, you should not have come out yourself, you should have sent. Has not Captain Ordie's arrival taken you by surprise?"

"I never was so much surprised," answered Mrs. Ordie, standing still, and not offering to stir. "I heard his footstep first, and knew it even in the distance. I am so glad! He must have come with James Beecher."

"Ay, we shall have James here to-morrow. But, my dear, let us not lose time. Is the child very ill?"

"She is not worse, there is no hurry," answered Mrs. Ordie, planting her back against a tree, as deliberately as if she meant to make it her station for the night, and gazing up at the casement which she knew belonged to their spare bedroom. Mrs. Beecher looked at her in surprise. "Will he be long?" she added. "There's no light."

"He will be here directly," said Mrs. Beecher; "he is finding his shoes. I suppose Kitty put them in some out-of-the-way place, ready for cleaning in the morning."

Another pause, and the curate appeared.

"O Mr. Beecher! you need not have got up," was Mrs. Ordie's greeting. "I am sorry to give you all this trouble."

"It is no trouble," he rejoined. "Do you want me to go for Mr. Percival?"

"You are very kind, but we shall not want the doctor to-night: at least I hope not. She has never woke up once since she was laid down. I have been watching her myself: I had her brought down to my own room. Nurse behaved shamefully over it, and I gave her warning. She shall leave to-morrow."

"Pray let us go on, and see how she is," said Mrs. Beecher, never supposing but they had been called up by the state of the child, and thinking Mrs. Ordie's words and delay very strange.

"When he comes. You say he will not be long. Had he undressed?"

"Had who undressed?"

"My husband."

Mrs. Beecher stared at her with amazement. "I do not understand you, Louisa. For whom are we waiting here?"

"For my husband, of course. You say he is finding his shoes."

Both Mr. and Mrs. Beecher thought her child's illness was turning her crazy. "Louisa, you are mystifying us. Is your husband coming out, here, into the garden? Are we to wait here for him?"

"Why, you know he is coming out, and of course I shall wait for him. Only think of his travelling in his regimentals! Just as if he were on duty."

"Where is Captain Ordie?" interposed the curate.

"Well, that's a sensible question, from you," laughed Mrs.

Ordie. "I suppose he is in your spare bedroom, though I see no light. Or else hunting for his shoes in your kitchen."

"Child," said Mrs. Beecher, taking hold of her tenderly, "you are not well. I told you to-day what it would be, if you excited yourself. Let us take you home."

"I will not go without my husband. There. And what makes him so long? I shall call to him." She advanced and turned the handle of the door, but it resisted her efforts.

"Why, you have locked it!" she exclaimed, turning to Mr. Beecher. "You have locked him in."

"Locked who in, child?" said Mrs. Beecher. "There's nobody in the house but Kitty."

"My husband is there. Did he not come to you, finding our house shut up?"

"No, certainly not. We have not seen him."

"Mr. Beecher," she impatiently uttered, "I asked you when you first came to the window, whether my husband had come here, and you said yes."

"My dear young lady, I must have misunderstood your question. You know I am a little deaf. All I heard, with reference to Captain Ordie, was, that he had come: I supposed to your house. He has certainly not been to ours."

"Then what were you talking of?" she reproachfully asked of Mrs. Beecher. "It was shameful to deceive me so! You said he had gone up-stairs in slippers, and was finding his shoes. You know you did."

"My dear child, I was speaking of Mr. Beecher. I did not know you thought your husband was here. Why did you think so?"

"If he is not here, where is he?" demanded Mrs. Ordie. "You need not look at me as though you thought I was out of my senses. Do you mean to say you have not seen Captain Ordie?"

"We have not, indeed. We went to bed at ten, and heard nothing, until you threw the gravel at the window."

"Where can he be? What can he have done with himself?" uttered Mrs. Ordie, in deep tribulation.

"Did he leave you to come to our house? What time did he arrive?"

"It was at twenty-five minutes after eleven. I had got baby in my room, as I told you, and I was sitting by her, reading the 'Vicar of Wakefield.' All at once I heard footsteps approaching from the upper gate, and I knew they were my husband's. He came close, and I looked out, and saw him, and called to him; he did not seem to hear me, but went in to the portico. I ran down to let him in, and to my surprise he was not there then, and I thought he must have come on to you."

"Then you have not yet spoken with him?" exclaimed Mr. Beecher.

"Not yet."

"Are you sure it was Captain Ordie? Who opened the gate to him?"

"No one. The gate is locked. There is the strange part of the business."

"My dear Mrs. Ordie! I fear it must be all a mistake. Captain Ordie would not arrive here on foot, even if he landed unexpectedly; and he could not have got through a locked gate. Perhaps you were asleep."

"Nonsense," peevishly replied Mrs. Ordie; "I was as wide awake as I am now. I was deep in the book, and had not felt sleepy. I had got to that part where the fine ladies from town had gone in to neighbor Flamborough's and caught them all at hunt-the-slipper, Olivia in the middle, bawling for fair play; where Mr. Burchell, afterwards, turns his back upon the company, and calls out 'fudge' at the ladies' high-lived conversation. The ballad 'Edwin and Angelina' came in, a few pages before, and that I skipped. I assure you I was perfectly awake."

"I do not think it possible to have been any thing but a delusion," persisted Mr. Beecher.

"How a delusion?" angrily asked the young lady; "I do not know what you mean. Delusions don't visit people who are wide awake, and in their sober senses. If my hearing had played me false, Mr. Beecher, my sight could not. I heard my husband, and saw him, and spoke to him: do you think I should speak to somebody I did not know? I am certain it was Captain Ordie. He was in his regimentals: were they a delusion?"

"This is very strange," said Mrs. Beecher.

"It is more than strange," was Louisa Ordie's answer, as she looked dreamily about. "He is in the grounds somewhere, and why he does not come forward, I don't know."

The mystery was not cleared up that night. The next day Mrs. Ordie sent for her father, to impart to him the strange circumstance. He adopted his curate's view of the affair, and indeed the universal view. Mrs. Ordie was much annoyed at their disbelief, and she actually, in spite of her friends, had Captain Ordie advertised for, in the local papers: he *was* in England, she said, and it would be proved so.

When letters next arrived from India, there was one from Captain Ordie, which gave proof positive that he was not, and had not been, in Europe. Mrs. Ordie was perplexed, and refused to speak of it further, for she only got ridicule.

The weeks went on, and the time fixed for the departure of Mrs. Ordie and her child drew near, but meanwhile the disastrous news had arrived of the outbreak in India, and it was deemed advisable to postpone it.

She was sitting one day in a gloomy mood; not a sorrowful one; more one of anger. She had not heard from her husband for some time, (his last letter was dated April,) and now, as she found, another mail was in, and no news from him. The rising at Delhi, where he was quartered, was known to her, but not as yet the details of its more disastrous features. She did not fear his having fallen, for had any thing happened to him, Mr. Main, or one of her sisters, would have written. They were all at Delhi. Mrs. Beecher came in, looking very pale and sad. Dr. and Mrs. Ling had gone off, in their pony carriage, to the county town, to pick up news. They were extremely uneasy.

"There has been another mail in these two days!" she exclaimed to Mrs. Beecher. "News travels slower to Enton than anywhere. Have you heard from James Beecher? You don't look well."

"He is come. He came overland."

"And you have been worrying yourselves that he is dead! How are things going on over there?"

"Very badly. They can not be worse."

"Does he know any thing of George?" continued Mrs. Ordie. "I think he might spare a minute from his fighting to write to me.

What *is* the matter with you? You have not bad news for me?" she added, her fears touched, and rising in excitement. "Oh! surely not! Not FOR ME!"

"James's news, altogether, is very dispiriting," returned Mrs. Beecher, at a loss how to proceed with her task. "My husband is gone to bring Dr. and Mrs. Ling back. We thought you might like them to be at home."

"Has George fallen in battle? Have those half-caste rebels shot him down? O——"

"Pray be calm, Louisa!" implored Mrs. Beecher; "if ever you had need of calmness in your life, you have need of it now. Affliction——"

"Is he wounded? Is he dead?" interrupted Mrs. Ordie, with a bitter shriek. "O George! dearest George! and I have been calling you hard names for not writing to me! What is it?"

"There is a great deal to be told, my child. James Beecher was at Delhi in the midst of it."

Mrs. Ordie suddenly rose from her seat and flew from the room. Mrs. Beecher supposed she had gone to her chamber, and followed her there. Not so. A thin man, looking fearfully ill, fair once, but browned by an Eastern sun, was lying on the sofa in the curate's parlor, when a young, excited woman came flying in.

"Mr. Beecher," she uttered, seizing his hands imploringly, "when did it happen? I am Mrs. Ordie."

"Has my sister-in-law told you—any thing?" he asked, hesitatingly.

"Yes, yes. I know the worst. I want particulars."

He had risen into an upright posture, though he could scarcely support himself, and she sat down beside him. He was a church missionary, a widower with children. "Are you sure that you can bear the details?" he asked, believing, from her words, that she knew the general facts.

"I am sure. Omit nothing. Mrs. Beecher says you were at Delhi."

"I went there in the spring, to say farewell to some friends, ere I came home. At Delhi I was taken worse, and lay ill there."

"But about the rising?"

"I am coming to it. On the second Monday in May, after

breakfast, bad news came in. The 3d Light Cavalry had dashed in from Meerut, fully armed, and were slaughtering the Europeans. Eighty-five of this regiment had been tried by court-martial at Meerut, for refusing to handle the greased cartridges, and sentenced to imprisonment. Their sentences were read out to them on parade on the previous Saturday, the 9th, and they were sent to jail. On the 10th, Sunday, the regiment rose, released the prisoners, massacred the European officers, their wives and children, and on the 11th came to Delhi, in open revolt. I struggled up, dressed myself, joined my friends where I was staying, and we waited further news. It came in too soon. The mutineers had gone towards Deriowgunge, shooting all the officers they encountered. The brigadier ordered out the 54th Native Infantry and two guns; and, I believe, a detachment of another regiment, but accounts varied. They met the rebels just outside the Cashmere gate, and it was all up, for the Sepoys deserted their officers, and shook hands with the Sowars. Every officer was killed: treacherous, cowardly wretches! they did not spare one."

She was biting her lips, and striving for calmness, determined to hear all. "Did the officers not resist?"

"All in their power, but they were unarmed," he said. "The next account that came in was, that the natives had risen and joined the insurrection, were firing the bungalows at Deriowgunge, and ransacking the European residences. The troopers were raging about, destroying life, and when their work was done, the Goojurs,[1] who had collected in great numbers, as they were sure to do, followed in their wake, and pillaged every thing, even to the matting. The bank was rifled."

Mr. Beecher paused, wondering whether he ought to proceed, but her studied calmness deceived him.

"No one knew where to fly for refuge, or what to do: none knew where to put the officers' wives and children. Many were taken to the Flagstaff Tower, but it was thought unsafe, and had to be abandoned. Some escaped—many, I hope—in conveyances,

1 A race of a peculiar caste, who congregate round Meerut and Delhi. They have been compared to our gipsy tribes, and live by plunder, even in times of peace. Some years ago a regiment was obliged to be raised especially to keep them under. [Author's note.]

or on horseback, or on foot. Some of the officers retreated to the cantonment, outside the gates, but the troopers got there when night came, killed them and their wives and children."

"Were any of *my* family with them?" she asked, still with unnatural composure.

"No. I will tell you. Before mid-day the ladies of our house, my host's wife and her cousin, escaped to a close hut, or outhouse, and I managed to hobble there with them. I don't know how: but it is astonishing the artificial strength that fear brings out. Others also took refuge there, about half a dozen ladies, your two sisters being amongst them, three or four children, and a poor little ensign, as ill and weak as I was. We hoped we were in safety; that the rebels would not think of looking for us there; and some old matting, well wetted, was hung up across the entrance, as if to dry. A Sepoy, who was really faithful, (and there were many such in the city,) sat before it to guard it: many a one, raging after prey, did he turn aside with a well-assumed story that his old mother was in there, dying—let her die in peace."

"Was my husband there?"

"Not then. No one came near us all day; they dared not, for our sakes; and we bore our suspense and apprehension as we best could, not knowing who was living or who dead, of those dearest to us. What a day that was! We had neither food nor drink; the heat of the weather was fearful; and so many of us stowed together, and closely shut up, rendered the air fetid. We thought it could not be less than 110 degrees. This was not the worst: there were the apprehensions of discovery. We men might brave it, at any rate to appearance, but the poor young women! I believe they would have been glad to die as they cowered there, rather than live to encounter an uncertain fate. I strove to speak comfort to them all, but it was difficult: one or two bore bravely up, and cheered the rest. Late at night, under cover of the darkness, Captain Ordie stole in."

She raised a faint cry at the name. "My husband!"

"He told us what he could of the progress of the day: it was horribly bad, yet I believed he softened it for their ears: and then began to talk of our own situation. It would be impossible, he said, to keep in the same place of concealment another day, and that we had better join a party who were about to make their escape towards Kurnaul. All seized at the idea eagerly, and wished to start without the delay of an instant. Just then, Mrs. Holt, my friend's wife, whom the idea of escape had aroused from lethargy inquired after her husband, whom she had not seen since morning.

" 'He is safe, and unharmed,' replied Captain Ordie.

" 'On your honor?' she said, fearing he might be deceiving her.

" 'On my honor. You will see him when we are fairly off; but it was not thought well for more than one of us to venture here.'

" 'And my husband?' added Mrs. Main, who had done nothing but clasp her baby to her breast all day, and weep silently. 'Is he safe?'

"Captain Ordie answered evasively," continued Mr. Beecher, "and I knew, by his words and by the turn of his face, that poor Main was gone."

"Was he? Is he dead?" shuddered Mrs. Ordie.

"I found he had been dead since the afternoon. The troopers had hacked him to pieces."

"Go on," she groaned. "George's turn comes next."

Mr. Beecher hesitated. "I will finish later," he suggested.

"No: finish now. You can not leave me in this suspense. It would be cruel."

"Captain Ordie spoke of the plan of departure. The officers had but three horses amongst them, and the ladies and invalids were to take it in turn to ride, two, with a child, on each horse. And all the party were to keep together. At that moment arose a yell, a horrible yell, which we knew proceeded only from a Sowar, and one of them appeared at the entrance, tearing down the matting. All the light we had was a night-wick in some oil, but we saw his dark face. The children shrieked; the ladies also, and huddled themselves together in a corner; and Captain Ordie advanced to the entrance, and dealt the man a blow on the temple with the butt-end of his pistol."

"I hope it killed him!" she uttered, her eyes sparkling.

"I think it did, for he lay motionless. Captain Ordie kicked him out of the way, and, throwing himself on his hands and knees, crawled out cautiously to reconnoitre. Alas! we soon heard a struggle outside: two more were upon him."

"And he was struck down! I *know* you are going to tell it me," she uttered, in a low, passionate wail.

Mr. Beecher sat silent, his countenance full of distress.

"Louisa, my darling, be composed," interrupted Mrs. Beecher, who had stolen in, in search of her. "You know the worst now."

"Yes, I know the worst," she moaned. "They killed him there and then."

"They did," whispered Mr. Beecher.

"You are *sure* he was dead?"

"Quite sure. It was instantaneous."

"Where was he wounded? Let me know. I can bear it."

"My child, you know enough," said Mrs. Beecher. "Be content."

"I will know it," she frantically said. "George, George! Did they cut him to pieces!"

"They beheaded him."

She turned sick, and shook violently. But, by a strong effort of control, spoke again. "Finish the history. What became of you, inside?"

"It was all commotion in a moment, dreadful commotion. The poor terrified women attempted to fly; some succeeded, and I hope escaped. Providentially there were only these two troopers; had more been upon us, none would have been left. The first thing I saw distinctly was, that one of them had got Mrs. Main's infant, tossing it on the point of his bayonet. She stretched her arms up after it, and its blood trickled down on to her face: her cries for mercy for it ring in my ear yet. He next seized her."

"Constance?" panted Mrs. Ordie.

"Yes. And killed her—killed her instantly. Be thankful."

Mrs. Ordie pressed down her eyeballs, as if she would shut out some unwelcome sight. "Constance murdered," she moaned. "And you tell me to be thankful!"

"Be ever thankful," impressively spoke the missionary. "Others met with a worse fate."

"Sarah Ann?" she shivered. "What became of her!"

"I am unable to tell you. I trust she escaped. At the moment of Mrs. Main's death, I fainted on the floor where I was lying, and that must have saved my life. Had the troopers thought I possessed any still, they would not have spared me. When I recovered, not a creature—living—was to be seen. The children were lying about; they had been put out of their misery; two of the ladies, and the ensign. Poor young fellow! he had told us, in the day, that he had no parents or near friends to mourn him, so the loss of a little griff, if they did kill him, would not count for much."

"Dead? All?"

"All. The two ladies were Mrs. Holt and Mrs. Main. Of the other ladies I saw no trace. I trust," he added, clasping his hands fervently, "that they escaped. We shall hear of many miraculous escapes: I pray theirs may be of the number."

"Now, Louisa, let me take you home," urged Mrs. Beecher. "You do know the worst."

"I must hear all," was the answer, uttered in a tone of frenzy. "If I thought there was a word, a recital, left untold to me, I must get up in the middle of the night, and come and ask for it."

"You have heard all," said Mr. Beecher—"all that I know. My own escape I will not trouble you with. It was wonderful: and I lost no time in coming home overland."

She leaned back on the sofa and closed her eyes. Mrs. Beecher was thinking of her random words—that she would rather lose every thing in the world than her child. But her thoughts had not grasped the dreadful possibility of losing her husband.

"When did this happen?" Mrs. Ordie suddenly asked. "What date?"

"I mentioned it," said Mr. Beecher. "Late on the night of the 11th of May."

She leaned forward breathless, her eyes staring. "How late? The exact hour? Speak?"

"It must have been near half past eleven. When Captain Ordie came in, we asked him the time, (for, strange to say, in our hurried hiding, not one of us put a watch about us,) and his watch said a quarter past eleven; and we were talking, after that, perhaps ten minutes. It must have been about twenty-five minutes after eleven when he was killed."

"Listen to that!" shrieked Louisa Ordie, seizing Mrs. Beecher by the arm. "It was the very hour I saw and heard him. How was he dressed?" she rapidly asked.

"In full regimentals."

"There! There! Do you believe me now, Mrs. Beecher? Ah! you, and all, ridiculed me; but hear it! It was my husband that came down the path here—appearing to me in the moment of his death."

The reader must judge of this mystery according to his own opinion. It happened; at least, to the positive belief of the lady, here called Mrs. Ordie; as her friends can testify. They reason with her in vain. They point out that twenty-five minutes after eleven in Delhi would not be twenty-five minutes after eleven here: they believe that it was, and could have been, nothing but her own vivid imagination, that her thoughts were probably running on her husband through the "George" in the "Vicar of Wakefield:" and they ask—even allowing (for the argument of the moment) that such things are permitted, that the spirits of the departing may, in rare instances, appear to their relatives in a distant place, and that it was George Ordie's which appeared to her—they ask to what end it came: what purpose was it to answer? They can see none. Neither can she; but she nevertheless believes, and will believe to the end of her life, that it was her husband's spirit.

# W. W. Fenn

# THE HAUNTED ROCK

## A LEGEND OF PORTH GUERRON COVE

WILLIAM WILTHEW FENN (1827-1906) *began a career as a painter, but an affliction of the eye and increasing blindness caused him to shift into the field of writing. He publicly recognized his wife's contributions to his publishing success, as she worked as his amanuensis to create the books published under his name.*[1] *After 1848, when the American press spread the story of the young Fox sisters using raps to communicate with a spirit bound to their house, the American Spiritualism movement quickly ignited.*[2] *The movement became a well-publicized force, one that had political ramifications. In 1854 the U.S. Senate was petitioned to appoint "a scientific committee to investigate spirit communication," and the death culture resulting from Civil War casualties further promoted spiritualism.*[3] *So, when the narrator of this tale returns from an 1877 trip to the United States, he finds himself fascinated with the new ideas of communicating with the dead, and he is ripe for an uncanny encounter and considers what it will take to lay the ghost. This tale first appeared in the Christmas number of* Illustrated London News *in 1881.*

P ORTH GUERRON IS IN CORNWALL. If you do not know the place it must be because, in your exploration of the hundred and one similar villages abounding on that romantic coast, you have overlooked the one—and that one must be Porth Guerron.

Like many of its fellows, it is situated in a little ravine in the

1 "William Wilthew Fenn," *The Biography and Review* (July 1881): 84-88.
2 Molly McGarry. *Ghosts of Futures Past: Spiritualism and the Cultural Politics of Nineteenth-Century America*. Berkeley: University of California Press, 2008, 1.
3 Bridget Bennett, *Transatlantic Spiritualism and Nineteenth-Century American Literature*. New York: Palgrave Macmillan, 2007, 7

dark serpentine rock running down to the sea from the higher land of gorse and heather-clad moor. Most of the thatched, and occasionally slate-roofed cottages, with their irregular patches of garden, nestle right and left among the ferny, craggy banks of the steep winding way by courtesy called a street, by which the traveller reaches the beach. Some few other dwellings, looking from the sea like huge white-winged gulls, are to be seen perched here and there upon apparently inaccessible ledges of cliff, whence they command many a fine peep across the "wide, wide world." The square-towered tiny church on the verge of a few green pastures and corn-fields stands at the head of the village, and the watermill, worked by a miniature mountain torrent, stands at the bottom. Only a little below this, begins a conglomeration of capstans, beach-houses, boats and boat-sheds, anchors, spars, chains, and the rest of the rumble-tumble of the fishing-trade, which holds high change on the shore. Here the coast, broadening out with a curve on either hand, forms a secluded cove between two arms of frowning precipitous cliff, which seem stretching forth to embrace this lapful of deep green-blue sea. The rugged and lofty formation of the land almost hides the existence of the little industrial hive until you come close upon it; and, so far as its importance in the world is concerned, you may be excused for overlooking it altogether—as you probably have done. But, if so, you have missed a very beautiful and romantic picture, and will scarcely have realised to its full extent the superstitious side of the Cornish mind, for there is attached to this place a legend in which many of the inhabitants believe with an almost religious intensity. It was told to me some years ago by a brave and intelligent old salt, one Jacob Sellar by name, a native of the village, whose implicit credence of the story supplied a strong example of the characteristics of his race.

I was returning from America in one of the Cunard boats. Sellar was a seaman on board, and spun for me many a yarn, ghostly and otherwise. I had lately witnessed some unaccountable spiritual manifestations in the States, and my natural scepticism on the question had, I confess, been considerably shaken—my mind was full of the subject, so that I listened with more interest than I might otherwise have done to this particular story, which greatly impressed me, not only from the man's manner of telling it, but from its weird nature, and I never forgot it.

Thus, when fate took me to the western crags of England in the autumn of 1877, and I came plump upon the nestling village of Porth Guerron, as most people do, before being aware of it, I recognised on the instant the feature in the landscape which marked it as the background to the legend I had heard from the lips of old Jacob.

This was a tall isolated mass of almost inaccessible rock, standing about two hundred yards away from the western headland of the cove. I call it "isolated," because it nearly always is so, for, except about an hour at the lowest of spring tides, in very calm weather, it is entirely cut off from the mainland. But on these occasions a narrow ridge of soft, sandy shingle is left bare, looking as if it would form an easy path to the rude promontory. Yet a little closer inspection soon shows this idea to be fallacious, inasmuch as, except by a boat, you cannot even reach the main shore end of the little causeway, jutting out as it does from the base of the sheer down cliff. Hence the Leopard's Head, as the crag is named, is never scaled, being inaccessible except at the one spot where its rocky spurs lose themselves in the sand of the narrow connecting ridge; thus it is left to the undisputed possession of the myriad sea-birds that make it their home.

The fishing-boats on their way to and from their anchorage in the cove always keep outside the Leopard's Head, and are never tempted to make a short cut westward by passing between it and the main land. However high the tide or calm the sea, they avoid this narrow channel, with its treacherous, never-absent ground swell; for, apart from its natural dangers, the superstition runs to the effect that a malignant demon stretches a huge iron net across the opening. Invisible to him until his craft is entangled within its fatal meshes, the mariner who, from ignorance or hardihood, should attempt the passage will, it is declared, struggle in vain to extricate himself, and must inevitably founder. So ran the legend, as told to me by the old salt aforesaid.

"Did he believe it?" I asked him.

"Yes, indeed, he did," he said; "he had good reason: he had seen the net once himself when a lad, and it was a terrible and strange business. It was the end of September, 1847, and a boat, during a heavy squall from the westward, was trying to make the cove by the short cut—and surely, just as she got betwixt the Leopard and the main land, in the Leopard's grip as the channel is called, she seemed to kind o' stick fast, although she had been running quite free the moment before. There was plenty of water, and she couldn't hardly have struck on the bar or little beach-way. But, howsomever, whether she did or not, she couldn't get through— the heavy seas broke over her of course, directly she was brought to—pooped her, in fact, and down she went with all hands, two men and a boy. The boy was my brother Isaac," continued Jacob Sellar, looking very grave when telling me the tale; "but he was saved; that is, he was picked up in the cove senseless, but they managed to restore him to life; the other two was never found even. There's a many curious things connected with that calamity, Sir, I can tell you," he added, "one of which is that, it being pretty nigh dark at the time, nobody couldn't exactly make out what did happen, 'cept that we all saw, as we stood on the beach, the net suddenly stretched across the channel, and could see that it was that as the craft got tangled in, as it brought her up, and turned her broadside on to the seas. The water was breaming at the time, you know, and this made the net plain to us, for it seemed to come up out of the sea just in front of the boat, and was sparkling all over its meshes just like silver, with the phosphorescent light."

"And you saw this?" I asked.

"That I did, Sir, with these very eyes."

"And the boy, your brother, when he came to his senses, what had he to say about it?"

"Ah! that's where 'tis, you see, Sir—poor chap, he never did come rightly to his senses—it gave him such a scare as he never got over—he's been kind o' cracky like ever since. He's a bit younger than I am, though elderly, you know, by this time. But he never quite got his wits back. He is harmless, don't you know, but dazed and silly, 'specially at times."

"And he could never give any account of how the accident happened? How it was the boat came to grief in the Leopard's Grip?"

"No, Sir; he warn't never able to tell nothing at all about it— never a word."

"Well," I remarked, after a pause, "it was true the poor fellows lost their lives, anyhow, whether the devil caught them in his net or not?"

"Yes, Sir; but another curious thing is, these two men—I remember them well—Tom Fenthall and Raymond Sass, were partners in the boat, and said to be great friends, and staunch to one another, but they were both in love with the same girl, Alice Dournelle, and it was said there had been words about her between 'em more than once, and especially just before they got lost. Another curious thing yet," went on old Jacob, presently, "is that some of the people looking on declared that, as well as seeing the net as I have just told you, when the boat foundered, they saw one of the men get ashore on the lower rocks of the Leopard's Head, and that he was seen standing there and waving his arms till night quite hid him."

"But could not they get him off?"

"No; no boat durst go near the place in such a sea."

"And next morning?"

"The next morning he was gone, been carried away again, if so be as he had ever been seen there at all—though I make no doubt he had."

"And the girl? What became of her?"

"Ah! that's the most curiousest part of it all," said the seaman, growing graver and graver and slower and slower in his utterances; "more curious than anything I've told you yet, Sir; and this I've seen myself, too, many times before I came away to sea. Poor Alice Dournelle took on terribly when she knew her lover was drownded; for she gave the preference, it was said, to Raymond Sass. Howsomever, a couple of years afterwards she died, in a kind o' decline, like; and she's the phantom of Porth Guerron Cove."

"What? haunts the place, I suppose?" I said, smiling.

"Yes; but you needn't laugh, Sir. This is a fact. I tell you I've seen her more than a score of times; and I do hear she may be seen even now, specially in September—about the anniversary, as you may say."

"Well, what does one see? What did you see?"

"Why, I've seen her standing in the dusk on the rocks of the

Leopard, all lighted up by the phosphorus, just as if she had come out of the sea, as we saw the net that night. Well, I've seen her just so. I remember her by sight, when she was alive, quite well, and I've seen her looking just as she did then, only all lighted up, as I say. Lots of the Porth Guerron folk have seen her; and they'll tell you so if you ever go there. My poor brother can always see her. He has a kind of gift that way. Like enough, you'd see her yourself."

"And what does she do?"

"Oh! do? Why, she seems to come out of the sea, as I tell you, and stand on the rocks, and then she'll go up higher and higher. Not seeming to clamber, but as if she was going up and up, as a spirit would, don't you know—floating like: rising, rising, till she reaches the flattish top of the Leopard's Head, and there she'll stay for hours passing to and fro, breaming with the light all the time."

"Why, then, she makes a sort of lighthouse," I said, still smiling; "a very useful phantom, truly."

"'Tain't no good for you to laugh, Sir," continued Jacob, yet more seriously, evidently not relishing my scepticism. "I tell you I've seen her over and over again, as you may if you ever goes to Porth Guerron."

And now I was at Porth Guerron; and now, as I have said, the old salt's story came back to my mind with a renewal of the interest it had originally created. The vexed question of how far we are permitted to have contact with the vast unseen has never ceased to interest me since my visit to the States, but a subsequent deep immersion in the stern realities of life had left me no opportunities for pursuing the subject. Here, however, was one at hand unexpectedly put before me; and, although I had attributed Jacob Sellar's strong belief to the natural superstition of the Cornish people, there was, nevertheless, an earnestness in his manner, and an intelligence peeping out beneath his uncultured speech, which forbade one to disregard it; and since, for the present, I was a wanderer and my time all my own, some of it I determined should be spent upon the scene of the mystery. I have given but the barest outline of my talk with Sellar. It was resumed over and over again, and it elicited so many circumstantial details, that, if they were not the result of a too fervid imagination, the phantom of Porth Guerron Cove was a manifestation equal to anything I had ever heard of, and well worth investigating.

Snug quarters at the little inn were readily obtained, and in the course of two or three days I had scraped acquaintance with many of the hearty, honest, kindly natives, including Jacob's brother, old Isaac Sellar, the poor chap who had been "kind o' cracky like" ever since that fatal time when he nearly lost his life in the Leopard's Grip. He was quite a feature of the place, much respected by his fellow-villagers, and not at all incapable of work. But I was told he had periodical fits of abstraction and wandering, which seemed to lift him quite above the world, and gave him a dazed and incoherent manner; otherwise, he was a strong, fine-looking man with a long grey beard, and with quite the air of a prophet and seer, as he professed himself to be. He was also a preacher at times, when the spirit moved him; and though undoubtedly "kind o' cracky," he was by no means bereft of intelligence.

All the fisher-folk were ready to talk about the phantom, and to believe in it; but I found very few after all, besides poor crazy Isaac, who admitted having seen it. In his garrulous, half-witted way, however, he was very strong on the point, throwing into it a sort of religious fervour, and they said it was the only one on which he was thoroughly sane. He confirmed many of the details given me by his brother. To wit, the spirit of Alice Dournelle was only to be seen by ordinary folk in the gloaming, and then only under conditions of tide and weather similar to those which had prevailed when her lover lost his life, now thirty years ago. About the anniversary, too, she was more frequently visible than at any other time. But he (Isaac Sellar) could see her almost whenever he liked, he said, because he had faith, and could see farther into things than most folk. He had been a dreamer and a seer all his life, he avowed; he saw many strange things, of which other people had no idea, but sometimes, when they would believe him, he could make them see strange things too. In fact, from his own account of himself, Isaac Sellar would have been considered a first-rate medium in America—he seemed endowed with all the qualifications. In answer to my inquiry if he thought he could make me see Alice Dournelle, he said he thought he could.

"I doubt not but ye will see her yourself," he added, after looking at me in an odd, vacant, yet penetrating manner; "ye have the eye of belief, the face of a believer. It all depends on faith, as the Scripture tells us—faith in something just beyond what ye can touch and lay hold of. If ye'll walk in the right way, Sir, ye'll have the gift vouchsafed ye."

After a pause, during which he removed his eyes from mine, and seemed to gaze into space, he continued fervently, "Ah! sweet Alice! I knew her when I was a child. She loved the lad Raymond truly. I knew that all along; he had no need to have told me. And now, she never leaves him, never strays far from him—as in life so in death."

"You mean," I said, "that her spirit never strays far from the place where he was drowned?"

"That is my meaning," answered Isaac; "she dwells with the sea-birds among the rocks of the Leopard's Head, and sometimes, with them, dives deep beneath the treacherous waters which encircle it; dives deep, I believe, to where he lies many a fathom down. Then when she comes up she breams with light, and waves her arms, often beckoning and pointing, and in the dusk, or by night, she will be visible even to some of those without faith: even the fool who hath said in his heart 'there is no God,' may see her then. But I—I can see her in all lights, at all times, as plainly as the birds with whom she skims and flies around the Head. Sometimes, too, I hear her voice mingling with their notes. Faint but clear it comes to me—a painful wailing cry that the unbeliever will tell you is naught but that of the kitty-wake and sea gulls; but I know the difference, though she speaks no word. Surely to-morrow will be, of all days, the day to look for her presence. Thirty years will then have come and gone to the very hour at nightfall when Raymond died. Early and late she will be there, and as the dawn creeps into the air ye shall see her if ye'll come and bide by me."

You will think me as crazy as poor Isaac himself, when I say that I listened with deep interest to these half mystic, half prophetic, but most earnestly delivered utterances. But we have all a crazy side to our characters (politely called a weakness), and I am bound to repeat that what I had seen in the States had vastly

developed this my weakness, and had left the truth of spiritualism quite a moot point in my mind. To me there was as much
reason in this man's pretensions to hold commune with the
spirits of the departed as any of the mediums with whom I had
come in contact; albeit he knew little of the ways in which such
powers were used. Why, then, should I not place myself in his
mediumistic hands, and see if he could put me *en rapport* with
this troubled spirit from the "vasty deep," after the manner of
some of my late American experiences? I determined to do so,
and it was arranged that I should meet him the following morning, between five and six, on that part of the shore commanding
the nearest view of the haunted rock.

Verily a wild-goose chase it might have appeared even to the
fisher-folk of Porth Guerron, had they known our purpose when
the few early movers among them saw us meet at the foot of
the village, and stroll away along the lonely shore in the semi-
darkness of that chill, grey, misty morning.

A perfect calm prevailed—but heavy banks of dense sea-fog
hung about the headlands, now shrouding and now slightly
revealing their gloomy masses. At first the Leopard stood
out gaunt and huge against the grey surroundings, but as we
approached it became more and more obscure. The tardy dawn
just gave enough light to indicate our whereabouts, lending a
most weird aspect to the scene. When we had gone about half
a mile round the western arm of the bay, Isaac, who kept in
advance of me, and scarcely ever spoke, suddenly stopped, and,
stretching back a hand, whispered—

"Hold on, Sir—I saw her but now—take my hand and turn
your eyes due west. See where she hovers with the sea-birds
round the Leopard's base!"

I gazed eagerly in the direction indicated, and faintly beheld
a form, which for one moment certainly did look like that of a
woman clothed in silver light, rising out of the sea, but in another,
like nothing but that of a fantastic wreath of mist. It was gone as
rapidly as it had appeared—as rapidly as though it had been but
the flashing whiteness from the outstretched pinions of the birds
that by myriads soared and swooped through the heavy folds of
the fog—gone as though it had been but a passing fancy, an ocular

illusion, momentary, vague, and unsubstantial as the misty air itself.

"Ye saw her, Sir, I doubt not," then went on my guide. "Silence, patience, and faith, and ye shall see her again."

We had reached the utmost limits of the shingly shore, where the frowning cliffs at the western horn of the cove stretched precipitously into the sea and stopped farther progress. Fifty yards beyond this barrier began the sandy causeway connecting the mainland with the Leopard. But had the tide been out even we could not have seen it from our position; and the Leopard, when the fog lifted a little, lay before us completely isolated. Nothing in nature could well have looked more weird and ghostly than did the scene, or more in harmony with our purpose. The day was breaking languidly, and still shedding but the faintest, palest light, whilst the restless fog-banks, swirling to and fro, might have been likened to giant spectres as they swept across the oily ocean, or clung to the towering cliffs in strange, fantastic forms. An intense chill was in the air, which was greatly increased when, every now and then, the grey mist enveloped us in its ghostly folds, shutting out everything beyond an arm's length, and seeming to cut us off from the world of fact and light.

During one of the densest of these visitations, I felt the rough, broad palm of Isaac close tightly on mine; and through a gap which suddenly appeared in the obscurity surrounding us I once more saw the female form in strong relief against the dark crags of the Leopard. Now there was no mistake about it. Bathed in the same translucent light, there it plainly was, floating in mid-air, as one has seen angels represented in pictures, and slowly waving one arm, half-beckoning and pointing upwards. Say it was some three hundred yards distant across the water—say that it was still vague and vapour-like, semi-transparent in parts, as the fog itself—say that I was out of my mind, or in a dream, or unduly acted on by those Transatlantic experiences and the imaginings arising therefrom, which old Isaac had rekindled: say all this, if you please; but I say distinctly that with these eyes I saw a woman's form, palpable, unmistakable, floating upwards across the face of the cliff, pointing and beckoning. The features at such a distance, of course, could not be discerned—nor do I say that I could see any details. All was merged into the unsubstantial substance—if I may use the paradox—of silvery light; but the form and action were distinct. For two minutes or more, it may have been, the vision was so far clearly before me; nor did it dissolve into the mist, of which, I admit, it seemed composed, until the figure reached, in its slow ascent, the topmost verge of the isolated crag. Then the fog again shut it all out, and for a while held us in its weird gloom. But soon after this it lifted, a soft breeze sprang up, and the cheering rays of the morning sun restored us to warmth and reality.

Beyond a momentary look of triumph which shot from old Isaac's lack-lustre eyes as he turned them on me, little or nothing passed between us as we retraced our steps, and I had full time to cogitate over this strange experience. At length I said, as we got back among the boats,

"How long is it since the Leopard was explored?" Isaac shook his head, as he answered,

"It never was explored; no one can land there—no one ever goes nearer to it than we have been. If they did, the iron net which the evil spirit of the place stretches across the channel, and which cost Raymond his life, and made my wits to wander, would wind itself round and strangle the life out of those who should dare to brave the dangers of the crag."

"But I am told," said I, "one could manage to land there, when the sand is exposed, at very low tide."

"Aye, but you would not bide there long—the net would be shot over you as surely as fate."

"There are spring tides now, I think," I went on; "when will the sand be clearest?"

"At this evening's ebb; it was nearly clear this morning when we were first there. This evening the tide will run out farther, and be dead low water somewhere nigh to five o'clock."

"Then," said I, decidedly, "if the sea holds smooth I'll land there myself, and have a closer look at the place where this troubled spirit wanders."

This determination was the result of my cogitation, for, notwithstanding what I had seen, I had no dread of, nor belief in the existence of this direful net—that part of the story was, doubt-

less, founded on some antique myth, as old as the crag itself. If I
understood spiritual manifestations aright, they always pointed
to a purpose, and it is nothing but man's own wilful blindness and
scepticism which hides from him their end and aim, and leads
him in his arrogance to ask, "What is their use; what good ever
comes from these departed souls 'revisiting the glimpses of the
moon,' and by sights, signs, or sounds, holding converse with us
of the visible world?"

Isaac's face was something to see as I announced my resolve,
and, in spite of all persuasion and argument, he entirely refused
to accompany me on the expedition. He declared his conviction
that I should never return alive, and that I should find no one in
Porth Guerron who would go with me, adding—

"I doubt whether they'll even lend ye a boat, if they know your
bent."

I was so fully determined, however, that by an hour before low
water that evening I had hired the lightest row-boat in the place,
and, keeping my object to myself, was afloat in the bay under
pretext of simple amusement. Old Isaac reluctantly promised to
say nothing of my intention, and, though doing all he could to
dissuade me, helped me to push the boat off from the beach. As
I pulled out, I saw his tall, gaunt figure passing along the shore
towards the point we had occupied in the morning.

It was a lovely, soft, windless, autumn evening, as the sun sank,
towards the west, and, keeping my eye upon the tide, I had lazily
pulled to within twenty boats' length of the sandy ridge when the
thin line of rippling breakers marking its position faded away and
left it bare. Then I gave way lustily, and in a few minutes the boat's
nose ran softly up on to the sand just below the spur of the fatal
crag. Springing ashore, I made her fast by the grapnel I had ready
in her bows. An athlete, and a fairish cragsman, I soon managed
to scale the lower declivities, and before long I had clambered
well-nigh to the top of the Leopard's Head. I will not stop to
describe the wild beauty of the scene stretching around me, nor
do more than hint at the strange undercurrent of feeling which
had prompted me to make this exploration; but a conviction had
taken root in my mind that I might by it gain some clue to the
purpose of the manifestation I had witnessed—a conviction, as

I have said, that there had been an object in it, and that I might trace this object out. Thus I began examining and surveying every rift and fissure, cleft, and ledge of this wild storm-beaten islet; this hitherto undisputed home of the sea-birds, which, astounded by my audacity, at first seemed so reluctant to move that I might almost have captured many with my hands. But at length the whole colony was on the wing—swirling, swooping, hovering, until the air was darkened with them as by a cloud, and their shrill, piping, and discordant notes nearly deafened me.

Half an hour passed, and by the time I had wandered wherever foothold was possible, all over and around the top of the plateau, twilight was setting in. I was descending by the way I had come, and had got a short distance down, when, upon a rocky shelf just below a strangely beetling crag, my eye fell upon an object which startled me, and instantly riveted my attention. Getting close to the edge of the overhanging rock the better to look down upon this discovery, I all but lost my footing through the shock which the spectacle then gave me, for there, partially coiled under shelter of the projecting cliff, lay a human skeleton, bleached and mouldering, with the face of the skull turned upwards to the sky—the hollow sockets of the eyes seeming to meet mine with a horrible, imploring expression. When the amazement caused by this ghastly sight a little subsided, I began to realise the fact that in it perhaps lay the very clue I was looking for! How had the unhappy being whose remains lay thus exposed before me come there? Instantly I thought of Raymond Sass, and the account Jacob Sellar had given me of either he or his companion being seen clinging to the rocks when their boat foundered in the Leopard's Grip, just thirty years ago this very night! If these bleaching bones were indeed those of the hapless fisherman, and it seemed the likely solution, had I not discovered the purpose for which the restless spirit of Alice Dournelle had ever since haunted this wild and supposedly inaccessible rock?

Well! not to prolong my tale, I got back to my boat, and as soon as it touched the shore of the cove, without waiting to answer the questions with which I was assailed, I hastened straight away to the vicarage, and communicated my discovery to the incumbent of the square-towered, tiny church at the head of the village. He was a pompous, unsociable man, whom I had rather avoided, and, although at first he seemed to entirely discredit my statement—for, unwisely, I told him how I had been led to visit the Leopard—I convinced him of its truth.

In the end, he took such steps as led to the interment in the churchyard, by the grave of Alice Dournelle, of the remains of poor Raymond Sass. That they were his there could be no doubt, inasmuch as, lying with them besides the remains of some other slowly perishable trifles, such as a tobacco-box, knife, &c., there was found a little trinket in the shape of a heart. On it was engraved his name, and that of Alice, the donor, and he had evidently worn it round his neck by the little chain to which it was attached.

One word more about Isaac Sellar and my fisher friends. Although I had, for a few of them, dispelled the fable of the iron net and had shown that access to the rock was easy, and without danger, he entirely refused to make one of the small party who were at length persuaded to accompany me on a second visit, to assist in the removal of all that was left of their lost comrade.

And as to the phantom? Well; it has never appeared again. Even Isaac Sellar, whom I had a talk with only last autumn, has never seen it, though three years have passed since I cleared up the mystery by restoring to rest and peace the erewhile troubled spirit of Alice Dournelle—for that I did this by procuring for her lover Christian burial I have no manner of doubt.

My experiences at Porth Guerron have finally determined my wavering belief in the truth of spiritual manifestations. I can no longer doubt that they have their object, and that they have a real existence for those whose minds are rightly attuned, and who can, as Isaac put it, have "faith in something just beyond what ye can touch and lay hold of."

# Margaret Oliphant

# THE LADY'S WALK

## A STORY OF THE SEEN AND UNSEEN

MARGARET OLIPHANT (1828-1897), *a Scottish writer, creates in this story a West Highland shrine to the "sister-mother," a hearth goddess tied to the house more tightly than any earth-bound ghost. Oliphant's narrator aptly recognizes that the country house existence may appear blissful, but shadows lurk beneath the mask of paradise. Oliphant's stories of the uncanny were particularly capable of revealing the fissures in seemingly stable façades: "More so than their male counterparts, female authors increasingly turned to the ghost story as a way to critique the economic problems in both the impoverished streets and wealthy ancestral homes of England, as well as to shine a light on the emotional grievances existing behind closed doors."[1] This story first appeared in two parts in* Longman's Magazine *in December 1882 and January 1883.*

## CHAPTER I

I WAS ON A VISIT TO SOME PEOPLE IN SCOTLAND when the events I am about to relate took place. They were not friends in the sense of long or habitual intercourse; in short, I had met them only in Switzerland in the previous year; but we saw a great deal of each other while we were together, and got into that cosy intimacy which travelling brings about more readily than anything else. We had seen each other in very great *déshabillé* both of mind and array in the chilly mornings after a night's travelling, which perhaps is the severest test that can be applied in respect to looks; and amid all the annoyances of journeys short and

---

1 Melissa Edmundson, "The 'Uncomfortable Houses' of Charlotte Riddell and Margaret Oliphant". *Gothic Studies* 12:1 (2010): 61-67.

long, with the usual episodes of lost luggage, indifferent hotels, fusses of every description, which is an equally severe test for the temper; and our friendship and liking (I am at liberty to suppose it was mutual, or they would never have invited me to Ellermore) remained unimpaired. I have always thought, and still think, that Charlotte Campbell was one of the most charming young women I ever met with; and her brothers, if not so entirely delightful, were nice fellows, capital to travel with, full of fun and spirit. I understood immediately from their conversation that they were members of a large family. Their allusions to Tom and Jack and little Harry, and the children in the nursery, might perhaps have been tedious to a harsher critic; but I like to hear of other people's relations, having scarcely any of my own. I found out by degrees that Miss Campbell had been taken abroad by her brothers to recover from a long and severe task of nursing, which had exhausted her strength. The little ones had all been down with scarlet fever, and she had not left them night or day. "She gave up seeing the rest of us and regularly shut herself in," Charley informed me, who was the younger of the two. "She would only go out for her walk when all of us were out of the way. That was the worst of it," the young fellow said, with great simplicity. That his sister should give herself up to the nursing was nothing remarkable; but that she should deny herself their precious company was a heroism that went to her brothers' hearts. Thus, by the way, I learned a great deal about the family. Chatty, as they called her, was the sister-mother, especially of the little ones, who had been left almost in her sole charge since their mother died many years before. She was not a girl, strictly speaking. She was in the perfection of her womanhood and youth—about eight-and-twenty, the age when something of the composure of maturity has lighted upon the sweetness of the earlier years, and being so old enhances all the charm of being so young. It is chiefly among young married women that one sees this gracious and beautiful type, delightful to every sense and every require-ment of the mind; but when it is to be met with unmarried it is more celestial still. I cannot but think with reverence that this delicate maternity and maidenhood—the perfect bounty of the one, the undisturbed grace of the other—has been the foundation of that adoring devotion which in the old days brought so many saints to the shrine of the Virgin Mother. But why I should thus enlarge upon Charlotte Campbell at the beginning of this story I can scarcely tell, for she is not in the strict sense of the word the heroine of it, and I am unintentionally deceiving the reader to begin.

They asked me to come and see them at Ellermore when we parted, and, as I have nothing in the way of a home warmer or more genial than chambers in the Temple, I accepted, as may be supposed, with enthusiasm. It was in the first week of June that we parted, and I was invited for the end of August. They had "plenty of grouse," Charley said, with a liberality of expression which was pleasant to hear. Charlotte added, "But you must be prepared for a homely life, Mr. Temple, and a very quiet one." I replied, of course, that if I had chosen what I liked best in the world it would have been this combination: at which she smiled with an amused little shake of her head. It did not seem to occur to her that she herself told for much in the matter. What they all insisted upon was the "plenty of grouse;" and I do not pretend to say that I was indifferent to that.

Colin, the eldest son, was the one with whom I had been least familiar. He was what people call reserved. He did not talk of everything as the others did. I did not indeed find out till much later that he was constantly in London, coming and going, so that he and I might have seen much of each other. Yet he liked me well enough. He joined warmly in his brother's invitation. When Charley said there was plenty of grouse, he added with the utmost friendliness, "And ye may get a blaze at a stag." There was a flavour of the North in the speech of all; not disclosed by mere words, but by an occasional diversity of idiom and change of pronunciation. They were conscious of this and rather proud of it than otherwise. They did not say Scotch, but Scots; and their accent could not be represented by any of the travesties of the theatre, or what we conventionally accept as the national utterance. When I attempted to pronounce after them, my own ear informed me what a travesty it was.

It was to the family represented by these young people that I was going when I started on August 20, a blazing summer day, with dust and heat enough to merit the name of summer if anything ever did. But when I arrived at my journey's end there was just change enough to mark the line between summer and autumn: a little golden haze in the air, a purple bloom of heather on the hills, a touch here and there upon a stray branch, very few, yet enough to swear by. Ellermore lay in the heart of a beautiful district full of mountains and lochs, within the Highland line, and just on the verge of some of the wildest mountain scenery in Scotland. It was situated in the midst of an amphitheatre of hills, not of any very exalted height, but of the most picturesque form, with peaks and couloirs like an Alpine range in little, all glowing with the purple blaze of the heather, with gleams upon them that looked like snow, but were in reality water, white threads of mountain torrents. In front of the house was a small loch embosomed in the hills, from one end of which ran a cheerful little stream, much intercepted by boulders, and much the brighter for the interruptions, which meandered through the glen and fell into another loch of greater grandeur and pretensions. Ellermore itself was a comparatively new house, built upon a fine slope of lawn over the lake, and sheltered by fine trees—great beeches which would not have done discredit to Berkshire, though that is not what we expect to see in Scotland: besides the ashes and firs which we are ready to acknowledge as of northern growth. I was not prepared for the luxuriance of the West Highlands—the mantling green of ferns and herbage everywhere, not to say the wealth of flowers, which formed a centre of still more brilliant colour and cultivation amid all the purple of the hills. Everything was soft and rich and warm about the Highland mansion-house, I had expected stern scenery and a grey atmosphere. I found an almost excessive luxuriance of vegetation and colour everywhere. The father of my friends received me at a door which was constantly open, and where it seemed to me after a while that nobody was ever refused admission. He was a tall old man, dignified but homely, with white hair and moustache and the fresh colour of a rural patriarch, which, however, he was not, but an energetic man of business, as I afterwards found. The Campbells of Ellermore were not great chiefs in that much-extended clan, but they were perfectly well known people and had held their little estate from remote antiquity. But they had not stood upon their gentility, or refused to avail themselves of the opportunities that came in their way. I have observed that in the great and wealthy region of which Glasgow is the capital the number of the irreconcilables who stand out against trade is few. The gentry have seen all the advantages of combining commerce with tradition. Had it not been for this it is likely that Ellermore would have been a very different place. Now it was overflowing with all those signs of ease and simple luxury which make life so smooth. There was little show, but there was a profusion of comfort. Everything rolled upon velvet. It was perhaps more like the house of a rich merchant than of a family of long descent. Nothing could be more perfect as a pleasure estate than was this little Highland property. They had "plenty of grouse," and also of trout in a succession of little lochs and mountain streams. They had deer on the hills. They had their own mutton, and everything vegetable that was needed for the large profuse household, from potatoes and cabbage up to grapes and peaches. But with all this primitive wealth there was not much money got out of Ellermore. The "works" in Glasgow supplied that. What the works were I have never exactly found out, but they afforded occupation for all the family, both father and sons; and that the results were of the most pleasing description as regarded Mr. Campbell's banker it was easy to see.

They were all at home with the exception of Colin, the eldest son, for whose absence many apologies, some of which seemed much more elaborate than were at all necessary, were made to me. I was for my own part quite indifferent to the absence of Colin. He was not the one who had interested me most; and though Charley was considerably younger than myself, I had liked him better from the first. Tom and Jack were still younger. They were all occupied at "the works," and came home only from Saturday to Monday. The little trio in the nursery were delightful children. To see them gathered about Charlotte was enough to melt any heart. Chatty they called her, which is not a very dignified name, but I got to think it the most beautiful in the world as it sounded all over that cheerful, much-populated house. "Where is Chatty?" was the first question everyone asked as he came in at the door. If she was not immediately found it went volleying through the house, all up the stairs and through the passages— "Chatty! where are you?"—and was always answered from somewhere or other in a full soft voice, which was audible everywhere though it never was loud. "Here am I, boys," she would say, with a pretty inversion which pleased me. Indeed, everything pleased me in Chatty—too much, more than reason. I found myself thinking what would become of them all if, for example, she were to marry, and entered into a hot argument with myself on one occasion by way of proving that it would be the most selfish thing in the world were this family to work upon Chatty's feelings and prevent her from marrying, as most probably, I could not help feeling, they would. At the same time I perceived with a little shudder how entirely the whole thing would collapse if by any chance Chatty should be decoyed away.

I enjoyed my stay beyond description. In the morning we were out on the hills or about the country. In the evening it very often happened that we all strolled out after dinner, and that I was left by Chatty's side, "the boys" having a thousand objects of interest, while Mr. Campbell usually sat in his library and read the newspapers, which arrived at that time either by the coach from Oban or by the boat. In this way I went over the whole "policy," as the grounds surrounding a country house are called in Scotland, with Chatty, who would not be out of reach at this hour, lest her father should want her, or the children. She would bid me not to stay with her when no doubt it would be more amusing for me to go with the boys; and when I assured her my pleasure was far greater as it was, she gave me a gracious, frank smile, with a little shake of her head. She laughed at me softly, bidding me not to be too polite or think she would mind if I left her; but I think, on the whole, she liked to have me with her in her evening walk.

"There is one thing you have not told me of," I said, "and that you must possess. I cannot believe that your family has been settled here so long without having a ghost."

She had turned round to look at me, to know what it was that had been omitted in her descriptions. When she heard what it was she smiled a little, but not with the pleasant mockery I had expected. On the contrary, it was a sort of gentle smile of recognition that something had been left out.

"We don't call it a ghost," she said. "I have wondered if you had never noticed. I am fond of it for my part; but then I have been used to it all my life. And here we are, then," she added as we reached the top of a little ascent and came out upon a raised avenue, which I had known by its name of the Lady's Walk without as yet getting any explanation what that meant. It must have been, I supposed, the avenue to the old house, and now encircled one portion of the grounds without any distinct meaning. On the side nearest the gardens and house it was but slightly raised above the shrubberies, but on the other side was the summit of a high bank sloping steeply to the river, which, after it escaped from the loch, made a wide bend round that portion of the grounds. A row of really grand beeches rose on each side of the path, and through the openings in the trees the house, the bright gardens, the silvery gleam of the loch were visible. The evening sun was slanting into our eyes as we walked along; a little soft yet brisk air was pattering among the leaves, and here and there a yellow cluster in the middle of a branch showing the first touch of a cheerful decay. "Here we are, then." It was a curious phrase; but there are some odd idioms in the Scotch—I mean Scots'—form of our common language, and I had become accustomed now to accept them without remark.

"I suppose," I said, "there must be some back way to the village or to the farm house under this bank, though there seems no room for a path?"

"Why do you ask?" she said, looking at me with a smile.

"Because I always hear some one passing along—I imagine down there. The steps are very distinct. Don't you hear them now? It has puzzled me a good deal, for I cannot make out where the path can be."

She smiled again, with a meaning in her smile, and looked at me steadily, listening, as I was. And then, after a pause, she said, "That is what you were asking for. If we did not hear it, it would make us unhappy. Did you not know why this was called the Lady's Walk?'

When she said these words I was conscious of an odd enough

change in my sensations—nay, I should say in my very sense of hearing, which was the one appealed to. I had heard the sound often, and, after looking back at first to see who it was and seeing no one, had made up my mind that the steps were on some unseen bye-way and heard them accordingly, feeling quite sure that the sound came from below. Now my hearing changed, and I could not understand how I had ever thought anything else: the steps were on a level with us, by our side—as if some third person were accompanying us along the avenue. I am no believer in ghosts, nor the least superstitious, so far as I had ever been aware (more than everybody is), but I felt myself get out of the way with some celerity and a certain thrill of curious sensation. The idea of rubbing shoulders with something unseen startled me in spite of myself.

"Ah!" said Charlotte, "it gives you an—unpleasant feeling. I forgot you are not used to it like me."

"I am tolerably well used to it, for I have heard it often," I said, somewhat ashamed of my involuntary movement. Then I laughed, which I felt to be altogether out of place and fictitious, and said, "No doubt there is some very easy explanation of it— some vibration or echo. The science of acoustics clears up many mysteries."

"There is no explanation," Chatty said, almost angrily. "She has walked here far longer than anyone can remember. It is an ill sign for us Campbells when she goes away. She was the eldest daughter, like me; and I think she has got to be our guardian angel. There is no harm going to happen as long as she is here. Listen to her," she cried, standing still with her hand raised. The low sun shone full on her, catching her brown hair, the lucid clearness of her brown eyes, her cheeks so clear and soft, in colour a little summer-brown, too. I stood and listened with a something of excited feeling which I could not control: the sound of this third person, whose steps were not to be mistaken though she was unseen, made my heart beat: if, indeed, it was not merely the presence of my companion, who was sweet enough to account for any man's emotion.

"You are startled," she said with a smile.

"Well! I should not be acting my part, should I, as I ought, if I did not feel the proper thrill? It must be disrespectful to a ghost not to be afraid."

"Don't say a ghost," said Chatty; "I think *that* is disrespectful. It is the Lady of Ellermore; everybody knows about her. And do you know," she added, "when my mother died—the greatest grief I have ever known—the steps ceased? Oh! it is true! You need not look me in the face as if there was anything to laugh at. It is ten years ago, and I was only a silly sort of girl, not much good to anyone. They sent me out to get the air when she was lying in a doze; and I came here. I was crying, as you may suppose, and at first I did not pay any attention. Then it struck me all at once—the Lady was away. They told me afterwards that was the worst sign. It is always death that is coming when she goes away."

The pathos of this incident confused all my attempts to touch it with levity, and we went on for a little without speaking, during which time it is almost unnecessary to say that I was listening with all my might to those strange footsteps, which finally I persuaded myself were no more than echoes of our own.

"It is very curious," I said politely. "Of course you were greatly agitated and too much absorbed in real grief to have any time to think of the other: and there might be something in the state of the atmosphere——"

She gave me an indignant look. We were nearly at the end of the walk; and at that moment I could have sworn that the footsteps, which had got a little in advance, here turned and met us going back. I am aware that nothing could sound more foolish, and that it must have been some vibration or atmospheric phenomenon. But yet this was how it seemed—not an optical but an aural delusion. So long as the steps were going with us it was less impossible to account for it; but when they turned and audibly came back to meet us! Not all my scepticism could prevent me from stepping aside to let them pass. This time they came directly between us, and the naturalness of my withdrawal out of the way was more significant than the faltering laugh with which I excused myself. "It is a very curious sound indeed," I said with a tremor which slightly affected my voice.

Chatty gave me a reassuring smile. She did not laugh at me,

which was consolatory. She stood for a moment as if looking after the visionary passenger. "We are not afraid," she said, "even the youngest; we all know she is our friend."

When we had got back to the side of the loch, where, I confess, I was pleased to find myself, in the free open air without any perplexing shadow of trees, I felt less objection to the subject. "I wish you would tell me the story; for of course there is a story," I said.

"No, there is no story—at least nothing tragical or even romantic. They say she was the eldest daughter. I sometimes wonder," Chatty said with a smile and a faint increase of colour, "whether she might not be a little like me. She lived here all her life, and had several generations to take care of. Oh no, there was no murder or wrong about our Lady; she just loved Ellermore above everything; but my idea is that she has been allowed the care of us ever since."

"That is very sweet, to have the care of you," I said, scarcely venturing to put any emphasis on the pronoun; "but, after all, it must be slow work, don't you think, walking up and down there for ever? I call that a poor sort of reward for a good woman. If she had been a bad one it might have answered very well for a punishment."

"Mr. Temple!" Chatty said, now reddening with indignation, "do you think it is a poor thing to have the care of your own people, to watch over them, whatever may happen—to be all for them and their service? I don't think so; I should like to have such a fate."

Perhaps I had spoken thus on purpose to bring about the discussion. "There is such a thing as being too devoted to your family. Are they ever grateful? They go away and marry and leave you in the lurch."

She looked up at me with a little astonishment. "The members may vary, but the family never goes away," she said; "besides, that can apply to us in our present situation only. *She* must have seen so many come and go; but that need not vex her, you know, because they go where she is."

"My dear Miss Campbell, wait a bit, think a little," I said: "where she is! That is in the Lady's Walk, according to your story. Let us hope that all your ancestors and relations are not there."

"I suppose you want to make me angry," said Chatty. "She is in heaven—have you any doubt of that?—but every day when the sun is setting she comes back home."

"Oh, come!" I said, "if it is only at the sunset that is not so bad."

Miss Campbell looked at me doubtfully, as if not knowing whether to be angry. "You want to make fun of it," she said, "to laugh at it; and yet," she added with a little spirit, "you were rather nervous half an hour ago."

"I acknowledge to being nervous. I am very impressionable. I believe that is the word. It is a luxury to be nervous at the fit moment. Frightened you might say, if you prefer plain speaking. And I am very glad it is at sunset, not in the dark. This completes the round of my Highland experiences," I said; "everything now is perfect. I have shot grouse on the hill and caught trout on the loch, and been soaked to the skin and then dried in the wind; I wanted nothing but the family ghost. And now I have seen her, or at least heard her——"

"If you are resolved to make a joke of it I cannot help it," said Chatty, "but I warn you that it is not agreeable to me, Mr. Temple. Let us talk of something else. In the Highlands," she said with dignity, "we take different views of many things."

"There are some things," I said, "of which but one view is possible—that I should have the audacity and impertinence to laugh at anything for which you have a veneration! I believe it is only because I was so frightened——"

She smiled again in her lovely motherly way, a smile of indulgence and forgiveness and bounty. "You are too humble now," she said, "and I think I hear some one calling me. It is time to go in."

And to be sure there was some one calling her: there always was, I think, at all hours of the night and day.

## CHAPTER II

To say that I got rid of the recollection of the Lady of Ellermore when I went upstairs after a cheerful evening through a long and slippery gallery to my room in the wing would be untrue. The curious experience I had just had dwelt in my mind with a feeling of not unpleasant perplexity. Of course, I said to myself, there must be something to account for those footsteps—some hidden way in which the sounds could come. Perhaps my first idea would turn out to be correct—that there was a bye-road to the farm, or to the stables, which in some states of the atmosphere—or perhaps it might even be always—echoed back the sounds of passing feet in some subterranean vibration. One has heard of such things; one has heard, indeed, of every kind of natural wonder, some of them no more easy to explain than the other kind of prodigy; but so long as you have science with you, whether you understand it or not, you are all right. I could not help wondering, however, whether, if by chance I heard those steps in the long gallery outside my door, I should refer the matter comfortably to the science of acoustics. I was tormented, until I fell asleep, by a vague expectation of hearing them. I could not get them out of my mind or out of my ears, so distinct were they—the light step, soft but with energy in it, evidently a woman's step. I could not help recollecting, with a tingling sensation through all my veins, the distinctness of the turn it gave—the coming back, the steps going in a line opposite to ours. It seemed to me that from moment to moment I must hear it again in the gallery, and then how could it be explained?

Next day—for I slept very well after I had succeeded in getting to sleep, and what I had heard did not by any means haunt my dreams—next day I managed to elude all the pleasant occupations of the house, and, as soon as I could get free from observation, I took my way to the Lady's Walk. I had said that I had letters to write—a well-worn phrase, which of course means exactly what one pleases. I walked up and down the Lady's Walk, and could neither hear nor see anything. On this side of the shrubbery there was no possibility of any concealed path; on the other side the bank went sloping to the water's edge. The avenue ran along from the corner of the loch half-way round the green plateau on which the house was planted, and at the upper end came out upon the elevated ground behind the house; but no road crossed it, nor was there the slightest appearance of any mode by which a steady sound not its own could be communicated here.

I examined it all with the utmost care, looking behind the bole
of every tree as if the secret might be there, and my heart gave
a leap when I perceived what seemed to me one narrow track
worn along the ground. Fancy plays us curious pranks even when
she is most on her guard. It was a strange idea that I, who had
come here with the purpose of finding a way of explaining the
curious phenomenon upon which so long and lasting a superstition had been built, should be so quickly infected by it. I saw the
little track, quite narrow but very distinct, and though of course
I did not believe in the Lady of Ellermore, yet within myself I
jumped at the certainty that this was her track. It gave me a curious sensation. The certainty lay underneath the scepticism as if
they were two things which had no connection with each other.
Had anyone seen me it must have been supposed that I was looking for something among the bushes, so closely did I scrutinise
every foot of the soil and every tree.

It exercised a fascination upon me which I could not resist.
The Psychical Society did not exist in those days, so far as I know,
but there are many minds outside that inquisitive body to whom
the authentication of a ghost story, or, to speak more practi-
cally, the clearing up of a superstition, is very attractive. I managed to elude the family arrangements once more at the same
hour at which Miss Campbell and I had visited the Lady's Walk
on the previous evening. It was a lovely evening, soft and warm,
the western sky all ablaze with colour, the great branches of the
beeches thrown out in dark maturity of greenness upon the flush
of orange and crimson melting into celestial rosy red as it rose
higher, and flinging itself in airy masses rose-tinted across the
serene blue above. The same wonderful colours glowed in reflection out of the loch. The air was of magical clearness, and earth
and sky seemed stilled with an almost awe of their own loveli-
ness, happiness, and peace.

> The holy time was quiet as a nun,
> Breathless with adoration.

For my part, however, I noticed this only in passing, being
intent on other thoughts. From the loch there came a soft tumult

of voices. It was Saturday evening, and all the boys were at home.
They were getting out the boats for an evening row, and the white
sail of the toy yacht rose upon the gleaming water like a little
white cloud among the rosy clouds of that resplendent sky. I
stood between two of the beeches that formed a sort of arch, and
looked out upon them, distracted for an instant by the pleasant
distant sound which came softly through the summer air. Next
moment I turned sharply round with a start, in spite of myself—
turned quickly to see who it was coming after me. There was, I
need not say, not a soul within sight. The beech leaves fluttered
softly in the warm air; the long shadows of their great boles lay
unbroken along the path; nothing else was visible, not even a
bird on a bough. I stood breathless between the two trees, with
my back turned to the loch, gazing at nothing, while the soft
footsteps came quietly on, and crossed me—passed me! with
a slight waft of air, I thought, such as a slight figure might have
made; but that was imagination perhaps. Imagination! was it not
all imagination? or what was it? No shadows or darkness to conceal a passing form by; full light of day radiant with colour; the
most living delightful air, all sweet with pleasure. I stood there
speechless and without power to move. They went along softly,
without changing the gentle regularity of the tread, to the end of
the walk, growing fainter as they went further and further from
me. I never listened so intently in my life. I said to myself, "If they
go out of hearing I shall know it is merely an excited imagination." And on they went, almost out of hearing, only the faintest
touch upon the ground; then there was a momentary pause, and
my heart stood still, but leaped again to my throat and sent wild
waves of throbbing to my ears next moment: they had turned
and were coming back.

I cannot describe the extraordinary effect. If it had been dark
it would have been altogether different. The brightness, the life
around, the absence of all that one associates with the supernatural, produced a thrill of emotion to which I can give no name. It
was not fear; yet my heart beat as it had never in any dangerous
emergency (and I have passed through some that were exciting enough) beat before. It was simple excitement, I suppose;
and in the commotion of my mind I instinctively changed the

pronoun which I had hitherto used, and asked myself, would *she* come back? She did, passing me once more, with the same movement of the air (or so I thought). But by that time my pulses were all clanging in my ears, and perhaps the sense itself became confused with listening. I turned and walked precipitately away, descending the little slope and losing myself in the shrubberies which were beneath the range of the low sun, now almost set, and felt dank and cold in the contrast. It was something like plunging into a bath of cold air after the warmth and glory above.

It was in this way that my first experience ended. Miss Campbell looked at me a little curiously with a half-smile when I joined the party at the lochside. She divined where I had been, and perhaps something of the agitation I felt, but she took no further notice; and as I was in time to find a place in the boat, where she had established herself with the children, I lost nothing by my meeting with the mysterious passenger in the Lady's Walk.

I did not go near the place for some days afterwards, but I cannot say that it was ever long out of my thoughts. I had long arguments with myself on the subject, representing to myself that I had heard the sound before hearing the superstition, and then had found no difficulty in believing that it was the sound of some passenger on an adjacent path, perhaps invisible from the Walk. I had not been able to find that path, but still it might exist at some angle which, according to the natural law of the transmission of sounds—Bah! what jargon this was! Had I not heard *her* turn, felt her pass me, watched her coming back? And then I paused with a loud burst of laughter at myself. "Ass! you never had any of these sensations before you heard the story," I said. And that was true; but I heard the steps before I heard the story; and, now I think of it, was much startled by them, and set my mind to work to account for them, as you know. "And what evidence have you that the first interpretation was not the right one?" myself asked me with scorn; upon which question I turned my back with a hopeless contempt of the pertinacity of that other person who has always so many objections to make. Interpretation! could any interpretation ever do away with the effect upon my actual senses of that invisible passer-by? But the most disagreeable effect was this, that I could not shut out from my mind the expectation of hearing those same steps in the gallery outside my door at night. It was a long gallery running the full length of the wing, highly polished and somewhat slippery, a place in which any sound was important. I never went along to my room without a feeling that at any moment I might hear those steps behind me, or after I had closed my door might be conscious of them passing. I never did so, but neither have I ever got free of the thought.

A few days after, however, another incident occurred that drove the Lady's Walk and its invisible visitor out of my mind. We were all returning home in the long northern twilight from a mountain expedition. How it was that I was the last to return I do not exactly recollect. I think Miss Campbell had forgotten to give some directions to the coachman's wife at the lodge, which I volunteered to carry for her. My nearest way back would have been through the Lady's Walk, had not some sort of doubtful feeling restrained me from taking it. Though I have said and felt that the effect of these mysterious footsteps was enhanced by the full daylight, still I had a sort of natural reluctance to put myself in the way of encountering them when the darkness began to fall. I preferred the shrubberies, though they were darker and less attractive. As I came out of their shade, however, some one whom I had never seen before—a lady—met me, coming apparently from the house. It was almost dark, and what little light there was was behind her, so that I could not distinguish her features. She was tall and slight, and wrapped apparently in a long cloak, a dress usual enough in those rainy regions. I think, too, that her veil was over her face. The way in which she approached made it apparent that she was going to speak to me, which surprised me a little, though there was nothing extraordinary in it, for of course by this time all the neighbourhood knew who I was and that I was a visitor at Ellermore. There was a little air of timidity and hesitation about her as she came forward, from which I supposed that my sudden appearance startled her a little, and yet was welcome as an unexpected way of getting something done that she wanted. *Tant de choses en un mot*, you will say—nay, without a word—and yet it was quite true. She came up to me quickly as soon as she had made up her mind. Her voice was very soft, but very peculiar, with a sort of far-away sound as if the veil or evening air interposed a visionary distance between her and me. "If you are a friend to the Campbells," she said, "will you tell them——" then paused a little and seemed to look at me with eyes that shone dimly through the shadows like stars in a misty sky.

"I am a warm friend to the Campbells; I am living there," I said.

"Will you tell them—the father and Charlotte—that Colin is in great trouble and temptation, and that if they would save him they should lose no time?"

"Colin!" I said, startled; then, after a moment, "Pardon me, this is an uncomfortable message to entrust to a stranger. Is he ill? I am very sorry, but don't let me make them anxious without reason. What is the matter? He was all right when they last heard——"

"It is not without reason," she said; "I must not say more. Tell them just this—in great trouble and temptation. They may perhaps save him yet if they lose no time."

"But stop," I said, for she seemed about to pass on. "If I am to say this there must be something more. May I ask who it is that sends the message? They will ask me, of course. And what is wrong?"

She seemed to wring her hands under her cloak, and looked at me with an attitude and gesture of supplication. "In great trouble," she said, "in great trouble! and tempted beyond his strength. And not such as I can help. Tell them, if you wish well to the Campbells. I must not say more."

And, notwithstanding all that I could say, she left me so, with a wave of her hand, disappearing among the dark bushes. It may be supposed that this was no agreeable charge to give to a guest, one who owed nothing but pleasure and kindness to the Campbells, but had no acquaintance beyond the surface with their concerns. They were, it is true, very free in speech, and seemed to have as little *dessous des cartes* in their life and affairs as could be imagined. But Colin was the one who was spoken of less freely than any other in the family. He had been expected several times since I came, but had never appeared. It seemed that he had a

way of postponing his arrival, and "of course," it was said in the
family, never came when he was expected. I had wondered more
than once at the testy tone in which the old gentleman spoke of
him sometimes, and the line of covert defence always adopted
by Charlotte. To be sure he was the eldest, and might naturally
assume a more entire independence of action than the other
young men, who were yet scarcely beyond the time of pupilage
and in their father's house.

But from this as well as from the still more natural and apparent reason that to bring them bad news of any kind was most
disagreeable and inappropriate on my part, the commission I
had so strangely received hung very heavily upon me. I turned it
over in my mind as I dressed for dinner (we had been out all day,
and dinner was much later than usual in consequence) with great
perplexity and distress. Was I bound to give a message forced
upon me in such a way? If the lady had news of any importance
to give, why did she turn away from the house, where she could
have communicated it at once, and confide it to a stranger? On
the other hand, should I be justified in keeping back anything
that might be of so much importance to them? It might perhaps
be something for which she did not wish to give her authority.
Sometimes people in such circumstances will even condescend to
write an anonymous letter to give the warning they think necessary, without betraying to the victims of misfortune that anyone
whom they know is acquainted with it. Here was a justification
for the strange step she had taken. It might be done in the utmost
kindness to them, if not to me; and what if there might be some
real danger afloat and Colin be in peril, as she said? I thought over
these things anxiously before I went downstairs, but even to the
moment of entering that bright and genial drawing-room, so
full of animated faces and cheerful talk, I had not made up my
mind what I should do. When we returned to it after dinner I was
still uncertain. It was late, and the children had been sent to bed.
The boys went round to the stables to see that the horses were
not the worse for their day's work. Mr. Campbell retired to his
library. For a little while I was left alone, a thing that very rarely
happened. Presently Miss Campbell came downstairs from the
children's rooms, with that air about her of rest and sweetness,

like a reflection of the little prayers she has been hearing and the infant repose which she has left, which hangs about a young mother when she has disposed her babies to sleep. Charlotte, by her right of being no mother, but only a voluntary mother by deputy, had a still more tender light about her in the sweetness of this duty which God and her goodwill, not simple nature, had put upon her. She came softly into the room with her shining countenance. "Are you alone, Mr. Temple?" she said with a little surprise. "How rude of those boys to leave you," and came and drew her chair towards the table where I was, in the kindness of her heart.

"I am very glad they have left me if I may have a little talk with you," I said; and then before I knew I had told her. She was the kind of woman to whom it is a relief to tell whatever may be on your heart. The fact that my commission was to her, had really less force with me in telling it, than the ease to myself. She, however, was very much surprised and disturbed. "Colin in trouble? Oh, that might very well be," she said, then stopped herself. "You are his friend," she said; "you will not misunderstand me, Mr. Temple. He is very independent, and not so open as the rest of us. That is nothing against him. We are all rather given to talking; we keep nothing to ourselves—except Colin. And then he is more away than the rest." The first necessity in her mind seemed to be this, of defending the absent. Then came the question, From whom could the warning be? Charley came in at this moment, and she called him to her eagerly. "Here is a very strange thing happened. Somebody came up to Mr. Temple in the shrubbery and told him to tell us that Colin was in trouble."

"Colin!" I could see that Charley was, as Charlotte had been, more distressed than surprised. "When did you hear from him last?" he said.

"On Monday; but the strange thing is, who could it be that sent such a message? You said a lady, Mr. Temple?"

"What like was she?" said Charley.

Then I described as well as I could. "She was tall and very slight; wrapped up in a cloak, so that I could not make out much, and her veil down. And it was almost dark."

"It is clear she did not want to be recognised," Charley said.

"There was something peculiar about her voice, but I really cannot describe it, a strange tone unlike anything——"

"Marion Gray has a peculiar voice; she is tall and slight. But what could she know about Colin?"

"I will tell you who is more likely," cried Charley, "and that is Susie Cameron. Her brother is in London now; they may have heard from him."

"Oh! Heaven forbid! oh! Heaven forbid! the Camerons of all people!" Charlotte cried, wringing her hands. The action struck me as so like that of the veiled stranger that it gave me a curious shock. I had not time to follow out the vague, strange suggestion that it seemed to breathe into my mind, but the sensation was as if I had suddenly, groping, come upon some one in the dark.

"Whoever it was," I said, "she was not indifferent, but full of concern and interest——"

"Susie would be that," Charley said, looking significantly at his sister, who rose from her chair in great distress.

"I would telegraph to him at once," she said, "but it is too late to-night."

"And what good would it do to telegraph? If he is in trouble it would be no help to him."

"But what can I do? what else can I do?" she cried. I had plunged them into sudden misery, and could only look on now as an anxious but helpless spectator, feeling at the same time as if I had intruded myself upon a family affliction: for it was evident that they were not at all unprepared for "trouble" to Colin. I felt my position very embarrassing, and rose to go away.

"I feel miserably guilty," I said, "as if I had been the bearer of bad news; but I am sure you will believe that I would not for any-thing in the world intrude upon——"

Charlotte paused to give me a pale sort of smile, and pointed to the chair I had left. "No, no," she said, "don't go away, Mr. Temple. We do not conceal from you that we are anxious—that we were anxious even before—but don't go away. I don't think I will tell my father, Charley. It would break his rest. Let him have his night's rest whatever happens; and there is nothing to be done to-night——"

"We will see what the post brings to-morrow," Charley said.

And then the consultation ended abruptly by the sudden entrance of the boys, bringing a gust of fresh night air with them. The horses were not a preen the worse though they had been out all day; even old grumbling Geordie, the coachman, had not a word to say. "You may have them again to-morrow, Chatty, if you like," said Tom. She had sat down to her work, and met their eyes with an unruffled countenance. "I hope I am not so unreasonable," she said with her tranquil looks; only I could see a little tremor in her hand as she stooped over the socks she was knitting. She laid down her work after a while, and went to the piano and played accompaniments, while first Jack and then Tom sang. She did it without any appearance of effort, yielding to all the wishes of the youngsters, while I looked on wondering, How can women do this sort of thing? It is more than one can divine.

Next morning Mr. Campbell asked "by the bye," but with a pucker in his forehead, which, being now enlightened on the subject, I could understand, if there was any letter from Colin? "No," Charlotte said (who for her part had turned over all her letters with a swift, anxious scrutiny). "But that is nothing," she said, "for we heard on Monday." The old gentleman uttered an "Umph!" of displeasure. "Tell him I think it a great want in manners that he is not here to receive Mr. Temple." "Oh, father, Mr. Temple understands," cried Charlotte; and she turned upon me those mild eyes, in which there was now a look that went to my heart, an appeal at once to my sympathy and my forbearance, bidding me not to ask, not to speak, yet to feel with her all the same. If she could have known the rush of answering feeling with which my heart replied! but I had to be careful not even to *look* too much knowledge, too much sympathy.

After this two days passed without any incident. What letters were sent, or other communications, to Colin I could not tell. They were great people for the telegraph and flashed messages about continually. There was a telegraph station in the little village, which had been very surprising to me at first, but I no longer wondered, seeing their perpetual use of it. People who have to do with business, with great "works" to manage, get into the way more easily than we others. But either no answer or nothing of a satisfactory character was obtained, for I was told no more.

The second evening was Sunday, and I was returning alone from a ramble down the glen. It was Mr. Campbell's custom to read a sermon on Sunday evenings to his household, and as I had, in conformity to the custom of the family, already heard two, I had deserted on this occasion, and chosen the freedom and quiet of a rural walk instead. It was a cloudy evening, and there had been rain. The clouds hung low on the hills, and half the surrounding peaks had retired altogether into the mist. I had scarcely set foot within the gates when I met once more the lady whose message had brought so much pain. The trees arched over the approach at this spot, and even in full daylight it was in deep shade. Now in the evening dimness it was dark as night. I could see little more than the slim straight figure, the sudden perception of which gave me—I could scarcely tell why—a curious thrill of something like fear. She came hurriedly towards me, an outline, nothing more, until the same peculiar voice, sweet but shrill, broke the silence. "Did you tell them?" she said.

It cost me an effort to reply calmly. My heart had begun to beat with an excitement over which I had no control, like a horse that takes fright at something which its rider cannot see. I said, "Yes, I told them," straining my eyes, yet feeling as if my faculties were restive like that same horse and would not obey me, would not look or examine her appearance as I desired. But indeed it would have been in vain, for it was too dark to see.

"But nothing has been done," she said. "Did they think I would come for nothing?" And there was again that movement, the same as I had seen in Charlotte, of wringing her hands.

"Pardon me," I said, "but if you will tell me who you are? I am a stranger here; no doubt if you would see Miss Campbell herself, or if she knew who it was——"

I felt the words somehow arrested in my throat, I could not tell why; and she drew back from me with a sudden movement. It is hard to characterise a gesture in the dark, but there seemed to be a motion of impatience and despair in it. "Tell them again Colin wants them. He is in sore trouble, trouble that is nigh death."

"I will carry your message; but for God's sake if it is so important tell me who sends it," I said.

She shook her head and went rapidly past me, notwithstanding the anxious appeals that I tried to make. She seemed to put out a hand to wave me back as I stood gazing after her. Just then the lodge door opened. I suppose the woman within had been disturbed by the sound of the voices, and a gleam of fire-light burst out upon the road. Across this gleam I saw the slight figure pass quickly, and then a capacious form with a white apron came out and stood in the door. The sight of the coachman's wife in her large and comfortable proportions gave me a certain ease, I cannot tell why. I hurried up to her. "Who was that that passed just now?" I asked.

"That passed just now? There was naebody passed. I thought I heard a voice, and that it was maybe Geordie; but nobody has passed here that I could see."

"Nonsense! you must have seen her," I cried hastily; "she cannot be out of sight yet. No doubt you would know who she was—a lady tall and slight—in a cloak——"

"Eh, sir, ye maun be joking," cried the woman. "What lady, if it werna Miss Charlotte, would be walking here at this time of the night? Lady! it might be, maybe, the schoolmaster's daughter. She has one of those ulsters like her betters. But nobody has passed here this hour back; o' that I'm confident," she said.

"Why did you come out, then, just at this moment?" I cried. The woman contemplated me in the gleam from the fire from top to toe. "You're the English gentleman that's biding up at the house?" she said. "'Deed, I just heard a step, that was nae doubt your step, and I thought it might be my man; but there has naebody, far less a lady, whatever she had on, passed my door coming or going. Is that you, Geordie?" she cried suddenly as a step became audible approaching the gate from the outer side.

"Ay, it's just me," responded her husband out of the gloom.

"Have ye met a lady as ye came along? The gentleman here will have it that there's been a lady passing the gate, and there's been no lady. I would have seen her through the window even if I hadna opened the door."

"I've seen no lady," said Geordie, letting himself in with considerable noise at the foot entrance, which I now remembered to have closed behind me when I passed through it a few minutes before. "I've met no person; it's no an hour for ladies to be about the roads on Sabbath day at e'en."

It was not till this moment that a strange fancy, which I will explain hereafter, darted into my mind. How it came I cannot tell. I was not the sort of man, I said to myself, for any such folly. My imagination had been a little touched, to be sure, by that curious affair of the footsteps; but this, which seemed to make my heart stand still and sent a shiver through me, was very different, and it was a folly not to be entertained for a moment. I stamped my foot upon it instantly, crushing it on the threshold of the mind. "Apparently either you or I must be mistaken," I said with a laugh at the high tone of Geordie, who himself had evidently been employed in a jovial way—quite consistent, according to all I had heard, with very fine principles in respect to the Sabbath. I had a laugh over this as I went away, insisting upon the joke to myself as I hurried up the avenue. It was extremely funny, I said to myself; it would be a capital story among my other Scotch experiences. But somehow my laugh died away in a very feeble sort of quaver. The night had grown dark even when I emerged from under the trees, by reason of a great cloud, full of rain, which had rolled up over the sky, quenching it out. I was very glad to see the lights of the house gleaming steadily before me. The blind had not been drawn over the end window of the drawing-room, and from the darkness without I looked in upon a scene which was full of warmth and household calm. Though it was August there was a little glimmer of fire. The reading of the sermon was over. Old Mr. Campbell still sat at a little table with the book before him, but it was closed. Charlotte in the foreground, with little Harry and Mary on either side of her, was "hearing their Paraphrase."[1] The boys were putting a clever dog through his tricks in a sort of clandestine way behind backs, at whom Charlotte would shake a finger now and then with an admonitory smiling look. Charley was reading or writing at the end of the room. The soft little chime of the children's voices, the suppressed laughter and whis-

1 The Paraphrases are a selection of hymns always printed along with the metrical version of the Psalms in use in Scotland, and more easy, being more modern in diction, to be learnt by heart. [Author's note.]

pering of the boys, the father's leisurely remark now and then, made up a soft murmur of sound which was like the very breath of quietude and peace. How did I dare, their favoured guest, indebted so deeply as I was to their kindness, to go in among them with that mysterious message and disturb their tranquillity once more?

When I went into the drawing-room, which was not till an hour later, Charlotte looked up at me smiling with some playful remark as to my flight from the evening reading. But as she caught my eye her countenance changed. She put down her book, and after a little consideration walked to that end window through which I had looked, and which was in a deep recess, making me a little sign to follow her. "How dark the night is," she said with a little pretence of looking out; and then in a hurried under-tone, "Mr. Temple, you have heard something more?"

"Not anything more, but certainly the same thing repeated. I have seen the lady again."

"And who is she? Tell me frankly, Mr. Temple. Just the same thing—that Colin is in trouble? no details? I cannot imagine who can take so much interest. But you asked her for her name?"

"I asked her, but she gave me no reply. She waved her hand and went on. I begged her to see you, and not to give me such a commission; but it was of no use. I don't know if I ought to trouble you with a vague warning that only seems intended to give pain."

"Oh yes," she cried, "oh yes, it was right to tell me. If I only knew who it was! Perhaps you can describe her better, since you have seen her a second time. But Colin has friends—whom we don't know. Oh, Mr. Temple, it is making a great claim upon your kindness, but could not you have followed her and found out who she was?"

"I might have done that," I said. "To tell the truth, it was so instantaneous and I was—startled."

She looked up at me quickly with a questioning air, and grew a little pale, gazing at me; but whether she comprehended the strange wild fancy which I could not even permit myself to realise I cannot tell; for Charley seeing us standing together, and being in a state of nervous anxiety also, here came and joined us, and we stood talking together in an under tone till Mr. Campbell called to know if anything was the matter. "You are laying your heads together like a set of conspirators," said the old gentleman with a half-laugh. His manner to me was always benign and gracious; but now that I knew something of the family troubles I could perceive a vein of suppressed irritation, a certain watchfulness which made him alarming to the other members of the household. Charlotte gave us both a warning look. "I will tell him to-morrow—I will delay no longer—but not to-night," she said. "Mr. Temple was telling us about his ramble, father. He has just come in in time to avoid the rain."

"Well," said the old man, "he cannot expect to be free from rain up here in the Highlands. It is wonderful the weather we have had." And with this the conversation fell into an easy domestic channel. Miss Campbell this time could not put away the look of excitement and agitation in her eyes. But she escaped with the children to see them put to bed, and we sat and talked of politics and other mundane subjects. The boys were all going to leave Ellermore next day—Tom and Jack for the "works," Charley upon some other business. Mr. Campbell made me formal apologies for them. "I had hoped Colin would have been at home by this time to do the honours of the Highlands: but we expect him daily," he said. He kept his eye fixed upon me as if to give emphasis to his words and defy any doubt that might arise in my mind.

Next morning I was summoned by Charley before I came downstairs to "come quickly and speak to my father." I found him in the library, which opened from the dining-room. He was walking about the room in great agitation. He began to address me almost before I was in sight. "Who is this, sir, that you have been having meetings with about Colin? some insidious gossip or other that has taken ye in. I need not tell you, Mr. Temple, a lawyer and an Englishman, that an anonymous statement——" For once the old gentleman had forgotten himself, his respect for his guest, his fine manners. He was irritated, obstinate, wounded in pride and feeling. Charlotte touched him on the arm with a murmured appeal, and turned her eyes to me in anxious deprecation. But there was no thought further from my mind than that of taking offence.

"I fully feel it," I said; "nor was it my part to bring any disagreeable suggestion into this house—if it had not been that my own mind was so burdened with it and Miss Campbell so clearsighted."

He cast a look at her, half affectionate, half displeased, and then he said to me testily, "But who was the woman? That is the question; that is what I want to know."

My eyes met Charlotte's as I looked up. She had grown very pale, and was gazing at me eagerly, as if she had divined somehow the wild fancy which once more shot across my mind against all reason and without any volition of mine.

## CHAPTER III

Mr. Campbell was not to be moved. He was very anxious, angry, and ill at ease; but he refused to be influenced in any way by this strange communication. It would be some intrusive woman, he said; some busybody—there were many about—who, thinking she might escape being found out in that way, had thought it a grand opportunity of making mischief. He made me a great many apologies for his first hasty words. It was very ill-bred, he said; he was ashamed to think that he had let himself be so carried away; but he would hear nothing of the message itself. The household, however, was in so agitated a state that, after the brothers departed to their business on Monday, I made a pretext of a letter calling me to town, and arranged my departure for the same evening. Both Charlotte and her father evidently divined my motive, but neither attempted to detain me: indeed she, I thought, though it hurt my self-love to see it, looked forward with a little eagerness to my going. This however, explained itself in a way less humiliating when she seized the opportunity of our last walk together to beg me to "do something for her."

"Anything," I cried; "anything—whatever man can."

"I knew you would say so; that is why I have scarcely said I am sorry. I have not tried to stop you. Mr. Temple, I am not shutting my eyes to it, like my father. I am sure that, whoever it was that spoke to you, the warning was true. I want you to go to Colin," she said abruptly, after a momentary pause, "and let me know the truth."

"To Colin?" I cried. "But you know how little acquainted we are. It was not he who invited me but—Charley——"

"And I——. You don't leave me out, I hope," she said, with a faint smile; "but what could make a better excuse than that you have been here? Mr. Temple, you will go when I ask you? Oh, I do more—I entreat you! Go, and let me know the truth."

"Of course I shall go—from the moment you bid me, Miss Campbell," I said. But the commission was not a pleasant one, save in so far that it was for her service.

We were walking up and down by the side of the water, which every moment grew more and more into a blazing mirror, a burnished shield decked with every imaginable colour, though our minds had no room for its beauty, and it only touched my eyesight in coming and going. And then she told me much about Colin which I had not known or guessed—about his inclinations and tastes, which were not like any of the others, and how his friends and his ways were unknown to them. "But we have always hoped this would pass away," she said, "for his heart is good; oh, his heart is good! You remember how kind he was to me when we met you first. He is always kind." Thus we walked and talked until I had seen a new side at once of her character and life. The home had seemed to me so happy and free from care; but the dark shadow was there as everywhere, and her heart often wrung with suspense and anguish. We then returned slowly towards the house, still absorbed in this conversation, for it was time that I should go in and eat my last meal at Ellermore.

We had come within sight of the door, which stood open as always, when we suddenly caught sight of Mr. Campbell posting towards us with a wild haste, so unlike his usual circumspect walk, that I was startled. His feet seemed to twist as they sped along, in such haste was he. His hat was pushed back on his head, his coat-tails flying behind him—precipitate like a man pursued, or in one of those panics which take away breath and sense, or, still more, perhaps as if a strong wind were behind him, blowing him on. When he came within speech of us, he called out hurriedly, "Come here! come here, both of you!" and turning, hastened back with the same breathless hurry, beckoning with his hand. "He must have heard something more," Charlotte said, and rushed after him. I followed a few steps behind. Mr. Campbell said nothing to his daughter when she made up to him. He almost pushed her off when she put her hand through his arm. He had no leisure even for sympathy. He hurried along with feet that stumbled in sheer haste till he came to the Lady's Walk, which lay in the level sunshine, a path of gold between the great boles of the trees. It was a slight ascent, which tried him still more. He went a few yards along the path, then stopped and looked round upon her and me, with his hand raised to call our attention. His face was perfectly colourless. Alarm and dismay were written on every line of it. Large drops of perspiration stood upon his forehead. He seemed to desire to speak, but could not; then held up his finger to command our attention. For the first moment or two my attention was so concentrated upon the man and the singularity of his look and gesture, that I thought of nothing else. What did he want us to do? We stood all three in the red light, which seemed to send a flaming sword through us. There was a faint stir of wind among the branches overhead, and a twitter of birds; and in the great stillness the faint lap of the water upon the shore was audible, though the loch was at some distance. Great stillness—that was the word; there was nothing moving but these soft stirrings of nature. Ah! this was what it was! Charlotte grew perfectly pale, too, like her father, as she stood and listened. I seem to see them now: the old man with his white head, his ghastly face, the scared and awful look in his eyes, and she gazing at him, all her faculties involved in the act of listening, her very attitude and drapery listening too, her lips dropping apart, the life ebbing out of her, as if something was draining the blood from her heart.

Mr. Campbell's hand dropped. "She's away," he said. "She's away"—in tones of despair; then, with a voice that was shaken by emotion—"I thought it was, maybe, my fault. By times you say I am getting stupid." There was the most heartrending tone in this I ever heard—the pained humility of old age, confessing a defect, lit up with a gleam of feverish hope that in this case the defect might be a welcome explanation.

"Father, dear," cried Charlotte, putting her hand on his arm—she had looked like fainting a moment before, but recovered herself—"It may be only a warning. It may not be desperate even now."

All that the old man answered to this was a mere repetition, pathetic in its simplicity. "She's away, she's away!" Then, after a full minute's pause, "You mind when that happened last?" he said.

"Oh, father! oh, father!" cried Charlotte. I withdrew a step or two from this scene. What had I, a stranger, to do with it? They had forgotten my presence, and at the sound of my step they both looked up with a wild eager look in their faces, followed by blank disappointment. Then he sighed, and said, with a return of composure, "You will throw a few things into a bag, and we'll go at once, Chatty. There is no time to lose."

They went up with me to town that night. The journey has never seemed to me so long or so fatiguing, and Mr. Campbell's state, which for once Charlotte in her own suspense and anxiety did not specially remark, was distressing to see. It became clear afterwards that his illness must have been coming on for some time, and that he was not then at all in a condition to travel. He was so feeble and confused when we reached London that it was impossible for me to leave them, and I was thus, without any voluntary intrusion of mine, a witness of all the melancholy events that followed. I was present even at the awful scene which the reader probably will remember as having formed the subject of many a newspaper article at the time. Colin had "gone wrong" in every way that a young man could do. He had compromised the very existence of the firm in business; he had summed up all his private errors by marrying a woman unfit to bear any respectable name. And when his father and sister suddenly appeared before him, the unfortunate young man seized a pistol which lay suspiciously ready to his hand, and in their very presence put an end to his life. All the horror and squalor and dismal tragedy of the scene is before me as I write. The wretched woman, whom (I felt sure) he could not endure the sight of in Charlotte's presence, the heap of letters on his table announcing ruin from every quarter, the consciousness so suddenly brought upon him that he had betrayed and destroyed all who were most dear to him, overthrew his reason or his self-command. And the effect of so dreadful an occurrence on the unhappy spectators needs no description of mine. The father, already wavering under the touch of paralysis, fell by the same blow, and I had myself to bring Charlotte from her brother dead to her father dying, or worse than dying, struck dumb and prostrate in that awful prison of all the faculties. Until Charley arrived I had everything to do for both dead and living, and there was no attempt to keep any secret from me, even had it been possible. It seemed at first that there must be a total collapse of the family altogether; but afterwards some points of consolation appeared. I was present at all their consultations. The question at last came to be whether the "Works," the origin of their wealth, should be given up, and the young men disperse to seek their fortune as they might, or whether a desperate attempt should be made to keep up the business by retrenching every expense and selling Ellermore. Charley, it was clear to me, was afraid to suggest this dreadful alternative to his sister; but she was no weakling to shrink from any necessity. She made up her mind to the sacrifice without a moment's hesitation. "There are so many of us—still," she said; "there are the boys to think of, and the children." When I saw her standing thus, with all those hands clutching at her, holding to her, I had in my own mind a sensation of despair. But what was that to the purpose? Charlotte was conscious of no divided duty. She was ready to serve her own with every faculty, and shrank from no sacrifice for their sake.

It was some time before Mr. Campbell could be taken home. He got better indeed after a while, but was very weak. And happily for him he brought no consciousness of what had happened out of the temporary suspension of all his faculties. His hand and one side were almost without power, and his mind had fallen into a state which it would be cruel to call imbecility. It was more like the mind of a child recovering from an illness, pleased with, and exacting constant attention. Now and then he would ask the most heartrending questions: what had become of Colin, if he was ill, if he had gone home? "The best place for him, the best place for him, Chatty," he would repeat; "and if you got him persuaded to marry, that would be fine." All this Charlotte had to bear with a placid face, with quiet assent to the suggestion. He was in this condition when I took leave of him in the invalid carriage they had secured for the journey. He told me that he was glad to go home; that he would have left London some time before but for Chatty, who "wanted to see a little of the place." "I am going to join my son Colin, who has gone home before us—isn't that so, Chatty?" "Yes, father," she said. "Yes, yes, I have grown rather doited, and very very silly,"[1] the old man said, in a tone of extraordinary pathos. "I am sometimes not sure of what I am saying; but Chatty keeps me right. Colin has gone on before; he has a grand head for business; he will soon set everything right—connected," he added, with a curious sense which seemed to have outlived his other powers, that somehow explanation of Colin's actions was necessary—"connected with my retirement. I am past business; but we'll still hope to see you at Ellermore."

I ought perhaps to say, though at the risk of ridicule, that up to the moment of their leaving London, I constantly met, or seemed to meet—for I became confused after a while, and felt incapable of distinguishing between feeling and fact—the same veiled lady who had spoken to me at Ellermore. Wherever there was a group of two or three people together, it appeared to me that she was one of them. I saw her in advance of me in the streets. I saw her behind me. She seemed to disappear in the distance wherever I moved. I suppose it was imagination—at least that is the most easy thing to say: but I was so convinced at the moment that it was not imagination, that I have hurried along many a street in pursuit of the phantom who always, I need not say, eluded me. I saw her at Colin's grave: but what need to linger longer on this hallucination, if it was one? From the day the Campbells left London, I saw her no more.

## CHAPTER IV

Then there ensued a period of total stillness in my life. It seemed to me as if all interest had gone out of it. I resumed my old occu-

---

1 Used in Scotland in the sense of weakness of body-invalidism. [Author's note.]

pations, such as they were, and they were not very engrossing. I had enough, which is perhaps of all conditions of life, if the most comfortable, the least interesting. If it was a disciple of Solomon who desired that state, it must have been when he was like his master, blasé, and had discovered that both ambition and pleasure were vanity. There was little place or necessity for me in the world. I pleased myself, as people say. When I was tired of my solitary chambers, I went and paid visits. When I was tired of England, I went abroad. Nothing could be more agreeable, or more unutterably tedious, especially to one who had even accidentally come across and touched upon the real events and excitements of life. Needless to say that I thought of the household at Ellermore almost without intermission. Charlotte wrote to me now and then, and it sometimes seemed to me that I was the most callous wretch on earth, sitting there watching all they were doing, tracing every step and vicissitude of their trouble in my own assured well-being. It was monstrous, yet what could I do? But if, as I have said, such impatient desire to help were to come now and then to those who have the power to do so, is political economy so infallible that the world would not be the better for it? There was not a word of complaint in Charlotte's letters, but they made me rage over my impotence. She told me that all the arrangements were being completed for the sale of Ellermore, but that her father's condition was still such that they did not know how to communicate to him the impending change. "He is still ignorant of all that has passed," Charlotte wrote, "and asks me the most heartrending questions; and I hope God will forgive me all that I am obliged to say to him. We are afraid to let him see anyone lest he should discover the truth; for indeed falsehood, even with a good meaning, is always its own punishment. Dr. Maxwell, who does not mind what he says when he thinks it is for his patient's good, is going to make believe to send him away for change of air; and this is the artifice we shall have to keep up all the rest of his life to account for not going back to Ellermore. She wrote another time that there was every hope of being able to dispose of it by private bargain, and that in the meantime friends had been very kind, and the "Works" were going on. There was not a word in the letter by which it would have been divined that to leave Ellermore was to the writer anything beyond a matter of necessity. She said not a word about her birthplace, the home of all her associations, the spot which I knew was so dear. There had been no hesitation, and there was no repining. Provided only that the poor old man, the stricken father, deprived at once of his home and firstborn, without knowing either, might be kept in that delusion—this was all the exemption Charlotte sought.

And I do not think they asked me to go to them before they left the place. It was my own doing. I could not keep away any longer. I said to Charlotte, and perhaps also to myself, by way of excuse, that I might help take to care of Mr. Campbell during the removal. The fact was that I could not stay away from her any longer. I could have risked any intrusion, thrust myself in anyhow, for the mere sake of being near her and helping her in the most insignificant way.

It was, however, nearly Christmas before I yielded to my impatience. They were to leave Ellermore in a week or two. Mr. Campbell had been persuaded that one of the soft and sheltered spots where Scotch invalids are sent in Scotland would be better for him. Charlotte had written to me, with a half despair, of the difficulties of their removal. "My heart almost fails me," she said; and that was a great deal for her to say. After this I could hesitate no longer. She was afraid even of the revival of life that might take place when her father was brought out of his seclusion, of some injudicious old friend who could not be staved off, and who might talk to him about Colin. "My heart almost fails me." I went up to Scotland by the mail train that night, and next day, while it was still not much more than noon, found myself at Ellermore.

What a change! The heather had all died away from the hills; the sunbright loch was steely blue; the white threads of water down every crevice in the mountains were swollen to torrents. Here and there on the higher peaks there was a sprinkling of snow. The fir-trees were the only substantial things in the nearer landscape. The beeches stood about all bare and feathery, with every twig distinct against the blue. The sun was shining almost as brightly as in summer, and scattered a shimmer of reflections everywhere over the wet grass, and across the rivulets that were running in every little hollow. The house stood out amid all this light, amid the bare tracery of the trees, with its Scotch-French *tourelles*, and the sweep of emerald lawn, more green than ever, at its feet, and all the naked flower-beds; the blue smoke rising peacefully into the air, the door open as always. There was little stir or movement, however, in this wintry scene. The out-door life was checked. There was no son at home to leave traces of his presence. The lodge was shut up, and vacant. I concluded that the carriage had been given up, and all luxuries, and the coachman and his family were gone. But this was all the visible difference. I was received by one of the maids, with whose face I was familiar. There had never been any wealth of male attendants at Ellermore. She took me into the drawing-room, which was deserted, and bore a more formal look than of old. "Miss Charlotte is mostly with her papa," the woman said. "He is very frail; but just wonderful contented, like a bairn. She's always up the stair with the old gentleman. It's no good for her. You'll find her white, white, sir, and no like herself." In a few minutes Charlotte came in. There was a gleam of pleasure (I hoped) on her face, but she was white, white, as the woman said, worn and pale. After the first greeting, which had brightened her, she broke down a little, and shed a few hasty tears, for which she excused herself, faltering that everything came back, but that she was glad, glad to see me! And then she added quickly, that I might not be wounded, "It has come to that, that I can scarcely ever leave my father; and to keep up the deception is terrible."

"You must not say deception."

"Oh, it is nothing else; and that always punishes itself. It is just the terror of my life that some accident will happen; that he will find out everything at once." Then she looked at me steadily, with a smile that was piteous to see, "Mr. Temple, Ellermore is sold."

"Is it so—is it so?" I said, with a sort of groan. I had still thought that perhaps at the last moment something might occur to prevent the sacrifice.

She shook her head, not answering my words, but the expression of my face. "There was nothing else to be desired," she said; and, after a pause, "We are to take him to the Bridge of Allan. He is almost pleased to go; he thinks of nothing further—oh, poor old man, poor old man! If only I had him there safe; but I am more terrified for the journey than I ever was for anything in my life."

We talked of this for some time, and of all the arrangements she had made. Charley was to come to assist in removing his father; but I think that my presence somehow seemed to her an additional safeguard, of which she was glad. She did not stay more than half an hour with me. "It will be dull, dull for you, Mr. Temple," she said, with more of the lingering cadence of her national accent than I had perceived before—or perhaps it struck me more after these months of absence. "There is nobody at home but the little ones, and they have grown far too wise for their age, because of the many things that they know must never be told to papa; but you know the place, and you will want to rest a little." She put out her hand to me again—"And I am glad, glad to see you!" Nothing in my life ever made my heart swell like those simple words. That she should be "glad, glad" was payment enough for anything I could do. But in the meantime there was nothing that I could do. I wandered about the silent place till I was tired, recalling a hundred pleasant recollections; even to me, a stranger, who a year ago had never seen Ellermore, it was hard to give it up; and as for those who had been born there, and their fathers before them, it seemed too much for the cruellest fate to ask. But Nature was as indifferent to the passing away of the human inhabitants, whose little spell of a few hundred years was as nothing in her long history, as she would have been to the fall-ing of a rock on the hillside, or the wrenching up of a tree in the woods. For that matter, of so small account are men, the rock and tree would both have been older dwellers than the Campbells; and why for that should the sun moderate his shining, or the clear skies veil themselves?

My mind was so taken up by these thoughts that it was almost inadvertence that took me, in the course of my solitary rambles about, to the Lady's Walk. I had nearly got within the line of the beech-trees, however, when I was brought hurriedly back to the strange circumstances which had formed an accompaniment to this family history. To hear once more the footsteps of the guard-ian of Ellermore had a startling effect upon me. She had come back then! After that first thrill of instinctive emotion this gave

me a singular pleasure. I stood between the trees and heard the
soft step coming and going with absolute satisfaction. It seemed
to me that they were not altogether abandoned so long as she was
here. My heart rose in spite of myself. I began to speculate on the
possibility even yet of saving the old house. I asked myself how it
could be finally disposed of without Mr. Campbell's consent and
signature; and tried to believe that at the last moment some way
might open, some wonderful windfall come. But when I turned
back to the house, this fantastic confidence naturally failed me.
I began to contemplate the other side of the question—the new
people who would come in. Perhaps "some Englishman," as
Charley had said with a certain scorn; some rich man, who would
buy the moors and lochs at many times their actual value, and
bring down, perhaps, a horde of Cockney sportsmen to banish
all quiet and poetry from Ellermore. I thought with a mingled
pity and anger of what the Lady would do in such hands. Would
she still haunt her favourite walk when all whom she loved were
gone? Would she stay there in forlorn faithfulness to the soil, or
would she go with her banished race? or would she depart altogether, and cut the tie that had bound her to earth? I thought—for
fancy once set out goes far without any conscious control from
the mind—that these were circumstances in which the intruders
into the home of the Campbells might be frightened by noises
and apparitions, and all those vulgarer powers of the unseen of
which we hear sometimes. If the Lady of Ellermore would condescend to use such instruments, no doubt she might find lower
and less elevated spirits in the unseen to whom this kind of play
would be congenial. I caught myself up sharply in this wandering of thought, as if I were forming ideas derogatory to a dear
friend, and felt myself redden with shame. She connect her lovely
being with tricks of this kind! I was angry with myself, as if I had
allowed it to be suggested that Charlotte would do so. My heart
grew full as I pursued these thoughts. Was it possible that some
mysterious bond of a kind beyond our knowledge connected her
with this beloved soil? I was overawed by the thought of what
she might suffer, going upon her solitary watch, to see the house
filled with an alien family—yet, perhaps, by-and-by, taking them
into amity, watching over them as she had done over her own,

in that sweetness of self-restraint and tender love of humankind which is the atmosphere of the blessed. All through this spiritual being was to me a beatified shadow of Charlotte. You will say all this was very fantastic, and I do not deny that the sentence is just.

Next day passed in something the same way. Charlotte was very anxious. She had wished the removal to take place that afternoon, but when the moment came she postponed it. She said "To-morrow," with a shiver. "I don't know what I am afraid of," she said, "but my heart fails me—my heart fails me." I had to telegraph to Charley that it was deferred: and another long day went by. It rained, and that was an obstacle. "I cannot take him away in bad weather," she said. She came downstairs to me a dozen times a day, wringing her hands. "I have no resolution," she cried. "I cannot—I cannot make up my mind to it. I feel that something dreadful is going to happen." I could only take her trembling hand and try to comfort her. I made her come out with me to get a little air in the afternoon. "You are killing yourself," I said. "It is this that makes you so nervous and unlike yourself." She consented, though it was against her will. A woman who had been all her life in their service, who was to go with them, whom Charlotte treated, as she said, "like one of ourselves," had charge of Mr. Campbell in the meantime. And I think Charlotte got a little pleasure from this unusual freedom. She was very tremulous, as if she had almost forgotten how to walk, and leant upon my arm in a way which was very sweet to me. No word of love had ever passed between us; and she did not love me, save as she loved Charley and Harry, and the rest. I think I had a place among them, at the end of the brothers. But yet she had an instinctive knowledge of my heart; and she knew that to lean upon me, to show that she needed me, was the way to please me most. We wandered about there for a time in a sort of forlorn happiness; then, with a mutual impulse, took our way to the Lady's Walk. We stood there together, listening to the steps. "Do you hear them?" said Charlotte, her face lighting up with a smile. "Dear lady! that has always been here since ever I mind!" She spoke as the children spoke in the utter abandonment of her being, as if returning for refreshment to the full simplicity of accent and idiom, the soft native speech to which she was born. "Will she stay after us, do ye think?" Charlotte said; and then, with a little start, clinging to my arm, "Was that a sound—was that a cry?"

Not a cry, but a sigh. It seemed to wander over all the woods and thrill among the trees. You will say it was only the wind. I cannot tell. To me it was a sigh, personal, heart-rending. And you may suppose what it was to her. The tears dropped from her full eyes. She said, speaking to the air, "We are parting, you and me. Oh, go you back to Heaven, and let us trouble you no more. Oh, go back to your home, my bonnie lady, and let us trouble you no more!'

"Charlotte!" I cried, drawing her arm more closely through mine. She cast me a glance, a smile, like one who could not even in the midst of the highest thoughts neglect or be unkind, but drew her hand away and clasped it in the other. "We are of one stock," she said, the tears always falling; "and the same heart. We are too anxious, but God is above us all. Go back to your pleasant place, and say to my mother that I will never leave them. Go away, my bonnie lady, go away! You and me, we must learn to trust them to God."

We waited, and I think she almost expected some reply. But there was none. I took her arm within mine again, and led her away trembling. The moment, the excitement had been too much for me also. I said, "You tell her to go, that she is too anxious, that she must trust you to God—and in the same breath you pledge yourself never to leave them. Do you think if God does not want her, He wants you to stand between Him and them?" I grasped her arm so closely and held it so to my side in my passion that I think I almost hurt her. She gave me a startled look, and put up her hand to dry her wet eyes.

"It is very different," she said; "I am living and can work for them. It has come to me all in a moment to see that She is just like me after all. Perhaps to die does not make a woman wise any more than life does. And it may be that nobody has had the thought to tell her. She will have imagined that she could stop any harm that was coming, being here; but if it was not God's pleasure to stop it, how could she? You know she tried," said Charlotte, looking at me wistfully; "she tried—God bless her for that! Oh, you know how anxious she was; but neither she nor I could do it—neither she nor I!"

At this moment we were interrupted by some one flying towards us from the house, calling, "Miss Charlotte, Miss Charlotte! you are wanted," in a wild and agitated tone. It was the woman who had been left in charge of Mr. Campbell, and Charlotte started at the sight of her. She drew her hand from my arm, and flew along the path. "Oh, Marg'ret, why did you leave him?" she said.

"It was no blame of mine," said the woman, turning, following her mistress. I hurried on, too, after them, and the explanation was addressed to both of us. "He would come down to the library: nothing would stop him. I tried all I could; but what could I do? And there is nothing to be frighted for, Miss Charlotte. Ah! I've nae breath to tell it. He is just real like himself!"

Charlotte flew along the path like a creature flying for life. She paused an instant at the door of the house to beckon me to follow her. The library, the room where her father had gone, was one of those which had been partially dismantled. The pictures had been taken down from the walls, a number of books which she meant to take with her collected on the tables. Mr. Campbell had displaced some of the books in order to seat himself in his favourite seat. He looked at her curiously, almost with severity, as she came in anxious and breathless. He was greatly changed. He had been robust and hale, like a tower, when I first entered Ellermore, not yet six months since. Now he had shrunken away into half his size. The coat which he had not worn for months hung loosely upon him; his white hair was long, and he wore a beard which changed his appearance greatly. All this change had come since the time I parted with him in London, when he told me he was going to join his son Colin; but there was another change more remarkable, which I with awe, and Charlotte with terror, recognised at a glance—the prostration of his mind was gone. He looked his daughter in the face with intelligent, almost sternly intelligent eyes.

"Oh, father, you have wanted me!" Charlotte cried. "I went out for a mouthful of air—I went out—for a few minutes——"

"Why should you not have gone out, Chatty?" he said. "And

why was Marg'ret left in charge of me? I have been ill, I make no doubt; but why should I be watched and spied about my own house?"

She gave me a glance of dismay, and then she faltered, "Oh, not that, father—not that!"

"But I tell you it was that. She would have hindered my coming downstairs, that woman"—he gave a little laugh, which was terrible to us in the state of our feelings—"and here are you rushing in out of breath, as if there was some cause of fear. Who is that behind ye? Is it one of your brothers—or——"

"It is Mr. Temple, father," she said, with a new alarm.

"Mr. Temple," he said, with a shade of displeasure passing over his face. Then he recovered himself, and his old-world politeness. "I am glad to see ye," he said. "So far as I can remember, the house was much disorganised when you were here before, Mr. Temple. You will think we are always out of order; but I've been ill, and everything has fallen out of gear. This is not a place," he added, turning to Charlotte, "to receive a stranger in. What is all this for?" he added, in a sharp tone, waving his hand towards the books, of which some were heaped at his feet on the floor.

Once more she made a pause of dismay. "They are some books to take with us," she said; "you remember, father, we are going away."

"Going away!" he cried, irritably. "Where are my letters? Where are your brothers? What are you doing with a gentleman visitor (I beg ye a thousand pardons, Mr. Temple!) and the place in such a state? It is my opinion that there is something wrong. Where are my letters? It is not in reason that there should be no letters. After being laid aside from business for a time, to have your letters kept back from you, you will allow, Mr. Temple," he said, turning to me with an explanatory air, "is irritating. It is perhaps done with a mistaken notion that I am not equal to them; but if you think I will allow myself to be treated as a child——"

He stammered a little now and then, in his anger, but made a great effort to control himself. And then he looked up at us, once more a little severely, and brought confusion to all our hopes with one simple question. "Where is Colin?" he said.

What could be more natural? Charlotte gave me one look, and

stood, white as death, motionless, her fingers twisting together. How truly she had said that falsehood was its own punishment, even such falsehood as this! She had answered him with ambiguous words when he was in the state of feebleness from which he had thus awoke, and he had been easily satisfied and diverted from too close inquiry. But now she was confounded by the sudden question. She could not confront with a subterfuge her father's serious eyes; her head drooped, her hands caught at each other with a pitiful clasp, while he sat looking at her with an authoritative, but as yet unalarmed, look. All this time the door had been left ajar, and Marg'ret stood waiting outside, listening to all that went on, too much interested and anxious to feel herself out of place. But when she heard this demand the woman was struck with horror. She made a step within the door. "Oh, Ellermore!" she cried. "Oh! my auld maister, dinna break her heart and mine! To hear ye asking for Colin! and Colin in his grave this four long months, poor lad, poor lad!" She threw her apron over her head as she spoke, and burst forth into loud sobs and tears. Charlotte had put out a hand to stop the revelation, but dropped it again, and stood by speechless, her head bent, and wringing her hands, a silent image of grief and guilt, as if it had been her from whom the blow came.

The old man sat and listened with a countenance growing ashy pale, and with intent eyes, that seemed to flicker as if beyond his control. He tried to speak, but in the trembling of his lips could articulate nothing. Then he slowly raised himself up and stood pallid and dizzy, like a man on the edge of a precipice.

"My son is dead, and I knew it not," he said slowly, pausing between the words. He stood with his trembling lips falling apart, his countenance all moving and twitching, transfixed, it seemed, by a sort of woeful amaze, wondering at himself. Then he turned upon Charlotte, with a piteous appeal. "Was I told, and have I forgotten?" he asked. The humiliation of that thought overpowered his re-awakened soul.

She came to him quickly and put her arm round him. "Father, dear, you were so ill, they would not let us tell you. Oh, I have known, I have known it would be so much the worse when it came!"

He put her away from him, and sat down again feebly in his chair. In that dreadful moment he wanted no one. The horror of the individual humiliation, the idea that he could have heard and forgotten, was more terrible even than the dreadful news which thus burst upon him. "I'm glad," he said, "I'm glad," babbling with his loose lips. I shrank away, feeling it a profanation to be here, a spectator of the last mystery of nature; but Charlotte made a faint motion that kept me from withdrawing altogether. For the first time she was afraid; her heart had failed her.

For some minutes her father continued silent in his chair. The sunset had faded away, the misty twilight was falling. Marg'ret, guilty and miserable, but still unable altogether to subdue her sobs, throwing her white apron from her head, and looking round with a deprecating, apologetic glance, had withdrawn to the other side of the room. All was silence after that broken interchange of words. He lay back, clasping and unclasping his hands, his lips and features all moving, whether with a wish to speak or with the mere workings of emotions unspeakable, I cannot tell. When suddenly, all at once, with the voice of a strong man loud and full, he broke out into the cry which has sounded through all the world—the utterance of every father's anguish. "Oh, Absalom, my son, my son! Would God that I had died for thee, my son, my son——"

We both rushed towards him simultaneously. He did not remark me, fortunately; but again he put Charlotte away. "What are you afraid for?" he said, almost sternly; "that I will fall back and be ill again? That is not possible. Ye think sorrow kills; but no, it stings ye back to life: it stings ye back to life," he repeated, raising himself in his chair. Then he looked round him solemnly. "Marg'ret, my woman, come here, and give me your hand. We're partners in trouble, you and me, and never shall we part. As long as this is my house there is a place in it for you. Afterwards, when it goes to——ah! when it goes to Charley," he cried, with a sudden burst of unforeseen sobs.

Charlotte looked at me again. Her face was white with despair. How was this last news to be broken to him?

"Father," she said, standing behind him, "you are sorely tried. Will you not come back to your room and rest till to-morrow, and then you will hear all? Then we will tell you—about all that has happened——"

Her voice shook like a leaf in the wind, but she managed to show no other sign of her terror and despair. There was a long pause after this, and we stood waiting, not knowing how the moment would terminate. I believe it was the sight of me that decided it after all. A quick movement of irritation passed over his face.

"I think you are right, Chatty," he said; "I think you are right. I am not fit, in my shattered state, and with the information I have just received, to pay the attention I would like to pay——" He paused, and looked at me fixedly. "It is a great trouble to me that we have never been able to show you proper attention, Mr. Temple. You see, my son was detained; and now he is dead—and I've never known it till this moment. You will excuse a reception which is not the kind of reception I would like to give you." He waved his hand. "You were my Colin's friend. You will know how to make allowances. Yes, my dear, I am best in my own chamber. I will just go, with Mr. Temple's permission—go—to my bed."

A faint groan burst from him as he said these words; a kind of dreary smile flickered on his lips. "To my bed," he repeated; "that is all we can do, we old folk, when we are stricken by God's hand. Lie down, and turn our faces to the wall—our faces to the wall." He rose up, and took his daughter's arm, and made a few steps towards the door, which I was holding open for him. Then he turned and looked round with the air of one who has a favour to bestow. "You may come too, Marg'ret," he said. "You can come and help me to my bed."

This strange interruption of all plans, which it was evident filled Charlotte with despair, gave me much to think of, as I stayed behind in the slowly-darkening room. It was evident that now nothing could be concealed from him; and who was there so bold as to tell the bereaved father, in his first grief for his first-born, what horrors had accompanied Colin's death, and what a penalty the family had to pay? It seemed to me that the premonition of some fresh calamity was in the air; and when Charlotte came down about half an hour later, like a ghost through the dim-coming shadows, I almost expected to hear that it had already occurred. But even in these depths of distress it was a happiness to me to feel that she came to me for relief. She told me that he had gone to bed without asking any further questions, and that Margaret, who had been Colin's nurse, seemed almost more agreeable to him than herself. He had turned his face to the wall as he had said, and nothing but a long-drawn, occasional sigh told that he was awake. "I think he is not worse—in body," she said. "He has borne it far better than we could have thought possible. But how am I to tell him the way it happened, and how am I to tell him about Ellermore?" She wept with a prostration and self-abandonment which alarmed me; but she stopped my remonstrances and entreaties with a motion of her hand. "Oh, let me cry! It is the only ease I have," she said.

When she had gone away from me, restless, anxious, afraid to be out of hearing, I went out, myself, as restless, as incapable of banishing all these anxieties from my mind as she. The night was almost dark, soft and mild. It was one of those nights when the moon, without being visible, softens and ameliorates the gloom, and makes of night a sort of twilight. While I went pacing softly about, to occupy myself, a soft small rain began to fall; but this did not affect me in any way. It was rather soothing than disagreeable. I went down to the side of the loch, where the pale light on the water was touched by innumerable dimplings of the rain, then up again, round and round the house, not caring where I went. At this hour I had always avoided the Lady's Walk, I can scarcely tell why. To-night, in my strange familiarity with everything, and carelessness of all but one subject, I suddenly turned into it with a caprice I could not account for, perhaps with an unexpressed wish for company, for somebody who might understand my thoughts. The mystic footsteps gave me a sort of pleasure. Whether it was habit or some new sense of human fellowship which Charlotte's impassioned words had caused, I can scarcely tell; but the excitement with which I had always hitherto regarded the mysterious watcher here was altogether gone out of my mind. I felt a profound and tender pity for her rising in me instead. Was it possible that a spirit could be "over-anxious," as Charlotte said, endeavouring vainly, and yet not undutifully, to take God's supreme guardianship out of His hands? The thought

was new to me. To think that a good and blessed creature could so
err, could mistake so humanly and persevere so patiently, though
never able to remedy the evils, seemed somehow more possible
than that a guardian from Heaven could watch and watch for
generations with so little result. This gave me a great compassion for the lonely watcher thus rebelling in a heavenly way of
love against the law of nature that separated her from visible life.
My old idea, that it might be Charlotte herself in an unconscious
shadow-shape, whose protecting motherly love made these
efforts unawares, glided gratefully into the feeling that it was an
earlier Charlotte, her very kin and prototype, who could not even
now let God manage her race without her aid. While I was thus
thinking, I was startled once more by the same sigh which I had
heard with Charlotte. Yes, yes, it might be the wind. I had no time
to bandy explanations with myself. It was a soft long sigh, such
as draws the very breath out of an over-laden bosom. I turned
half round, it was so near to me; and there, by my side, so close
that I could have touched her, stood the Lady whom I had seen
so often—the same figure which I had met in the London streets
and in the woods of Ellermore. I suppose I stepped back, with a
little thrill of the old sensations, for she seemed to put out a hand
in the pale gloom, and began to speak softly, quickly, as if there
was scarcely time enough for what she had to say.

"I am going away like the rest," she said. "None of them have
ever bid me go before; but it is true—it is true what she says. I have
never done any good—just frightened them, or pleased them. It
is in better hands—it is in better hands."

With this there came the familiar movement, the wringing of
the hands, which was like Charlotte, and she seemed to weep; but
before I could say anything (and what could I have said?) she cried
with eagerness, "I came to you because you loved her, but you
were too late—and now again, again! you may help if you will. It
will be set before you to help, if you will."

"How can I help?" I cried. "Tell me, Lady, whoever you are; I
will do it, I will do it!—but how can I do it? Tell me——"

I put out my hand to touch her dress, but it melted out of my
hold. She withdrew with a swift, shy movement. "It will be set
before you," she said, with a breathless faintness as if of haste;

and already her voice was further off breathing away. "It will be set before you—I must not say more. One can never say more."

"What can I do?" I cried; so much had I forgot the old terror that I put myself in her path, stopping the way. "Tell me how, how! Tell me, for God's sake, and because of Charlotte!"

The shadowy figure retreated before me. It seemed to fade, then reappeared, then dissolved altogether into the white dimness, while the voice floated away, still saying, as in a sigh, "You may help, you may help, you may save——" I could hear no more. I went after this sighing voice to the end of the Walk; it seemed to me that I was pursuing, determined to hear her message, and that she softly fled, the hurrying footsteps becoming almost inaudible as they flew before me. I went on hotly, not knowing what I did, determined only to know what it was; to get an explanation, by what means I did not care. Suddenly, before I knew, I found my steps stumbling down the slope at the further end, and the pale water alive with all the dimplings of the rain appearing at my very feet. The steps sank upon the loch-side, and ceased with a thrill like the acutest sound. A silence more absolute than any I have heard in nature ensued. I stood gasping, with my foot touching the edge of the water; it was all I could do to arrest myself there.

I hurried back to the house in a state of agitation, which I cannot describe. It was partly nervous dread. I do not disguise this; but partly it was a bewildered anxiety and eagerness to know what the chance was which was to be set before me. That I had the most absolute faith in it I need hardly say. "You may help them if you will! You may help them if you will! I said it over and over to myself a thousand times with a feverish hurry and eagerness. Indeed, I did nothing but repeat it. When Charlotte came down late to tell me her father was asleep, that the doctor who had been sent for had pronounced his recovery real, I was walking up and down the half-lighted drawing-room, saying these words over and over to myself.

"He says it is wonderful, but it may be complete recovery," Charlotte said; "only to tell him nothing we can help, to keep all the circumstances from him; especially, if it is possible, about Ellermore. But how is it possible? how can I do it? 'Help if you will?' Mr. Temple, what are you saying?"

"It is nothing," I said; "some old rhyme that has got possession of me."

She looked very anxiously into my face. "Something else has happened? You have seen or heard——" Her mind was so alive to every tone and glance that it was scarcely possible to conceal a thought from her.

"I have been in the Walk," I said, "and being excited and restless, it was more than my nerves could bear."

She looked at me again wistfully. "You would not deceive me, Mr. Temple," she said; then returned to her original subject. The doctor was anxious, above all things, that Mr. Campbell should leave Ellermore to-morrow, that he should go early, and above all that he should not suspect the reason why. She had the same dread of the removal as ever, but there was no alternative, and not even a day's delay was to be thought of, for every day, every hour, made the chances of discovery more.

"But you cannot keep up the delusion for ever," I said, "and when it is found out?"

Again she wrung her hands. "It is against my judgment; but what can I do?" She paused a moment, and then said, with a melancholy dignity, "It can but kill him, soon or syne. I would not myself have my life saved by a lie; but I am weak where my father is concerned, and God understands all. Oh, I am beginning to feel that so, Mr. Temple! We search and search, and think what is best, and we make a hundred mistakes, but God sees the why and the wherefore. Whoever misunderstands, He never misunderstands."

She went away from me in the calm of this thought, the secret of all calm. It seemed to me that I, in my blind anxiety guessing at the enigma that had been given to me, and my poor Lady vagrant from the skies, still trying to be the providence of this house, were left alike behind.

Next morning Charlotte came down to breakfast with me, which she had not done before. She told me that her father had passed a good night, that he had shed tears on awaking, and began to talk tenderly and calmly of Colin, and that everything seemed to promise that the softening and mournful pre-occupation of grief, distracting his mind from other matters, would be an advantage to him. He was pleased to be left with Margaret, who had adored her nursling, and who had been fully warned of the necessity of keeping silence as to the circumstances of Colin's death. The post-bag came in while we were talking. It lay on the table for a few minutes untouched, for neither of us were anxious for our correspondence. We were alone at table, and Charlotte had rested, though I had not, and was almost cheerful now that the moment had arrived for the final severance. The necessity of doing inspired her; and perhaps, though I scarcely dared to think so, this tranquil table at which we sat alone, which might have been our table, in our home, in a new life full of peace and sober happiness, soothed her. The suggestion it conveyed made the blood dance in my veins. For the moment it seemed as if the hope I dared not even entertain, for one calm hour of blessedness and repose, had come true.

At last she gave me the key, and asked me to open the bag. "I have been loth to disturb this peaceful moment," she said, with a smile which was full of sweetness and confidence, "and nothing outside seems of much consequence just now; but the boys may have something to tell, and there will be your letters—will you open it, Mr. Temple?" I, too, was loth, more loth than she, to disturb the calm, and the outside world was nothing to me, while I sat here with her, and could fancy her my own. But I did what she told me. Letters are like fate, they must be encountered with all that is good and evil in them. I gave her hers, and laid out some, probably as important to them, though they seemed to me so trifling and unnecessary, that were for the servants. Then I turned to my own share. I had two letters, one with a broad black border, which had been forwarded from one place to another in search of me, and was nearly ten days old; for, like most people, I examined the outside first; the other a large, substantial blue letter, which meant business. I can remember now the indifference with which I opened them, the mourning envelope first. There were so many postmarks on it, that that of its origin, which would have enlightened me at once, never struck me at all.

Heaven above! what was this that met my eyes? An announcement, full of the periphrasis of formal regret, of the death of my old cousin Jocelyn ten days before. I gave a sort of fierce cry—I can hear it now—and tore open the second, the official letter. Of course I knew what it was; of course I was aware that nothing could interfere; and yet the opportuneness of the announcement was such, that human nature, accustomed to be balked, would not allow me to believe in the possibility. Then I sprang from my seat. "I must go," I cried; "there is not a moment to lose. Stop all proceedings—do nothing about the going, for God's sake, till I come back."

"Mr. Temple, what has happened? Charley——," cried Charlotte, blanched with terror. She thought some other catastrophe had happened, some still more fatal news that I would not tell her. But I was too much absorbed in my own excitement to think of this.

"Do nothing," I said; "I will meet Charley on the way, and tell him. All will be right, all will be right, only wait till I come back." I rushed to the door in my haste, then came back again, not knowing what I did, and had caught her in my arms before I was aware—not in my arms, but with my hands on her shoulders, holding her for one wild moment. I could hardly see her for the water in my eyes. "Wait," I said, "wait till I come back! Now I can do what she said! Now my time is come; do nothing till I come back." I let my hands drop down to hers, and caught them and kissed them in a wild tremor, beyond explanation. Then I rushed away. It was a mile or more to the little quay where the morning boat carried communications back to the world. I seemed to be there as on wings, and scarcely came to myself till I descended into the noise, the haze, the roar of the damp streets, the crowds and traffic of Glasgow. Next moment (for time flew and I with it, so that I took no note of its progress or my own) I was in the clamour of the "Works," making my way through the grime and mud of a great courtyard, with machinery clanging round me on every side, from the big skeleton houses with their open windows—into the office, where Charley, in close converse with a stranger, jumped up with terror at the sight of me. "What has happened?" he cried; "my father?" I had scarcely breath enough to say what I had to say. "Your father," I cried, "has come to himself. You can make no sale without him—every arrangement must be stopped at once." All that I was capable of knowing was with a certainty, beyond all proof, that the man with whom Charley was talking, a sportsman in every line of his countenance and clothes, was the intending purchaser of Ellermore.

I remember little of the conversation that followed. It was stormy and excited, for neither would Charley be convinced nor would the other consent to be off his bargain. But I made my point clear. Mr. Campbell having recovered his faculties, it was clear that no treaty could be concluded without his consent. (It could not have been legal in any case, but I suppose they had in some way got over this.) I remember Charley turning upon me with a passionate remonstrance, when, almost by violence and pertinacity, I had driven his Cockney sportsman away. "I cannot conceive what is your object, Temple," he said. "Are you mad? my father must give his consent; there is no possibility of a question about it. Ellermore must be sold—and as well to him as to another," he said, with a sigh. I took out my blue letter, which I had huddled into my pocket, and laid it before him. "It is to me that Ellermore must be sold," I said.

My inheritance had come—there was nothing wonderful about it—it was my right; but never did inheritance come at a more suitable moment. Charley went back with me that afternoon, after a hurried conference with his young brothers, who came round me, shaking my arms nearly off, and calling to each other in their soft young basses, like rolls of mild thunder, that, whatever happened, I was a good fellow, a true friend. If they had not been so bashful they would have embraced me, less I verily believe from the sense of escape from a great misery which they had scarcely realised, than from generous pleasure in what they thought a sort of noble generosity: that was their view of it. Charley perhaps was more enlightened. He was very silent during the journey, but at one point of it burst out suddenly upon me. "You are doing this for Chatty, Temple. If you take her away, it will be as bad as losing Ellermore." I shook my head. Then, if never before, I felt the hopelessness of the position. "There is but one thing you can do for me: say not a word of that to her," I said.

And I believe he kept counsel. It was of her own accord that Charlotte came up to me after the hurried interview in which Charley laid my proposal before her. She was very grave, though the sweetness of her look drew the heart out of my breast. She held out her hands to me, but her eyes took all warm significance out of this gesture. "Mr. Temple," she said, "you may think me bold to say it, but we are friends that can say anything to one another. If in your great generosity there may yet be a thought— a thought that a woman might recompense what was done for her and hers——" Her beautiful countenance, beautiful in its love and tenderness and noble dignity, but so pale, was suddenly suffused with colour. She took her hands out of mine, and folded them together—"That is out of my power—that is out of my power!" she said.

"I like it better so," I cried. God help me! it was a lie, and so she knew. "I want no recompense. It will be recompense enough to know you are here."

And so it has remained ever since, and may, perhaps, for ever—I cannot tell. We are dear friends. When anything happens in the family I am sent for, and all is told to me. And so do I with her. We know all each other's secrets—those secrets which are not of fortune or incident, but of the soul. Is there anything better in marriage than this? And yet there is a longing which is human for something more.

That evening I went back to the Lady's Walk, with a sort of fanciful desire to tell her, the other, that I had done her bidding, that she had been a true guardian of her race to the last. I paced up and down through the dim hour when the sun ought to have been setting, and later, long into the twilight. The rain fell softly, pattering upon the dark glistening leaves of the evergreens, falling straight through the bare branches. But no soft step of a living soul was on the well-worn track. I called to her, but there was no answer, not even the answer of a sigh. Had she gone back heart-sick to her home in Heaven, acknowledging at last that it was not hers to guard her race? It made my heart ache for her to think so; but yet it must have been a sweet grief and easily healed to know that those she loved were most safe in God's only care when hers failed—as everything else must fail.

# Arthur Conan Doyle

# THE CAPTAIN OF THE "POLE-STAR"

*This story takes place well within the Arctic Circle. It contains
some of the same features as other stories in this anthology: a doctor
invited to observe but not fully understand a patient's encounter with
the uncanny; the mysterious power of the sea; and the pretensions
of authenticity.* ARTHUR CONAN DOYLE (1859-1930) *also realized
that to fully explain a ghostly encounter is to do away with some of
its power. The author, who was to go on to write the first Sherlock
Holmes story four years later, already knew the power of mystery.
Doyle himself took a medical post aboard an arctic whaling ship from
February to August of 1880. Twenty-one at the start of the voyage,
Conan Doyle would eventually come to see this experience as one that
changed his life and served as a rite of passage into adulthood.*[1] *This
story first appeared in* Temple Bar *in January 1883.*

[Being an extract from the journal of John McAlister Ray, student
of medicine, kept by him during the six months' voyage in the
Arctic Seas of the steam-whaler "Pole-star," of Dundee, Captain
Nicholas Craigie.]

*September 11th.* Lat. 81° 40′ N.; Long. 2° E.—Still lying-to amid
enormous ice-fields. The one which stretches away to the
north of us, and to which our ice-anchor is attached, cannot be
smaller than an English county. To the right and left unbroken
sheets extend to the horizon. This morning the mate reported
that there were signs of pack ice to the southward. Should this
form of sufficient thickness to bar our return, we shall be in a
position of danger, as the food, I hear, is already running somewhat short. It is late in the season and the nights are beginning

1 Jon Lellenberg and Daniel Stashower. Introduction. *Dangerous Work: Diary
of an Arctic Adventure.* Chicago: University of Chicago Press, 2012.

to reappear. This morning I saw a star twinkling just over the foreyard—the first since the beginning of May. There is considerable discontent among the crew, many of whom are anxious to get back home to be in time for the herring season, when labor always commands a high price upon the Scotch coast. As yet their displeasure is only signified by sullen countenances and black looks, but I heard from the second mate this afternoon that they contemplated sending a deputation to the captain to explain their grievance. I much doubt how he will receive it, as he is a man of fierce temper, and very sensitive about anything approaching to an infringement of his rights. I shall venture after dinner to say a few words to him upon the subject. I have always found that he will tolerate from me what he would resent from any other member of the crew.

Amsterdam Island, at the north-west corner of Spitzbergen, is visible upon our starboard quarter—a rugged line of volcanic rocks, intersected by white seams, which represent glaciers. It is curious to think that at the present moment there is probably no human being nearer to us than the Danish settlements in the south of Greenland—a good nine hundred miles as the crow flies. A captain takes a great responsibility upon himself when he risks his vessel under such circumstances. No whaler has ever remained in these latitudes till so advanced a period of the year.

9 P.M.—I have spoken to Captain Craigie, and though the result has been hardly satisfactory, I am bound to say that he listened to what I had to say very quietly and even deferentially. When I had finished he put on that air of iron determination which I have frequently observed upon his face, and paced rapidly backwards and forwards across the narrow cabin for some minutes. At first I feared that I had seriously offended him, but he dispelled the idea by sitting down again, and putting his hand upon my arm with a gesture which almost amounted to a caress. There was a depth of tenderness too in his wild, dark eyes which surprised me considerably. "Look here, doctor," he said, "I'm sorry I ever took you—I am indeed—and I would give fifty pounds this minute to see you standing safe upon the Dundee quay. It's hit or miss with me this time. There are fish to the north of us. How dare you shake your head, sir, when I tell you I saw them blowing from

the masthead!"—this in a sudden burst of fury, though I was not conscious of having shown any signs of doubt. "Two and-twenty fish in as many minutes, as I am a living man, and not one under ten foot.[1] Now, doctor, do you think I can leave the country when there is only one infernal strip of ice between me and my fortune? If it came on to blow from the north to-morrow we could fill the ship and be away before the frost could catch us. If it came on to blow from the south—well, I suppose, the men are paid for risking their lives, and as for myself it matters but little to me, for I have more to bind me to the other world than to this one. I confess that I am sorry for *you*, though. I wish I had old Angus Tait who was with me last voyage, for he was a man that would never be missed, and you—you said once that you were engaged, did you not?"

"Yes," I answered, snapping the spring of the locket which hung from my watch-chain, and holding up the little vignette of Flora.

"Blast you!" he yelled, springing out of his seat, with his very beard bristling with passion. "What is your happiness to me? What have I to do with her that you must dangle her photograph before my eyes?" I almost thought that he was about to strike me in the frenzy of his rage, but with another imprecation he dashed open the door of the cabin and rushed out upon deck, leaving me considerably astonished at his extraordinary violence. It is the first time that he has ever shown me anything but courtesy and kindness. I can hear him pacing excitedly up and down overhead as I write these lines.

I should like to give a sketch of the character of this man, but it seems presumptuous to attempt such a thing upon paper, when the idea in my own mind is at best a vague and uncertain one. Several times I have thought that I grasped the clue which might explain it, but only to be disappointed by his presenting himself in some new light which would upset all my conclusions. It may be that no human eye but my own shall ever rest upon these lines, yet as a psychological study I shall attempt to leave some record of Captain Nicholas Craigie.

[1] A whale is measured among whalers not by the length of its body, but by the length of its whalebone. [Author's note.]

A man's outer case generally gives some indication of the soul within. The captain is tall and well-formed, with dark, handsome face, and a curious way of twitching his limbs, which may arise from nervousness, or be simply an outcome of his excessive energy. His jaw and whole cast of countenance is manly and resolute, but the eyes are the distinctive feature of his face. They are of the very darkest hazel, bright and eager, with a singular mixture of recklessness in their expression, and of something else which I have sometimes thought was more allied with horror than any other emotion. Generally the former predominated, but on occasions, and more particularly when he was thoughtfully inclined, the look of fear would spread and deepen until it imparted a new character to his whole countenance. It is at these times that he is most subject to tempestuous fits of anger, and he seems to be aware of it, for I have known him lock himself up so that no one might approach him until his dark hour was passed. He sleeps badly, and I have heard him shouting during the night, but his room is some little distance from mine, and I could never distinguish the words which he said.

This is one phase of his character, and the most disagreeable one. It is only through my close association with him, thrown together as we are day after day, that I have observed it. Otherwise he is an agreeable companion, well-read and entertaining, and as gallant a seaman as ever trod a deck. I shall not easily forget the way in which he handled the ship when we were caught by a gale among the loose ice at the beginning of April. I have never seen him so cheerful, and even hilarious, as he was that night, as he paced backwards and forwards upon the bridge amid the flashing of the lightning and the howling of the wind. He has told me several times that the thought of death was a pleasant one to him, which is a sad thing for a young man to say; he cannot be much more than thirty, though his hair and moustache are already slightly grizzled. Some great sorrow must have overtaken him and blighted his whole life. Perhaps I should be the same if I lost my Flora—God knows! I think if it were not for her that I should care very little whether the wind blew from the north or the south to-morrow. There, I hear him come down the companion and he has locked himself up in his room, which shows that he is still in an amiable mood. And so to bed, as old Pepys would say, for the candle is burning down (we have to use them now since the nights are closing in), and the steward has turned in, so there are no hopes of another one.

*September 12th.*—Calm, clear day, and still lying in the same position. What wind there is comes from the south-east, but it is very slight. Captain is in a better humor, and apologized to me at breakfast for his rudeness. He still looks somewhat *distrait*, however, and retains that wild look in his eyes which in a Highlander would mean that he was "fey"—at least so our chief engineer remarked to me, and he has some reputation among the Celtic portion of our crew as a seer and expounder of omens.

It is strange that superstition should have obtained such mastery over this hard-headed and practical race. I could not have believed to what an extent it is carried had I not observed it for myself. We have had a perfect epidemic of it this voyage, until I have felt inclined to serve out rations of sedatives and nerve-tonics with the Saturday allowance of grog. The first symptom of it was that shortly after leaving Shetland the men at the wheel used to complain that they heard plaintive cries and screams in the wake of the ship, as if something were following it and were unable to overtake it. This fiction has been kept up during the whole voyage, and on dark nights at the beginning of the seal-fishing it was only with great difficulty that men could be induced to do their spell. No doubt what they heard was either the creaking of the rudder-chains, or the cry of some passing sea-bird. I have been fetched out of bed several times to listen to it, but I need hardly say that I was never able to distinguish anything unnatural. The men, however, are so absurdly positive upon the subject that it is hopeless to argue with them. I mentioned the matter to the captain once, but to my surprise he took it very gravely, and indeed appeared to be considerably disturbed by what I told him. I should have thought that he at least would have been above such vulgar delusions.

All this disquisition upon superstition leads me up to the fact that Mr. Manson, our second mate, saw a ghost last night—or, at least, says that he did, which of course is the same thing. It is quite refreshing to have some new topic of conversation after the eternal routine of bears and whales which has served us for so many months. Manson swears the ship is haunted, and that he would not stay in her a day if he had any other place to go to. Indeed the fellow is honestly frightened, and I had to give him some chloral and bromide of potassium this morning to steady him down. He seemed quite indignant when I suggested that he had been having an extra glass the night before, and I was obliged to pacify him by keeping as grave a countenance as possible during his story, which he certainly narrated in a very straightforward and matter-of-fact way.

"I was on the bridge," he said, "about four bells in the middle watch, just when the night was at its darkest. There was a bit of a moon, but the clouds were blowing across it so that you couldn't see far from the ship. John McLeod, the harpooner, came aft from the foc'sle-head and reported a strange noise on the starboard bow. I went forrard and we both heard it, sometimes like a bairn crying and sometimes like a wench in pain. I've been seventeen years to the country and I never heard seal, old or young, make a sound like that. As we were standing there on the foc'sle-head the moon came out from behind a cloud, and we both saw a sort of white figure moving across the ice-field in the same direction that we had heard the cries. We lost sight of it for a while, but it came back on the port bow, and we could just make it out like a shadow on the ice. I sent a band aft for the rifles, and McLeod and I went down on to the pack, thinking that maybe it might be a bear. When we got on the ice I lost sight of McLeod, but I pushed on in the direction where I could still hear the cries. I followed them for a mile or maybe more, and then running round a hum-mock I came right on to the top of it standing and waiting for me seemingly. I don't know what it was. It wasn't a bear anyway. It was tall and white and straight, and if it wasn't a man nor a woman, I'll stake my davy it was something worse. I made for the ship as hard as I could run, and precious glad I was to find myself aboard. I signed articles to do my duty by the ship, and on the ship I'll stay, but you don't catch me on the ice again after sundown."

That is his story, given as far as I can in his own words. I fancy what he saw must, in spite of his denial, have been a young bear erect upon its hind legs, an attitude which they often assume when alarmed. In the uncertain light this would bear a resemblance to a human figure, especially to a man whose nerves were already somewhat shaken. Whatever it may have been, the occurrence is unfortunate, for it has produced a most unpleasant effect upon the crew. Their looks are more sullen than before and their discontent more open. The double grievance of being debarred from the herring fishing and of being detained in what they choose to call a haunted vessel, may lead them to do something rash. Even the harpooners, who are the oldest and steadiest among them, are joining in the general agitation.

Apart from this absurd outbreak of superstition, things are looking rather more cheerful. The pack which was forming to the south of us has partly cleared away, and the water is so warm as to lead me to believe that we are lying in one of those branches of the Gulf Stream which run up between Greenland and Spitzbergen. There are numerous small Medusæ and sea-lemons about the ship, with abundance of shrimps, so that there is every possibility of "fish" being sighted. Indeed one was seen blowing about dinner time, but in such a position that it was impossible for the boats to follow it.

*September 13th.*—Had an interesting conversation with the chief mate Mr. Milne upon the bridge. It seems that our captain is as great an enigma to the seamen, and even to the owners of the vessel, as he has been to me. Mr. Milne tells me that when the ship is paid off, upon returning from a voyage, Captain Craigie disappears, and is not seen again until the approach of another season, when he walks quietly into the office of the company, and asks whether his services will be required. He has no friend in Dundee, nor does any one pretend to be acquainted with his early history. His position depends entirely upon his skill as a seaman, and the name for courage and coolness which he had earned in the capacity of mate, before being entrusted with a separate command. The unanimous opinion seems to be that he is not a Scotchman, and that his name is an assumed one. Mr. Milne thinks that he has devoted himself to whaling simply for the reason that it is the most dangerous occupation which he could select, and that he courts death in every possible manner. He mentioned several instances of this, one of which is rather curious, if true. It seems that on one occasion he did not put in an appearance at the office, and a substitute had to be selected in his place. That was at the time of the last Russian and Turkish war. When he turned up again next spring he had a puckered wound in the side of his neck which he used to endeavor to conceal with his cravat. Whether the mate's inference that he had been engaged in the war is true or not I cannot say. It was certainly a strange coincidence.

The wind is veering round in an easterly direction, but is still very slight. I think the ice is lying closer than it did yesterday. As far as the eye can reach on every side there is one wide expanse of spotless white, only broken by an occasional rift or the dark shadow of a hummock. To the south there is the narrow lane of blue water which is our sole means of escape, and which is closing up every day. The captain is taking a heavy responsibility upon himself. I hear that the tank of potatoes has been finished, and even the biscuits are running short, but he preserves the same impassible countenance and spends the greater part of the day at the crow's nest, sweeping the horizon with his glass. His manner is very variable, and he seems to avoid my society, but there has been no repetition of the violence which he showed the other night.

7.30 P.M.—My deliberate opinion is that we are commanded by a madman. Nothing else can account for the extraordinary vagaries of Captain Craigie. It is fortunate that I have kept this journal of our voyage, as it will serve to justify us in case we have to put him under any sort of restraint, a step which I should only consent to as a last resource. Curiously enough it was he himself who suggested lunacy and not mere eccentricity as the secret of his strange conduct. He was standing upon the bridge about an hour ago, peering as usual through his glass, while I was walking up and down the quarterdeck. The majority of the men were below at their tea, for the watches have not been regularly kept of late. Tired of walking, I leaned against the bulwarks, and admired the mellow glow cast by the sinking sun upon the great ice-fields which surround us. I was suddenly aroused from the reverie into which I had fallen by a hoarse voice at my elbow, and starting round I found that the captain had descended and was standing by my side. He was staring out over the ice with an expression in which horror, surprise, and something approaching to joy were contending for the mastery. In spite of the cold, great drops of perspiration were coursing down his forehead and he was evidently fearfully excited. His limbs twitched like those of a man upon the verge of an epileptic fit, and the lines about his mouth were drawn and hard.

"Look!" he gasped, seizing me by the wrist, but still keeping his eyes upon the distant ice, and moving his head slowly in a horizontal direction, as if following some object which was moving across the field of vision. "Look! There, man, there! Between the hummocks! Now coming out from behind the far one! You see her, you *must* see her! There still! Flying from me, by God, flying from me—and gone!"

He uttered the last two words in a whisper of concentrated agony which shall never fade from my remembrance. Clinging to the ratlines he endeavored to climb up upon the top of the bulwarks as if in the hope of obtaining a last glance at the departing object. His strength was not equal to the attempt, however, and he staggered back against the saloon skylights, where he leaned panting and exhausted. His face was so livid that I expected him to become unconscious, so lost no time in leading him down the companion, and stretching him upon one of the sofas in the cabin. I then poured him out some brandy, which I held to his lips, and which had a wonderful effect upon him, bringing the blood back into his white face and steadying his poor shaking limbs. He raised himself up upon his elbow, and looking round to see that we were alone, he beckoned to me to come and sit beside him.

"You saw it, didn't you?" he asked, still in the same subdued, awesome tone so foreign to the nature of the man.

"No, I saw nothing."

His head sank back again upon the cushions. "No, he wouldn't without the glass," he murmured. "He couldn't. It was the glass that showed her to me, and then the eyes of love—the eyes of love. I say, doc, don't let the steward in! He'll think I'm mad. Just bolt the door, will you?"

I rose and did what he had commanded.

He lay quiet for a little, lost in thought apparently, and then raised himself up upon his elbow again, and asked for some more brandy.

"You don't think I am, do you, doc?" he asked as I was putting the bottle back into the after-locker. "Tell me now, as man to man, do you think that I am mad?"

"I think you have something on your mind," I answered, "which is exciting you and doing you a good deal of harm."

"Right there, lad!" he cried, his eyes sparkling from the effects of the brandy. "Plenty on my mind—plenty! But I can work out the latitude and the longitude, and I can handle my sextant and manage my logarithms. You couldn't prove me mad in a court of law, could you, now?" It was curious to hear the man lying back and coolly arguing out the question of his own sanity.

"Perhaps not," I said, "but still I think you would be wise to get home as soon as you can and settle down to a quiet life for a while."

"Get home, eh?" he muttered with a sneer upon his face. "One word for me and two for yourself, lad. Settle down with Flora—pretty little Flora. Are bad dreams signs of madness?"

"Sometimes," I answered.

"What else? what would be the first symptoms?"

"Pains in the head, noises in the ears, flashes before the eyes, delusions——"

"Ah! what about them?" he interrupted. "What would you call a delusion?"

"Seeing a thing which is not there is a delusion."

"But she *was* there!" he groaned to himself. "She *was* there!" and rising, he unbolted the door and walked with slow and uncertain steps to his own cabin, where I have no doubt that he will remain until to-morrow morning. His system seems to have received a terrible shock, whatever it may have been that he imagined himself to have seen. The man becomes a greater mystery every day, though I fear that the solution which he has himself suggested is the correct one, and that his reason is affected. I do not think that a guilty conscience has anything to do with his behavior. The idea is a popular one among the officers, and, I believe, the crew; but I have seen nothing to support it. He has not the air of a guilty man, but of one who has had terrible usage at the hands of fortune, and who should be regarded as a martyr rather than a criminal.

The wind is veering round to the south to-night. God help us if it blocks that narrow pass which is our only road to safety! Situated as we are on the edge of the main Arctic pack, or the "barrier" as it is called by the whalers, any wind from the north has the effect of shredding out the ice around us and allowing our escape, while a wind from the south blows up all the loose ice behind us and hems us in between two packs. God help us, I say again!

*September 14th.*—Sunday, and a day of rest. My fears have been confirmed, and the thin strip of blue water has disappeared from the southward. Nothing but the great motionless ice-fields around us, with their weird hummocks and fantastic pinnacles. There is a deathly silence over their wide expanse which is horrible. No lapping of the waves now, no cries of seagulls or straining of sails, but one deep, universal silence in which the murmurs of the seamen, and the creak of their boots upon the white, shining deck, seem discordant and out of place. Our only visitor was an Arctic fox, a rare animal upon the pack, though common enough upon the land. He did not come near the ship, however, but after surveying us from a distance fled rapidly across the ice. This was curious conduct, as they generally know nothing of man, and being of an inquisitive nature become so familiar that they are easily captured. Incredible as it may seem, even this little incident produced a bad effect upon the crew. "Yon puir beastie kens mair, aye an' sees mair nor you nor me!" was the comment of one of the leading harpooners, and the others nodded their acquiescence. It is vain to attempt to argue against such puerile superstition. They have made up their minds that there is a curse upon the ship, and nothing will ever persuade them to the contrary.

The captain remained in seclusion all day except for about half an hour in the afternoon, when he came out upon the quarter-deck. I observed that he kept his eye fixed upon the spot where the vision of yesterday had appeared, and was quite prepared for another outburst, but none such came. He did not seem to see me although I was standing close beside him. Divine service was read as usual by the chief engineer. It is a curious thing that in whaling vessels the Church of England Prayer-book is always employed, although there is never a member of that Church among either officers or crew. Our men are all Roman Catholics or Presbyterians, the former predominating. Since a ritual is used which is foreign to both, neither can complain that the other is preferred to them, and they listen with all attention and devotion, so that the system has something to recommend it.

A glorious sunset, which made the great fields of ice look like a lake of blood. I have never seen a finer and at the same time more ghastly effect. Wind is veering round. If it will blow twenty-four hours from the north all will yet be well.

*September 15th.*—To-day is Flora's birthday. Dear lass! it is well that she cannot see her boy, as she used to call me, shut up among the ice-fields with a crazy captain and a few weeks' provisions. No doubt she scans the shipping list in the *Scotsman* every morning to see if we are reported from Shetland. I have to set an example to the men and look cheery and unconcerned; but God knows, my heart is very heavy at times.

The thermometer is at nineteen Fahrenheit to-day. There is but little wind, and what there is comes from an unfavorable quarter. Captain is in an excellent humor; I think he imagines he has seen some other omen or vision, poor fellow, during the night, for he came into my room early in the morning, and stooping down over my bunk whispered, "It wasn't a delusion, doc, it's all right!" After breakfast he asked me to find out how much food was left, which the second mate and I proceeded to do. It is even less than we had expected. Forward they have half a tankful of biscuits, three barrels of salt meat, and a very limited supply of coffee beans and sugar. In the after-hold and lockers there are a good many luxuries such as tinned salmon, soups, haricot mutton, etc., but they will go a very short way among a crew of fifty men. There are two barrels of flour in the storeroom, and an unlimited supply of tobacco. Altogether there is about enough to keep the men on half rations for eighteen or twenty days—certainly not more. When we reported the state of things to the captain, he ordered all hands to be piped, and addressed them from the quarterdeck. I never saw him to better advantage. With his tall, well-knit figure and dark, animated face, he seemed a man born to command, and he discussed the situation in a cool, sailor-like way which showed that while appreciating the danger he had an eye for every loophole of escape.

"My lads," he said, "no doubt you think I brought you into this fix, if it is a fix, and maybe some of you feel bitter against me on account of it. But you must remember that for many a season no ship that comes to the country has brought in as much oil-money as the old 'Pole-star,' and every one of you has had his share of it. You can leave your wives behind you in comfort while other poor fellows come back to find their lasses on the parish. If you have to thank me for the one you have to thank me for the other, and we may call it quits. We've tried a bold venture before this and succeeded, so now that we've tried one and failed we've no cause to cry out about it. If the worst comes to the worst, we can make the land across the ice, and lay in a stock of seals which will keep us alive until the spring. It won't come to that, though, for you'll see the Scotch coast again before three weeks are out. At present every man must go on half rations, share and share alike, and no favor to any. Keep up your hearts, and you'll pull through this as you've pulled through many a danger before." These few simple words of his had a wonderful effect upon the crew. His former unpopularity was forgotten, and the old harpooner whom I have already mentioned for his superstition, led off three cheers, which were heartily joined in by all hands.

*September 16th.*—The wind has veered round to the north during the night, and the ice shows some symptoms of opening out. The men are in a good humor in spite of the short allowance upon which they have been placed. Steam is kept up in the engine-room, that there may be no delay should an opportunity for escape present itself. The captain is in exuberant spirits, though he still retains that wild "fey" expression which I have already remarked upon. This burst of cheerfulness puzzles me more than his former gloom. I cannot understand it. I think I mentioned in an early part of this journal that one of his oddities is that he never permits any person to enter his cabin, but insists upon making his own bed, such as it is, and performing every other office for himself. To my surprise he handed me the key to-day and requested me to go down there and take the time by his chronometer while he measured the altitude of the sun at noon. It is a bare little room containing a washing-stand and a few books, but little else in the way of luxury, except some pictures upon the walls. The majority of these are small cheap oleographs, but there was one water-color sketch of the head of a young lady which arrested my attention. It was evidently a por-trait, and not one of those fancy types of female beauty which sailors particularly affect. No artist could have evolved from his own mind such a curious mixture of character and weakness. The languid, dreamy eyes, with their drooping lashes, and the broad, low brow unruffled by thought or care, were in strong contrast with the clean-cut, prominent jaw, and the resolute set of the lower lip. Underneath it in one of the corners was written "M. B., æt. 19." That any one in the short space of nineteen years of existence could develop such strength of will as was stamped upon her face seemed to me at the time to be well-nigh incred-ible. She must have been an extraordinary woman. Her features have thrown such a glamour over me that though I had but a fleeting glance at them, I could, were I a draughtsman, reproduce them line for line upon this page of the journal. I wonder what part she has played in our captain's life. He has hung her picture at the end of his berth so that his eyes continually rest upon it. Were he a less reserved man I should make some remark upon the subject. Of the other things in his cabin there was nothing worthy of mention—uniform coats, a camp-stool, small looking-glass, tobacco-box and numerous pipes, including an Oriental hookah—which by-the-bye gives some color to Mr. Milne's story about his participation in the war, though the connection may seem rather a distant one.

11.20 P.M.—Captain just gone to bed after a long and interest-ing conversation on general topics. When he chooses he can be a most fascinating companion, being remarkably well-read, and having the power of expressing his opinion forcibly without appearing to be dogmatic. I hate to have my intellectual toes trod upon. He spoke about the nature of the soul, and sketched out the views of Aristotle and Plato upon the subject in a masterly manner. He seems to have a leaning for metempsychosis and the doctrines of Pythagoras. In discussing them we touched upon modern spiritualism, and I made some joking allusion to the impostures of Slade, upon which, to my surprise, he warned me most impressively against confusing the innocent with the guilty, and argued that it would be as logical to brand Christianity as an error, because Judas who professed that religion was a villain. He shortly afterwards bade me good-night and retired to his room.

The wind is freshening up, and blows steadily from the north. The nights are as dark now as they are in England. I hope to-morrow may set us free from our frozen fetters.

*September 17th.*—The bogie again. Thank Heaven that I have strong nerves! The superstition of these poor fellows, and the circumstantial accounts which they give, with the utmost earnestness and self-conviction, would horrify any man not accustomed to their ways. There are many versions of the matter, but the sum-total of them all is that something uncanny has been flitting round the ship all night, and that Sandie McDonald of Peterhead and "lang" Peter Williamson of Shetland saw it, as also did Mr. Milne on the bridge; so, having three witnesses, they can make a better case of it than the second mate did. I spoke to Milne after breakfast and told him that he should be above such nonsense, and that as an officer he ought to set the men a better example. He shook his weatherbeaten head ominously, but answered with characteristic caution. "Mebbe aye, mebbe na, doctor," he said; "I didna ca' it a ghaist. I canna' say I preen my faith in sea bogles an' the like, though there's a mony as claims to ha' seen a' that and waur. I'm no easy feared, but maybe your ain bluid would run a bit cauld, mun, if instead o' speerin' aboot it in daylicht ye were wi' me last night, an' seed an awfu' like shape, white an' gruesome, whiles here, whiles there, an' it greetin' and ca'ing in the darkness like a bit lambie that hae lost its mither. Ye would na' be sae ready to put it a' doon to auld wives' clavers then, I'm thinkin'." I saw it was hopeless to reason with him, so contented myself with begging him as a personal favor to call me up the next time the spectre appeared—a request to which he acceded with many ejaculations expressive of his hopes that such an opportunity might never arise.

As I had hoped, the white desert behind us has become broken by many thin streaks of water which intersect it in all directions. Our latitude to-day was 80° 52′ N., which shows that there is a strong southerly drift upon the pack. Should the wind continue favorable it will break up as rapidly as it formed. At present we can do nothing but smoke and wait, and hope for the best. I am rapidly becoming a fatalist. When dealing with such uncertain factors as wind and ice a man can be nothing else. Perhaps it was the wind and sand of the Arabian deserts which gave the minds of the original followers of Mahomet their tendency to bow to *kismet*.

These spectral alarms have a very bad effect upon the captain. I feared that it might excite his sensitive mind, and endeavored to conceal the absurd story from him, but unfortunately he overheard one of the men making an allusion to it, and insisted upon being informed about it. As I had expected, it brought out all his latent lunacy in an exaggerated form. I can hardly believe that this is the same man who discoursed philosophy last night with the most critical acumen, and coolest judgment. He is pacing backwards and forwards upon the quarterdeck like a caged tiger, stopping now and again to throw out his hands with a yearning gesture, and stare impatiently out over the ice. He keeps up a continual mutter to himself, and once he called out, "But a little time, love—but a little time!" Poor fellow, it is sad to see a gallant seaman and accomplished gentleman reduced to such a pass, and to think that imagination and delusion can cow a mind to which real danger was but the salt of life. Was ever a man in such a position as I, between a demented captain and a ghost-seeing mate? I sometimes think I am the only really sane man aboard the vessel—except perhaps the second engineer, who is a kind of ruminant, and would care nothing for all the fiends in the Red Sea, so long as they would leave him alone and not disarrange his tools.

The ice is still opening rapidly, and there is every probability of our being able to make a start to-morrow morning. They will think I am inventing when I tell them at home all the strange things that have befallen me.

12 P.M.—I have been a good deal startled, though I feel steadier now, thanks to a stiff glass of brandy. I am hardly myself yet however, as this handwriting will testify. The fact is that I have gone through a very strange experience, and am beginning to

doubt whether I was justified in branding every one on board as madmen, because they professed to have seen things which did not seem reasonable to my understanding. Pshaw! I am a fool to let such a trifle unnerve me, and yet, coming as it does after all these alarms, it has an additional significance, for I cannot doubt either Mr. Manson's story or that of the mate, now that I have experienced that which I used formerly to scoff at.

After all it was nothing very alarming—a mere sound, and that was all. I cannot expect that any one reading this, if any one ever should read it, will sympathize with my feelings, or realize the effect which it produced upon me at the time. Supper was over, and I had gone on deck to have a quiet pipe before turning in. The night was very dark—so dark that standing under the quarter boat, I was unable to see the officer upon the bridge. I think I have already mentioned the extraordinary silence which prevails in these frozen seas. In other parts of the world, be they ever so barren, there is some slight vibration of the air—some faint hum, be it from the distant haunts of men, or from the leaves of the trees, or the wings of the birds, or even the faint rustle of the grass that covers the ground. One may not actively perceive the sound, and yet if it were withdrawn it would be missed. It is only here in these Arctic seas that stark, unfathomable stillness obtrudes itself upon you in all its gruesome reality. You find your tympanum straining to catch some little murmur, and dwelling eagerly upon every accidental sound within the vessel. In this state I was leaning against the bulwarks when there arose from the ice almost directly underneath me, a cry, sharp and shrill, upon the silent air of the night, beginning, as it seemed to me, at a note such as prima donna never reached, and mounting from that ever higher and higher until it culminated in a long wail of agony, which might have been the last cry of a lost soul. The ghastly scream is still ringing in my ears. Grief, unutterable grief, seemed to be expressed in it and a great longing, and yet through it all there was an occasional wild note of exultation. It seemed to come from close beside me, and yet as I glared into the darkness I could make out nothing. I waited some little time, but without hearing any repetition of the sound, so I came below, more shaken than I have ever been in my life before. As I came down the companion I met Mr. Milne, coming up to relieve the watch. "Weel, doctor," he said, "maybe that's auld wives' clavers tae? Did ye no hear it skirling? Maybe that's a supersteetion? what d'ye think o't noo?" I was obliged to apologize to the honest fellow, and acknowledge that I was as puzzled by it as he was. Perhaps to-morrow things may look different. At present I dare hardly write all that I think. Reading it again in days to come, when I have shaken off all these associations, I should despise myself for having been so weak.

*September* 18th.—Passed a restless and uneasy night still haunted by that strange sound. The captain does not look as if he had had much repose either, for his face is haggard and his eyes bloodshot. I have not told him of my adventure of last night, nor shall I. He is already restless and excited, standing up, sitting down, and apparently utterly unable to keep still.

A fine lead appeared in the pack this morning, as I had expected, and we were able to cast off our ice-anchor, and steam about twelve miles in a west-sou'-westerly direction. We were then brought to a halt by a great floe as massive as any which we have left behind us. It bars our progress completely, so we can do nothing but anchor again and wait until it breaks up, which it will probably do within twenty-four hours, if the wind holds. Several bladder-nosed seals were seen swimming in the water, and one was shot, an immense creature more than eleven feet long. They are fierce, pugnacious animals, and are said to be more than a match for a bear. Fortunately they are slow and clumsy in their movements, so that there is little danger in attacking them upon the ice.

The captain evidently does not think we have seen the last of our troubles, though why he should take a gloomy view of the situation is more than I can fathom, since every one else on board considers that we have had a miraculous escape, and are sure now to reach the open sea.

"I suppose you think it's all right now, doctor?" he said as we sat together after dinner.

"I hope so," I answered.

"We mustn't be too sure—and yet no doubt you are right. We'll all be in the arms of our own true loves before long, lad, won't we? But we mustn't be too sure—we mustn't be too sure."

He sat silent a little, swinging his leg thoughtfully backwards and forwards. "Look here," he continued. "It's a dangerous place this, even at its best—a treacherous, dangerous place. I have known men cut off very suddenly in a land like this. A slip would do it sometimes—a single slip, and down you go through a crack and only a bubble on the green water to show where it was that you sank. It's a queer thing," he continued with a nervous laugh, "but all the years I've been in this country I never once thought of making a will; not that I have anything to leave in particular, but still when a man is exposed to danger he should have everything arranged and ready—don't you think so?"

"Certainly," I answered, wondering what on earth he was driving at.

"He feels better for knowing it's all settled," he went on. "Now if anything should ever befall me, I hope that you will look after things for me. There is very little in the cabin, but such as it is I should like it to be sold, and the money divided in the same proportion as the oil-money among the crew. The chronometer I wish you to keep yourself as some slight remembrance of our voyage. Of course all this is a mere precaution, but I thought I would take the opportunity of speaking to you about it. I suppose I might rely upon you if there were any necessity?"

"Most assuredly," I answered; "and since you are taking this step, I may as well——"

"You! you!" he interrupted. "*You're* all right. What the devil is the matter with *you?* There, I didn't mean to be peppery, but I don't like to hear a young fellow, that has hardly begun life, speculating about death. Go up on deck and get some fresh air into your lungs instead of talking nonsense in the cabin, and encouraging me to do the same."

The more I think of this conversation of ours the less do I like it. Why should the man be settling his affairs at the very time when we seem to be emerging from all danger? There must be some method in his madness. Can it be that he contemplates suicide? I remember that upon one occasion he spoke in a deeply reverent manner of the heinousness of the crime of self-destruction. I shall keep my eye upon him however, and though I cannot obtrude upon the privacy of his cabin, I shall at least make a point of remaining on deck as long as he stays up.

Mr. Milne pooh-poohs my fears, and says it is only the "skipper's little way." He himself takes a very rosy view of the situation. According to him we shall be out of the ice by the day after to-morrow, pass Jan Meyen two days after that, and sight Shetland in little more than a week. I hope he may not be too sanguine. His opinion may be fairly balanced against the gloomy precautions of the captain, for he is an old and experienced seaman, and weighs his words well before uttering them.

The long-impending catastrophe has come at last. I hardly know what to write about it. The captain is gone. He may come back to us again alive, but I fear me—I fear me. It is now seven o'clock of the morning of the 19th of September. I have spent the whole night traversing the great ice-floe in front of us with a party of seamen in the hope of coming upon some trace of him, but in vain. I shall try to give some account of the circumstances which attended upon his disappearance. Should any one ever chance to read the words which I put down, I trust they will remember that I do not write from conjecture or from hearsay, but that I, a sane and educated man, am describing accurately what actually occurred before my very eyes. My inferences are my own, but I shall be answerable for the facts.

The captain remained in excellent spirits after the conversation which I have recorded. He appeared to be nervous and impatient however, frequently changing his position, and moving his limbs in an aimless, choreic way which is characteristic of him at times. In a quarter of an hour he went upon deck seven times, only to descend after a few hurried paces. I followed him each time, for there was something about his face which confirmed my resolution of not letting him out of my sight. He seemed to observe the effect which his movements had produced, for he endeavored by an overdone hilarity, laughing boisterously at the very smallest of jokes, to quiet my apprehensions.

After supper he went on to the poop once more, and I with him. The night was dark and very still, save for the melancholy soughing of the wind among the spars. A thick cloud was coming up from the north-west, and the ragged tentacles which it threw out in front of it were drifting across the face of the moon, which only shone now and again through a rift in the wrack. The captain paced rapidly backwards and forwards, and then seeing me still dogging him, he came across and hinted that he thought I should be better below—which I need hardly say had the effect of strengthening my resolution to remain on deck.

I think he forgot about my presence after this, for he stood silently leaning over the taffrail, and peering out across the great desert of snow, part of which lay in shadow, while part glittered mistily in the moonlight. Several times I could see by his movements that he was referring to his watch, and once he muttered a short sentence of which I could only catch the one word "ready." I confess to having felt an eerie feeling creeping over me as I watched the loom of his tall figure through the darkness, and noted how completely he fulfilled the idea of a man who is keeping a tryst. A tryst with whom? Some vague perception began to dawn upon me as I pieced one fact with another, but I was utterly unprepared for the sequel.

By the sudden intensity of his attitude I felt that he saw something. I crept up behind him. He was staring with an eager, questioning gaze at what seemed to be a wreath of mist, blown swiftly in a line with the ship. It was a dim, nebulous body devoid of shape, sometimes more, sometimes less apparent, as the light fell on it. The moon was dimmed in its brilliancy at the moment by a canopy of thinnest cloud, like the coating of an anemone.

"Coming, lass, coming," cried the skipper, in a voice of unfathomable tenderness and compassion, like one who soothes a beloved one by some favour long looked for, and as pleasant to bestow as to receive.

What followed, happened in an instant. I had no power to interfere. He gave one spring to the top of the bulwarks, and another which took him on to the ice, almost to the feet of the pale, misty figure. He held out his hands as if to clasp it, and so ran into the darkness with outstretched arms and loving words. I still stood rigid and motionless, straining my eyes after his retreating form, until his voice died away in the distance. I never thought to see him again, but at that moment the moon shone out brilliantly through a chink in the cloudy heaven, and illuminated the great field of ice. Then I saw his dark figure already a very long way off, running with prodigious speed across the frozen plain. That was the last glimpse which we caught of him—perhaps the last we ever shall. A party was organized to follow him, and I accompanied them, but the men's hearts were not in the work, and nothing was found. Another will be formed within a few hours. I can hardly believe I have not been dreaming, or suffering from some hideous nightmare as I write these things down.

7.30 P.M.—Just returned dead beat and utterly tired out from a second unsuccessful search for the captain. The floe is of enormous extent, for though we have traversed at least twenty miles of its surface, there has been no sign of its coming to an end. The frost has been so severe of late that the overlying snow is frozen as hard as granite, otherwise we might have had the footsteps to guide us. The crew are anxious that we should cast off and steam round the floe and so to the southward, for the ice has opened up during the night, and the sea is visible upon the horizon. They argue that Captain Craigie is certainly dead, and that we are all risking our lives to no purpose by remaining when we have an opportunity of escape. Mr. Milne and I have had the greatest difficulty in persuading them to wait until to-morrow night, and have been compelled to promise that we will not under any circumstances delay our departure longer than that. We propose therefore to take a few hours' sleep, and then to start upon a final search.

*September 20th, evening.*—I crossed the ice this morning with a party of men exploring the southern part of the floe, while Mr. Milne went off in a northerly direction. We pushed on for ten or twelve miles without seeing a trace of any living thing except a single bird, which fluttered a great way over our heads, and which by its flight I should judge to have been a falcon. The southern extremity of the ice-field tapered away into a long, narrow spit which projected out into the sea. When we came to the base of this promontory the men halted, but I begged them to continue to the extreme end of it, that we might have the satisfaction of knowing that no possible chance had been neglected.

We had hardly gone a hundred yards before McDonald of Peterhead cried out that he saw something in front of us, and began to run. We all got a glimpse of it and ran too. At first it was only a vague darkness against the white ice, but as we raced along together it took the shape of a man, and eventually of the man of whom we were in search. He was lying face downwards upon a frozen bank. Many little crystals of ice and feathers of snow had drifted on to him as he lay, and sparkled upon his dark seaman's jacket. As we came up some wandering puff of wind caught these tiny flakes in its vortex, and they whirled up into the air, partially descended again, and then, caught once more in the current, sped rapidly away in the direction of the sea. To my eyes it seemed but a snowdrift, but many of my companions averred that it started up in the shape of a woman, stooped over the corpse and kissed it, and then hurried away across the floe. I have learned never to ridicule any man's opinion, however strange it may seem. Sure it is that Captain Nicholas Craigie had met with no painful end, for there was a bright smile upon his blue, pinched features, and his hands were still outstretched as though grasping at the strange visitor which had summoned him away into the dim world that lies beyond the grave.

We buried him the same afternoon with the ship's ensign around him, and a thirty-two-pound shot at his feet. I read the burial service, while the rough sailors wept like children, for there were many who owed much to his kind heart, and who showed now the affection which his strange ways had repelled during his lifetime. He went off the grating with a dull, sullen splash, and as I looked into the green water I saw him go down, down, down until he was but a pale flickering patch of white hanging upon the outskirts of eternal darkness. Then even that faded away and he was gone. There he shall lie, with his secret and his sorrows and his mystery all still buried in his breast, until that great day when the sea shall give up its dead, and Nicholas Craigie come out from among the ice with the smile upon his face, and his stiffened arms outstretched in greeting. I pray that his lot may be a happier one in that life than it has been in this.

I shall not continue my journal. Our road to home lies plain and clear before us, and the great ice-field will soon be but a remembrance of the past. It will be some time before I get over the shock produced by recent events. When I began this record of our voyage I little thought of how I should be compelled to finish it. I am writing these final words in the lonely cabin, still starting at times and fancying I hear the quick, nervous step of the dead man upon the deck above me. I entered his cabin to-night as was my duty, to make a list of his effects in order that they might be entered in the official log. All was as it had been upon my previous visit, save that the picture which I have described as having hung at the end of his bed had been cut out of its frame, as with a knife, and was gone. With this last link in a strange chain of evidence I close my diary of the voyage of the "Pole-star."

[NOTE by Dr. John McAlister Ray, senior.—"I have read over the strange events connected with the death of the captain of the 'Pole-star,' as narrated in the journal of my son. That everything occurred exactly as he describes it I have the fullest confidence, and, indeed, the most positive certainty, for I know him to be a strong-nerved and unimaginative man, with the strictest regard for veracity. Still, the story is, on the face of it, so vague and so improbable, that I was long opposed to its publication. Within the last few days, however, I have had independent testimony upon the subject which throws a new light upon it. I had run down to Edinburgh to attend a meeting of the British Medical Association, when I chanced to come across Dr. P——, an old college chum of mine, now practising at Saltash, in Devonshire. Upon my telling him of this experience of my son's, he declared to me that he was familiar with the man, and proceeded, to my no small surprise, to give me a description of him, which tallied remarkably well with that given in the journal, except that he depicted him as a younger man. According to his account, he had been engaged to a young lady of singular beauty residing upon the Cornish coast. During his absence at sea his betrothed had died under circumstances of peculiar horror."]

# F. Marion Crawford

# THE DOLL'S GHOST

FRANCIS MARION CRAWFORD (1854-1909) *wrote many short stories in the horror genre, the most famous being "The Upper Berth,"* *originally published in* Unwin's Christmas Annual. *This Italian-born American novelist rated as one of the most popular at the end of the nineteenth century. While his tales of horror represent a small fraction of his writing, they are his most enduring work.*[1] *Dog ghosts occasionally feature in Victorian stories, but the active spirits typically belong to dead people until the late nineteenth century. At that point, the "many late Victorian horror stories concerning objects seem to be at least in part a reaction to developments in late nineteenth century capitalism and consumer culture."*[2] *In this tale, originally published in the* Illustrated London News *Christmas Supplement in 1896, Crawford finds ghostly inspiration in a seemingly innocuous store-bought object, a child's toy.*

IT WAS A TERRIBLE ACCIDENT, and for one moment the splendid machinery of Cranston House got out of gear and stood still. The butler emerged from the retirement in which he spent his elegant leisure, two grooms of the chambers appeared simultaneously from opposite directions, there were actually house-maids on the grand staircase, and those who remember the facts most exactly assert that Mrs. Pringle herself positively stood upon the landing. Mrs. Pringle was the housekeeper. As for the head nurse, the under nurse, and the nursery-maid, their feelings cannot be described. The head nurse laid one hand upon the polished marble balustrade and stared stupidly before her, the under

---

1  S. T. Joshi, *The Evolution of the Weird Tale.* New York: Hippocampus Press, 2004.

2  Jonathan Maximilian Gilbert, "The Horror, The Horror": *The Origins of a Genre in Late Victorian and Edwardian Britain, 1880-1914.* Diss. Rutgers State University of New Jersey, 2008, 153.

nurse stood rigid and pale, leaning against the polished marble wall, and the nursery-maid collapsed and sat down upon the polished marble step, just beyond the limits of the velvet carpet, and frankly burst into tears.

The Lady Gwendolen Lancaster-Douglas Scroop, youngest daughter of the ninth Duke of Cranston, and aged six years and three months, picked herself up quite alone and sat down on the third step from the foot of the grand staircase in Cranston House.

"Oh!" ejaculated the butler, and he disappeared again.

"Ah!" responded the grooms of the chambers, as they also went away.

"It's only that doll," Mrs. Pringle was distinctly heard to say, in a tone of contempt.

The under nurse heard her say it. Then the three nurses gathered round Lady Gwendolen, and patted her and gave her unhealthy things out of their pockets, and hurried her out of Cranston House as fast as they could, lest it should be found out upstairs that they had allowed the Lady Gwendolen Lancaster-Douglas-Scroop to tumble down the grand staircase with her doll in her arms. And as the doll was badly broken, the nursery-maid carried it, with the pieces, wrapped up in Lady Gwendolen's little cloak. It was not far to Hyde Park, and when they had reached a quiet place they took means to find out that Lady Gwendolen had no bruises. For the carpet was very thick and soft, and there was thick stuff under it to make it softer.

Lady Gwendolen Douglas-Scroop sometimes yelled, but she never cried. It was because she had yelled that the nurses had allowed her to go downstairs alone with Nina, the doll, under one arm, while she steadied herself with her other hand on the balustrade, and trod upon the polished marble steps beyond the edge of the carpet. So she had fallen, and Nina had come to grief.

When the nurses were quite sure that she was not hurt, they unwrapped the doll and looked at her in her turn. She had been a very beautiful doll, very large and fair and healthy, with real yellow hair, and eyelids that would open and shut over very grown-up dark eyes. Moreover, when you moved her right arm up and down she said "Pa-pa," and when you moved the left she said "Ma-ma," very distinctly.

"I heard her say 'Pa' when she fell," said the under nurse, who heard everything. "But she ought to have said 'Pa-pa.'"

"That's because her arm went up when she hit the step," said the head nurse. "She'll say the other 'Pa' when I put it down again."

"Pa," said Nina, as her right arm was pushed down, and speaking through her broken face. It was cracked right across, from the upper corner of the forehead, with a hideous gash, through the nose and down to the little frilled collar of the pale green silk Mother Hubbard frock, and two little three-cornered pieces of porcelain had fallen out.

"I'm sure it's a wonder she can speak at all, being all smashed." said the under nurse.

"You'll have to take her to Mr. Puckler," said her superior. "It's not far, and you'd better go at once."

Lady Gwendolen was occupied in digging a hole in the ground with a little spade, and paid no attention to the nurses.

"What are you doing?" inquired the nursery-maid, looking on.

"Nina's dead, and I'm diggin' her a grave," replied her ladyship thoughtfully.

"Oh, she'll come to life again all right," said the nursery-maid.

The under nurse wrapped Nina up again and departed. Fortunately a kind soldier, with very long legs and a very small cap, happened to be there; and, as he had nothing to do, he offered to see the under nurse safely to Mr. Puckler's and back.

Mr. Bernard Puckler and his little daughter lived in a little house in a little alley, which led out of a quiet little street not very far from Belgrave Square. He was the great doll-doctor, and his extensive practice lay in the most aristocratic quarter. He mended dolls of all sizes and ages, boy dolls and girl dolls, baby dolls in long clothes and grown-up dolls in fashionable gowns, talking dolls and dumb dolls, those that shut their eyes when they lay down, and those whose eyes had to be shut for them by means of a mysterious wire. His daughter Else was only just over twelve years old, but she was already very clever at mending dolls' clothes and at doing their hair, which is harder than you might think, though the dolls sit quite still while it is being done.

Mr. Puckler had originally been a German, but he had dissolved his nationality in the ocean of London, many years ago, like a great many foreigners. He still had one or two German friends, however, who came on Saturday evenings, and smoked with him and played picquet or "skat" with him for farthing points, and called him "Herr Doctor," which seemed to please Mr. Puckler very much.

He looked older than he was, for his beard was rather long and ragged, his hair was grizzled and thin, and he wore horn-rimmed spectacles. As for Else, she was a thin, pale child, very quiet and neat, with dark eyes and brown hair that was plaited down her back and tied with a bit of black ribbon. She mended the dolls' clothes and took the dolls back to their homes when they were quite strong again.

The house was a little one, but too big for the two people who lived in it. There was a small sitting-room on the street, and the workshop was at the back, and there were three rooms upstairs. But the father and daughter lived most of their time in the workshop, because they were generally at work, even in the evenings.

Mr. Puckler laid Nina on the table and looked at her a long time, till the tears began to fill his eyes behind the horn-rimmed spectacles. He was a very susceptible man, and he often fell in love with the dolls he mended, and found it hard to part with them when they had smiled at him for a few days. They were real little people to him, with characters and thoughts and feelings of their own, and he was very tender with them all. But some attracted him especially from the first, and when they were brought to him maimed and injured, their state seemed so pitiful to him that the tears came easily. You must remember that he had lived among dolls during a great part of his life, and understood them.

"How do you know that they feel nothing?" he went on to say to Else. "You must be gentle with them. It costs nothing to be kind to the little beings, and perhaps it makes a difference to them."

And Else understood him, because she was a child, and she knew that she was more to him than all the dolls.

He fell in love with Nina at first sight, perhaps because her beautiful brown glass eyes were something like Else's own, and he loved Else first and best, with all his heart. And, besides, it was a very sorrowful case. Nina had evidently not been long in the world, for her complexion was perfect, her hair was smooth where it should be smooth, and curly where it should be curly, and her silk clothes were perfectly new. But across her face was that frightful gash, like a sabre-cut, deep and shadowy within, but clean and sharp at the edges. When he tenderly pressed her head to close the gaping wound, the edges made a fine, grating sound, that was painful to hear, and the lids of the dark eyes quivered and trembled as though Nina were suffering dreadfully.

"Poor Nina!" he exclaimed sorrowfully. "But I shall not hurt you much, though you will take a long time to get strong."

He always asked the names of the broken dolls when they were brought to him, and sometimes the people knew what the children called them, and told him. He liked "Nina" for a name. Altogether and in every way she pleased him more than any doll he had seen for many years, and he felt drawn to her, and made up his mind to make her perfectly strong and sound, no matter how much labour it might cost him.

Mr. Puckler worked patiently a little at a time, and Else watched him. She could do nothing for poor Nina, whose clothes needed no mending. The longer the doll-doctor worked, the more fond he became of the yellow hair and the beautiful brown glass eyes, he sometimes forgot all the other dolls that were waiting to be mended, lying side by side on a shelf, and sat for an hour gazing at Nina's face, while he racked his ingenuity for some new invention by which to hide even the smallest trace of the terrible accident.

She was wonderfully mended. Even he was obliged to admit that: but the scar was still visible to his keen eyes, a very fine line right across the face, downwards from right to left. Yet all the conditions had been most favourable for a cure, since the cement had set quite hard at the first attempt and the weather had been fine and dry, which makes a great difference in a dolls' hospital.

At last he knew that he could do no more, and the under nurse had already come twice to see whether the job was finished, as she coarsely expressed it.

"Nina is not quite strong yet," Mr. Puckler had answered each time, for he could not make up his mind to face the parting.

And now he sat before the square deal table at which he worked, and Nina lay before him for the last time, with a big brown paper box beside her. It stood there like her coffin, waiting for her, he thought. He must put her into it, and lay tissue-paper over her dear face, and then put on the lid, and at the thought of tying the string his sight was dim with tears again, he was never to look into the glassy depths of the beautiful brown eyes any more, nor to hear the little wooden voice say "Pa-pa" and "Ma-ma." It was a very painful moment.

In the vain hope of gaining time before the separation, he took up the little sticky bottles of cement and glue and gum and colour, looking at each one in turn, and then at Nina's face. And all his small tools lay there, neatly arranged in a row, but he knew that he could not use them again for Nina. She was quite strong at last, and in a country where there should be no cruel children to hurt her she might live a hundred years, with only that almost imperceptible line across her face, to tell of the fearful thing that had befallen her on the marble steps of Cranston House.

Suddenly Mr. Puckler's heart was quite full, and he rose abruptly from his seat and turned away.

"Else," he said unsteadily, "you must do it for me. I cannot bear to see her go into the box."

So he went and stood at the window, with his back turned, while Else did what he had not the heart to do.

"Is it done?" he asked, not turning round. "Then take her away, my dear. Put on your hat, and take her to Cranston House quickly, and when you are gone I will turn round."

Else was used to her father's queer ways with the dolls, and, though she had never seen him so much moved by a parting, she was not much surprised.

"Come back quickly," he said, when he heard her hand on the latch. "It is growing late, and I should not send you at this hour. But I cannot bear to look forward to it any more."

When Else was gone, he left the window and sat down in his place before the table again, to wait for the child to come back.

He touched the place where Nina had lain, very gently, and he recalled the softly tinted pink face, and the glass eyes, and the ringlets of yellow hair, till he could almost see them.

The evenings were long, for it was late in the spring. But it began to grow dark soon, and Mr. Puckler wondered why Else did not come back. She had been gone an hour and a half, and that was much longer than he had expected, for it was barely half a mile from Belgrave Square to Cranston House. He reflected that the child might have been kept waiting, but as the twilight deepened he grew anxious, and walked up and down in the dim workshop, no longer thinking of Nina, but of Else, his own living child, whom he loved.

An undefinable, disquieting sensation came upon him by fine degrees, a chilliness and a faint stirring of his thin hair, joined with a wish to be in any company rather than to be alone much longer. It was the beginning of fear.

He told himself in strong German-English that he was a foolish old man, and he began to feel about for the matches in the dusk. He knew just where they should be, for he always kept them in the same place, close to the little tin box that held bits of sealing-wax of various colours, for some kinds of mending. But somehow he could not find the matches in the gloom.

Something had happened to Else, he was sure, and as his fear increased, he felt as though it might be allayed if he could get a light and see what time it was. Then he called himself a foolish old man again, and the sound of his own voice startled him in the dark. He could not find the matches.

The window was grey still; he might see what time it was if he went close to it, and he could go and get matches out of the cupboard afterwards. He stood back from the table, to get out of the way of the chair, and began to cross the board floor.

Something was following him in the dark. There was a small pattering, as of tiny feet upon the boards, he stopped and listened, and the roots of his hair tingled. It was nothing, and he was a foolish old man. He made two steps more, and he was sure that he heard the little pattering again. He turned his back to the window, leaning against the sash so that the panes began to crack, and he faced the dark. Everything was quite still, and it smelt of paste and cement and wood-filings as usual.

"Is that you, Else?" he asked, and he was surprised by the fear in his voice.

There was no answer in the room, and he held up his watch and tried to make out what time it was by the grey dusk that was just not darkness. So far as he could see, it was within two or three minutes of ten o'clock. He had been a long time alone. He was shocked, and frightened for Else, out in London so late, and he almost ran across the room to the door. As he fumbled for the latch, he distinctly heard the running of the little feet after him.

"Mice!" he exclaimed feebly, just as he got the door open.

He shut it quickly behind him, and felt as though some cold thing had settled on his back and were writhing upon him. The passage was quite dark, but he found his hat and was out in the alley in a moment, breathing more freely, and surprised to find how much light there still was in the open air. He could see the pavement clearly under his feet, and far off in the street to which the alley led he could hear the laughter and calls of children, playing some game out of doors. He wondered how he could have been so nervous, and for an instant he thought of going back into the house to wait quietly for Else. But instantly he felt that nervous fright of something stealing over him again. In any case it was better to walk up to Cranston House and ask the servants about the child. One of the women had perhaps taken a fancy to her, and was even now giving her tea and cake.

He walked quickly to Belgrave Square, and then up the broad streets, listening as he went, whenever there was no other sound, for the tiny footsteps. But he heard nothing, and was laughing at himself when he rang the servants' bell at the big house. Of course, the child must be there.

The person who opened the door was quite an inferior person—for it was a back door—but affected the manners of the front, and stared at Mr. Puckler superciliously under the strong light.

No little girl had been seen, and he knew "nothing about no dolls."

"She is my little girl," said Mr. Puckler, tremulously, for all his anxiety was returning tenfold, "and I am afraid something has happened."

The inferior person said rudely that "nothing could have happened to her in that house, because she had not been there, which was a jolly good reason why"; and Mr. Puckler was obliged to admit that the man ought to know, as it was his business to keep the door and let people in. He wished to be allowed to speak to the under nurse, who knew him; but the man was ruder than ever, and finally shut the door in his face.

When the doll-doctor was alone in the street, he steadied himself by the railing, for he felt as though he were breaking in two, just as some dolls break, in the middle of the backbone.

Presently he knew that he must be doing something to find Else, and that gave him strength. He began to walk as quickly as he could through the streets, following every highway and byway which his little girl might have taken on her errand. He also asked several policemen in vain if they had seen her, and most of them answered him kindly, for they saw that he was a sober man and in his right senses, and some of them had little girls of their own.

It was one o'clock in the morning when he went up to his own door again, worn out and hopeless and broken-hearted. As he turned the key in the lock, his heart stood still, for he knew that he was awake and not dreaming, and that he really heard those tiny footsteps pattering to meet him inside the house along the passage.

But he was too unhappy to be much frightened any more, and his heart went on again with a dull, regular pain, that ground its way all through him with every pulse. So he went in and hung up his hat in the dark, and found the matches in the cupboard and the candlestick in its place in the corner.

Mr. Puckler was so much overcome and so completely worn out that he sat down in his chair before the work-table and almost fainted, as his face dropped forward upon his folded hands. Beside him the solitary candle burned steadily with a low flame in the still, warm air.

"Else! Else!" he moaned against his yellow knuckles.

And that was all he could say, and it was no relief to him. On the contrary, the very sound of the name was a new and sharp pain that pierced his ears and his head and his very soul. For every time he repeated the name it meant that little Else was dead, somewhere out in the streets of London in the dark.

He was so terribly hurt that he did not even feel something pulling gently at the skirt of his old coat, so gently that it was like the nibbling of a tiny mouse. He might have thought that it was really a mouse if he had noticed it.

"Else! Else!" he groaned, right against his hands.

Then a cool breath stirred his thin hair, and the low flame of the one candle dropped down almost to a mere spark, not flickering as though a draught were going to blow it out, but just dropping down as if it were tired out. Mr. Puckler felt his hands stiffening with fright under his face; and there was a faint rustling sound, like some small silk thing blown in a gentle breeze. He sat up straight, stark and scared, and a small, wooden voice spoke in the stillness.

"Pa-pa," it said, with a break between the syllables.

Mr. Puckler stood up in a single jump, and his chair fell over backwards with a smashing noise upon the wooden floor. The candle had almost gone out.

It was Nina's doll-voice that had spoken, and he should have known it among the voices of a hundred other dolls. And yet there was something more in it, a little human ring, with a pitiful cry and a call for help, and the wail of a hurt child. Mr. Puckler stood up, stark and stiff, and tried to look round, but at first he could not, for he seemed to be frozen from head to foot.

Then he made a great effort, and he raised one hand to each of his temples, and pressed his own head round as he would have turned a doll's. The candle was burning so low that it might as well have been out altogether, for any light it gave, and the room seemed quite dark at first. Then he saw something. He would not have believed that he could be more frightened than he had been just before that. But he was, and his knees shook, for he saw the doll standing in the middle of the floor, shining with a faint and ghostly radiance, her beautiful glassy brown eyes fixed on his. And across her face the very thin line of the break he had mended shone as though it were drawn in light with a fine point of white flame.

Yet there was something more in the eyes too; there was something human, like Else's own, but as if only the doll saw him through them, and not Else. And there was enough of Else to bring back all his pain and to make him forget his fear.

"Else! My little Else!" he cried aloud.

The small ghost moved, and its doll-arm slowly rose and fell with a stiff, mechanical motion.

"Pa-pa," it said.

It seemed this time that there was even more of Else's tone echoing somewhere between the wooden notes that reached his ears so distinctly and yet so far away. Else was calling him, he was sure.

His face was perfectly white in the gloom, but his knees did not shake any more, and he felt that he was less frightened.

"Yes, child! But where? Where?" he asked. "Where are you, Else?"

"Pa-pa!"

The syllables died away in the quiet room. There was a low rustling of silk, the glassy brown eyes turned slowly away, and Mr. Puckler heard the pitter-patter of the small feet in the bronze kid slippers as the figure ran straight to the door. Then the candle burned high again, the room was full of light, and he was alone.

Mr. Puckler passed his hand over his eyes and looked about him. He could see everything quite clearly, and he felt that he must have been dreaming, though he was standing instead of sitting down, as he should have been if he had just waked up. The candle burned brightly now. There were the dolls to be mended, lying in a row with their toes up. The third one had lost her right shoe, and Else was making one. He knew that, and he was certainly not dreaming now. He had not been dreaming when he had come in from his fruitless search and had heard the doll's footsteps running to the door. He had not fallen asleep in his chair. How could he possibly have fallen asleep when his heart was breaking? He had been awake all the time.

He steadied himself, set the fallen chair upon its legs, and said to himself again very emphatically that he was a foolish old man. He ought to be out in the streets looking for his child, asking questions, and inquiring at the police-stations, where all accidents were reported as soon as they were known, or at the hospitals.

"Pa-pa!"

The longing, wailing, pitiful little wooden cry rang from the passage, outside the door, and Mr. Puckler stood for an instant with white face, transfixed and rooted to the spot. A moment later his hand was on the latch. Then he was in the passage, with the light streaming from the open door behind him.

Quite at the other end he saw the little phantom shining clearly in the shadow, and the right hand seemed to beckon to him as the arm rose and fell once more. He knew all at once that it had not come to frighten him but to lead him, and when it disappeared, and he walked boldly towards the door he knew that it was in the street outside, waiting for him. He forgot that he was tired and had eaten no supper, and had walked many miles, for a sudden hope ran through and through him, like a golden stream of life.

And sure enough, at the corner of the alley, and at the corner of the street, and out in Belgrave Square, he saw the small ghost flitting before him. Sometimes it was only a shadow, where there was other light, but then the glare of the lamps made a pale-green sheen on its little Mother Hubbard frock of silk; and sometimes, where the streets were dark and silent, the whole figure shone out brightly, with its yellow curls and rosy neck. It seemed to trot along like a tiny child, and Mr. Puckler could almost hear the pattering of the bronze kid slippers on the pavement as it ran. But it went very fast, and he could only just keep up with it, tearing along with his hat on the back of his head and his thin hair blown by the night breeze, and his horn-rimmed spectacles firmly set upon his broad nose.

On and on he went, and he had no idea where he was. He did not even care, for he knew certainly that he was going the right way.

Then at last, in a wide, quiet street, he was standing before a big, sober-looking door that had two lamps on each side of it, and a polished brass bell-handle, which he pulled.

And just inside, when the door was opened, in the bright light, there was the little shadow, and the pale-green sheen of the little silk dress, and once more the small cry came to his ears, less pitiful, more longing.

"Pa-pa!"

The shadow turned suddenly bright, and out of the brightness the beautiful brown glass eyes were turned up happily to his, while the rosy mouth smiled so divinely that the phantom doll looked almost like a little angel just then.

"A little girl was brought in soon after ten o'clock," said the quiet voice of the hospital doorkeeper. "I think they thought she was only stunned. She was holding a big brown paper box against her, and they could not get it out of her arms. She had a long plait of brown hair that hung down as they carried her."

"She is my little girl," said Mr. Puckler, but he hardly heard his own voice.

He leaned over Else's face in the gentle light of the children's ward, and when he had stood there a minute the beautiful brown eyes opened and looked up to his.

"Papa!" cried Else softly. "I knew you would come!"

Then Mr. Puckler did not know what he did or said for a moment, and what he felt was worth all the fear and terror and despair that had almost killed him that night. But by and by Else was telling her story, and the nurse let her speak, for there were only two other children in the room, who were getting well and were sound asleep.

"They were big boys with bad faces," said Else, "and they tried to get Nina away from me, but I held on and fought as well as I could till one of them hit me with something, and I don't remember any more, for I tumbled down, and I suppose the boys ran away, and somebody found me there. But I'm afraid Nina is all smashed."

"Here is the box," said the nurse. "We could not take it out of her arms till she came to herself. Should you like to see if the doll is broken?"

And she undid the string cleverly, but Nina was all smashed to pieces. Only the gentle light of the children's ward made a pale green sheen in the folds of the little Mother Hubbard frock.